APPLEWOOD

As a general rule, except when weather threatened the harvest, Pierre-Edouard did not work on Sundays. Instead he made use of this day to survey his property quietly, noting the fine growth of the crops, the vigour of the trees and vines. He loved these walks, and took great pleasure in them.

Sometimes Mathilde and the children accompanied him. Then, whilst the children galloped ahead, they remembered the paths walked and the years gone by since that morning in September 1917 when they had met, up there among the broom and juniper bushes of the White Peak. Pierre-Edouard had never for a moment regretted that day, the sudden urge which had thrown them together and united them for all time with an oft-renewed fervour. Their love grew stronger and deeper, quickened afresh by the daily round of work on the land they loved, enlivened by the births of their children and the happiness and vitality they brought with them . . .

Claude Michelet was born in Brive in Limousin in 1938. He still lives on his land at Marcillac, close to Brive, where one of his six children now farms with him. He is the author of a trilogy about the people of Saint-Libéral which begins with *Firelight and Woodsmoke* and many other works, including a biography of his father, Edmond Michelet, who was a minister in General de Gaulle's government.

ALSO BY CLAUDE MICHELET

Firelight and Woodsmoke
Scent of Herbs

APPLEWOOD

Claude Michelet

Translated by Sheila Dickie

ORION

An Orion paperback
First published in Great Britain in 1994 by Orion Books Ltd
Orion House, 5 Upper St Martin's Lane,
London WC2H 9EA

Third impression 1995

A CIP catalogue record for this book is available from
the British Library.

Typeset at The Spartan Press Ltd,
Lymington, Hants

Printed and bound in Great Britain by
Clays Ltd, St Ives plc

La plénitude des arbres séculaires émanait de leur masse, mais l'effort par quoi sortaient de leurs énormes troncs les branches tordues, l'épanouissement en feuilles sombres de ce bois, si vieux et si lourd qu'il semblait s'enfoncer dans la terre et non s'en arracher, imposaient à la fois l'idée d'une volonté et d'une métamorphose sans fin.

André Malraux
Les Noyers de l'Altenburg

The richness of the century-old trees emanated from their size, but the energy of the twisted branches springing from the enormous trunks, the dark leaves spreading from the wood, so old and so heavy that it seemed to be burrowing into the ground rather than rising from it, imposed at the same time the idea of ceaseless strength and growth.

André Malraux
The Walnut Trees of Altenburg

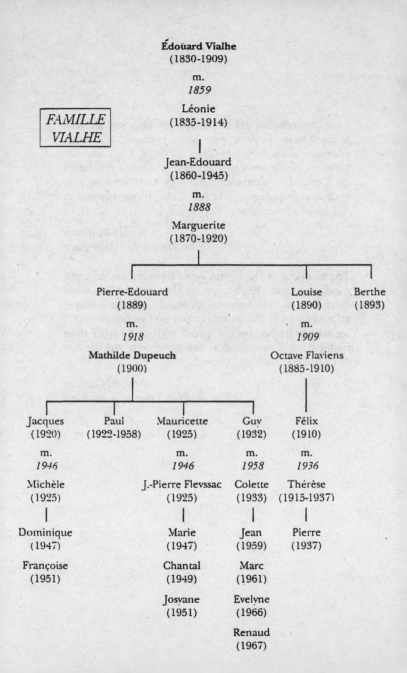

FAMILLE VIALHE

Édouard Vialhe
(1830-1909)

m.
1859

Léonie
(1835-1914)

Jean-Edouard
(1860-1945)

m.
1888

Marguerite
(1870-1920)

Pierre-Edouard
(1889)

m.
1918

Mathilde Dupeuch
(1900)

Louise
(1890)

m.
1909

Octave Flaviens
(1885-1910)

Berthe
(1893)

Jacques
(1920)

m.
1946

Michèle
(1925)

Dominique
(1947)

Françoise
(1951)

Paul
(1922-1958)

Mauricette
(1925)

m.
1946

J.-Pierre Flevssac
(1925)

Marie
(1947)

Chantal
(1949)

Josvane
(1951)

Guy
(1932)

m.
1958

Colette
(1933)

Jean
(1959)

Marc
(1961)

Evelyne
(1966)

Renaud
(1967)

Félix
(1910)

m.
1936

Thérèse
(1915-1937)

Pierre
(1937)

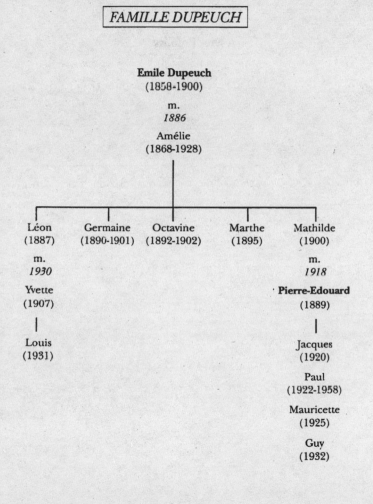

FAMILLE DUPEUCH

Emile Dupeuch
(1858-1900)

m.
1886

Amélie
(1868-1928)

Léon	Germaine	Octavine	Marthe	Mathilde
(1887)	(1890-1901)	(1892-1902)	(1895)	(1900)

Léon — m. *1930* — Yvette (1907) — Louis (1931)

Mathilde — m. *1918* — **Pierre-Edouard** (1889)

Jacques (1920)

Paul (1922-1958)

Mauricette (1925)

Guy (1932)

A Mes Enfants

PART ONE

Saint-Libéral-sur-Diamond

PART ONE

Chapter 1

THEY ran quickly and silently, darting like the agile lizard which passes in a grey blur across a sunny old wall. The grass rustled against their bare legs, and their tousled hair captured occasional petals from the drift falling from the plum and cherry trees across the whole countryside. Warblers, stonechats and dunnocks were chirruping from each tiny bush, announcing the spring on every side; they sang on the peaks and hillsides and in the woods which surrounded the village of Saint-Libéral. The oft-repeated call of the cuckoo echoed the monotonous chant of the hoopoe. As far as the eye could see the fruit trees shook their haloes, like angels preparing for a wedding. The air smelled of pollen, honey and fertile, fresh earth.

The two children jumped nimbly over the Diamond. The white pebbles on the bed of the stream had been washed and rewashed by the winter floods and were now revealed beneath the spring cascades of water so pure, so limpid, that it seemed almost invisible.

They cut across a damp pasture, already bright with buttercups reflecting the sun, with the purple tears of wild orchids and the white tracery of Queen Anne's Lace. An angry blackbird shot out of the dark bushes as they slipped through a hedge and crept along the edge of a meadow. They lay on their stomachs among the vetch and then rose slowly to their elbows and watched, their hearts thumping.

The men were working about three hundred metres away; a large group of them were busy around a tall metal derrick.

'You'll see, they're going to lift it,' whispered the older boy.

'I know,' cut in his brother.

And down below, suspended from a rope hauled by the workers, rose a tall column of white concrete, straight and slender as a Lombardy poplar – magnificent! It joined the others which were already fixed in concrete and rose in a perfectly straight line, scaling the heights and plunging into the ravines, disappearing out of sight. These were the advance guard of the approaching electricity line which would soon throw light into the houses of Saint-Libéral.

The work had started in October 1929, but the site had been deserted all winter. First of all the holes meant for the pylons had filled with water as fast as they were dug out, and then a period of bitter frost prevented any concreting, for each pole had to be solidly embedded and immovable.

'Did you see, they've put on the saucers,' remarked the younger boy.

The two lads had watched over the work impatiently as it slowly advanced. They made sure they came twice a week, on Sunday afternoons and on Thursdays; it was now Thursday 24 April 1930.

'They're beautiful,' agreed the older one, gazing at the four glass insulators which decorated the top of a pylon nearby. It had been put up a week ago, there in the middle of the meadow, only fifteen paces from them.

'Bet you I can knock one off,' whispered the little one.

Jacques Vialhe turned quickly and gave his brother a cuff.

'You're mad, don't do it!'

'Bet you!'

'No, come away! Anyway, we must go and look after the animals.'

They had left them up on Combes-Nègres, four hundred metres away. In theory the cows would not leave the pasture, too happy enjoying the freshly growing grass, but you never knew with them! If old Pig left to go exploring, for example, it would be enough to set the whole herd off after her. Jacques felt worried; he imagined the Limousin cows spreading out into the fields, vineyards and orchards which adjoined Combes-Nègres, and the inevitable punishment which would result from this lack of care. He was ten years old and would be held responsible. But just at the moment, the cows' behaviour worried him less than his brother's.

Paul was two years younger than him, but almost as tall and strong. He was driven primarily by a spirit of audacity, of sheer nerve which bordered on madness. For him life had no

4

real meaning, was not worth living, unless he could enliven it by doing everything which the grown-ups tried to proscribe. Such as, among other things, going secretly one night to the public wash-house and diving in to pull out the plug, just to enjoy the cries of the housewives, faced with a huge empty basin and piles of dirty linen next morning. Or again – this impious deed had taken place two weeks ago – taking advantage of his role as altarboy to climb into the bell tower on Maundy Thursday and wrap rags and old sacks round the clapper of the big bell; he experienced several minutes of intense pleasure as he watched the consternation of the faithful worshippers on Easter morning, when, instead of the cheerful call of the great bell in the Gloria, they heard only the muffled rumbling of bronze in bandages!

Of course these little jokes attracted paternal retribution, that was only fair. But it was less fair that the blows fell indiscriminately; Paul had all the outrageous ideas and carried them out, but Jacques always shared the beating which followed.

To be quite frank he readily admitted that, although Paul was the inventor and instigator of the pranks, he himself was the craftsman; without the string which he had given Paul, the rags and sack would never have stayed around the clapper of the big bell . . .

Though an accomplice, Jacques, unlike his brother, was always aware of the enormity of the crimes committed, and above all of the inevitable consequences. So he did his utmost to dissuade Paul. It was a waste of time! His brother, crouching in the vetch, was already stretching out his catapult in the direction of the four insulators which challenged them.

'Don't be a fool!' begged Jacques, without also, as he should have done, grabbing Paul's arm. The pebble hummed away, just missed the insulator, bounced off the concrete and shot into the sky.

'Amateur!' cried Jacques.

This was not true, for no one could teach Paul anything about catapults.

'Amateur yourself! The pebble was no good,' explained the marksman. He searched his pockets and smiled as his fingers met a fine round stone, the size of a pigeon's egg.

'I could blow it up with the first shot!' said Jacques, fingering the handle of his weapon, which hung around his neck.

Once more, Paul envied his brother's magnificent catapult. It was a superb tool: the boxwood fork had a perfect angle of curvature – not any old V-shaped fork, but two slender branches moulded into a perfect half oval. The bands fixed to them were of white rubber, easy to pull but with incredible strength and power. It was Uncle Léon, Jacques' godfather, who had given him this little marvel, with strict instructions not to use it for any mischief . . .

Jacques now felt in his own pockets, and suddenly in his palm he held a shiny steel marble.

'Ooooh,' breathed Paul, 'where's that from?'

'My godfather. He gave me a dozen of them, they're ball bearings.'

'Give me one, just one!'

'Uh, uh,' replied Jacques, as he slid the projectile into the leather pouch of his catapult. He crouched, tensed his arm, and closed his left eye. The dry crack of the elastic was almost overtaken by the shattering noise as the insulator exploded under the impact; lumps of glass scattered over several metres. It was a fine shot!

'Did you see that?' said Jacques, beginning to smile. But he was already gripped with panic. What stupidity, he thought. 'Come on, we'd better get going,' he said briskly.

'Let me shoot!' protested Paul. 'Look, I'm aiming for the third one.' And that insulator vanished into thin air just like the other. 'And I haven't even got ball bearings! Never mind, I can still bust a few things . . .'

'Let's go!' insisted Jacques. 'The cows will have gone off somewhere!'

Paul gazed covetously at the untouched insulators. They were so tempting!

'Okay,' he sighed, 'but we'll come back, eh?'

'You must be mad! When our parents find out . . .'

'And how will they know, we're not the only ones who can shoot!'

Jacques shrugged his shoulders; that was his brother's reasoning! Of course other kids in the village had catapults, and used them in the same way – and at the same targets, if they got the chance – but those lucky devils had parents who were blind, easy to deceive, who believed the most shameless lies. That was by no means the case for them, the sons of Pierre-Edouard and Mathilde Vialhe. Their parents knew everything, and straight away. They were not fooled by any lies or subterfuges. They were in charge.

Jean-Edouard Vialhe sat in the sun in front of the house, and smiled as he watched the little girl holding out her plump hands towards him. Mad with impatience, she moved from one side to the other, clinging to his trousers, clambering on his clogs, and trying desperately to get hold of the object he was making for her; her big eyes shone with desire and wonder.

'Give it to me, Pépé, give it to me!' the little one repeated.

She came up to his knee, was covered in delightful dimples, and was amazingly precocious. Mauricette was five years old and understood perfectly how to control the whole household. Obstinate and fiery as a true Vialhe, but quiet and coaxing like her mother, she got what she wanted from her elder brothers, Jacques and Paul, who were always kind to her and indulged her every whim.

'God knows how those rascals got the devilment in them,' thought Jean-Edouard, 'especially the second one! It's incredible what they dream up, those kids! And it's not that they haven't been properly brought up!'

He smiled as he thought how that did not prevent the two young imps from adding to their escapades and adventures; the deeds were reprehensible, of course, but they had the gift of making you laugh until you cried.

He had decided right from the start never to intervene in the organisation of the farm or the conduct of the family. He had not taken this decision easily or happily, but he had kept to it for eight years. Nor did he regret it: it was better so, more sensible and peaceful. He was respected as the older man and he had never, in all the eight years, experienced the least lack of due deference. As for everything else – his authority, the management of the farm and the family – he had willingly given that up once and for all in favour of his son, for he

7

understood that this was the only way to remain on good terms with him.

This abdication had been painful, and during the years following the death of his wife he had struggled to delay the inevitable decision. For two years, alone on the farm, he had tried to get to grips with things, to accustom himself to the miserable loneliness, to his own unhappiness, his weakness even. For he could see how everything was going downhill; first of all the animals, but above all the land, which he became less and less able to tend alone. And when his neighbours, like Jeantout and Gaston, had kindly come to help him, he had felt mortified each time, for everyone knew that his own son Pierre-Edouard was up there on his miserable steading at Coste-Roche, just waiting for the word to return and take his place as head of the family.

Yes, Pierre-Edouard was just waiting for one word: 'Come.' But it still remained to be spoken, and for that Jean-Edouard had to climb up to the cottage and say: 'I will step down. From now on, you are the boss.'

How simple that seemed in hindsight, now that everything had returned to normal, eight years later! But at the time it was an admission that he was stepping aside to let his son take over, that he accepted almost all Pierre's past opinions; that he would forget all their years of quarrelling, his son's snide comments, the fact that he took his sisters' side, and finally his marriage. He had condemned this union from the start, when Pierre-Edouard returned from that terrible war at the end of 1918, and presented them with a *fait accompli* by introducing Mathilde.

It had not been easy to forget all that, or to admit to himself that not all the faults had been on Pierre-Edouard's side: that he himself and his obstinacy had contributed to the sad situation; he, one of the most able farmers in the village, had neglected his land and let his farm go to ruin, simply because he had quarrelled with his eldest son. Just as he had fallen out with his two daughters! They, unlike Pierre-Edouard, had left the Corrèze and never returned.

All this had held him back, for two years, from going to see his son. At first he had hoped that Pierre-Edouard would return of his own accord, and that he would gradually let him take the reins, discreetly, as the years passed. But that did not allow for the Vialhe character. Pierre-Edouard was too proud, and too wise, to ask anything of his father. So, after two years of waiting and reflecting in solitude, it was he who had to take the first step.

The announcement of the expected birth of a second child, Paul, had made up his mind; even stimulated him. He had harnessed the horse and driven it up to Coste-Roche, on the slope leading to the plateau, on the edge of the parish. Then, once he had taken that first step, it all seemed plain and simple, and they talked without embarrassment or constraint.

'I know you're expecting another child; that's good, it's very good. But this one should be born at home, under our roof – well, your roof, if you prefer . . . '

Jacques, the eldest of the Vialhe grandchildren, had seen the light of day here, in this pitiful hovel where the young family were living.

'You want it to be born at our place, is that what you're saying?' Pierre-Edouard needed to get it clear.

'Yes, you come back. You can see very well that I'm just struggling along since your dear mother died. You've seen the fields . . . '

'Yes, I have, they're dreadful, they need a bit of effort put into them . . . '

A few years earlier a comment like that would have made his blood boil, but now he just shrugged his shoulders.

'No, there's no lack of effort, but at sixty-two, however hard I work it's not worth a quarter of what you could do. You're young, and so's your wife; that's what it needs. I can't cope with it any more. So there it is; come back, set up home there. And don't worry, I know what you're like, I won't give you any excuse to grumble about me. When you're living there you can do as you think fit with the land and the animals, just whenever and however you think best. It won't be my business any more . . . '

He had kept his word. It had not been easy, and he had often felt the urge to interfere with his son's ideas and ways of doing things. But he had always managed to remain silent, to keep the ironic and bitter comments to himself although they were on the tip of his tongue. It was much better like that.

Besides, he had been forced to recognise that Pierre-Edouard was an excellent farmer and a good son, Mathilde the best of daughters-in-law, and the three grandchildren adorable rascals.

However, even with them he had to adjust to a new sort of relationship. In his time, children would never have dared to be so familiar with their parents, and certainly not with their grandparents, as to address them as 'tu'. But nowadays the young ones did not say 'father', they said 'papa'. The word grandfather meant nothing to them, replaced by the strange-sounding Pépé! As for the formal 'vous', that was reserved for strangers, outside the family.

'Now, Pépé, give it to me, yes!' insisted the little girl, pulling at his waistcoat.

'I'll give it to you in exchange for a smacker,' he said, turning his cheek towards her.

She placed a wet kiss on his rough cheek, and wrinkled her nose. 'You prickle, you should shave off those scratches,' she said, rubbing her tiny forefinger over her little pink chin with its smiling dimple. 'Go on, give it to me, you promised!'

He held out the willow basket which he had just woven, and was touched to see her so happy with such a simple gift. She slipped her arm jauntily through the handle of bent chestnut twigs and trotted happily into the house.

Pierre-Edouard glanced in the direction of Paul, who was greedily eating his soup. Then he looked at Mathilde, sitting opposite him, and smiled at her discreetly; she responded by winking in agreement.

'Why have you been playing about with the reaper?' he asked his sons.

They lowered their noses to their plates and contemplated the globules of fat on the clear soup with great interest. They were amazed that their father was so quickly aware of their activities. It was Paul, yet again, who had had the absurd idea to check whether the reaper was equipped with any bearings which could be extracted to provide some fine missiles for their catapults. Their efforts had been in vain: the ball bearings were completely inaccessible. But who the devil could have seen them when, having returned from their expedition to the building site and brought the cows back home, the two of them had slipped into the barn? Their parents? Surely not; at the time when Paul was attacking the impenetrable gearing with a hammer, they were planting potatoes on the Meeting Field, up on the plateau, more than a kilometre away! Who could it be then? Pépé? No, he was busy with the animals and certainly would not have heard anything; he had grown a little deaf in his old age. Mauricette? She had not left her grandfather's side, she was so delighted to help him bed down the animals by proudly carrying a handful of straw in her brand-new basket.

'Well?' Pierre-Edouard asked again, and wrinkled his brow quizzically. 'What did you want with the reaper, eh?'

'Oh, nothing!' Jacques assured him.

'No, nothing!' his brother confirmed.

'Well, why were you messing about with it then – just for fun? Don't you know that's dangerous? If the cutter falls on your head it'll crush you! I've already told you that.'

'And how do you know that we touched it?' Paul ventured to ask; his father's gift for being everywhere simultaneously filled him with admiration.

'I know, that's enough, and Maman knows too.'

'Did you see us?' Jacques had a turn at trying to find out.

'Just as if we were there!' his mother assured him, ruffling his hair. 'Go on with you,' she responded to his air of amazement, 'it's not so difficult. Look at your nails, you mucky pups, they're black with oil!'

'Damn!' groaned Paul, sorry now that he had put so much effort into washing his hands. Really, if that was the outcome it was enough to put you off soap and water for life! He looked at his fingers; of course, they should have cleaned their nails as well! Annoyed, he made a note to watch out for telltale signs like that the next time he went in search of ball bearings.

'Guess what,' Jacques told them, 'Godfather came by just now, he said he wanted to see you both at his place this evening.'

'Great!' cried Paul, 'we're going to Uncle Léon's.'

'Oh no you're not,' interrupted his mother, 'you're going to bed. Anyway, he said he wanted to see us two; that's the two of us, Papa and me.'

'And why doesn't Uncle Léon ever come to our house?' asked Paul.

'Don't you bother about that, just eat up.' Pierre-Edouard changed the subject.

The matter of Léon was the only sticking point on which Jean-Edouard had consistently refused to make the slightest concession. Too much bitterness, hatred even, had built up between himself and his daughter-in-law's brother. The two men had avoided each other and not spoken for years. If Léon paid one of his rare, fleeting visits to the house, Jean-Edouard would pointedly leave the room to go and shut himself in his bedroom. This behaviour, embarrassing for everyone, quickly made Léon understand that he was not welcome; that the old man could never forgive his actions and his attitude in times past.

Furthermore, Jean-Edouard could not forgive Léon for succeeding to the mayoralty at the elections in May 1925. At the time Jean-Edouard had let it be known that he was retiring from the contest, that he was not even interested in the humbler position of councillor. But there was no doubt that his political strategy would have been different if he had suspected that Léon Depeuch would succeed him. And masterfully, since, no sooner elected, he had moved heaven and earth to get water laid on, just as the electors had demanded. However, blinded by his resentment towards Léon, he refused to accept that his enemy was the best choice for Mayor of Saint-Libéral. He was as obstinate as he was prejudiced, and finally convinced himself that the electors would reject Léon —that lout, that crook, that faithless and lawless stock-dealer who had amassed a veritable fortune by plundering the market places all around! When it came to these elections he had really hoped that his son would throw himself into the fray. Unfortunately Pierre-Edouard did not feel attracted by the sash of office; he was not interested in the job, and had only reluctantly accepted the position of deputy which the new mayor had offered him.

These reasons were quite sufficient to justify Jean-Edouard's lasting animosity, but his anger was also fuelled by the solid friendship which allied his son to that toad

Léon. An old friendship, forged in their youth, and now reinforced by family ties since Pierre-Edouard's marriage to Mathilde. An unshakeable friendship, which was a constant source of irritation to him.

Léon was aware of all this; he felt no need to turn the knife in the wound, poison the abscess of hatred, and so he restricted his visits to the Vialhes as much as possible. But that did not prevent him from maintaining a very good relationship with his sister, brother-in-law, nephews and niece; his house was always open to them.

Chapter 2

LÉON poured coffee into the wide earthenware bowls, and replaced the coffee-pot on the wood-burning stove. Since his mother had died fifteen months earlier – Mathilde was still wearing her mourning black – he had lived entirely in one room of the vast mansion which he had had built just before the war. Unmarried and engrossed in his work, he lived away from home more often than under his own roof. He took all his meals at the inn, often slept in Brive or Tulle, even in Limoges or Paris, and never bothered with housekeeping as such. So the single room which he used had become a real slum; but it was a slum without any dust, for Mathilde cleaned it every week, upset to see it turned into a pigsty.

The room was therefore clean but cluttered, invaded – drowned, almost – by an accumulation of strange objects; of washing, paperwork, dishes. Even the grand fireplace, where he never lit the fire, was full of calving-ropes, harness and wooden yokes.

'Well, what's new?' asked Pierre-Edouard, as he searched the sideboard to try to unearth the sugar tin. At last he found and opened it: it was full of nails. 'So that's your sugar?' he teased.

'Ask your wife! It's she who tidies it away, it seems that sugar should be in a sugar bowl! Look, it's over there, on the chair, in the pot marked Heather Honey.'

'You wanted to see us?' Pierre-Edouard continued as he returned with the container.

'Yes, sit down. Here,' said Léon, pushing a bottle of plum brandy towards him, 'help yourself, take a good drop, you're going to need it . . . ' He sat down as well, looked at them both, and smiled at his sister. 'It's amazing, you never look any older! Of course you're still young, only thirty! Ah, if only I were still thirty!'

He deftly unstrapped the prosthesis on the end of his left

arm – a souvenir of the battles on the Piava river – laid the metal claw on the table, and rubbed the swollen, purplish stump which had replaced his fist.

'*Miladiou*, it doesn't half itch in the evenings!' he grumbled as he scratched himself.

'Come on, stop mucking about,' demanded Pierre-Edouard, 'you didn't ask us here to talk about your fleas!'

He knew his brother-in-law well, and guessed he was feeling embarrassed and inhibited.

'Have you done something stupid?' Mathilde was worried. She had a secret horror, a fear, of seeing her brother entangled in some unsavoury dealings over animals, for he was not overburdened with scruples. He had an enormous turnover of stock, a lot of money passed through his hands, and he probably amassed a tidy sum from one year to the next. He was certainly as cunning as a fox, but you could never be sure: he swam with sharks, and perhaps one day he would meet one more ruthless than himself.

'Hey, what do you take me for! Stupid? Would I do something I shouldn't? No, that's not my style. Now, as it happens,' he turned to his brother-in-law, 'I've rented six more hectares on the plain at Varetz, not far from Castel Novel; good pasture land, you must come and have a look at it.'

'Okay,' Pierre-Edouard agreed, and stirred his coffee. Now he was sure it must be something serious, important, and Léon was trying to delay his confession with red herrings.

'So,' he tried again, 'you're not going to have us stay the night, are you? What's up?'

Léon shrugged, and poured himself a generous slug of brandy.

'I'm going to get married,' he said with a smile.

'Oh, so that's it . . .' Pierre-Edouard gasped. He was as surprised as he had been twenty years earlier, when his newly-widowed sister Louise had announced her intention to remarry just as abruptly.

'Now,' he hesitated, 'you're not teasing?'

'Tell us, Léon, is it a joke?' Mathilde was not sure either, just as flabbergasted as her husband.

'My God! Anyone would think you were upset about it! I'm not that old!'

'We're not at all upset!' protested Pierre-Edouard. 'Quite the opposite! But you always told us that you didn't want a wife.'

'Well, yes, I know, I always preferred other people's . . . but a fellow can change his mind, can't he? I'm fed up with running after the girls! Oh, don't look at me like that, little sister. Just because your husband keeps you happy, it doesn't mean it's like that for all wives! Basically I was doing the poor lasses a favour; thanks to me they've known a little affection . . .'

'So that was it,' she interrupted, 'you did it all out of kindness! That's very fine, you should try explaining it to the priest like that, it'd make him very happy . . .'

Mathilde was a good Christian. She never missed Mass on Sundays, and made sure that her boys attended catechism classes regularly. She felt a little sad that Pierre-Edouard so rarely accompanied her to the service, but she knew that in his own way he too had respect for religion. He took Communion at Easter, and got on well with Father Verlhac, who did them the honour of coming to share the family dinner three or four times a year.

But as far as her brother was concerned, she had good reason to be worried about his religious practices. Not that he was violently anti-clerical – he was on the best of terms with the priest – but that was no proof of Faith; all the former soldiers in the parish got on well with the cleric because he too was a war veteran. Apart from this relationship, Léon was totally indifferent to Church matters; he did not deride religion or argue about it but he declared 'I don't give a damn about all that!'

'Go on, no more kidding, is it a joke?' Pierre-Edouard insisted.

'Not at all! For God's sake, what's so extraordinary about it? Dammit, I'm not so old! Do you feel old yourself?' he asked his brother-in-law. 'No? Well then! Okay, I'm two years older than you, but it's no big deal to be forty-three! Think of that moron Léonard Bouyssoux at the Heath; he was over forty before he got married! And Gaston's second son-in-law, how old was he, eh? And Doctor Delpy, he was over fifty! So what?'

'That's not the problem,' his sister interrupted, 'it's just that we hadn't pictured you with a wife, that's all. Besides, who is she? Is she from round here?'

'No; well, yes . . .' he explained, fiddling with the prongs of his false hand. 'Bloody hell,' he burst out suddenly, 'you don't seem to like it very much! No, but it's true, you've given me the hump!'

'You've got it wrong,' Pierre-Edouard reassured him earnestly. 'We're surprised, that's all; put yourself in our shoes, we didn't expect to have a sister-in-law.'

'Who is she?' asked Mathilde again.

'You don't know her; she's from Brive, Chantalat's daughter . . .'

'Chantalat! The biggest wholesale butcher in the Corrèze! Well, my friend,' exclaimed Pierre-Edouard, 'you *are* aiming high!'

'What do you know about it! It's not like that . . .'

'I hope not!' Mathilde interrupted. 'How old is she?'

'Well . . .' he muttered in embarrassment. 'All right, she's twenty-three. Oh, I know what you're going to say! She's too young. She'll like going to dances. She'll need lots of dresses, and then I'm old enough to be her father, and so on and so on! Well, maybe I am, but so what? I don't care! You can say what you like, I shall marry her anyway!'

'Don't get upset,' said Pierre-Edouard, putting a hand on his arm, 'we won't say anything.'

'Maybe you won't, but they'll be gossiping in the village!'

'It'll soon pass,' Pierre-Edouard tried to comfort him. 'And after all, as you say, you're not the first person to marry someone younger than yourself!'

'Yes, I know,' said Léon gloomily. 'And I know better than you what young people need . . . so there! All I ask of her is that she gives me a child, a child like yours.' He was embarrassed to show a new side to his character. 'I'd like to have a son – yes, a son! And if he'd like to study, I'll pay for it. If he wants to be a doctor or even a government minister, then he'll be one! I've had enough of being alone with my pile of money! I don't know what to do with it all! The more I pay out, the more I get back, and it's no real use to me! Look, here, I've leased all the land and grazing belonging to the château and to the solicitor, that's sixty-two hectares, plus forty on the Rivière plain, another twenty-two at Larche, eight at Daudevie and six more at Varetz! I employ ten workers and I pay them well! I have a turnover of hundreds of calves, cows, bullocks and horses every year! And what's it all for? To live in this dump!' He waved his arm at the room. 'To end up all alone like a bad-tempered old boar! No, it can't go on like this. So, I'm going to get married, we'll have a child, and then it'll be worth earning some money.'

'You're right,' said Mathilde, 'and what's her name?'

'Yvette. She's not very pretty – no, she wouldn't hold a candle to you. She's not a beauty, but she is kind and gentle, and she has lovely eyes. And then, she's not marrying me for my money, she's got more than me! Just think, Chantalat's only child! So it's all settled, we're getting married in Brive on the twelfth of July, it's a Saturday. You will come, won't you? And the children too?'

'Of course,' said Mathilde.

'Good, so Pierre-Edouard will be my witness. I was really worried that you'd be cross with me, especially you,' he said, looking at his sister, 'you've always watched me like a cat watches her kittens! Well, I was worried that you wouldn't want to have anything to do with a sister-in-law. So, if you think it's a good idea, will you help me?'

'What with?'

'To sort things out here, get the house ready, all that. You see, I don't know much about women – well, what I mean is, what I know isn't any good for . . .'

'I understand,' Mathilde interrupted. 'Don't worry, we'll prepare a fine home for her. And you'll see, everyone in the village will be pleased to know that their mayor is settling down at last.'

Jacques turned over again in bed and envied his brother, who was deep in untroubled sleep, curled up at his side. He pushed him away roughly, and heard the familiar and irritating sound of greedy sucking. Not only did Paul fall asleep as soon as he got into bed, he also still sucked his thumb, despite being eight years old.

Jacques concluded that this babyish habit, and the fact that he could fall into sweet dreams in a few moments, proved that his brother lacked a conscience. Father Verlhac maintained that the guilty were tortured and often lay awake half the night. Not so! The priest was wrong, and that devil Paul was proof of it! It wasn't he who was gnawed by remorse, or the sneaking anxiety it engendered; *his* sleep was as calm and peaceful as a new-born babe's!

Yet, there were plenty of things to worry about and to dread in the next few days. For Jacques had no doubt that the damage they had caused would be discovered tomorrow, perhaps had been already. The workers putting up the line could not fail to notice how the insulators had been broken. They would naturally report this crime to the Mayor, and then it would not be Godfather or Uncle Léon, but a very strict grown-up who would instruct Alfred, the town sergeant, to investigate the matter immediately. 'Alfred wouldn't set the world on fire,' thought Jacques, remembering an expression his father had used, 'it's true that he's a fool, and he can't run because of losing a foot in the war, but still, he knows that we mind the cattle on Combes-Nègres and it's not far from the building site . . . No, it was a stupid idea to take my shooter!' He cursed himself again.

Then he thought that Paul would have broken the insulators anyway, and he would have been accused of aiding and abetting him. So, if you weighed it all up, at least he would deserve whatever he got . . .

He heard his grandfather going to bed on the other side of the partition. The springs creaked a little and then silence fell in the bedroom again, the only sounds the gentle breathing of little Mauricette, who lay beside her parents' bed, and the vulgar snuffling of that lucky devil Paul.

Jacques wondered what time his parents would return. They often went to see Léon after dinner; normally he was not aware of their return, for the noise they made going to bed and the light of their paraffin lamp did not wake him. But would it be the same, soon, when they turned on the electricity?

Everything was ready for it. Already a porcelain shade

hung from the ceiling of the bedroom, and when the moment came his father would connect one of the bulbs which now stood in the top of the wardrobe. There were six of them, and according to his father each would be as bright as twenty-five candles! What a marvel that such a little sphere of glass could emit such a light! Six bulbs, one for each of the two bedrooms of the house, another for the main room, one to light the yard in winter and the last two for the barn and piggery.

A lot of the villagers considered this a waste of money — one had to have plenty to spare to install electricity for the animals! But Pierre-Edouard replied that, since the electricians were coming to do work at his place, he might as well make the most of the opportunity.

True, the installation must have been expensive. Jacques did not know exactly what the final cost was, but the few conversations which he had happened to interrupt or over-hear made him think his father must have paid out at least 1,500 francs. That was considerable, the price of a young heifer. Jacques was proud of this extravagance, and regarded his friends at school with a certain air of condescension, for their parents were content with the minimum provision necessary and, for the sake of economy, would continue to milk by the light of an oil-lamp, or even with a candle, as they had done in the past! He even knew some, real barbarians these, who had refused to allow the electricity into their homes; they proclaimed that it would attract lightning towards the houses of those who had clamoured for this foolish innovation!

This was stupid, and the schoolmaster had told them so; he had even explained how electricity worked! Naturally you should not touch the wires, or put fingers or nails into the sockets; that was obvious, anyone could understand it! Of course — this thought depressed him — you should not break the insulators with catapult shots either . . .

He heard the front door creak, and the footsteps of his parents. He turned towards the wall, covered his nose with the sheet, and pretended to be asleep.

Just as Jacques had anticipated, the foreman of the work-team from the Gas Fusion company, which held the contract to install the line, stormed over to the mairie early next morning, described the damage, and demanded immediate action.

'You must understand,' he explained to Léon, 'if we do nothing there won't be a single insulator left when we come to attach the wire! It's bound to be some local kids up to mischief!'

'From this community? You have no proof,' Léon retorted, for he felt allegiance to his villagers and their offspring. 'But never fear, I'll look into it.'

But he had plenty of other things to do, and forgot the incident. Towards the end of the morning he noticed the children coming out of school, and this jogged his memory. He smiled when he saw his godson, Jacques, followed by his brother, who was kicking along an old tin with great thuds of his clogs. Then he rememberd the foreman's complaint, and called to his nephews.

There was no cause to suspect them in particular among the forty or so children dispersing across the square – except that Paul had a certain reputation. When he saw their faces he knew that he was on the right track. He forced himself to adopt a formidable expression, although he really had no wish to treat them harshly. He loved the two boys, knew that their parents kept them on a short rein, and did not want to be responsible for the punishment awaiting them, if they actually were guilty. And he had his own memories too. What had he *not* done, at that age! And Pierre-Edouard as well, always with his sister Louise in tow, had never been slow to join in Léon's outrageous escapades then.

'Well, young fellows,' he called to them, 'how's it going at school? Yes, I'm sure it's fine, you both work well . . . And my catapult, is that working well?'

It was Paul who saved the situation. Jacques had made Paul swear he would not whisper a word to anyone of the conversation overheard the previous evening, at a time when he was supposed to be asleep; now he was annoyed that he had confided in Paul, and blushed from head to toe.

'Hey, uncle, is it true that you're going to get married?' asked Paul with an innocent expression.

'Who told you that?' Léon was startled. He had asked his

sister and brother-in-law to be discreet; he intended to announce the news himself during the next meeting of the town council. 'Well, who told you?'

'It was Jacques,' blurted out the boy as he cleared out his nose with an experienced forefinger. He scrutinised the digit and then licked it clean. 'It's great you're getting married, we'll go to the wedding!'

'Bloody hell, where did you get that from, eh?' asked Léon, examining his godson.

'It was yesterday evening, I wasn't asleep when my parents came back from your place,' Jacques admitted, and hung his head. 'But we haven't told anyone,' he reassured his uncle.

'Honest,' added Paul, 'we haven't said anything yet . . . '

'Oh no? You're two rascals who'd be quite capable of breaking some insulators on the electricity line, wouldn't you? You haven't heard anything said about that by any chance, have you?'

'Well . . . ' Paul took evasive action. 'Tell us, is it true that you're going to buy yourself a car?'

'My God!' exclaimed Léon with a great guffaw, 'you'll get by okay, you've got the gift of the gab all right! Fine,' he said and suddenly became serious, 'I don't want to know which little scamps broke the insulators – it couldn't have been you, could it, eh? The Mayor's nephews couldn't do that! What would people think of me then, eh? And your parents! If they found out they'd tan your backsides pretty quickly . . . Go on, get out of here, and make sure you're not caught hanging about near the electricity pylons, or someone might get suspicious . . . Understand?'

'Yes, yes,' they chorused back.

'But you won't say anything to Papa, will you?' begged Jacques.

'No, I won't,' his godfather reassured him. 'This time, and this time only, I think it was those ragamuffins from Perpezac or Yssandon who came and did it, so that won't concern your father . . . '

Pierre-Edouard shrugged his shoulders, folded his newspaper and got up.

'I must go,' he said, glancing at the big pendulum clock.

It was his duty to attend the meeting of the town council, and he was sorry to give up this peaceful April evening for it. The children had been in bed for the last half-hour and were already quiet. His father had also gone to his bedroom, and only the hissing of the fire and the clicking of Mathilde's knitting-needles disturbed the peace and quiet of the room.

'I'll wait up for you,' said his wife from the settle.

'That's nice of you. Do you want the newspaper?'

'Oh no, I make do with watching your face as you read it!' she joked.

'You may be better off with that! I wonder what will come of it all!'

He slipped on his jacket, bent over Mathilde to kiss her, and went out.

It was fresh, almost cold, and the sky was quite clear, punctuated by a reddish arc, the first quarter of the new moon.

'If it doesn't cloud over, that russet moon will cause some losses,' he thought as he started down the main street.

There was no need for natural forces to add to their troubles and make things even more difficult. The country was in crisis; if Pierre-Edouard shrugged his shoulders as he read the paper, it was because there was nothing else he could do. All those idiotic politicans quarrelling over their share of the cake were not worth anything more. Because anyone with any sense was fed up with ministers who came and went; since the sad departure of Poincaré they had been led by a series of puppets – Briand, Tardieu, Chautemps. All those time-servers had achieved was a fall in the price of corn; six months ago it had dropped from 161.50 francs a quintal to 139.50. They really had something to be proud of! Proud of the slump in the price of meat too, and the growing difficulties which beset the farmers on all sides!

Despite this, Pierre-Edouard would not be drawn into militant political action, although he was never slow to give his opinion. He mistrusted those who made a living out of politics – and a good living – too much to want to imitate them and support one party or another.

He reserved the right to praise or criticise whoever he saw fit, whatever their political colour, and he exercised this right freely. Up till now he had managed to remain on good terms with all his friends, whether they were liberal and apolitical, like Dr Delpy; on the right, like his next-door neighbour Maurice, Edouard Lapeyre or even Pierre Delpeyroux; moderate like his brother-in-law Léon; or frankly leftist like Martin Tavet, Jean Bernical or Louis Brousse. All these men were members of the town council and did their best to promote the well-being of the community of Saint-Libéral-sur-Diamond.

Exclamations and laughter exploded from the mairie and echoed along the main street: Pierre-Edouard realised that his brother-in-law had just announced his impending marriage, and quickened his pace. Now he was in a hurry to see the expression of the prospective bridegroom of forty-three, and in a hurry to join in the jokes which would probably take up a good part of the meeting. He pushed open the door of the mairie and was himself greeted with shouts.

'You knew about this, did you?' cried Maurice.

'Only since the day before yesterday, no longer,' he confessed.

'Are we all here?' bawled Léon. 'Perhaps we ought to get down to a bit of work!'

'The doctor can't come,' Pierre Delpeyroux informed them, 'he's gone to the Mazière farm, it looks as if the father won't last the night . . . '

The mood darkened immediately, and the men nodded their heads. Old Firmin Mazière was eighty-seven, the patriarch of the village and well liked by everyone. He had never harmed anyone, was a good neighbour and an honest man. He was one of the last who could still recall the old way of life and evoke memories of an age when there were almost 1,300 people living in the parish of Saint-Libéral; when every patch of land was lovingly tended, when the village could feed everyone who wanted to take the trouble to work, and young people had no need to leave for the towns.

Alas, a bygone era! Today there were only 594 inhabitants, and the land left fallow extended further each year, just as the exodus of the young also gathered strength. Nothing could halt this flight, for nothing could relieve the poverty which forced them from their homes.

'Say what you like, old Mazière was a fine man,' Léon continued. And everyone agreed.

After the meeting they all repaired to the inn, for Léon's engagement had to be suitably celebrated, and there they learned of Mazière's death. He had passed away an hour earlier. The landlady had the news from the doctor, whom she saw returning from the house of the deceased.

'He died just as we were talking of him,' remarked Martin Tavet.

'Bah,' their hostess interrupted, 'he was old enough, wasn't he? What can I get you?'

No one said a word, but gave their orders without commenting on Suzanne's thoughtlessness and lack of respect; such a remark would never have been tolerated when the Chanlats were running the place. The Chanlat couple were local; they knew everyone, and they respected the dead. But with Suzanne, they would have to overlook it . . .

After all, she was an outsider, born in Tulle, and then, everyone agreed that she was slightly crazy. You would have to be, to buy an inn which was on its last legs – the bedrooms had remained desperately empty during the three years of her ownership. But she hadn't balked at the amount, had paid the asking price, cash on the nail. Since then business had been neither good nor bad, but Suzanne did not complain. As a war widow, she had a good pension anyway.

Her first husband had been killed on the Marne in September 1914 when she was only eighteen; his faded portrait adorned the wall on the left side of the mirror behind the bar. However, they were all of the opinion that this unfortunate private was not the one who had made her fortune. On the contrary, she was beholden to her second husband, a sergeant-major; he had just found time to give her a daughter before stupidly stepping on a mine in August 1918. Since then she banked a regular income to live on and raise her daughter, thanks to the good man whose photo and medals hung on the right of the mirror; the modest takings from the inn were almost superfluous.

But the two bereavements she had suffered before she was

twenty-three had left another legacy, besides the pension. She was seized by terrible bouts of melancholia, when she dissolved into tears, and all the unmarried men in the area were seized by an insatiable urge to console her. These crises of despair were invariably followed by a period of euphoria during which she sang like a blackbird, willingly served anyone, and even gave credit to all those who wanted to share in her happiness.

In fact it was an open secret that she changed her partner every four or five months; she drowned her sorrows in curaçao for a week or so, and revived again as soon as she could lay her hands on a sympathetic man who had his health and strength. Yes, she was a foolish woman and her remarks were often indiscreet, but all her customers were fond of her. As for the women of the village, they considered her a dangerous and depraved female.

'Come on, give us another of those,' demanded Léon, holding out his empty glass.

'Well now, it's my turn, in honour of your marriage,' announced Suzanne, with a touch of bitterness in her voice. She cherished unmistakable but unreciprocated feeling for Léon, who had always rebuffed her advances. He was very circumspect in the matter of his conquests; although a terrible skirt-chaser, he had the prudence of a fox and, like them, did not hunt on his home patch.

'I bet you haven't heard the latest news, have you?' added Suzanne. She paused to increase the suspense, and was satisfied when she noticed that everyone was listening; she drew herself up —you were forced to admire her bust, everyone said as much.

'Yes,' she continued, 'I had it from Maître Chardoux, from his own lips, he stopped by this evening on his way back from the château . . . '

'And so what?' asked Léon.

Everyone knew that Maître Chardoux took care of her ladyship's affairs. Since she had been widowed during the war, the old lady had not returned to the village. She was living in Paris with her second daughter, and left to her solicitor the business of renting the land and maintaining the château, which had been empty for nearly fifteen years. The arrival of the solicitor in Saint-Libéral was therefore nothing unusual.

'And so what?' mimicked Suzanne. 'Well, her ladyship is going to come back to live here soon, and her daughter too . . .'

'Incredible!' cried the men.

They were pleased at this decision, for everyone was sad to see the great building deteriorate from year to year, when it had once been so full of life. Nothing was more forlorn than the closed shutters overgrown with ivy and wild vines, the steps overrun by briars and nettles, the terraced gardens invaded by scrub, the old trees in the orchard smothered in old man's beard and honeysuckle.

If the squire's wife returned, all that would be brought back to life, renovated, and the village would be enhanced in the process. Furthermore, the restoration would give the craftsmen some work – the tiler, the joiner, the stonemason; there was so much to do to repair the neglect of years! Then the lady would certainly need a housekeeper, a gardener, and perhaps even a steward, as before. Her return really was good news.

Chapter 3

As a general rule, except when weather threatened the harvest, Pierre-Edouard did not work on Sundays. Instead he made use of this day to survey his property quietly, noting the fine growth of the crops, the vigour of the trees and vines. He loved these walks, and took great pleasure in them.

Sometimes Mathilde and the children accompanied him. Then, whilst the children galloped ahead, they remembered the paths walked and the years gone by since that morning in September 1917 when they had met, up there among the broom and juniper bushes of the White Peak. Pierre-Edouard had never for a moment regretted that day, the sudden urge which had thrown them together and united them for all time with an oft-renewed fervour. Their love grew stronger and deeper, quickened afresh by the daily round of work on the land they loved, enlivened by the births of their children and the happiness and vitality they brought with them.

There had been difficulties enough, and worries still beset them, but these did not daunt them or weaken their resolve; instead each problem drew them together, strengthened their unity, as comrades in adversity support, encourage and complement one another.

Pierre-Edouard entered the field called the Meeting. He was alone on his walk on this the first Sunday in June, for Mathilde had preferred to remain at home to look after Mauricette, who was feeling low after a persistent cold. As for Jacques and Paul, as soon as High Mass was over, they had joined their Sunday School friends in a game of rugby, with Father Verlhac as referee, and would return elated but covered in bruises.

He stopped in front of the field of potatoes, took out his pipe and filled it while contemplating the vast expanse of the plateau and the pattern of fields. Here, at least, the land was clean and in good heart. The slopes where the gradient demanded hand digging and manual cultivation were quite a different matter.

Abandoned since the war for lack of manpower, most were now covered with brushwood and undergrowth. It was a pity to think that beneath the saplings a fine rich loam lay hidden, just right for spring vegetables and fruit trees; but what was to be done about it? No one had the time or opportunity to work as in the past. Just a few plots, the more accessible ones between the briars and gorse, displayed a variety of vegetables in rows: peas, onions and salad greens. But this area dwindled from year to year; it was enough for a grandfather or grandmother to die for the tiny oasis which they tended with such care to perish with them.

Fortunately, it was a different matter on the plateau. The fields were level, easy to plough, and the soil was productive when well cared for. Many of the farmers of Saint-Libéral owned plots up here. But the best pieces, the largest, were undoubtedly those of the Vialhe family.

Over there the Big Field, covered in wheat; then the Malides, where winter barley was growing; further on the Perrier field, with its lines of young but vigorous plum trees, and to the right the Long Piece with its twenty-eight walnut trees; these were nearly thirty years old, and had grown into magnificent specimens. Nearer to him lay the land called the Letters, which had belonged to Léon and then Mathilde, and in front of him the patch called the Meeting.

Eight years ago all this land had been neglected, the soil exhausted by his father's poor system of crop rotation. Pierre-Edouard had taken it in hand and restored it. Rough work, to which he and Mathilde had devoted time and effort unstintingly – and now their labours were bearing fruit.

From his time on a farm near Paris, Pierre-Edouard had brought back modern ideas and techniques. Some had made his neighbours laugh, but eventually they were forced to admit that he knew what he was doing. They had been compelled to acknowledge that the seeds and fertilisers he used gave excellent results, and that his methods of work were an improvement on theirs.

Now no one disputed his position as the best farmer in the community, just as his father had been before him. Year in, year out, he managed a return of seventeen quintals – an old measure, approximately equal to a hundredweight – of corn from each hectare; that was about eight more than the average yield in the area. As for his pure-bred Limousin cows, they compared well with the championship animals which Léon exhibited at the agricultural shows all around. He also raised pigs, a dozen sows and a boar which everyone admired. The breeding stock had been ordered from the farm where he had spent four years before the war, following the quarrel with his father. These Yorkshire piglets were fatter, longer and faster growing than the black and white local breed common to the area.

All this justified the decision, taken by the majority of the farmers, to entrust him with the office of president of the farmers co-operative society, the buying syndicate. He had therefore replaced his father at the head of this organisation and everyone benefited from his professional skill and judicious advice.

However, there was a cloud on the horizon, a threat to the future. Although Pierre-Edouard had earnestly requested it, his father had never set his affairs in order. Most of the land – seventeen hectares of it – the farm and the outbuildings, were still in Jean-Edouard's name, and while he was alive they would remain so. Of course Pierre-Edouard was in charge; it was he and he alone who managed the farm and ran it in his own way, just as he managed the five hectares which were his and Mathilde's own property.

There was nothing to prevent his sisters from one day reclaiming their share of this inheritance. He would have preferred it to happen during his father's lifetime, if only to know where he stood, resolve the uncertainty of his situation.*

But Jean-Edouard would never give in. He had probably forgiven his daughters their past behaviour, but not so fully that he would allow them to benefit from his prosperity while he was still there!

Pierre-Edouard was therefore making economies, to pre-pare for the day when his father died and his sisters would

---

*In France all children inherit equally if the father dies intestate.

exercise their rights to the property. He did not mind paying them compensation, that was a legitimate principle, but his fear was that Louise or Berthe would refuse the money, would choose the land. They might force him to divide up the Vialhe estate, which for almost two centuries had increased in size and beauty. It was his pride, and he intended to pass it on to one of his sons, whichever he judged best able to succeed him. But for the time being, the farm was not even in his own name!

He reassured himself: his sisters would not want land, what could they do with it? Especially Berthe! You could say she had been successful, but what a life she led! You might get the flavour of it by looking at some of the postcards she sent each year: London, New York, Rio, Berlin, Rome. She had widened her field of operations and, without abandoning her first great success – her remarkable talent as a milliner – had expanded into haute couture, and now toured the world to present her collections or to open new showrooms.

Pierre-Edouard was full of admiration for her, but he also had his reservations. He admired her because he knew what she had suffered on the farm until that day in August 1914 when she had at last attained her majority and taken to the road. What a change since then! What boldness and business sense, to know how to set up an enterprise like that! But he could not accept the way of life she had chosen; it embarrassed him. A life of luxury, of a liberated woman, who preferred to remain unmarried and seek *affaires*, rather than the calm and ordered role which befitted a worthy daughter of the house of Vialhe. Berthe really threw him off-balance.

It was not the same with Louise. Despite the distance which separated them and the fact that they had not seen each other for ten years, he still felt the same bond with her that had linked them all their youth.

She also wrote regularly, as did her son Félix, who was Pierre-Edouard's godson. Louise continued as governess in the château in Brenne, where she looked after her employer's three children, and never complained. As for Félix, he was completing his military service; he was in Morocco and enjoying it. After his discharge he would become a forest warden, like the stepfather whom he had hardly known but greatly admired, to the point of sharing the same love of trees

31

and the forest.

Louise, Berthe and himself: what paths they had travelled in the last twenty years!

Pierre-Edouard lit his pipe, tamped the tobacco with his thumb, and walked on into the potato field. They were fine strong plants; he had earthed them up during the week and they were in good order.

He bent down and fingered the leaves. He was pleased with his choice of seed potatoes; for the first time he had chosen 'Early Round', a variety similar to 'Orléans Yellow', which was supposed to do well in this area and produce fifteen to twenty tons a hectare. He straightened a slightly withered shoot, stared at the plant and suddenly swore: 'My God, they've arrived . . . '

He took a few steps and immediately saw them: dozens of yellow and red beetles with ten black stripes running down the body. He could not be mistaken – the colony which was currently devouring his potatoes was that dreaded parasite, the Colorado beetle!

It was not really a surprise. For years all the farmers had been expecting just such an attack; for years they had discussed the inexorable approach of these destructive insects. The beetles had made their first appearance in 1920 in the Bordeaux area, and caused such losses that the whole farming community of France had been worried. But that had not prevented the pests from spreading further each year, from reaching Charentes, the Dordogne, Vienne and Haute Vienne and then, two years ago, part of the Corrèze. Up till now nobody in the village had been affected by this curse, this catastrophe. Now it was fact; the Colorado beetles were there.

Pierre-Edouard bent down again, turned over several leaves and pulled a face as he saw dozens of minute yellow eggs stuck to the underside of the foliage. On some of the plants the sticky, obese larvae were already crawling about, orangey-red caterpillars with black patches.

'Now we're for it!'

The most fantastic stories were told about Colorado beetles. Some people were certain that they came from

America, secretly despatched by the government over there in order to ruin French farmers, so that the Americans could export their surplus potatoes. Other rumours swore that the blow had been struck by the Germans as revenge for their defeat. The latest gossip pointed to the pesticide salesmen, who were supposed to have come by night and shaken out sacks of insects from aeroplanes over the areas which were not yet infested.

This rubbish was not worth listening to; Pierre-Edouard knew, from reading about it in one of the farming reviews, that it was much simpler than any of that. It was true that the infestation had begun in 1920 in the Gironde area, true that it had originated in America, but it was accidental, not deliberate; the pests had been imported in a cargo of potatoes. All the rest was lies, and those who accused the Germans were ignorant, because it was well known that the beetle – discovered in 1824 in Colorado – had first appeared in Germany in 1876! However, it *was* true to say that they were very poorly equipped to defend themselves against this invader.

Pierre-Edouard strode swiftly through the field. He then cut across the plateau and hurried towards the village.

Just as he had expected and hoped, plenty of men were taking a drink at Suzanne's. He went in and leaned towards Maurice.

'Go and tell the men who are at Lamothe's to come here. Yes, yes, it's important, they must come!'

The Lamothe daughter kept the other bistro in the village. She had followed in the footsteps of her mother, Ma Eugène, whose reputation had been more than questionable in the early 1900s. It was enough to make you believe that vice was hereditary, for Noémie Lamothe was even more slatternly than her mother, according to the old men, and that was saying something ... Thirty-five years old, with a bold eye, not ugly, but careless of her appearance, she survived thanks to a small but loyal clientele of old bachelors who did not mind the tittle-tattle and preferred to visit her rather than a brothel. It was closer to home, friendlier and cheaper; the only inconvenience was that you could not be in a hurry – the wench was hard to satisfy and took her time. Compared to

33

that slut, the beautiful Suzanne almost passed for a saint. Two or three episodes a year practically raised her to the rank of a decent woman.

Pierre-Edouard elbowed his way to the bar and ordered a Pernod. He was just finishing his glass when the half-dozen customers from Noémie's rounded up by Maurice entered the auberge.

'Good God! What's up with you?' complained Mathieu Fayette. He was furious because Maurice had fetched him back from halfway up the staircase which led to Noémie's bedroom. 'Well, what do you want?' he repeated. 'I've got other things to do besides coming to your meetings!'

This comment was greeted with coarse laughter and plenty of improper suggestions, but Pierre-Edouard did not feel like laughing.

'I don't want to call a meeting! I've just come down from the plateau and look, lads, up there it's covered in Colorado beetles . . .'

'God damn it!' cried the men.

'I told you,' shouted one of the drinkers, 'it's you who brought them here, with your blasted special seeds! They're not on *our* plants, those pests won't touch *us*!'

'Don't talk rubbish,' interrupted Pierre-Edouard. 'On my way back I crossed your potato field; it's worse affected than mine! And covered in blight as well! I told you to spray with copper sulphate, but as usual you don't listen to anything!'

'The beetles are on my land?' the heckler was reduced to murmuring.

'Yes, on your land! On Maurice's too, on Bernical's, my brother-in-law's and yours, Edmond; I didn't see any on yours, Pierre, that was the only one.'

They were all struck dumb by the news. Eventually, Louis Brousse spoke out: 'But we must do something!'

'Well, yes,' replied Pierre-Edouard quietly, 'but what? I know we need lead arsenate, but I haven't any in the store – the pest control officer gave me some, but I passed it on to Léon.'

'Why didn't you keep it! It's your business to have some in the co-op!' cried one of the group.

'Go and get lost!' Pierre-Edouard shouted at him. 'If you

34

want my job, you can have it. You don't think I was going to keep that poison in stock? It's full of arsenic, that stuff!'

'So we must contact Léon,' suggested Maurice.

'It's Sunday, who knows where he'll be!'

'He'll have gone off to look under the leaves with his lady-friend,' cried a joker.

But there was little laughter in response to this comment, for they were all thinking about the beetles eating their crops.

Father Verlhac was the first to launch an attack on the pests. As soon as he heard the news, that is to say just after lunch, he went to Pierre-Edouard and explained his idea. He was not the first to think of it; he admitted that it came from reading an article in the *Pélerin*. In the badly affected areas, the schoolchildren had collected up the insects and leaves bearing eggs, and this had slowed down the infestation.

'But they'll trample on all the plants!' exclaimed Jean-Edouard. 'Your cure will be worse than the illness!'

He had been considering the best way to stop the invasion ever since his son had told him what he had seen. He had never been the sort to give up, and he intended to fight this battle too. He had experienced so many of these struggles between man and nature in his lifetime! The Colorado beetles were a new plague; they had to survive it and beat it if possible.

'Yes,' he repeated, 'your kids will crush everything.'

'I'm not so sure,' said Pierre-Edouard, 'if we explain it carefully, it might work. If we put one or two of them in each row, with a box to throw the pests into, that's not so complicated!'

'No,' said Paul, 'but what if they pinch our fingers?'

'Stupid! They don't sting!' his brother snapped at him. 'That's right, isn't it, Papa, they can't hurt us?'

'No, only the potatoes.'

'So, what's the decision?' asked Father Verlhac.

'We'll do as you suggest, but we'll have to contact the teacher first so that he can get all the kids together; it's a matter of explaining carefully how to do it.'

'All right, I'll go and see him.'

The relationship between the priest and Charles Deplat, the

primary school teacher, was most peculiar. The two men were almost the same age, getting on for fifty, and had arrived in the village in the years just before the war. There followed a long period of stealthy observation and of extreme circumspection; each did his best not to provide any ammunition for the other to attack him.

The four years of war had changed all that, and when they met again it was not as enemies but as brothers-in-arms. Brothers sometimes have little family quarrels, of course; ideological differences, nothing of consequence, they were settled in battles of words. One would wave the latest article by Herriot or Briand, the other defended his position every inch of the way by quoting long tirades from the latest Papal Encyclical, *Divini illius Magistri* – concerning Christian education – or, if it was a really serious matter, denounce him in the words of Léon Daudet!

When, at the end of arguments, they resorted to calling each other Bolshevik, Communist lackey, Fascist or Royalist, reconciliation was in sight. This was usually sealed with a glass of aperitif, in which each combatant toasted the health of his own party.

'To the socialists of the world and long live the class struggle!' the teacher would gravely announce.

'To the Christians martyred by you Reds, and long live God!' responded the priest.

The whole village understood this mild guerilla warfare and found it amusing, except the hardline militants who made themselves ridiculous by fiercely advocating either Marx or Christ! The former accused the schoolmaster of complacency in confronting the enemy, the latter – a few men and a horde of bigoted women – scolded their pastor, for he not only consorted with a disciple of the Devil, he also encouraged vice and debauchery by drinking at Suzanne's, the fallen woman. They had even written to the bishop deploring the laxity of their priest.

Father Verlhac knew their opinion of him, but he did not worry about it any more than he did about his best cassock. All that concerned him was that through the rugby team, which he organised with the help of the teacher, the boys continued to come and see him, even after their First

Communion.

It had the desired effect, and that was only a start! He was still laughing at the underhand blow he had just dealt the anti-church faction; he had secretly purchased a magnificent miniature film projector, bleeding himself white to pay for it. Thanks to this machine and some good films, he was confident, as soon as electricity was connected in the village, of increasing the number of children within his realm of influence. His acquisition had enraged the teacher, furious that he had not been the first with such a brilliant idea! The two men had called each other names, and then drank together to seal a truce.

The priest found the teacher in his garden. He was weeding a long row of carrots, with the help of his wife; the clergyman was sorely tempted to criticise them for working on a Sunday. He swallowed his words, remembering that he had come with the aim of setting the children to work; this idea, worthy of an arch-pagan, was all his own.

An hour later, all the children were on the plateau. There were also many men and women curious to see what the beetles looked like and what damage they caused. After they had expressed their horror and outrage, they augmented the teams spread out in the various plots and joined the hunt.

They worked until evening, filling their buckets or tins and then going to empty them into a basin half-full of paraffin. When it began to get dark and they were about to go back down to the village, Pierre-Edouard had an argument with several of the women who wanted to keep what they had collected – to feed their hens, they explained.

'No, no! In the first place I don't know whether chickens eat these creatures, and secondly they can fly, so if you take them to the village, some are bound to escape and you'll have spread the plague a bit further, is that what you want to do?'

'Pierre-Edouard is right,' agreed the teacher as he wiped his fingers, sticky and yellow from crushing many insects, on the grass. 'We must not spread these evil creations of our good Lord!' he called out in the direction of the priest.

'Of the Devil, my friend, of the Devil,' the priest firmly stated. 'You're in a good position to know that Satan is the ruler in this world . . . '

'Yes, yes,' interrupted Pierre-Edouard, not in the mood to referee the slanging match he felt was imminent. He was tired but more, very worried, for after a few steps through the rows of potatoes, he could already see that many of the beetles had escaped being collected.

'Yes,' he repeated, 'we don't give a damn whether they come from God or the Devil! All I know is,' he took out his lighter, 'I'm going to set fire to the horrible mess. Mind out!' he shouted, as he lit a handful of dry grass.

The bowl instantly blazed up with a clear, high flame, the wing cases and bodies sparkling and sputtering as they burned.

'There's a good job done,' he announced, 'but we must spray the plants, starting tomorrow. My God, we didn't need this! Come on, I must get back.'

They fell into step with him and strode down towards the village, which was already bathed in darkness.

A council meeting took place as early as possible the following morning, to implement a proper plan of action.

'Do you know where you can get this preparation?' asked Léon, turning to his brother-in-law, 'because the amount you gave me won't be enough.'

'In Objat.'

'And do you know what we need?'

'Yes, lead arsenate and lime.'

'Well, go and get some straight away. Since we've decided to treat the fields, there's no point in waiting till the evening train for delivery. Take your cart and get going. My God, how long have I been saying that I should buy a car! To think I missed that old one belonging to Monsieur Lardy!'

The former solicitor, who had retired ten years ago, had sold his Renault six months earlier, but Léon had carelessly missed the chance to buy it. Now only the doctor owned a motor-car, and he certainly would not have time to run over to Objat on a Monday morning!

'I'll take your tilbury instead,' Pierre-Edouard informed him. 'My mare won't get there and back without losing at least one of her shoes, they're so worn down at the moment.

And now I think of it, we must count how many sprayers we've got, we'll need to use them all.' Not all the farmers had spraying-machines. Only those with good-sized vineyards had bought one of these devices for spreading the copper sulphate, and there was no guarantee that they were in working order.

'Yes, I'll get Alfred to see to that, starting this morning. Come on, get going, you should have left already! And don't forget,' he called out, 'I bought my horse from the army, he's just as idle as an adjutant!'

Everyone laughed, for they all knew that Pierre-Edouard had ended the war with that rank.

Pierre-Edouard returned during the afternoon; no horse could dawdle along with him, who had broken in plenty of them. As soon as he emerged into the main square he noticed a row of at least twenty spraying-machines in front of the fountain, and carts lined up with barrels of water and tubs on them, to prepare the mixture. The men were waiting, sitting under the lime trees or on the terrace of Suzanne's bar.

'You didn't hang around,' Léon said admiringly, patting the sweat-soaked flanks of his horse.

'He's a fine beast, I suspect you don't now how to talk to him,' replied Pierre-Edouard as he jumped down.

'He's a good-for-nothing, I told you,' maintained Léon stubbornly as he began to unload the boxes, 'but if you like I'll let you have him at cost price!'

'Keep talking!' cried Pierre-Edouard as he set off home, 'I'm going to get a bite to eat, I didn't have time earlier. I'll join you up there. Oh, and if it's any comfort to you, we're not alone; it seems there are beetles right across the plain. They multiplied in that humidity, that's why there are so many all at once.'

They worked until darkness fell, taking turns to carry the heavy, metal machines; the straps cut into their shoulders, and their right arms, which had to pump continuously, swelled up, and the weight rested agonisingly on the small of the back.

Towards eight o'clock, while it was still light, the women

came up with food. The men ate hungrily but with wrinkled noses, for their hands and clothes were impregnated with the chemicals, and a revolting smell hung over the plateau. Then they resumed their dogged march to and fro, walking with the slow step of exhausted foot soldiers.

When they finally stopped, all the potatoes on the plateau had received their dose of poison. They returned to the village believing that they had won the battle.

But a week later, the beetles appeared in the fields on the edge of the village. In a fortnight they reappeared on the high ground. The men repeated the treatment. They knew that from now on they would have to reckon with this pest. It seemed ineradicable, like midges, lice or mosquitoes. So they might as well get used to it; it was just another enemy to fight.

Chapter 4

SINCE the new moon in mid-June the weather had been superb, warm, just right for the haymaking. The whole village set to work in haste, to try to make up for the days lost at the beginning of the month, when it had been too stormy. They rose at dawn to the whetting of the scythe and the scratching of the reaper blades on the sandstone grinder, and they fell asleep late at night while the chains rattled on the well-coping and the water gushed from the last buckets the workers poured over themselves. The air grew balmy, and as the last swathes were cut their slightly bitter, coarse smell mingled with the heavy perfume of drying hay which transpired in the relative cool of the barns.

Pierre-Edouard was washing his face one last time in front of the well, his chest bare and trousers rolled up to the knee; he dried himself roughly with his sweat-soaked shirt, and smiled as he watched his sons. For once they were not being stingy with the water; they usually ran away from the tap over the sink, but now they seemed to be enjoying washing themselves. They really had sweated themselves out, helping him to load the last cartful of hay.

'Come on,' he called to them, 'you've watered yourselves enough now. Maman and Pépé will have finished seeing to the animals, you'd better get dressed, it's supper-time.' He walked into the main room and his bare feet slapped on the tiles. 'Good God, it's as dark as an oven in here!' He felt along the plaster moulding above the fireplace in search of matches.

He pulled down the paraffin lamp hanging above the table, lit it and was pleased to see that everything was ready for the meal; the table laid, the lettuce ready to be tossed, the jugs filled. As for the soup, it was simmering gently on the dying embers of the fire. He poured himself half a glass of wine, topped it up with water and swallowed it in one, then he slipped on his clogs and went out again to join Mathilde in the stable. Beside the well, the children were still splashing about in fits of giggles.

'You got everything under cover?' asked Jean-Edouard, as he poured a measure of wine into the bottom of his soup bowl.

'Yes, and I had help!' said Pierre-Edouard, lifting his chin towards Jacques and Paul.

'You do as you think best,' continued his father, 'but if I were you I wouldn't mow tomorrow, the sun set in a watery haze . . . '

'I saw it. But don't worry, I don't need that to tell me that a storm's coming . . . '

'Your leg?' asked Mathilde.

She was resting on the settle and gently stroking Mauricette's head; the child had fallen asleep on her lap.

'Yes,' he replied, 'since midday.'

He had been seriously wounded during the final months of the war, and bore a long deep scar on his left thigh which reacted to the slightest change in the weather with a nagging pain. It did not hurt enough to incapacitate him, just enough to warn him.

'Well, we'll see what tomorrow brings; anyway we've done most of it,' he said, sliding a portion of omelette on to his plate. He served his sons, and then suddenly pointed his fork towards the paraffin lamp. 'Speaking of tomorrow, do you remember?'

The children nodded. Of course they remembered! The electricity was going to be connected, they had been looking forward to the day for ages!

'It's an important date,' continued Pierre-Edouard. 'Have a good look at this paraffin lamp; we won't be needing it after tomorrow.'

'So we could smash it!' cried Paul, full of excitement at the thought of such a fine target.

'And what for?' growled his father. 'All you ever think of is destroying things! No, we won't smash it up, we don't need that!'

'Well, if it isn't any use any more . . . ' Paul tried again.

'Be quiet! Then eat up and get to bed, there's school tomorrow!'

'Yes, and we won't be able to see the electricity when it comes on,' Jacques complained.

'Yes, you will,' Mathilde reassured him, 'I'm sure the teacher will test it in school. What time are they connecting us?' she asked her husband.

'At eleven o'clock. And afterwards there's a reception at the mairie and everyone is invited — especially former town councillors,' he added casually.

He knew his father would not deign to appear, particularly if it involved congratulating Léon! But at least he could not say that he had not been informed about it!

'Right, I'm going to bed,' observed Jean-Edouard drily.

He leaned towards his grandsons, offered his grey stubbly cheek to be kissed, and then went into his room. The door slammed behind him.

Mathilde looked at Pierre and shrugged her shoulders almost imperceptibly; the gulf between her brother and her father-in-law could not be bridged, and even the inauguration of the electricity supply would not change that.

Everyone in the village was happy to have electricity at last, so they came in great numbers to celebrate its arrival. A few pessimists gravely foretold that this step forward would cost them their eyesight, but the majority of the inhabitants were proud of the brand-new posts beside the main road, and the transformer on the edge of the village, just beyond the railway station.

But the heavens were not propitious. The clouds were already dense and low as dawn broke, and all those who had hay on the ground were in a bad mood as they rushed to the meadows to try to gather the drying fodder into tall heaps. It was no use: the first shower came pattering down at about nine o'clock, short but violent, and drenched all the crops. It also soaked all the workers, who came back angrily cursing the clouds. Towards ten o'clock the thunder rolled over Terrasson.

'Bah, the morning storm doesn't deter the traveller,' cried Léon to the men who had already arrived at the town hall.

'No,' replied Louis Brousse seriously, 'but it rots the hay . . .'

He was reproaching himself bitterly for having cut a large part of his meadow the previous evening, and he almost regretted paying 1,850 francs for his reaper. For he too, like many others, had finally given in to the temptation to mechanise. What alternative was there? Seasonal workers were few and far between now, and the occasional young man who offered his services hardly knew how to use a scythe, let alone sharpen it without ruining the blade! It was really sad. A far cry from the teams of mowers of twenty years ago who cut the majority of the hay-meadows in the village. Nowadays only the steeply sloping fields echoed to the swish of the scythe; the rest was ruled by machinery.

He had nothing against the machines. They were efficient – too efficient perhaps, for they made it all too easy and encouraged you to work on, each swathe calling to its brother as it fell! That was what made Louis Brousse so cross with himself: he had not known when to stop. Now, because of that wretched machine which mowed so quickly, half his meadow was soaking up the water! He would not have suffered such damage if he had stuck to his good old scythe. The effort required for the work meant that a man was never tempted to mow more than he could bring in. He cut a section, turned it, gathered it up and stored it under shelter. Then he took up his blade again and set quietly to mowing a fresh portion of grass. Pacing oneself like that, the amount of hay spoiled never caused any loss of sleep, even if a storm came. Whereas now more than half a hectare had been exposed to the downpour . . .

'Have you got hay on the ground?' Léon asked him.

'You could say so! All the top part of my holding!'

'Everyone has got some on the ground,' said Bernical, 'that's the way it is with the mechanical reapers, nothing comes in half measures!'

'That's just what I said,' grumbled Louis Brousse, 'we're fools to let ourselves be controlled by machines!'

He shrugged his shoulders and moved to the window, pensively watching the rain pour down.

The storm broke at ten to eleven. It was not one of those huge terrifying onslaughts which leave you breathless and counting anxiously as you await the next peal of thunder. It was quiet, frightened no one, and moved away after five or six warning flashes.

Unfortunately one of these broke the circuit in the trans-former, which made Léon look ridiculous. As eleven o'clock struck, having said a few well-chosen words on the benefits of scientific progress, he intended to illuminate the hall of the mairie. He lowered the switch and the assembly looked up towards the porcelain lamp-shade.

'Bloody hell, what's up! It's not working!' murmured Léon, flicking the little copper switch up and down to no avail. 'Well now,' he called to the chief engineer, 'so that's your electrical magic? It doesn't seem much of a miracle!'

'The storm must have blown a fuse in the transformer,' explained the engineer. 'It will be quickly repaired.'

He sent off one of his men immediately to have a look at the transformer. The expert returned very soon and confirmed the diagnosis.

'So, this time is it going to work?' asked Léon. 'Yes? Good, let's go.'

He moved the switch and swore when he observed that nothing had happened; a murmur of discontent rumbled around the hall.

'*Miladiou*! Are you trying to make a fool of me, or what?' groaned Léon.

'The problem must lie here,' declared the engineer crossly. 'Are you sure your meter is switched on?'

'What an idea! I'm not stupid!'

'Let's make sure, all the same,' suggested the engineer, and strode to the little cupboard which concealed the black box. But he had to believe the evidence of his eyes. The meter was working.

'Very well, very well,' he said, forcing a smile. He ran his hand through his hair and scratched his head. 'The whole sector must be out,' he pronounced authoritatively, 'because of the storm. It happens sometimes . . .'

'That's not much use,' cried one of the men. 'If the light goes out every time a cloud farts sideways, it wasn't worth all that expense!'

'That's right,' added his neighbour, 'say what you like, that doesn't happen with a candle.'

'Just the opposite,' joked Maurice. 'At my house my wife lights the Candlemas candle as soon as she hears a peal of thunder!'

'So, what shall we do?' asked Léon. 'Will it take a long time?'

'No, no,' the engineer reassured him, 'my colleagues must be mending it already, believe me.'

'We-e-ell, all right.' Léon was somewhat sceptical. 'Fine, we'll drink to it anyway,' he decided, and turned to the table laden with bottles and glasses. 'Come along, help yourselves,' he invited.

But however much they clinked their glasses and told jokes, their hearts were not in it. They felt frustrated and soon began to slip away.

'Ah, now it's working!' Léon noticed after everyone had left.

'Simply an accident,' the engineer tried to reassure him.

'Yes, yes,' added Pierre-Edouard, 'and it'll be more use this evening, your electricity. You'll see then, it'll be fine.'

The current was actually switched on at about half-past twelve, although it had been expected at eleven, and most people were not even aware of it, for they had very wisely switched off at the meter because of the thunderstorms rumbling around the hills. So it was not until night-time that everyone could at last appreciate the advantages of electric lighting. Alas, the electricity was cut off again less than an hour and a half later; it was greeted with cries of protest from every household.

Days later they learned that the tiny storm at Saint-Libéral had erupted violently elsewhere; branches had fallen on the wires and caused short-circuits. Very disappointed, the villagers retired to bed grumbling.

But they were so little used to the whole business of switches that many left theirs on. When the supply was finally reconnected at about midnight, a large part of the village suddenly lit up. The customers cursed progress as they were woken from their sleep to get up and switch off those blasted bulbs: stupid things which did not work when you needed them and lit up without a by-your-leave! That never happened with a paraffin lamp.

The return of the squire's wife did not pass unnoticed. A rich elderly lady was expected, the embodiment of luxury and comfort, but it was an old woman of very modest appearance who got down from the evening train in Saint-Libéral on Wednesday 25 June.

Helped by her daughter, she climbed carefully down from the carriage and waited patiently while the porter unloaded her luggage and piled it on the dusty platform.

Apart from their trunks and cases – of beautifully polished leather, with a few old labels from grand hotels to recall past splendours – nothing else gave the impression that the two passengers had once known the leisured and gilded existence of those who could live on their unearned income. Even the station manager, who remembered full well the lady of pre-war years, hesitated before approaching this elderly woman; he hardly recognised her as the widow of the late lamented Jean Duroux. And then he was amazed to see her climbing into Julien's charabanc a little later; she settled down amongst the luggage and endured, without batting an eyelid, the jolts and creaks of the dilapidated cart which was commonly used to transport calves and pigs.

Hardly had this outfit set off up the road to the château than the station-master, still in a state of shock, ran to Suzanne's, where he was sure the regulars would be fascinated by the incredible news: the lady of the manor had returned, but instead of arriving in a beautiful motor-car as everyone expected, she had just disembarked from the railcar, like an ordinary village wife coming back from market at Objat!

'Well, that's hard to believe,' murmured one of the drinkers. 'And you say they climbed into Julien's cart?'

'I swear they did!'

'Well, well,' sighed the man, 'then we really will have to accept that she has no money left! But look here, you knew that, didn't you?' he asked, turning to the back of the room, where the former solicitor was playing billiards all alone.

Maître Lardy shrugged, struck another ball, then replaced the cue and came to the bar.

'Yes, I knew that,' he admitted. 'Oh, I can tell you, I'm not bound by professional confidentiality any longer, anyway it's not a secret. You'll soon see, the lady doesn't own much any more . . .'

'But how the devil's that!' asked the man.

They could not begin to understand how the Duroux family's solid fortune could have disappeared without trace.

'Ah, my dear fellows,' the solicitor exhaled slowly, 'the really hard task these last ten years hasn't been earning money, but keeping it!'

'But good God!' his neighbour persisted, 'the squire in his time owned property and, and . . . what do you call them, those bits of paper?'

'Stocks and shares,' the old notary laughed sarcastically. 'Of course he did. And his widow is proof positive that no one can be protected from injudicious investments . . . His property? Sold at the end of the war! As for his shares, they lost four-fifths of their value in ten years! And then there were the Russian loans . . . No, believe me, the fine times at the château are over, well and truly finished. All that Madame Duroux has left are the farm rents paid by Léon and, I think, the income from a small flat in Paris. She can still live off that, but she'll have to be careful . . .'

'My God! You could have told us earlier! She owes me money!' cried Edouard Feix. He was a slater, and had just spent a fortnight renovating the roof of the château; now he feared that he would not be paid.

'Complain to my colleague in Terrasson, he's looking after the last remains of Madame Duroux's estate,' Maître Lardy reminded him.

'I know,' grumbled the other, now annoyed that he had undertaken more than 500 francs'-worth of repairs. 'Tell me, do you think she'll still be able to pay me?'

'Of course. Don't make it worse than it is, she's not a beggar yet!'

'Maybe not yet,' agreed one of the customers, 'but all the same, if you'd told me that one day she would travel up to the château in Julien's cart! Well!'

The return of the squire's wife and her daughter enlivened the village gossip for several days. A few evil tongues made the most of the station-master's and Julien's reports, assuring everyone that the old lady was not only completely ruined but also burdened with debt, and the shopkeepers should beware of demands for credit which would not be long in coming.

But that malicious tittle-tattle did not circulate for long after it was discovered that Edouard Feix had his bill for 518 francs settled without any difficulty. Roger Traversat, the carpenter, who had repaired a few shutters and several square metres of parquet flooring lifted by the damp, promptly climbed up to the château, politely presented his invoice, and pocketed the 1,027 francs he was owed. Then everyone had to admit that even if the lady no longer enjoyed her former riches, she still had enough to live on, provided she confined herself to a modest way of life.

So they became accustomed to seeing her walking into the village to make her necessary purchases of groceries. Always accompanied by her daughter, she never failed to greet all the elderly people whom she had known in former times. Often she stopped for a little chat, asked for news of such and such a one, or enquired after the health of those whom she remembered. But many of these were missing, carried off by the war, old age or illness. Then she would shake her head and murmur: 'How time passes . . .' and continue her walk.

A devout Christian, she attended Mass every morning, naturally resuming her place in the old pew reserved for the lords of the manor; it still stood between the fourth and fifth rows of chairs, to the left of the altar. No one had dared to sit in that stall since the departure of the Duroux family fifteen years earlier.

'Are you ready? asked Pierre-Edouard, pushing open the door of the bedroom. He went in, smiled, then strode over to Mathilde, picked her up in his arms and twirled her round.

'You're crazy! We're not the ones getting married!' she protested with a laugh, 'you'll spoil my things!'

He kissed her on the neck, enraptured. She looked ravishing in a beautifully cut, diaphanous blue dress which suited her perfectly.

She had made the outfit herself, following an example

49

shown in *Petit Echo de la Mode*; not content to copy it exactly, she had improved it by using some remnants of tulle to add delicate touches to the cuffs, collar and bodice. For the first time since her mother's death she had left off her mourning dress, in honour of her brother, and felt quite young again.

'You'll look much more beautiful than the bride,' he assured her as he turned her round at arm's length. 'Right, this is too important to be late, are the children ready?'

'Of course, but they're hanging about outside and . . . I hope they haven't got dirty!'

'Yes, it's time to go, come on, into the gig,' he said, holding out his hand to her.

The cart was waiting by the door, and Mathilde noticed that Pierre-Edouard had polished the harness; the horse-collar shone like the sun, the copper rivets glowed, and even the bit had been rubbed with fine sand and sparkled in the horse's mouth.

'Wait for us! Wait for us!' shouted the children, running out of the barn.

'What have you been up to in there?' Pierre-Edouard frowned at them, but then smiled at their sheepish expressions, and with one arm lifted up little Mauricette – pink from head to foot in her pink dress – and placed her on the seat of the cart.

'Climb in, I'll be back in a minute,' he said and moved towards the stable. 'We're going now,' he called to his father.

Jean-Edouard loaded a forkful of dung onto the wheelbarrow and nodded. 'All right.'

'I expect we'll be back very late.'

'Yes, of course. Go on, don't worry, the house won't be empty, the animals will be seen to, I'm here . . . '

'Good. Right then, we're going,' repeated Pierre-Edouard, and went out.

Once again he was a little embarrassed not to be able to share this happiness, just because Léon was involved. If only his father could forget his old grudges, and stop adopting a frosty expression whenever there was any mention of Léon! It was getting boring, and annoying, because Mathilde could not even invite her brother in. And the children were not stupid, they asked more and more often why their uncle never came to spend an evening at their house.

'We'll have to find a way,' he thought, 'especially now that he'll have a wife! Bloody hell, she'll be our sister-in-law!'

But it was a difficult problem to resolve, for no one could force his father to open his home to someone he disliked. The house belonged to him; he had the right to let Léon know that his presence was not welcome.

The big Mathis automobile slid along the kerbstone and stopped in front of the entrance to the mairie. Behind it a sparkling eight-cylinder Amilcar drew in to park, then a Morris-Léon-Bollée, and finally two Renault Vivasix.

The curious positioned on every street corner, and the customers who paraded the length of the market stalls in Place St Martin, all nodded their heads like experts. Marriages took place frequently at Brive, especially on Saturday afternoons, but a wedding with so many guests and such luxurious vehicles was a rare sight.

All the bystanders joined in a good-natured conspiracy which inspired each to chatter spontaneously to his closest neighbour; soon they were all informed as to the identity of the husband and wife to be. A lively commentary ensued on the age of the bride, the price of her dress, the size of her dowry and her father's estate. The naïve might exclaim at the great difference in age between the bride and the groom, and the cynics ramble on as Léon took his young fiancée's arm in his and entered the mairie, but the majority of onlookers declared unanimously that successful, lasting marriages were based on similarities of position in life, on alliances of wealth and eventually, as a result of these, on mutual esteem. For love and fresh water is fine for giddy girls or the thoughtless, but not for serious people who know how hard life can be, what things cost and what dangers lie in wait for marriages based solely on blind passion.

'The mayor must be blind!' cried one joker. 'Or otherwise he'll have to put a paper bag over his head tonight. Blimey, that's no Mistinguett he's marrying! What a beanpole!'

This observation was cruel and unjust. Certainly Yvette Chantalat was no Venus, but she was really not ugly, as the connoisseur of female beauty had just implied. Not ugly, but dull and faded, too thin and puny; despite her magnificent dress, which had been designed to show off her best points, everyone suspected it concealed a fleshless backside and a charmless façade.

In spite of all this, she radiated a sort of goodness and kindness which was attractive. It derived from her gaze, so sweet, so serene, and also from her infectious smile – delicate, sometimes tinged with an air of sadness – which seemed to be apologising to the world. A little as if the young girl knew well enough that she was not beautiful, but she could not remedy that and would have to be accepted as she was.

Léon had the honesty to declare quite openly to her that he was not looking for a beauty or a fortune, but simply a good honest wife, and for that reason she had accepted his offer of marriage. She was grateful for his candour, and had chosen him because he was the only man who had not lied to her. There were other suitors circling around, hypocrites who declared they were madly in love with her, with her charm, with her elegance – some even dared to vow her beauty!

How could those idiots think that she would be taken in by their monkey-tricks? All those dowry-hunters in love with her? Get away! Self-interested or morally corrupt, yes! The youngest of them was two years older than Léon, and she knew via her father that he was a spendthrift and gambler, to such an extent that he had run through a fine fortune within a few years of inheriting it from his parents! As for the others who had been trying their luck since her eighteenth birthday, they were no better!

But Léon was different. Her father and he had known each other for many years; they often worked together, and respected each other. And then Léon had behaved very delicately, almost prudishly, had hardly allowed himself more than an occasional kiss; but he had been very attentive, and had promised to do everything to make her happy. What more could she hope for, when no boy her own age looked at her without sneering?

Chapter 5

PIERRE-EDOUARD looked at Mathilde, caught her eye and smiled at her. But he was feeling for her, because he guessed that she was ill at ease. The banquet was in full swing and, judging by the menu, it would not be possible to leave the table for at least three or four hours.

After High Mass at St Martin's and the photo session on the church steps, the whole wedding party was taken to the Truffe Noire hotel, where Chantalat senior provided drinks for his numerous friends and relations before they repaired to the dining room.

Pierre-Edouard and Mathilde soon realised that they did not belong to the same class as the other guests; that they were nothing but peasants who had strayed into a world which rather despised them. This world was one of meat trading, money, big business. Lots of wholesale butchers, transport agents and stock dealers were there, and to Pierre-Edouard they were the enemy who all, or almost all, owed their plump bellies, florid countenances, flamboyant dress and flashy, painted wives to the dirty tricks which they had played on him and all the other farmers. What's more he was not rich, not to them, and that was a definite fault.

Even Léon and Mathilde's own sister was judging them with a critical eye. She had married, eleven years earlier, an employee from the préfecture, the local seat of government. He was an elegant man, no doubt a good husband and father, but he was haughty and bumptious, proud of being an official, and he enjoyed reminding everyone that his frequent professional promotions were due entirely to his own abilities and achievements.

Pierre-Edouard had no liking for this bureaucrat, whom he regarded as an idler paid to do nothing. He loathed his pedantic style and his way of wrinkling his nostrils and feigning disgust on the rare occasions he condescended to visit

Saint-Libéral, and there encountered muddy gutters, cow-pats and dung-heaps; anyway, he had not set foot in the village since the death of his mother-in-law two years earlier.

Mathilde and her sister were completely alienated from each other because of him. Now, since the announcement of his marriage, this sister had grown closer to Léon; she felt that her brother was making a good move, an alliance that raised him to the ranks of suitable people, with whom the wife of an official might possibly associate without demeaning herself.

Even their only son, a lad the same age as Jacques, had adopted the same habits, and behaved like the worthy heir of his pretentious father. Pierre-Edouard, watching the child, suddenly felt anxious for him.

He was sitting right at the end of the table, between Jacques and Paul, who had immediately realised that their cousin was an arsehole, but that they were not going to give him the chance to fart over them. From there it was a small step to dreaming up a few innocent little tricks to enliven the day . . . Pierre-Edouard knew his sons well, and feared they might be planning to settle some accounts.

He looked back towards Mathilde and pitied her, suffering the imbecilities of a fat, red-faced man who was already well away and trying to whisper down her neck. The wedding party had been at table for two hours, and the men were already taking off their jackets and loosening their ties.

Jacques and Paul were busily stuffing their faces, drinking hard and beginning to feel their ears turning pink. They were enjoying to the full the freedom allowed them there, right at the end of the table, where they ate what they wanted, when they felt like it, and as much of it as they desired. They frequently poured themselves half glasses of Sauterne, but with natural caution diluted it with fresh water.

The foie gras garnished with truffles had been served with a Château-Yquem as sugary as a fruit cordial, and almost as heavy; the children loved it so much that Paul cleverly spirited away three half-bottles while the courses were changed.

Jacques and Paul were good trenchermen, but quite frankly their cousin's observations were beginning to exasperate them. This fellow from Tulle was upsetting their digestive systems, if not exactly their appetites, his remarks irritating them like horseflies in August. What did it matter to them that he had a bicycle, a wrist-watch and a fountain pen? And what was this sixth form and this Lycée which he was to attend in October? It was the beginning of the holidays, and the idiot was talking about going back to school! A real imbecile!

'I'm going for a pee,' said Paul, getting up.

He winked to his brother, who instantly announced that he too was dying to go.

'He's a bloody fool, that one!' declared Paul, after they had admired the cleanliness and sophistication of the toilets. 'And he doesn't even know how to fire a catapult!' he added, as he admired the bubbles he was making in the lavatory bowl.

'And I have a red bicycle with a headlamp and a wrist-watch too!' Jacques imitated him in a sing-song voice. 'I bet he can't tell a magpie from a crow!'

'We'll have to get him drunk,' decided Paul.

'Don't be a dummy!' his brother warned him. 'They'll tan our backsides!'

'Oh, no, they won't.' Paul was sure of himself. 'We'll have a competition to see who can drink the most.'

'You must be mad! We'll get tiddly too!'

'Oh no! Listen, you talk to him, and meanwhile I'll fill my glass three-quarters full of water with a drop of wine to colour it, and then I'll fill his glass. While we're drinking, you do the same – lots of water and hardly any wine – and then we'll begin again. He won't be so full of himself after a few of those . . .'

'But what if the grown-ups see us at it?'

'Huh, they're too busy drinking themselves! Come on, we'll miss the guinea-fowl. So we'll do that, okay?'

'We'll get another hiding,' Jacques forecast fatalistically.

Their cousin's pride was a great help to them. He quickly saw through their game but believed that he was stronger than them; he resolved to show these country bumpkins how they drank in the towns.

'Hey, look at that! You're swallowing that like milk!' exclaimed Paul in false admiration, when the second glass had been emptied in one go.

'You'd better stop now, or you'll be ill,' Jacques sweetly advised, attacking a wing of guinea-fowl.

'Ill, me? Let me tell you, my father gives me wine with the dessert every Sunday, and livelier than that one!' their cousin assured them, as he filled his glass.

He drank, but his sudden pallor allerted the brothers, who decided to provide themselves with a convincing alibi; they rose and sauntered out into the courtyard of the hotel.

A few stifled cries, then some laughter – the scene they had prepared had been enacted. They returned with innocent expressions, their spirits revived by the fresh air, to find that the boy had disappeared; his place setting had been removed and a waiter was wiping up under the table.

'I hope you're not going to do the same?' demanded a fat lady.

'What happened?' asked Jacques.

'What happens to children who are too fond of wine!'

'Oh, I'm not surprised!' exclaimed Paul, 'he did nothing but drink from the moment he sat down. We told him he'd be ill, eh Jacques, didn't we tell him?'

His brother firmly agreed. But one look from his father assured him that their game had not escaped him; he was amazed when Pierre-Edouard winked at him and smiled conspiratorially.

It was a beautiful evening, warm and echoing to the chirp of the crickets, and in a sky sparkling with stars shone the pale arc of a quarter moon.

Leaning against Pierre-Edouard, gently rocked by the swaying cart, Mathilde dozed a little. Behind her, stretched out on a rug, the three children were sleeping soundly. Overcome by fatigue and their overloaded digestive systems, they had drifted off even before the carriage left the suburbs of Brive.

Now the horse was trotting smoothly across the Larche Plain; it knew the way and was making good progress without too much effort. Lulled by the regular rhythm of movement and the beat of the hooves on the ground, Pierre-Edouard felt his own eyelids grow heavy, and would gladly have copied the children, whose deep breathing he could hear behind him. But he reckoned that they would be on the road for at least an hour before reaching Saint-Libéral, so he filled and lit his pipe. The high flame from his fat copper lighter disturbed Mathilde's doze; she sat up and examined the shadows.

'Where are we?' she asked, staring wide-eyed about her.

'Just coming to Daudevie. Were you asleep?'

'Nearly. What a day!'

They had not been able to speak privately since the morning, and now had a lot to say to each other.

'It was a really fine wedding, after all,' she admitted with a yawn.

'Yes, and what a meal!'

'Oh, that . . . Old man Chantalat was certainly generous!'

'But it must have cost him a fortune . . . Tell me, weren't you bored between those two fat pig-dealers?'

'No, and how did you get on?'

'I was all right. You have to experience all sides of life,' he said with a shrug.

'We were a bit out of place, weren't we? I hope you weren't ashamed of me?'

'Don't be silly. You were the most beautiful woman there, by a long chalk!'

'Well, I'm sure I was the only one who had made her own dress. It wasn't too obvious?'

'Don't be daft,' he said, pulling her close to him, 'anyone would think you hadn't seen the old goat and the fat sausage on either side of me! They may have had beautiful outfits and all that jewellery, but I swear they were jealous of you!'

'Do you think so? Well, Léon's married at last . . . Tell me, do you think he'll turn out like them?'

'How do you mean?'

'I was thinking of those people there . . . Well, you can see perfectly well that they don't live like us, so I was wondering whether Léon . . . '

'No, no,' he reassured her, 'anyway, he won't be leaving Saint-Libéral.'

'That's true. And what did you think of Yvette?'

'I think she's very nice,' he said with sincerity.

But he did not tell her what else he was thinking. He was

having difficulty in accepting the idea that his brother-in-law could find contentment with such a thin and unattractive wife, especially after tumbling so many pretty girls in the straw. And yet he seemed to be, not exactly in love, but very tenderly disposed towards her, and very considerate. Hadn't he thought to install a real bathroom in his house in Saint-Libéral, like they had in the towns, with an indoor toilet! Apart from the doctor, he was the only person in the village to enjoy such a luxury. Despite having water piped in, the other houses only had one little tap above the sink.

The other point which proved how far he was prepared to go to please his wife was this honeymoon trip – to Paris, of all places! That set him apart from the rest. Only the idle rich – a type unheard of in Saint-Libéral – could afford such an expensive adventure. Léon had justified it to Pierre-Edouard – who had not requested any explanation – by demonstrating that he could make use of his time in the capital to contact some of the wholesale horse-dealers in La Villette.

On the other hand it was probable, and in line with his character, that all this generosity was a demonstration; a bid to prove to the world that he had no need of his wife's dowry, but owed his prosperity to his own ability and hard work. Yes, perhaps it was his pride which forced him to compete with a show of wealth.

But if that was the case he had a lot to do, for that little Chantalat was really rich! Everything proclaimed it, starting with the car given to her by her father on her twenty-first birthday, which she drove with amazing competence. Pierre-Edouard only knew two women drivers, his new sister-in-law and Dr Vialle's second daughter. The man who had saved his leg in 1918 still lived in Brive, and Pierre-Edouard visited him every Christmas without fail, taking four pairs of chickens, or a leveret, or six woodcock; it was during one of these calls that he saw the girl driving a motor car. And to think that his sister-in-law had the same prowess! That had spurred on Léon. How else to explain his sudden haste to pass his driving test? He had talked about buying a car for a long time, but had never seriously addressed the problem of getting a licence until a few months ago. It was enough to see his fiancée at the steering wheel; he immediately decided to take the test.

There again he had reacted typically. Pierre-Edouard knew him well; that would not be the last proof of his pride. The Dupeuchs attached importance to the ideal of honour; such an inflexible ideal that Léon and Mathilde's father had died of it, thirty years earlier . . .

They had just passed through Brignac when a pair of headlights lit up the cart from behind. Pierre-Edouard turned round, screwed up his eyes at the approaching car, and directed his horse on to the verge. The B2 overtook them and continued in the direction of Perpezac-le-Blanc.

'I would say that's the doctor's car,' remarked Mathilde.

'Yes, it's his,' agreed Pierre-Edouard, who had recognised the number plate.

'I didn't know he had patients so far away.'

'Perhaps he's just spent the evening with friends, in Brive or in Larche.' Pierre-Edouard skated round the subject.

Mathilde had great faith in the doctor, and he did not want her to know what Léon had confided to him six months earlier, first extracting a promise that he would not repeat it to anyone. It was a sad story, which would spoil the doctor's reputation if it became known, make him a laughing stock and probably force him to move. A doctor could not treat people who made fun of him behind his back, or even despised him.

Pierre-Edouard really liked Dr Delpy. Of course he did not have the style and renown of his predecessor, Dr Fraysse, who had died eight years earlier and was still mourned by the village; nevertheless, nobody questioned his professional competence, his dedication or his honesty. He was one of the village personalities, who gave very good advice on town business and even on family matters. It was therefore important not to say anything which might lower his public standing. Otherwise spiteful gossip would take over and make his life hell.

Two years earlier he had married a beautiful, distinguished young woman, the widow of one of his colleagues in the Saint-Yrieix area. Unfortunately he was seventeen years older than her. In addition, although she had done all she could to persuade him, he refused to abandon his patients in Saint-Libéral and open, as she had begged him to, a practice in Tulle; he was a country doctor and intended to remain one. 'Besides, as I told her, at my age you don't change your way of life!'

A wise principle, which he should have considered before he sacrificed his comfortable bachelor life at the age of fifty-two! His loyalty to the people of Saint-Libéral deserved their respect, and called for discretion concerning his misfortunes. If Léon had talked of what he knew to his brother-in-law it was only so that he could help, whenever necessary, to scotch the unpleasant rumours which had been circulating the countryside for the last year.

Already several vicious gossips – the sort who raise frigidity to a virtue and want to make it universal and compulsory – those nasty pieces of work were suggesting that the doctor's wife was possibly not looking after her sick mother when she was away two weeks in every month . . . Other equally evil and no less sterile minds whispered that the young woman was getting on very well with a young lawyer in Tulle, said to be her cousin . . . The sad part of the story was that the lying devils were not far from the truth.

It was Léon who, one day, had discovered and understood everything when his business had led him as far as Limoges. For it was not in Tulle but in Limoges that this warm and dimpled blonde spent a fortnight each month. Léon had seen her in the rue du Clocher, looking in the window of Demerliac, the jeweller's; a very handsome man had his arm round her waist. Léon did not know whether he was a lawyer, but he was certainly not her cousin. No family ties, however close, could give a couple such an air of perfect harmony, nor drive two people to hold each other so close, exchange such burning gazes full of understanding and promise; still less to talk so intimately.

The young woman was so completely preoccupied by her companion that she did not see Léon, who was blushing two metres away and already looking for an excuse, as though he were the guilty party! He had made off as fast as he could and, when he got back, warned Pierre-Edouard that the matter was serious. He had decided straight away to do all he could to keep it a secret, and always changed the subject when some mean spirit happened to make a ribald comment about the number of trips undertaken by the doctor's wife.

Since then, still without seeking to know, Léon had also learned – from one of his business contacts – that the poor doctor went to Brive to console himself in the arms of a sympathetic mistress, whom he had visited for a long time before his marriage and who held no grudge against him for his short-lived defection. So the doctor had probably not been visiting the sick, but his lady-friend.

'Tell me,' asked Mathilde suddenly, 'do you believe that, that he . . . well, goes to Brive to see women?'

Pierre-Edouard had never lied to his wife and hoped he would never have to. So before replying he tried to find out what prompted her to ask such a question.

'Who told you that rubbish?'

'Oh, it was at the wash-house, you know how it is, people talk . . . But it was Germaine who was saying it most. And she's positive that his wife is deceiving him, too. It's not true, is it?'

Mathilde had lofty ideals when it came to conjugal fidelity; Pierre-Edouard shared her ideals, but knew that some of his friends did not attach quite the same importance to them; he did not stick his nose into their business, that was their problem, not his. But he knew that his wife was too frank, too honest, too innocent perhaps, to be able to conceal her feelings if he revealed the whole story to her. Of course she would not pass judgement, as many did. Despite her disappointment she would say nothing, but he knew that she would be quite unable to speak frankly and naturally to the doctor, let alone his wife, as if nothing had happened. Her attitude to them would change because her good opinion of them had been destroyed, and she would be unhappy.

'And did you believe her, silly old Germaine?' he asked, as he filled his pipe.

'No.'

'Well, go on that way, then. You know gossip is like a blow-fly, it comes from carrion and loves to foul up everything. I suppose that's what it's meant to do.'

*

Twelve years earlier Pierre-Edouard had entrusted Mathilde with the management of their finances, and it was a point of honour with her to acquit herself well as guardian of the purse. She kept careful accounts and knew to within about twenty sous the exact total of their available funds. Economical without being mean or grasping, she saw to it that the volume of their investments grew as much as possible, in anticipation of the day when Pierre-Edouard would have to compensate his sisters.

Over the course of the years she had calculated what they had lost through the weakness of the currency, so that she had no confidence in bank notes. As soon as she could, she entrusted her small savings to Léon, who transformed them, by means of various discreet transactions, into honest-to-goodness gold coins. Pierre-Edouard made fun of her little precautions, like the provident ant in the fable stocking up for winter, but at heart he was very happy to have a wife with such foresight, and very relieved that thanks to her he was rid of the burden of doing the accounts.

One morning at the end of October, the day of the monthly market in Saint-Libéral, Mathilde drew several notes from the box which she kept at the back of her wardrobe, took her shopping bag, called Mauricette who was playing in the yard, and set out towards the main square.

She was pleased to see that there was a good turn-out of animals and numerous buyers and sellers, altogether a fine crowd. That would gladden the hearts of all those in the village who had been worrying for years about declining markets. Some had been so sparsely attended that the town council had considered abolishing them, although in former days the markets had stimulated the finances of the whole town. They were convenient too, not only for the farmers, who were saved the difficulties of taking their produce to Objat, Brive, Tulle or Terrasson, but also for the housewives, who found what they needed to buy, thanks to the stall-holders.

Mathilde pushed her way towards a group of horse-dealers in black overalls who were haggling in front of the inn, reached her brother and pulled his sleeve.

'Oh, it's you,' he said, turning round. He kissed her and

Mauricette, and then guided her towards a quieter corner. 'I've some news,' he blurted out. 'It's not a cold that's making Yvette feel tired!'

She smiled, and marvelled that a man of his age could be so naïve as to confuse a touch of 'flu with the obvious signs of early pregnancy. She had seen her sister-in-law the previous evening and known then that the young woman was expecting; the symptoms were unmistakable to a mother. But she did not want to tell her brother that she had guessed, and allowed him the pleasure of announcing the great news.

'This time it's definite!' he said triumphantly. 'Yvette is expecting a baby! Just imagine, it will be born in May!'

He beamed proudly at her.

'Are you sure?' she teased him. 'I haven't noticed anything, and I see Yvette every day.'

'Yes, of course. The doctor said so,' he insisted. Then he saw that she was joking and began to laugh. 'Huh, so you're making fun of me, are you? Well, never mind, I'm really happy!'

'And so are we!'

'Look, you'll keep an eye on her, won't you? Make sure she doesn't do anything silly, eh? And at the birth, you'll come and help her?'

'But of course. And don't worry, it's not an illness!'

'Yes, yes, I'm really happy,' he repeated. 'Just imagine, I'm going to have a baby!'

'I expect Yvette's happy too?'

'Oh yes, and how! Really I could never have hoped . . . You know,' he admitted, 'she's a truly wonderful wife. Yes, she is. At the beginning I was a bit worried, you knew that, she doesn't come from here, and her family, well . . . So I said to myself she'll have difficulty in getting used to it, and everything. Well, it's not like that at all. She, she — I don't know how to put it, but I think she likes it here.'

'And I'm sure of it; she told me so.'

'Really?'

'Truly,' she assured him.

'Well, I owe that to you; you welcomed her as a sister, and your kids are always popping into our place! It seems they were needing an aunt!'

'They did. Yvette spoils them with sweets and cakes!'

'That's because she loves them. Well, I'd better be getting back to work. Is Pierre-Edouard around?'

'Yes, he should be at the syndicate.'

'Now, will you come to our house tonight to celebrate?'

'With pleasure. You know, I'd like to be able to invite you to my home too, but . . .'

'Don't worry about it, it's not worth quarrelling with your father-in-law over a little thing like that, it isn't important.'

'That's not how Pierre-Edouard feels, nor me,' she admitted a little sadly. Then she shrugged and moved on.

'How much are these?' asked Mathilde, brandishing a pair of woollen stockings.

'Nine francs fifty,' replied the trader.

'Oh well, I like knitting, and it's obviously worth doing,' she remarked, and put them down again. 'And the men's shirts?'

'The pure wool American ones are eighteen francs fifty, the wool-mixture is thirteen francs, or linen at twelve francs fifty.'

'But,' she protested, 'the last ones I bought from you cost two or three francs less! And that was only two years ago!'

'You're talking ancient history, dear! Haven't your chickens gone up in the last two years? The last one I bought cost me six francs a pound!'

'Not that much!' she protested. 'But if you want to talk about chickens I'll talk about our wheat; that's lost more than twenty francs a quintal in two years! And this, how much is it?' she asked, pointing to a pair of children's shorts with the Petit Bateau trade mark.

'Eight francs fifty.'

'And you think that's worth more than two pounds of chicken! Anyone can tell you don't breed them,' she cried, as she continued to rummage on the stall.

She chose what she needed with great care and held out her purchases to the trader, but alerted him with one of those special smiles she had.

'I'm a good customer of yours, you should give me a discount. Look how much I'm buying.'

The man shook his head, and began to add it up in a low

voice: 'Two shirts at twelve-fifty, three Petit Bateau at eight-fifty, two boys' shirts at eleven . . . '

'What! Eleven francs for those shirts?' she interrupted. 'But they're not worth it, the children will have them in shreds within two months!'

The man shrugged and continued his counting. 'One hundred and thirty francs twenty-five,' he announced, 'let's say one-thirty because you're sweet.'

'Oh no, no,' she said, pretending to leave, 'unless perhaps you add this,' she decided, picking up a zip fastener twenty centimetres long. She was in the process of making a sweater for Pierre-Edouard, and realised that a zip would finish it off nicely.

'You must be joking! That cost me almost seven francs! It's the very best!'

'Well, that's all I can afford!' she said quite insincerely, a lie worthy of her cattle-dealer brother.

'No, no! Okay, the zip, I'll let you have it for five francs, but I'm losing by it. All right, a hundred and thirty-five francs for the lot. And look, I'll throw in these sweets for your little girl, and for you, this nice pair of suspenders. They're pretty, · aren't they? They cost me more than a franc, your husband will like them! The lucky devil, what a fine time he'll have taking them off . . . '

'I don't need *them* to give him a fine time! Oh, all right, a hundred and thirty francs and we're quits,' she said, briskly seizing the pink suspenders, which went to join the zip fastener at the bottom of her bag.

'Now come on! You're taking all my profits!' protested the salesman.

'Far from it,' smiled Mathilde, offering her money. 'So, it's agreed? Because I can always buy from the fellow next door if you prefer . . . '

'Fine,' the tradesman capitulated, and took what he was owed. 'But if all my customers were like you . . . '

'Well, then life would be less expensive,' she assured him as she moved away, 'and then everyone would get on better.'

PART TWO

The Ungrateful Land

Chapter 6

THE harvest was at its height when Mathilde realised that her
fourth pregnancy had just started. She had suspected as much
for a week, and the wave of giddiness which swept over her, as
she was tying sheaves in the Peuch field, confirmed it.

She was forced to lean against a plum-tree and wait for the
galaxy of stars twirling in her brain to disperse. Her dizziness
disappeared quite quickly, but was replaced by nausea which
gave her the feeling of having her stomach between her teeth,
whilst an icy wave washed across her back.

She breathed slowly, calmly, made herself take a few steps
and felt better. Then, so that no one should become aware of
her condition, she took up the sheaf she had dropped and
bound it with a flick of the wrist. She saw that, luckily,
nobody had noticed her moment of weakness.

Twenty paces ahead worked her father-in-law and Paul,
with little Mauricette chirruping along beside them, whilst
right at the end of the field Pierre-Edouard and Jacques were
guiding the reaping-machine. As for Léon's farm-hand,
whom Pierre-Edouard hired for the heavy work, he was even
further away, busy opening a corridor for the machine with
the scythe.

The wheat crop was not bad, and anyone but Pierre-
Edouard would have been quite satisfied, but not he. He
found it a poor return. 'When you think what I put down, it's
hardly worthwhile! No, what we should do is plough deeper,
like they do up in the north, but that's impossible with our
cows. Like it or not, I should buy a pair of oxen; with those
and my new Brabant swivel, I could plough it beautifully!'

This statement had almost caused an outbreak of hostilities
between himself and his father. Old Jean-Edouard, with the
confidence of seventy-one years' experience, had questioned
the efficacy of deep ploughing.

'Ten, twelve centimetres, that's quite enough. After that

you bring up cold earth that's never seen the sun and is no use for anything! Believe me, I know this soil. And then, oxen – they eat enough for four cows and don't give any milk or calves. Really, anyone would think you had money to burn!'

'In any case, it's *my* money,' grumbled Pierre-Edouard, 'and as for knowing the soil . . .'

The dispute had been cut short, for Mathilde calmed her husband with a smile. He had stated his case and she accepted that he planned to buy oxen; she knew him well enough to realise that he would carry out his project. Besides, he was sure to be right. She picked up a new sheaf, and then suddenly thought how the arrival of a baby would upset their lives for the next year.

Firstly, despite her determination and strength, her ability to work would gradually lessen during the final three months, and Pierre-Edouard needed her help to get through all his work. Then, and this was the most worrying thing, there were the problems of accommodation. There were already five of them sleeping in the same room, and it would be difficult to fit in another child, especially a baby whose crying would be sure to wake the other children during the night.

She recalled the pathetic squalling of a new-born baby, and smiled to herself over the fond memories.

'We'll put the boys in the main room,' she planned, 'after all, that's where Pierre slept when he was their age. Anyway, if there's another baby it's his fault, and if he's forgotten when he made it, I'll remind him! But I'm sure he won't have forgotten,' she decided, laughing silently to herself.

It was impossible that he could have forgotten. There are moments in a couple's life which are engraved for ever on their minds. They shape the memories which lend such secret and confiding tenderness to the looks exchanged by very old couples much later in life, at least by those who are still united in love.

The day of Louis' birth was one of those events which mark the calendar, such is the happiness and celebration surrounding them. Léon's son was born a week after Paul Doumer was elected as the new President of the Republic. Léon and Yvette's joy, as they leant over the cradle, was so great that Pierre-Edouard and Mathilde had shared it, adopted it and made it their own. When night came, the happiness was still with them. It was so beautiful on that May evening, so good to walk beneath the stars, to embrace and whisper to each other like two lovers who happen to find a soft nest of moss by a path and lie down to enjoy an hour of perfect love . . .

Pierre-Edouard could not have forgotten that evening; it was impossible. No more than he could forget all those evenings up there at Coste-Roche, in their little cottage, where they could live and love without thinking about the children who now slept or didn't sleep within two metres of them in the same room; without worrying about that moonbeam which cast an indiscreet ray of light through the heart-shaped hole in the shutter, so that the little ones would observe you with an astonished and curious eye if they awoke; not to mention the squeaking springs whose rattling might amuse or wake her father-in-law, whose expression in the morning would seem weighted with meaning.

But *that* night! Ah! that night, even the moon was welcome, when it later softly illuminated the peaceful, relaxed face of Pierre-Edouard, asleep under the Milky Way.

'Are you certain?' asked Pierre-Edouard, watching her closely.

Mathilde had waited till night fell, until children and grandfather were in bed and the workman had disappeared down the path which led to the village. Then she had told him, in two words. She looked at him and thought she discerned a shadow of annoyance in his expression, but it was only the effect of tiredness after a full day of harvesting.

'I hope you're not cross with me?' she questioned, nonetheless.

'Oh no,' he said, smiling. 'We'll have to tighten our belts a bit more, that's all.' He looked her up and down and drew her to him. 'And I bet you're going to tell me that it was all because of that evening in May, when the moon was so beautiful?' he murmured.

'Well, yes. I was sure you'd remember it.'

'Are you sorry?'

'No, not at all, quite the opposite. And you?'

'No, I'm not sorry either. We're not so old, we're still of an age to make tomorrow's children. Just imagine, this baby will only be sixty-eight in the year 2000; that's fantastic when you think about it!'

'So it's all right,' she repeated. 'You're not cross with me?'

He shook his head, then stroked her cheek with the back of his hand.

'No, I'm actually very happy. You see, this little one will force us to fight on. We felt younger when we made it. I reckon the good Lord must have seen us. With that moon he would have had to be blind not to! Yes, he must have seen us, all young and in love, so he sent us this child to keep us young and in love. And I'm also happy because it will just show your brother!' he joked. 'Since he's had a son, he thinks he's the only one who knows how to make them!'

Pierre-Edouard did not turn to his brother-in-law when he decided to buy a pair of oxen, for fear of spoiling their friendship; they both knew that you should never mix business and pleasure. Léon owned several pairs, beautiful beasts grazing his pasture, probably good workers too.

'But,' as he said to Pierre-Edouard, 'you're right, I'd prefer to sell them to someone else. One never knows, eh; suppose they went lame or something? That'd make trouble between us, and I don't want that.'

'Me neither, but what you can do is take me to the market at Turenne and help me choose. Two pairs of eyes are always better than one.'

On the appointed day, one fine morning in September, the two men climbed into Léon's Renault – a beautiful piece of engineering which he drove with ease and confidence, despite his false arm. It was a second-hand model in excellent condition which had cost him nearly 4,000 francs, but he did not regret the purchase. Thanks to this comfortable fast car, he no longer had to catch the train at impossible times in order to reach the markets when they opened. An end to the white nights at station buffets, waiting for connections to Treignac, Meymac, Bugeat or Saint-Privat! From then on he got behind the wheel and proceeded to the other side of the département with no trouble at all. Now he was often managing to research the markets of Lot or Creuse or Haut-Vienne.

They reached Turenne three-quarters of an hour before the market opened, which allowed them time to take a cup of coffee and then saunter around the market-place and have a look at the animals.

'It's a small market,' observed Léon. 'If you'd seen the last one with fat stock, the one on the Thursday after Passion Sunday, there must have been more than a thousand animals, and good ones at that!'

'Yes but I'm not looking for fat stock. Look over there; those two aren't bad.'

'Keep moving,' ordered Léon, pulling him away. 'I know that salesman, he's a colleague – a wide boy, and I know what I'm talking about! Cast an eye over those over there. Tough-looking, eh?'

They circled the animals, two superb Limousins with short heads, wide foreheads crowned by pale broad horns, thick necks, strong shoulders, solid well-muscled limbs, with wide hocks and short cannon-bones.

'A bit heavy, really,' Pierre-Edouard criticised them, 'and still quite young; seven or eight, do you think?'

'Have to look at their teeth, but I think you're right. We'll come back and look at them, all the same. I may well buy them myself.'

They strolled about for another ten minutes, looking at the other yokes of oxen, and Pierre-Edouard identified a pair of young ones among them which seemed to him outstanding. So, as soon as the drumbeat announced the beginning of the market, Léon and he sauntered carelessly around these animals. Prudently, the seller left them to it. He was a little old man with thin lips and a crafty expression. He knew what his animals were worth, but did not intend to sing their praises just at the moment.

'Well,' said Pierre-Edouard, after observing them for several minutes, 'they're a bit thin, aren't they? Especially this one,' he said, feeling the animal's rump.

Léon joined in the game. 'That one! Oh dear, oh dear, it's been suffering! That one hasn't always had enough to eat, it'll never reach eight quintals. And then, you see, there's a risk of a lop-sided team, because his partner will push harder . . . '

'That may be so, but he's eighteen months older!'

'Quite possibly . . . How old?' Léon asked the seller.

'You only have to look, my friend!' said the little old man, calmly rolling a cigarette.

Léon grasped the beast's muzzle, separated the lips and shook his head. Then he studied the second animal's teeth.

'That one is getting on for five,' he said, pointing to the first one, 'and he's only just three and a half . . .'

'That's not true!' cried the owner, forced to break his silence by such an outrageous statement.

'How's that, not true?' repeated Pierre-Edouard. 'That one has the corner teeth developing, and this one is just getting his second intermediates! So?'

'It's not true!' repeated the old man, who now took his turn at opening the animal's mouth. He pushed his nicotine-stained index finger in towards the row of teeth. 'Where are these corner teeth you can see? Are those them, there? No! It's just the second intermediates coming through! My oxen are forty months old, both of them!'

'I'm not so sure, I'm not so sure,' insisted Léon, who knew very well that the good man was telling the truth, to within two or three months.

'All the same,' slipped in Pierre-Edouard, 'they're not very heavy for their age.'

'Not heavy? Just you see here!' protested the seller. 'Those oxen, they'll reach thirteen quintals.'

'Oh, oh, my friend!' cried Léon with a laugh, 'now you're joking!'

He stepped back and measured them with narrowed eyes.

'Look, I bet if you took them to the weighing-machine, they wouldn't make eleven quintals. But I put them at . . . one thousand and sixty-five, no more!'

'How did that go again?' the old man asked sarcastically, shrugging his shoulders. But he was furious; he had weighed his animals two hours earlier and knew that Léon had a formidable eye for a beast. He had guessed right, to within two kilos!

'I hope they're docile?' asked Pierre-Edouard.

'Of course, isn't it obvious that they're trained?'

'Get them to walk a bit.'

The man obediently called the animals, who followed him

quietly.

'What do you think of them?' Pierre-Edouard whispered in Léon's ear.

'They're good, very good. Look, they move forward together, and in a straight line, and believe me at ten years old, if they're well treated, they'll be on the verge of eighteen quintals.'

'That's what I thought. Well, how much do you want for them?' he asked, as soon as the owner had brought back the team.

The old man pretended to consider it; pushed his beret on to the back of his head, scratched his bald patch, spat and then sighed.

'5,250 francs – including the yoke of course . . .'

'Hah!' Léon exploded with a great laugh. 'Look, we'll take them without the yoke! A good ash yoke, with attachments and everything, is worth eighty francs, and you're asking us a thousand for it! You're not going to tell us that those little oxen are worth what you're asking!'

'Yes, I am, they're worth it, absolutely! 5,250 francs, no less!'

'Well then, no sale,' warned Pierre-Edouard.

'So, you're not the only ones at the market, are you?' was the seller's riposte.

'That's right,' Léon admitted gently, 'but shall I tell you something? Your bullocks there, at a thousand and sixty kilos, what would they give in meat, eh? They're thin, you know, you wouldn't get fifty-five per cent of the live weight in meat, let's say at a pinch fifty-three per cent, that would give you . . . call it five hundred kilos. And do you know what meat is worth, at La Villette? Eight francs fifty . . . So you see what that makes them? 4,250 francs, not a sou more, and that would be a good price! Believe me, I'd be amazed if you got more, but you can always try. Have a good day!'

'I'll shepherd him, the fool!' he continued, when they were thirty paces from the man.

Turning a seller into a shepherd was one of his specialities. All he had to do was draw two of his colleagues into the game and ask them, in return for doing the same for them some time, to go and negotiate with the chosen victim, and come to an understanding with him – or almost. In this case, since the old man was asking for 5,250 francs, that meant he would be ready to accept 4,900. So someone had to feed him the bait with an offer of 4,800 and then disappear for ever. Then the second accomplice would come along and offer 4,100 francs. The seller would laugh in his face, certain that he could do much better, but would be a little worried not to see that pleasant, honest buyer returning, and sorry, now, that he had let him go. For already, in his mind, 4,800 was a very good price that he ought to guard, as a shepherd watches over his ewes . . .

There would follow two hours of torture during which the trickster would periodically badger him, hovering around like a marauding wolf, but always making the same ridiculously low offer, sapping his resolve to hold out.

Towards midday, as activity in the market slackened and the seller found himself alone, cursing himself for having missed a good deal, it would be easy to strike a bargain. Remembering too late that a bird in the hand is worth two in the bush, the man would welcome any customer whose offer was nearer to the price suggested by the first 'wolf'; the original price was long forgotten.

'Yes,' continued Léon. 'I noticed Chassaing and Delmond – I'll prime them, and we'll shepherd him, the ass! How much do you want to part with?'

'4,300,' said Pierre-Edouard, 'but I don't like your system very much. Don't you think we should simply bargain with him?'

'No, you don't know a thing about it! These old guys, you've got to squeeze them! 4,300, you say? They're worth it; you could even go to 4,400, but more than that would be too much. Good, wait there; I'll prime my colleagues and come back to you.'

Pierre-Edouard watched him walk away and shook his head as he filled his pipe. Léon was a bloody good dealer!

Once the trap had been set, Pierre-Edouard and Léon strolled about the market, pretending complete lack of interest in the coveted animals.

Léon put in a bid for the first pair which they had seen

before the fair opened, just for the fun of it and to have something to do, but the seller was greedy. Besides, Léon discovered a weakness in the rear hoof of one of the beasts. The heel had split, and though the scar was hardly visible and looked well on the way to complete recovery, there was no guarantee that it would not open up on the first stone it struck.

'Keep your oxen,' said Léon as he left, 'their feet are too fragile for my liking.'

Dealing tailed off earlier than expected, so it was towards half-past eleven when Pierre-Edouard and Léon returned to circle around their quarry. The old man, now realising that he was out-manoeuvered, glared at them vengefully. He feared the worst.

'So you're still here?' commented Léon genially.

'Seriously, now, do you want to sell, or have you just come out to give your animals some fresh air? asked Pierre-Edouard, offering his tobacco pouch and cigarette papers.

The old man rolled himself a cigarette, lit it and shrugged.

'If I don't sell today, I'll be here at the next market.'

'That's easy to say, but very rarely worth the trouble,' Léon intervened. 'So, how much?'

'4,800, that's the lowest I'll go!'

'No, no,' said Pierre-Edouard, 'we have to talk seriously, the market's nearly over and I have to get home. So let's shake on 4,250, and I'll pay for lunch.'

'You're mad! Animals like that!'

'*Miladiou*, we're not going to argue about it; you must know the price is too high, since they're still here! All right, I'll add five pistoles and it's done!' proposed Pierre-Edouard, holding out his hand.

'The devil take me if I'll let them go at that price!' protested the seller, turning away.

'Come on, you'll have to come to an agreement,' said Léon. 'How about we split the difference? All right, let's say he adds eight pistoles. Come on, shake on it.'

'No, twelve!' insisted the man. 'Not one less!'

'I'll go for twelve,' Pierre-Edouard conceded. 'That brings them to 4,370 – a high price for those little oxen!'

But he was delighted with his purchase.

*

77

Most of the inhabitants of St Libéral shared the feeling of unease which affected the country during the autumn, but few of them realised the seriousness of the crisis. Probably only the old solicitor and the doctor understood the significance of, for example, the complete financial collapse in Germany, the crash of the Viennese bank Kreditanstalt, and the forty per cent devaluation of the English pound following the abandonment of the gold standard in Britain.

For in St Libéral they were only vaguely aware of the existence of the Bourse, so when they learned that the market was falling it did not appear to be a catastrophe. In the eyes of most people, there did not seem to be any connection between strangely named shares and the price of a quintal of wheat.

Nevertheless, there was a sense of foreboding, without any perception of what the danger was, and the atmosphere in the village grew sombre. Since Léon had a sixth sense about this sort of thing, and perhaps also because he remembered the Wall Street crash – without really knowing what had happened, except for the waves of bankruptcies and suicides, which in themselves told him enough – he toured all the markets in the region and filled his pastures and sheds with heifers, young bullocks and other animals which could be fattened up. That stock, he was hoping, would not lose its value. Then he suggested that Pierre-Edouard do the same. But his brother-in-law was not worried about his savings; they were meagre, and therefore less vulnerable.

However, Pierre-Edouard also smelt danger, and made a substantial investment in supplies of seed and various fertilisers; he decided to plant as much land as he could, and set to ploughing. This season he could at last plough to a proper depth, as he had long wanted to do.

His oxen, Red and Fawn, were perfectly trained, despite being so young, and their strength was promising. They pulled the Brabant plough without apparent difficulty, and if Pierre-Edouard did not set it quite as deep as he would have liked – he did not want to exhaust his team – he improved on his previous ploughing by at least four good centimetres. Though they seemed to move so slowly, he succeeded in turning over a third of a hectare of land in a single day, thanks to these oxen – one whole plot more than with his cows.

Even Jean-Edouard had to admit that the exposed soil was of a fine consistency, with a promising, fresh appearance and a respectable colour. He gladly helped his son to sow the seed, then to harrow all the plateau fields, which were planted, according to their aspect and yield, with wheat, winter barley and rye on the poorest plots.

When all the crops were sown, Pierre-Edouard, following an old custom, fixed a small cross, shaped roughly out of straw, in the middle of each field. Mathilde attached importance to this practice. She saw it firstly as a sort of tribute to the land and to the work, and also as a discreet appeal to Heaven, a little wink at the Lord, as if to say to him: 'Look, we've done all we should do, as well as we could; now it's up to You to do the rest.'

Guy Vialhe, a strong baby of over seven pounds, saw the light of day on Wedneday, 24 February 1932. He had not caused his mother any problems for nine months, and now he was born just as easily. He announced his arrival quietly, towards eight o'clock in the morning, as his elder brothers were having breakfast before going to school, and he welcomed them back with his squalling when they returned at midday.

The boys might have believed in a miracle considering the speed of the birth, but they were accustomed to seeing animals coupling and to long hours watching calves and lambs being born. You go off in the morning, leaving your mother by the fireside, and you come back to find her in bed with a totally red baby beside her; it howls worse than a stuck pig, and your father is leaning over it with a soppy expression.

'Well, that was quick!' murmured Jacques.

'Hm, yes, it was!' echoed Paul, trying to sound as though everything was normal.

He was very shy, not sure whether it was quite proper to see his mother in bed. Especially as Mauricette, jealous as a broody hen, clung to her mother's nightdress and had pulled it half-open to reveal two breasts heavy with milk.

'Come and give me a kiss,' Mathilde told them. She hugged them and ruffled their hair.

'He's sweet, your little brother, isn't he?' asked Pierre-Edouard.

'Yes, yes,' they lied in chorus, for they really could not say what they were thinking. Just imagine, their brother was as ugly as a freshly skinned leveret!

And yet even their grandfather, who was talking to the doctor at the back of the room, seemed to think he was superb. As for their Aunt Yvette, busy changing the marvel, it was quite obvious she had gone completely mad, with her 'gouzi-gouzi' and ridiculous fussing. Her behaviour was so bizarre that the two boys did not even realise it was the first time she had entered their house.

The non-Communist Socialists campaigned fiercely during the first round of elections to the legislative assembly, and were well received by the electors in Saint-Libéral. Many had appreciated the moderate speeches made by Léon Blum. At least he did not have his eye on people's private property; he had given a guarantee to all the farmers that his party would help them to keep their land.

That was certainly more reassuring than the proletarian revolution proposed by others. Even when the Reds in St Libéral proclaimed that they too would respect the property of small farmers, many people mistrusted their word. St Libéral might be a long way from the centre of the world, but they still read the newspapers and what they knew of the Soviet experience was food for disturbing thoughts.

It was towards five o'clock in the afternoon, two days before the second round of the elections should have taken place as normal, that the dreadful news broke. Yvette Dupeuch was the first to know. Six months earlier Léon had given her a big wireless, on which she picked up the programmes from Radio Limoges *and* those from Paris. Her receiver, the only one like it in the village, was the envy of all – the doctor owned one, but it was a crystal set with comparatively poor reception. The next-door neighbours were happy when Yvette opened her window; then they all enjoyed the tunes, concerts and songs broadcast by the beautiful machine – for free.

Léon was in the stable when his wife came to inform him of the crisis. He put down his brush and currycomb, and leaned on the horse he had been grooming.

'My God, it reminds me of poor old Jaurès . . . '

Then he went out to tell his brother-in-law. As he entered the courtyard he bumped into Jean-Edouard, who gave him a baleful look and turned his back.

'Is Pierre there?' asked Léon.

'What's that to you?' muttered Jean-Edouard, moving away.

He's a bloody fool, that old man, groaned Léon inwardly. He hesitated, nearly decided to leave, and then suddenly called out: 'This is a fine time to have the sulks! They've just murdered the President of the Republic!'

'What's that you said?' whispered Jean-Edouard, turning back.

'A Russian shot him, not two hours ago, in Paris. He's not dead, but it's just like when . . . '

'Ah, well, yes . . . like Sadi Carnot . . . A Russian, you said? That doesn't surprise me, those Bolshevik pigs!' The old man was carried away; for him, all Russians were Reds, after 1917.

His feelings towards those whom he accused of making a pact with the Germans in the middle of the war were such that no one could get him to see that Gorguloff, despite being Russian, was a White, an anarchist and, to cap it all, mentally deranged.

'That's what I'm saying!' he insisted, 'a real Bolshevik! And clear out of my way, you and your newspapers!' He pushed away the ones his son shoved under his nose the following morning.

And that evening he cursed all the Marxists in creation as he turned on his heel, walked into the house and slammed the door.

'He'll never accept me, the queer old fish!' grumbled Léon, left standing in the middle of the farmyard.

So it was not until it grew dark, when Pierre-Edouard came down from the plateau where he had been planting maize, that he learned the news. It saddened him. He respected the President of the Republic for, as he explained to his sons during dinner:

'A man who has lost four sons out of five in the war can't be a bad man. He must be an honest man, because he could have

81

protected them from having to enlist if he'd wanted to. Yes, four sons out of five. And now it's him they're firing at . . . Well, perhaps he'll survive it . . . '

In the early morning, the village discovered that Paul Doumer had rendered up his soul at sunrise, at exactly 4.37 a.m.

The financial crisis, which everyone had been expecting for several months, spared no one in Saint-Libéral, not even Léon. During the summer of 1932 the price of wheat fell sharply from the level it had been at for the last two years, about 140 francs to 117 a quintal –and those who could get rid of it at that price were well content, for it fell again in the months that followed. As for meat, the rate fell by twenty per cent.

For many small farmers, who were already finding it difficult to make a living and could not economise further, it was truly terrible. They sank into miserable poverty, and did not even have the solution of seeking a living in the towns, for unemployment was already rife there.

The whole commercial life of the village was affected, and Saint-Libéral fell into a torpor; soon there was very little cash in any household. As a logical reaction, the only thing that might save them, the farms tried to turn in on themselves, become self-sufficient, undertaking nothing which required the slightest capital outlay. For the few sous which did come in were essential to settle the vital bills – the local taxes, the fire insurance, the electricity, the medical expenses in families where someone was sick. And then, for many farmers, there were also the annual interest payments on loans.

All the shopkeepers and craftsmen in the village suffered from the scarcity of money; a few could save their businesses, come what may – some charitable ones even gave credit – but others could not keep afloat for long, and they disappeared.

So it was that Jean Breuil, one of the two carpenters, went away, and also Edouard Feix, the last slater. And then one evening, having carefully swept up the golden shavings which drifted across the floor of his workshop, put away all his tools, placed his last pair of sabots on the shelf, the old clog-maker climbed stiffly up to his attic, where the walnut logs were stored. He rolled one of them into the middle of the room, sat down on it, placed his chin over the mouth of his old Flobert – a 12-bore with pin-fire cartridges and black powder – and blew out his brains.

His death distressed the whole community, for the old man, who was going on for eighty, had been part of the life of the village. As he had been a widower for ten years and had no children, the town council arranged a civil funeral, attended by a thoughtful crowd. Everyone approved of the presence of Father Verlhac, who, disregarding the precepts, came to pray by the open grave; then, turning to the congregation, explained to them that this old man had the right to prayers, despite his suicide, for despair, loneliness and poverty had prompted him to an irrational act which should be forgiven.

No one ever knew that this charitable impulse, denounced to the bishop by several devotees, earned him a scolding the following week from an elder of the Church who would not compromise over the regulations.

On top of these deaths and failures, the schoolteacher retired, and he and his wife left the village. He had held his post in Saint-Libéral since 1906; they had integrated into the community, and if some felt they were politically biased to the left, all were unanimous in recognising their professional competence as above criticism. Thanks to them, and the twenty-six years they had devoted to teaching, numerous inhabitants now possessed a School Certificate. Added to that were the many services rendered, the good advice and even the helping hand which they had never hesitated to offer.

Everyone was sorry to see them go. Few men therefore missed the leaving party organised by the council, and all were moved to hear the warmth and emotion in the teacher's voice when he thanked them.

'As for you, Father,' he concluded, 'you know that we don't work in the same way, neither with the same weapons nor the same aims. Nevertheless, I must say that I've always found you an honest and outspoken opponent, and I can admit – for everyone is aware of it – that you were my enemy when we first knew each other, but have become my friend, as has everyone else here. To conclude, I hope that my young successor, who has won his teaching spurs in Objat, will find as much happiness here as I have done, and that everyone will give him the welcome he deserves.'

The new teachers, Jacques and Germaine Sourzac, arrived at the beginning of September. It was soon obvious that he too was a radical Socialist, more politically committed than his predecessor and more extreme in his views. But the situation was so bad, the mood so bitter, that his acid comments and opinions passed unnoticed. No one needed him to tell them that things were not going well!

During the course of his life, Pierre-Edouard had often been forced to struggle against discouragement, tiredness and pessimism, but he had never doubted his vocation until this slump came. Following a poor harvest, a storm or a severe frost, he had experienced the dragging depression which haunts the lives of all those who wrestle with nature, but he had reacted by telling himself that next year would perhaps be better.

Even at the beginning of their marriage, when he and Mathilde had fought to survive on their tiny farm, they had continued the battle by telling themselves that the future would smile on them. The poverty they suffered was the natural reward of those who lacked land and so could not produce more, but it would be over as soon as they could increase their output.

But those times, when all you had to do was work your fingers to the bone to develop and increase the crops, were long gone. Since the market had fallen there was no point in killing yourself to get the harvest in; you still had to sell, and count yourself lucky when the prices covered the expense of production.

This situation worried Pierre-Edouard; its illogicality made him doubt his vocation. For the first time, he began to question what use and value there was in his profession.

For several months he drifted in a haze of discouragement, scepticism and bitterness. Finally he reacted, with all the strength and aggression of a Vialhe, but he never forgot the lesson of those chaotic years, when he fought against real poverty, despite full storage lofts and generous harvests.

The threat hanging over the whole farming world forced

him to open his eyes to the future facing his own children. Up till then – faithful to long family tradition – he had nurtured the hope that the most capable of his sons would succeed him. The crisis threw everything into disarray, showing him that this sequence was not as reliable as he had thought. The one who inherited the farm would not necessarily be the lucky one; it might be a millstone.

This realisation shook him. However, because he had never given up, he refused to despair, and did not abandon the idea of one day leaving in the hands of Jacques, Paul or Guy that land which had fed the Vialhes for almost two centuries.

But he was prudent. He surmised that owning land was no longer a sufficient advantage, and he decided, in agreement with Mathilde, to do his best to equip his sons for the battle of life: this crrisis might be only the forerunner of worse to come.

All these worries, all these doubts, forced Pierre-Edouard and Mathilde to throw themselves into the struggle. For a while they drifted in despair, sleepwalking through the minimum work necessary, but their awakening was sudden and violent.

The spirit which had helped them surmount the first trials, fourteen years earlier, took hold of them again. They joined forces and plunged into the thick of battle.

Mathilde was the first to react. One evening at the end of that sad year, 1932, when the children were asleep, Grandfather was ensconced on the settle reading *La Montagne* – they had subscribed to it for the past two years – and Pierre-Edouard was flicking through a back number of *Chasseur Français*, Mathilde pushed a school exercise book covered in figures towards him.

'Do you want to discourage me completely?' he reproached her, glancing at the rows of figures.

'Of course not. Look, here . . .'

He did as she asked, remembering fondly that evening more than twelve years ago when, as now, she had shown him the results of her calculations and suggested what he should do to extricate them from their difficulties.

'Fine,' he said, having surveyed her accounts, 'and so what?'

'So what? Come on, look here, don't you see?' she replied,

pointing to one column with her forefinger. 'Don't you see that the only product to hold its price is tobacco?'

'I've known that for a long time; there's no need to tell me!'

'Yes, you know, but you don't draw the right conclusions!'

On the settle, Jean-Edouard nervously turned the pages of his newspaper. He admired his daughter-in-law, respected her, but he could not accept her meddling in a subject which, in his opinion, was no business of hers. Pierre-Edouard was the head of the farm, and his wife, however charming, should not stick her nose in. But as he had sworn never to get mixed up in this sort of discussion, he resumed his reading; he was startled to hear his son's reply.

'All right, dear,' joked Pierre-Edouard, 'you should know by now that you married an idiot! So what should we do? Your ideas are bound to be better than mine!'

'We must plant three or four times as much tobacco!'

'Oh, that's all? We put in ten thousand this year, and you'd like to do forty thousand? A hectare, eh? Nothing puts you off, does it?'

'That's the only thing which gives any results,' she repeated. 'First you'll have to get permission to increase your production, but that's no problem, Léon will get it for you – he's already done battle with the new director of the Tobacco Board. Then we'll have to get down to it, starting this year!'

'*Mais miladiou*!' he grumbled, 'anyone would think you didn't know the work involved! That's what's preventing me doing it! If it were up to me I'd have planted another 25,000 at least two years ago! Bloody hell, there are only three of us here! And that's only because Father is willing to help us! Tell me, don't you think we work long enough hours as it is?'

'We'll *have* to manage it!' she insisted. 'We can't go on like this. All you have to do is take on some day labourers – Léon would like nothing better than to loan you two or three of his workers.'

'Sure! At ten or twelve francs a day, plus food! And where am I going to find money like that? By selling our wheat, perhaps? Nobody wants it!'

'We must grow more tobacco,' she repeated. 'It's the only way out, think about it.'

*

He thought about it. But it was a whole month later before he took the step; he was almost pushed into it by other events.

First of all, in January, there was a gloomy meeting of the town council during which Léon announced the closing down of the shuttle connection which had replaced the main-line trains since 1924. This decision, supposedly taken following a very serious accident – there had in fact been deaths – was actually for economic reasons.

The railway line, which had opened Saint-Libéral to the world at the beginning of the century, made possible the markets, the shows, and trade with other areas, was running at a loss. Without it, Saint-Libéral would sink back into loneliness and isolation. A bus was promised to replace the train, but that was no use to transport the tons of plums, cherries, peas and beans produced in the commune to Brive and Objat. They would have to load up their carts as in the old days, and set off in the middle of the night so as not to miss the opening of the wholesale markets. Or buy a van, but nobody could afford one of those.

All the villagers took the closure of the line as a personal insult. They also saw it as proof that those up there in Limoges or Paris who had taken this decision could not care less about the consequences, were completely indifferent to the future of the village; it could die, for all they would worry about it.

What was Saint-Libéral to the smart men in suits? Nothing. It was only a hamlet in a remote corner of the Corrèze. Whether it lived or died did not concern them; did they even know of its existence?

The second event which shook Pierre-Edouard was the deterioration of the political situation, and the certain knowledge that this had caused the terrible impasse in which he was stuck, like millions of his colleagues, unable to find a way out.

After Herriot was overthrown on 14 December 1932, Paul-Boncour was the next to fall, only six weeks later. It was Léon who announced this news to him when they met out hunting on Sunday, 29 January. But it was nothing unusual: it was only the fifth government to flounder in eighteen months.

'My God!' swore Pierre-Edouard. 'When are they going to stop fooling about! It's incredible, we'll never get out of this!'

87

Léon shrugged, and looked down at his dog, who was wagging his tail and stretching his nose towards an oak spinney.

'Look out,' he alerted Pierre. 'He might flush out a woodcock.'

But it was only a blackbird, which shot out at knee height, piping its alarm call.

'Yes,' Léon replied eventually, 'they're in a complete muddle up there, it'll all end in disaster . . . '

'But what's to become of us? Bloody hell, we've got to live! I've got four kids, after all!'

'All you have to do is plant more tobacco!' joked Léon.

'Oh, so Mathilde's been talking to you about her plans! She's a fine one, your sister . . . '

'Yes, when she wants something, it's quite something . . . but her idea holds up.'

'Maybe . . . Maybe, and tobacco's the only way to get anything out of the State!'

When he returned home at midday, he had taken the decision.

'All right,' he said, 'we can't go on like this. If we get permission, we'll sow 40,000 tobacco plants this year.'

'I knew you'd come round to it,' said Mathilde, putting the soup tureen on the table. 'You'll see, we'll get out of this.'

And her smile warmed his heart.

The following evening, Saint-Libéral learned that Germany had chosen a new Chancellor, one Adolf Hitler. But nobody took any interest in the news.

'Besides,' as one of Suzanne's customers put it, 'what's all the fuss about that pig of an Austrian; *he* won't give us back our trains or improve the price of wheat!'

When spring came the whole village saw that Pierre-Edouard had decided to launch an offensive; instead of submitting passively to the effects of the crisis (and there was no end in sight) he was preparing to tempt fate.

The old men smiled, and reminded the younger ones that Pierre-Edouard had something to live up to; at the beginning of the century his father had also amazed everyone with his determination to work hard and take risks. He had realised what profit could be made from the building of the railway line, and had put the work in hand to benefit from it. And the greybeards, who still remembered and admired the enterprise which had made him rich, had no doubt that his son knew what he was doing, that his plan was considered, matured, with every detail thought out.

Despite that, they were absolutely astonished. They knew the Viahles, they were ready for anything. But even Jean-Edouard could not believe his ears when his son announced that he would not be growing a single grain of wheat while the prices remained so low.

'No more wheat? You can't be serious! The wheat, that's the . . . that's the pride of the farm!'

'Huh, pride! I don't give a damn about that; it's costing me too dear, your pride!'

'My God! Think of the neighbours! What will they say?'

'I don't give a damn about the neighbours either.'

'And your bread? Eh? What about your bread?'

'What about my bread? I'll buy it, that's all!'

'But, good God, it won't be your own!'

'Oh, so you think that the baker keeps our flour separate from his? Oh well! I suppose he puts more chalk in it!'

Up till then the Vialhes, and all the farmers in the village, had got their bread by bartering their flour for it. Since the death of the miller the water-mill at St Libéral lay silent, so they took their grain down to the factory-mill at Brignac, collected their flour and their bran and returned, happy in the knowledge that they would not lack bread in the year to come. By deciding not to grow wheat any more, Pierre-Edouard was flouting an ancient tradition; to his father it was worse than insulting, it was criminal.

'*Per moun arme*!' Jean-Edouard swore an old oath. 'On my word, while I live, this farm will provide a portion of wheat! I'm seventy-three years old, but in the name of God, I am still capable of holding the plough and sowing my wheat!'

It was the first time that he had protested since he had handed over the farm to his son. He had closed his eyes to many things, but this was going too far. It was Mathilde who saved the situation.

'Now, now, Father, don't worry. Remember, the wheat has

been sown for this year, you've seen it; the "Dattel" crop is doing well and so is the "Good Farmer", and there's almost four hectares of it! What Pierre means is that he won't drill in the autumn, unless the market improves. If it climbs back up, he'll sow, that's a promise—just enough for us, but he'll sow it. If the price stays down he'll keep back double the amount of corn for our flour, that's all. And perhaps things will be looking better the year after.'

'But why don't you want to sow any more wheat?' grumbled Jean-Edouard, a little reassured but not convinced.

'Because I'm losing money on it!'

'And what are you going to put in its place?'

'It doesn't matter what – maize, tatties, tobacco, barley, that's what's selling least badly.'

'Never mind that.' His father was stubborn. 'No wheat on the farm, it's hardly a proper farm!'

'We'll talk about it again when it's time to sow,' said Pierre-Edouard, shrugging his shoulders, 'but I'm telling you, if wheat doesn't recover its price, I won't sow a single handful!'

'Yes, Father, we'll talk about it another time,' Mathilde interrupted, placing her hand on her husband's arm. 'Just now Pierre wants to plant our land with potatoes, maize and tobacco, not forgetting vegetables. It'll be a lot of work for us.'

When Mathilde spoke of 'our' land, she meant the fields which belonged specifically to them, to Pierre-Edouard and herself – the Meeting Field, Léon's Letters, Mathilde's, the Peaks. The Vialhe fields she only ever referred to as 'the' land, and everyone understood.

'So besides 40,000 tobacco plants, you want a hectare of potatoes and the same of maize, and vegetables as well! You must be mad, you'll never manage it!' predicted Jean-Edouard, who knew full well just how much work such areas required.

'Yes, we will,' Pierre-Edouard assured him. 'We'll manage it because we have no choice.'

There were many in the village who shared Jean-Edouard's scepticism. Some felt that Pierre-Edouard was aiming too high, embarking on work of such a scale that he would never accomplish the hoeing of such areas with only his wife and father to help him. The old man might be strong, but you could see his age. As for Mathilde, she was a plucky one, but she had plenty to keep her busy; her little one was now thirteen months old and took a lot of looking after – the other children too, not to mention the cows, ewes, pigs and the fowl in the yard.

'Well then,' Maurice interrupted one evening at Suzanne's when the conversation turned to Pierre-Edouard's plans, 'he'll take on Léon's workers, that's how he'll do it! I'm not worried about him!'

'Maybe, but labourers are only good at eating up the profits.' Bernical was sure of it. 'No, he'll break his back, that's for sure!'

'And that would please you, eh?' joked Louis Brousse.

They all knew that, while Bernical was not a bad man, he was envious and resentful by nature; he saw every neighbour's success as a personal affront, so he had plenty to vent his spleen on when it came to the Vialhes.

'Me?' he replied. 'I don't give a damn! He can do what he likes, it's his farm!'

'All the same,' continued Maurice, 'I know him well, I'm sure he'll come out of it all right. And his idea of not wanting to plant any more wheat, it's not so stupid as all that. Believe me, he's right about that too.'

'So why don't you do the same?' asked his neighbour.

They all knew the answer. Although he was getting on for forty-two and remained on good terms with his father, Maurice was not the owner. At the farm it was his father, old Jeantout of seventy-two, who took all the decisions, and it would be like that until he died. Maurice was not going to copy Pierre-Edouard; even if the price of wheat fell further, it would never be said that Jeantout's land grew no wheat. He too felt that a farm was judged by its wheat-store.

Nicolas arrived in Saint-Libéral one evening in May 1933. He walked in long strides, with the supple, rhythmic gait of one accustomed to the high road; he marched like a man who was not afraid of 50 kilometres at a go, or a journey of 500 leagues. And at his back, swinging from a stout elm cudgel across his shoulder hung the bundle which is common to all those who can tie up their fortune and all their belongings in a simple linen cloth.

He stopped in the middle of the square and looked slowly around him. The few old women chatting under the lime trees noticed that he looked like a hawk, one of those spirited birds of prey whose gaze mesmerises.

Tall and well built, he had a haughty air and a severe expression accentuated by a generous shock of white hair; an angular, scraggy face with sparkling pale blue, almost grey, eyes. Dressed in black corduroys, worn but very clean, and a blue shirt open to reveal a powerful tanned chest, he was impressive, with his noble bearing, his stature and his haughty manner of narrowing his eyelids and throwing back his white mane as he looked about him. After he had examined each house and glanced coldly in the direction of the gossips, he turned on his heel and marched towards the mairie.

Alfred, the town sergeant, who was sipping an absinthe at Suzanne's, had noticed the stranger's arrival and did not know quite how to classify him. The bundle denoted a tramp, but the figure demanded respect. These two totally contradictory facts provoked an uncontrollable outbreak of sweat on his balding forehead. He pushed his kepi on to the back of his neck, mopped his brow, then, to restore his confidence, fingered the shining copper badge proudly pinned over his heart. He stepped out into the square and called to the newcomer.

The man turned round and, from the steps of the mairie, looked down at the representative of law and order hobbling towards him.

Alfred, whom the fortunes of war had assigned to St Nazaire in 1917, had lost a foot while helping to unload an American cargo ship. But he was very proud of his pegleg, exhibited it with great complacency and used it to convince the younger generation that he had received this wound during the terrible battles of Mort-Homme. The old men sniggered at this blatant lie and assured everyone gravely that Alfred was the one who had received the most 'sardines' during the war, those coveted chevrons which were the pride of all the veterans. The wicked men knew that foolish Alfred had received a crate on his foot, accidentally released from a crane; the crate contained a ton of sardines in oil.

'There's no one at the mairie at the moment!' he advised, as he struggled up the four steps.

He fiddled with his badge again, and stared hard at the stranger to try to discover what his business was. For Alfred, the human race was divided into two groups, the good and the bad. The former were clean, hard-working, honest and had the right to be addressed respectfully; they did not wander the byways or frequent places of ill-repute, and could produce their papers in good order at a moment's notice. The latter were quite the opposite.

His examination of the tall fellow who stood before him plunged him into agonising confusion. This person was definitely a tramp, for he carried the bundle of a poor man and had arrived on foot. But he had the bearing of a colonel in a cavalry regiment, and his gaze penetrated your brain, which absolutely contradicted the first impression; a traveller would never give him the feeling that he should stand up straight and prepare to salute. Racked by doubts, Alfred opted for the cautious approach.

'Are you by any chance looking for someone?'

'Mayor!' said the other, after a moment's hesitation.

'The mayor? He's not there yet.'

'Where I find mayor?' insisted the man, in a strong accent which sounded picturesque to Alfred's ear.

He's a dago! he thought, and this discovery put him at his ease. Everything fell into place; the suspect, despite his grand manner, was indeed a poor beggar, and it would give him real pleasure to accompany this interloper to the parish boundary and use his boot too, if necessary! He drew himself up and frowned, which accentuated the sluggishness of his bovine expression.

'What do you want with the mayor then, eh?'

'Where he, mayor?' repeated the other.

He doesn't understand a thing, the mug! Alfred was in control: 'Come on, show me your papers,' he ordered abruptly. And to intimidate his victim he took a step forward, hoping that this would provoke action. 'Move a muscle and I'll clap you inside for assaulting a police officer. Articles 228 and 230 of the penal code!' he recited in delighted anticipation. 'Right, these papers, where in hell are they!'

'Oh, papers!' said the man, fumbling in his jacket. He took out a well-used wallet, but its fine leather and gold initials caught the sergeant's eye.

I bet he stole that, he rejoiced inwardly, and pictured himself arresting the fellow.

'Give me those,' he ordered, eagerly seizing the identity cards which the stranger held out to him.

He glanced over the writing, furrowed his brow, then laboriously spelt out in a low voice: 'Nicolas Kra-jha-lo-vic, born 30 June 1893 at . . . at Kra-gu-je-vac, Serbia. Dammit, a Russian! Well, what's he up to here, this Cossack! Eh? What are you wandering around here for? What a turn up!' he said, scratching his head. He turned round towards the square to enlist the women as witnesses, for they had strolled nearer.

Heaven granted that Father Verlhac emerged at that moment from the presbytery, to go to recite the Angelus. He saw the gathering and came over.

'What's going on?' he asked the sergeant.

'There's this Russian, looks a bit fishy to me, wants to see Léon.'

'A Russian?'

'Well, yes, see here,' said Alfred, holding out the papers to him.

The priest studied them, and smiled. 'He's no more Russian than you! He's a Serbian – or to be more precise, a Yugoslavian for the last two years.'

'Oh well, it's all the same, isn't it?' protested Alfred, in annoyance.

The priest shrugged his shoulders and turned to the man.

'Do you speak French?' The stranger looked confused. He continued: 'German? Italian?'

Then, suddenly, the man launched into a long speech, a mixture of Italian, German and French. The priest listened, asked a few questions, and turned to Alfred.

'He wants to see Léon because he's looking for work. He's come from Marseilles, on foot. He left his country in 1930 and he's spent two years in Italy; his papers and his residence permit are all in order.'

'Oh, all right,' said Alfred, quite cast down. 'Well, he'll just have to wait for the mayor, it's not my business then.' And he went off grumbling to himself.

Léon arrived half an hour later. He had chanced upon Father Verlhac and been alerted to the situation, so he called upon the few scraps of Italian he had learned during the war and tried to find out what this strange creature wanted. But the man, before replying to the question, pointed his finger at Léon's metal hook.

'War?'

'Yes,' said Léon. 'Why?'

'Me too, war,' said the man, opening his shirt.

'My God! They really made a mess of you!' gasped Léon as he viewed a deeply scarred hole the size of a man's fist carved in the man's stomach.

'Demis-Kapou,' explained the stranger, buttoning up his shirt. Then he clicked his heels and cried out: 'Long live Franchet d'Esperey, Marshal of France!'

'Well, you're a card!' murmured Léon, quite won over. 'So you're looking for work? Any sort of work? Yes? Well, old chap, I can't give you any, I've got all the workers I need! But come on, I know who might be able to find you something.'

Chapter 7

PIERRE-EDOUARD untied the young calf, who bounded immediately to his mother and butted her stomach, furiously and clumsily, with his head. Pierre-Edouard guided him to the udder swollen with milk and pushed his muzzle towards a teat; the calf snatched at it greedily and sucked long and appreciatively. His tail quivered almost in time with the rhythm of his swallows and a thick foam bubbled out at the corners of his lips.

'You're a fine one, you are,' Pierre-Edouard said again, leaning against the cow, 'I do need a worker, but not just anyone! I don't know this fellow! It may be that he's never touched a tool in his life!'

'Don't be stupid,' said Léon, 'did you see his hands? You can't believe that they got calloused like that by resting his backside on a chair as a clerk?'

'Mmmm.' Pierre-Edouard gave him that. 'Perhaps he does know how to grip a handle.'

He sucked on his unlit pipe and sighed. He was exhausted and not in the mood for taking decisions. He had spent the day hoeing in the company of Mathilde, his father and two of Léon's hands, and now he could feel the drag of tired muscles in his back and sides.

'What do you think?' he asked Mathilde.

The young woman shrugged her shoulders evasively, and continued her work. She was milking briskly, and the powerful jets of milk hissed into the bucket which she gripped between her knees.

'He seems to be honest, and one more man wouldn't come amiss,' she said at last.

'Well, you could always give him a try,' insisted Léon, 'you'll soon see whether he's up to it!'

Pierre-Edouard sized the man up and reckoned that his height, his bearing and, most of all, his serious manner, spoke in his favour. His quietness too: since he had entered the cowshed, the stranger had not said a word. He had simply greeted them by bowing his white head in their direction, then he had stood still and straight, with an almost haughty expression, as if what Léon was saying to explain his presence did not really concern him. But his intense blue eyes contradicted his distant attitude; it was evident that despite his apparent passivity, he was trying to understand what they were saying.

'Are you sure that he's only forty?' asked Pierre-Edouard.

'Yes, according to his papers. Of course, with his white hair . . . I think he must have had some dreadful . . . '

'Yes, but he can't speak French, it's not very practical! And then you know, I haven't even space to house him!'

'Bah, you've got a loft, haven't you, and straw and hay? Eh, would that do for you?' asked Léon, turning to the man: 'To sleep!' he indicated the loft with a wave of his arm.

'You really wish to work?' asked Pierre-Edouard more formally. Unlike his brother-in-law he found it difficult to adopt a familiar tone, address a stranger as 'tu'. 'All right, twelve francs a day, plus food, of course; will that do?'

'No,' said the man, at last breaking his silence.

'Oh-ho!' cried Léon, 'you're not going to turn up your nose at that! Twelve francs is excellent pay!'

'No, not twelve francs,' repeated the stranger. 'Eight francs and four of those,' he explained, pointing to the bucket of milk.

And as neither Pierre-Edouard nor Léon understood, he moved to a corner of the shed and signalled to them to follow. Intrigued, they moved closer. The man made sure that Mathilde could not see, and then unbuttoned his shirt.

'For this, four!' he said, pointing to the terrible scar gouged in his stomach. He smiled, and lifted the neck of an imaginary bottle to his mouth. 'Drink only milk, four!' he repeated, buttoning up his shirt.

'*And* he's a cripple,' said Pierre-Edouard, 'he won't make much of a worker!' But he was impressed by the stranger's sense of decency: the man had not wanted to expose himself in front of a woman, that was in his favour. 'You want four litres of milk and eight francs a day?' he asked, after some thought.

'Yes, yes! Four and eight francs!'

'Well, you won't be the loser,' slipped in Léon to his brother-in-law, 'at sixty centimes a litre!'

'All right, agreed,' Pierre-Edouard confirmed it, 'and you sleep in the loft, but no smoking there! Understood? No smoking, forbidden!'

The man smiled and shook his head.

'Never smoking.' He felt around in his pocket, brought out a little black horn with a silver cap at one end, and shook it.

'He takes snuff,' explained Léon, 'he won't set you on fire. Good, I'll leave you. You know, if I'd had work for him, I'd have kept this fellow. I'm sure you'll be pleased with him.'

'Maybe,' conceded Pierre-Edouard. 'We'll have to see how it goes. And what's his name?'

'Me, Nicolas,' said the man, 'You, boss, she, madame,' he said, pointing to Mathilde. Then he looked at Léon and added: 'And he, Mayor.'

'Good for you, Nicolas,' said Pierre-Edouard, and held out his hand to seal their agreement.

As soon as he heard from Jacques, who had listened to this conversation, that his son had taken on a guy with white hair, and a foreigner to boot, Jean-Edouard could not contain his disapproval. It was bad enough to have to seat Léon's workhands at the table – they had to be fed, after all – but to break bread with someone who did not even speak French, whom you knew absolutely nothing about; what if he were a good-for-nothing? So he gave Pierre-Edouard a frosty welcome when he came in, and pretended not to see Nicolas at all as he followed him into the room.

'I told you that you were aiming too high!' was his immediate reproach, 'and now you see, you have to take on foreigners to finish the hoeing!'

'Well, what does it matter, if he works! Anyway, it's me who's paying him, isn't it?' retorted Pierre-Edouard, who was too tired to be diplomatic.

'Suit yourself! But don't come complaining afterwards! Those sort of people, they're all thieves, drunkards and idlers! That's why they're on the road, you'll see.'

'And so what? I had to take to the road too!' remarked Pierre-Edouard drily.

This barb found its mark. His father hated to be reminded of certain events which he would have preferred forgotten.

'Fine, if you're going to take it like that!' he said, getting up. And to underline his anger, he ostentatiously left the room and shut himself in his bedroom.

'Old gentleman not happy . . .' commented Nicolas apologetically.

'It'll pass!' muttered Pierre-Edouard. *Unless you give him cause to complain*, he added to himself.

Nicolas won over the whole Vialhe family in less than a week; even Jean-Edouard was converted. He would not acknowledge it straight away, for he hated to admit his mistakes, but everyone knew that he accepted, even appreciated, the newcomer when, one evening after supper, he took a packet of snuff out of his pocket and pushed it towards Nicolas.

'He doesn't smoke . . .' he explained.

Pierre-Edouard nodded; he understood. Unable to share his tobacco pouch as a mark of esteem and friendship, his father had found this device. Modest though it was, his gift was generous in spirit. It announced loud and clear that he recognised the white-haired foreigner as a real man of the soil – dependable, conscientious, and whose strength commanded admiration.

That was the opinion of everyone who had watched him at work. To see him handling a hoe, you could believe that he had done nothing else all his life. Yet other signs – his impeccable table manners for example, or his even more refined behaviour towards Mathilde – proved that he had not always earned his living in the fields.

It was only as the months passed, gradually, as a result of his efforts to learn French, that Nicolas revealed a minute section of his history. A few facts, a few remnants of an existence which remained shrouded in mystery and secrecy, were all that he deigned to reveal.

Thus one day he admitted to Pierre-Edouard that back there, in his country, he had been for more than ten years steward of a beautiful estate, so vast that it took two whole days in the saddle to ride around it all!

'So why d'you leave, then?' asked Pierre-Edouard, who had finally adopted the familiar form of address for convenience.

'Politics, bad thing, very bad thing . . .' explained Nicolas, before enclosing himself in an impenetrable silence.

Several weeks passed before he revealed a few more snippets of information. Yes, he had been steward; a fine, enjoyable position which he had inherited from his father. And no one had ever questioned his ability, for the lands which he managed gave their maximum yield and all the peasants under his orders loved and respected him. He was happy and his young wife, fifteen years his junior, could live like a princess.

Politics had spoiled everything, destroyed everything. Nicolas had never accepted the rule imposed by Alexander I. Immediately in conflict with the government of Pasic, he had even gone so far as to join the resistance, the Croatian Nationalists – although they were sworn enemies of the Serbs – had plotted with them, done all he could to overthrow a regime he detested.

What followed was unfortunately nothing unusual: his house surrounded in the middle of the night, gunfire suddenly ringing out, his wife shot in the neck as they fled and he, heartbroken and inconsolable at her death, forcing his mount on, setting course southwards, leaving behind his whole life and all he owned. Exile, in Albania at first. Then Italy, and there again a prudent flight, away from a police state which showed no sympathy towards penniless foreigners. Finally France, and now Saint-Libéral – but for how long?

'As long as you like!' Pierre-Edouard reassured him.

The story he had just heard made a deep impression on him. All the more so because Nicolas had, as he confided in him, never lost his slightly detached, rather ironic smile, as if the meagre memories he was quietly relating were not really his own but those of another man, whose pitiful life had undergone such dramatic changes that you had to be amused by it, or weep at it. But he was not a man to cry over spilt milk. The talented steward, the determined conspirator, even the refugee, were long dead. Now he was nothing but an emigrant, a man for ever cut off from his roots, a simple farm labourer. Only his hawk-like gaze, amazing white hair and wallet with gold initials testified to another and very different past.

Adopted by the Vialhes, he was also accepted by the people of Saint-Libéral. It quickly became known that he was sober, quiet, pleasant and did not run after women. And on the day old Jean-Edouard admitted that, without him, Pierre-Edouard and Mathilde would never have been able to pursue their intensive crop cultivation, he became a full member of the community.

Nicolas was the one who made it possible to plant, among other things, a hectare of tobacco; the revenue from this helped them to confront the crisis, and implement the other project which they had planned for many months – ever since Pierre-Edouard had realised that the land would no longer provide an unassailable haven for his sons.

Jacques accepted his parents' decision without saying a word, but Paul, as was his wont, protested enough for two and fought like ten men. They had been warned at the beginning of the year that, barring accidents, they would start the next school year as boarders in Brive, so the two boys had had plenty of time to get used to the idea. This had not prevented them from praying for frost, hail and storms to destroy the 40,000 tobacco plants on which their fate depended.

Unfortunately for them, the weather was exceptionally mild, good for growing things. The plum trees were weighed down with fruit, and even the twenty-eight walnut trees on the Long Field played their part in helping Pierre-Edouard and Mathilde to pay for their sons' boarding school.

It was enough to make you lose faith in the Lord! Paul was on bad terms with Him anyway, since overhearing a conversation between his father and Abbé Verlhac. For it was he who had encouraged their parents, he who had pointed out the new school due to open in October. Paul considered this such a terrible betrayal that he no longer felt at all guilty when he swigged the communion wine and munched the unconsecrated wafers after Mass; these reprisals were mere trifles compared to the perfidy of Father Verlhac.

Furthermore, he was furious with himself. Why had he not realised earlier that his zeal and competence at school just strengthened his parents' determination to see him continue his studies! He had landed himself with all those good marks and was beginning to regret it; the only result – a fine reward in his opinion – was to speed his entry into the sixth form at Bossuet School in Brive. As for Jacques, he had just been awarded his School Certificate with excellent marks, and would join the fourth form at the same establishment.

Jacques was just as upset as his brother at the idea of having to leave his parents, the farm and the village, everything which shaped his world. But in contrast to his younger brother, he accepted it in principle; fate had decreed the catastrophe and there was no use fighting it. Sometimes his brother irritated and worried him with his obsessive search for a means of escape from the boarding-school which was to be their prison.

'Well, what if we were to be ill?' Paul suggested to him on one of those September afternoons when the skies are such clear blue and the air so mild, that it seems nothing in the world can be better than to lie on your back on the warm moss, gazing up at the heavens while the cows you are minding graze around you.

'It wouldn't make any difference,' Jacques shrugged. 'Anyway, they'd soon see that it wasn't true.'

'Then we'll have to leave here before term starts!'

'Are you mad? Where would you go?'

'Papa left, that time!'

'Yes, but he was old, he was at least twenty-one!'

'It's a real pity that Pépé isn't in charge. If it were up to him, we'd stay here!'

The announcement that his grandsons were going to boarding-school had put Jean-Edouard in a rage; he could not help showing his feelings, and thumped the table like in the old days. It was to no avail; Pierre-Edouard would not give in.

'If they study, they'll be no use on the land!' cried the old man. 'The priest and the teacher wanted you to study, a long time ago, and we refused! And if your grandfather and I had listened to them, those smooth talkers, you wouldn't be here today!'

'Yes I would, and I'd be managing just as well, probably better. There are a lot of things that pass me by, which I might understand if I'd studied a bit longer!'

'It's a waste of time when you're working on the land. And then, they'll get ideas in their heads in the town. You'll see, they'll never want to come back to the farm!'

'They'll come back here if they want to. I say we must give them something else besides the land. Don't you see that it's betraying us! It can't feed its own people any longer! It's staring you in the face! You've seen the price of wheat? So? Is that what you want for them, poverty?'

'*Lo diable m'estel*! It's better to live poor at home than rich amongst strangers! What have your children done to you that you want to get rid of them? And you,' he cried to Mathilde, 'don't you care about your children being abandoned in the town?'

'Yes, of course I do. But they won't be unhappy. You must understand, Father, they have to study. One day you'll be proud to have a grandson who's an agricultural engineer, or even a teacher!'

'Huh, I don't give a damn for that! They'll be so posh they won't want to know me. Or you either. That's what'll happen, I can see it: children who despise you, and your land lying fallow!'

'We haven't come to that yet,' Pierre-Edouard had interrupted him. 'Anyway, if neither Jacques nor Paul want the farm, Guy will take it over.'

'Bloody hell! He's not even two yet, your heir! A lot of things can happen between now and him learning how to plough! You're still young, but that doesn't mean you can't fall ill! Who'd do the work then, eh? Jacques at least could be a help to you already, he's strong, he has a taste for the work and he's the oldest . . . He should follow you. When I was his age I was doing a man's work, almost, and so were you, not learning all that nonsense in schools, in the town!'

'Times have changed. Our children are clever enough to study and they're going to do it, and that's that!'

'It'll bring you nothing but misery, making your sons forget where they come from. You'll see, nothing but misery, I tell you, you're asking for bad luck!'

'Good God! Do I have to listen to this? Tell me, do you know what year it is? It's 1933! It's time you realised that! How do you think we got electricity, cars, aeroplanes, radios, all that! You think they appear all by themselves? People who studied invented all those things!'

'Huh, for all the good they do us!'

'You didn't always say that! In your day, you had the finest, most up-to-date farm in the area, and that's still the case, because I've continued it, to the best of my ability. And whoever comes after me will do the same, and the farm will be more efficient and modern, just so long as he's capable of working it.'

'No need to go to school to do that!'

'Yes there is. Anyway, I don't know why I'm bothering to argue. Say what you like, it won't change a thing!'

So the argument ended there, but Paul, who had overheard the whole conversation from his bedroom, had felt a surge of affection for his grandfather. He had the right arguments! Unfortunately, it was not him making the decisions!

Chapter 8

MATHILDE had to call on all her reserves of strength not to weaken or show her distress when she accompanied her sons to the school. The journey from Saint-Libéral to Brive was sad, for it was obvious that Pierre-Edouard's heart was heavy, too. He pretended to be light-hearted and flippant, tried to joke with Jacques and Paul, made believe that he was jealous of their fine uniforms, but nobody was fooled; it was a mournful occasion. Even the gentle trot of the mare sounded funereal as each click of the hooves, each tinkle of the bells attached to the collar, each creak of the cart-axles marked the passage of time, the progress towards the town, to school and the approaching separation which, in less than two hours' time, would divide the family unit; until that day they had never been apart.

Pierre-Edouard and Mathilde felt it deeply; a page was about to be turned. From now on, life in the house would never be quite the same again. Two voices would be missing, and in the evening, at supper-time, the two empty places would leave a gap at the table which would affect them all. Not forgetting Mauricette's plaintive questions about her brothers, and grandfather's disapproving silence.

Despite this, Pierre-Edouard and Mathilde did not regret their decision, or the various sacrifices which it had forced on them. If all went well, the time would come when the children would thank them. At the moment they were bravely controlling their tears, and probably did not understand why they had to be sent away to the town. But one day they would appreciate all the advantages acquired during their years of study. Then, strengthened by a good education, they would be free to choose whatever job they wanted – perhaps even farming . . .

Night was coming on as the cart left the rue de Bossuet and set off towards Estavel. Mathilde turned round and strained to hear the racket made by the pupils in the playground, where they were supposed to be getting into line. A bell rang, and the murmuring of children's voices petered out into silence.

'That's it . . . ' sighed the young woman.

Pierre-Edouard looked at her, and despite the shadows he could see her lips trembling, and the tears shining in her eyes. He pulled her to him and hugged her.

'Come on, come on, they'll be fine there, it's not a barracks! And,' he continued, 'we'll be coming to see them all the time. Léon and Yvette will visit too.'

'I'll miss them, I miss them already . . .'

'Me too, but we can't always follow our feelings.'

'I know,' she said, wiping her cheeks briskly with the back of her hand. 'You know,' she continued, 'I'm afraid your father won't get over this . . .'

'Go on, don't be silly!'

'No, it's true, I know him well. To him, this separation is dreadful, he loves them so much, our children!'

'He'll do the same as us, he'll get used to it.'

'No, because he's convinced that there's no point in sending them to this school. He's sure that neither of them will want to take over the farm in the future. So, you know what we should do to comfort him a bit? We should sow a square of wheat, just to please him.'

'Bloody hell! Have you seen the market price? 117 francs last year, 85 francs this year! I'm not going to sow even a handful!'

'Yes you are; you're going to plant it, to please me.'

'But you agreed! It's you who keeps the accounts, you know very well that it's a waste of time and money!'

'That doesn't matter; we must sow a bit, just to comfort your father. Because if you take away our children *and* his plot of wheat, I'm convinced it will kill him. You know very well that for him, only wheat counts. Promise me you'll sow the Léon's Letters field. After all, that's my land,' she said with a smile, 'I have the right to do what I want with it!'

'The whole field?' he protested.

'No, half of it, just the five strips where we had potatoes. We carried lots of manure on to it, it won't take much effort to get a beautiful crop.'

'You've been working it all out, as usual. Oh, you, honestly!'

'So, you promise? Then we could tell your father straight away, it would cheer him up.'

'All right,' he said with a laugh, 'anyway, I'm getting used to it, it's always you who wins! I'll send Nicolas to plough it, starting tomorrow.'

She kissed him on the cheek and hugged him to her.

'Tell me, about Nicolas, do you reckon on keeping him on long-term?'

'Oh, don't try to tell me that he costs us too much! I'm keeping Nicolas, and I won't change my mind about that!'

'You are stupid, you know,' she joked. 'I'm not suggesting you get rid of him! I know we'd never find anyone better. Everyone envies us, even Léon's sorry to have let him come to us!'

'Well then, why are you talking about him?'

'Winter's coming . . . '

'Yes, so what?'

'Well, you can't leave him to sleep in the hay! The poor man will freeze out there. And I feel ashamed; someone may say that we don't know how to look after our workers. So you're going to build a room in the shed, beside the calf boxes. It won't take many planks for him to have a home and be in the warm. We'll bring down the old bed from the attic, and that way Nicolas will be comfortable.'

He nodded and smiled.

'You really are something; you think of everything. Me, I'd never even have thought that our trusty Nicolas would be frozen, and I hadn't seen that my father needs to be consoled by sowing a square of wheat for him. You understood straight away what had to be done, and you're right. I'm just an old fool, I do believe.'

Jacques threw himself into his studies to escape the terrible depression which threatened to engulf him, but Paul reacted in quite a different way. He changed from one day to the next; whereas at school in Saint-Libéral he had always been noted for his lively spirit, now he retreated into a deep silence from which nobody could draw him out. With stubborn bad temper, he methodically undermined any hope that he might be considered an outstanding pupil.

Cunning and guileful, he nevertheless took care not to attract the masters' attention by sinking into idleness; his marks were never bad, not even poor, just absolutely average.

As he was bored to tears, and working way below his capabilities, he expended his excess energy at games, and by causing trouble and picking fights. He hit out hard and fast, and never hesitated to take on the big boys who were more than a head taller than him; he collected plenty of knocks, but built himself a fine reputation as a fighter.

Ignoring his brother's warnings, he became the instigator of, and chief actor in, all the escapades which could be devised by a child who refuses to fit in, a lad much too proud to cry in public, but who, every evening, wept out his soul into his pillow, clenching his fists and teeth so that his neighbours guessed none of it.

It was he who slipped into the refectory one evening towards midnight, silently collected up all the bowls set out for breakfast, and stuffed them all into the lavatory pans. He who slashed the teachers' bicycle tyres one night a week later. In memory of his adventures in Saint-Libéral, he also succeeded in climbing up to the bell on a subsequent evening; he unhooked the rope which he then tied across the stairway leading to the masters' rooms, at ankle height.

Vigorous enquiries were made by the disciplinary prefect, but they led nowhere. No one suspected him except Jacques, who immediately detected a familiar little spark of revenge in his brother's eye. Paul did not deny it.

'But you're crazy!' protested Jacques. 'If they catch you, they'll expel you, and then Papa will . . .'

'That's all the same to me, at least I'll be at home! Anyway they won't catch me, they're all a load of sissies!'

And then one evening, about a week before Christmas, he could take it no longer. As soon as he was sure that the dormitory monitor was sleeping, he got up, dressed and left. Holding his shoes in one hand, he bounded along the corridors, hurtled down the stairs, and jumped down into the courtyard from one of the classroom windows.

Once outside, he put on his shoes and ran silently to the street wall, which he nimbly climbed. The soil of the kitchen garden which lay behind the school softened his fall. He was free.

Free but terrified, worried sick and deathly cold. It was freezing hard, and the ridged earth cracked beneath his feet like glass. Here and there, the raucous barking of dogs greeted him from sleeping farms as he passed. He had been running for more than fifteen minutes, and could already make out the dark shape of the railway embankment ahead of him. He turned towards the Estavel bridge and at last reached the road.

The darkness frightened him, as did the distance to Saint-Libéral, more than thirty kilometres. But he swallowed his tears, tried not to think that he would have to run all night to see home again, and set off along the macadam.

In the hour that followed, he had to stop running three times to crouch in the ditch as cars passed. He was on the slope down to Saint-Pantaléon, and about to cross the bridge which spanned the bend in the road, when another car appeared behind him. He attempted to hide on the verge, but the beam of the headlights suddenly engulfed him, blinding him.

Petrified, cowering against a blackberry bush, he ducked his head between his shoulders and tried, in a last desperate reflex, to hide his face in his hands. The headlights passed over him, swept across the archway of the bridge and stopped there, a huge yellow stain curdled by a few wisps of mist. A door clicked and the beam of a torch investigated the corner where the boy was sobbing convulsively, paralysed with fear.

'You, upon my word! What are you up to here? Well, if anyone had told me . . .'

Paul felt a hand placed on his shoulder, and blinked towards the lights which were dazzling him.

'God in heaven, you're freezing, poor child! Come on with me! Do you recognise me, at least?'

Paul nodded, sprang towards his rescuer, and clung to his chest.

'Come, come.' Dr Delpy calmed him by gently stroking his

hair. 'Come on, let's go and warm you up in the car. I'll give you a sugar cube with a few drops of mint spirit on it, that'll buck you up. And after that you can tell me, if you like, what you're doing on this road at one o'clock in the morning. Okay?'

'Oh, yes!' said Paul.

He was ready to confess everything, to explain everything, just so long as the doctor did not leave him there, alone on the road which seemed it would never reach Saint-Libéral.

'I understand,' the doctor comforted him, after Paul had finished his story.

He gave the boy's knee a friendly pat, and nodded. Say what you like, this boy snuggled up beside him had brains.

The car purred along gently and a pleasant warmth suffused Paul's legs, all wrapped in a rug. The car was approaching the hill up to Perpezac-le-Blanc.

'And what will your father say?' asked the doctor, after a little while.

'Oh well, he's bound to beat me,' forecast Paul. But his tone of voice showed quite clearly that this very logical result was nothing compared to the three months of hell he had just endured, or the two traumatic hours of flight.

'Yes, he's bound to beat you, as you say; what's more, you deserve it, don't you? No, what's worrying me is waking up your parents at this time of night, because of your grand-father, you understand? At his age this sort of excitement is not recommended, and as he's just had a bad attack of bronchitis . . .'

'I could go to Uncle Léon's,' suggested the boy.

'If you think he'd be happy to be got out of bed in the middle of the night!'

'Well then, I'll go to the cowshed, I'll sleep with Nicolas. Mama told me that he's built himself a room next to the calf-boxes.'

'That's not a bad idea, that's what we'll do. You see, I'd take you to my place, but you know my old Marthe, she's not happy just to keep house for me! She tells everyone everything she sees, so if she finds you with me tomorrow, the whole village will know about it. You don't want it all to come out, do you? Think how ashamed your parents would be!'

'That's true, people would be only too pleased . . . It's better if I go and sleep with Nicolas.'

Despite the knowledge that punishment would follow, Paul trotted along the main street of Saint-Libéral with a joyful heart. The dogs barked as he passed, but he knew them all and quietened them with a word. The squat shape of his house came into view at the end of the street; he smiled and hurried on.

He was pushing open the door of the cowshed without a sound when suddenly a beam of light transfixed him, and a fist grasped him firmly. He jumped with fright.

'Well, well!' said Nicolas with a smile, putting down the heavy stave he was brandishing. 'It you, my little fellow! And what you do here? I thinking to catch a thief!'

'I'll explain it to you,' whispered Paul, moving into the barn. He took several steps, and then could not resist the temptation to stroke old Moutonne. The cow, resting on a bed of dried chestnut leaves, stretched out her damp nose towards the hand which was patting her.

'She's had her calf?' asked Paul.

'There,' Nicolas pointed.

'Oh, he's super!' cried the child admiringly, hugging the little animal's curly head.

'What you do here?' asked Nicolas once more. 'You left town, eh? Not good, that! Boss will use his belt!'

'Well yes, but I must explain it to you. Say, it's quite good, this room of yours!' commented Paul as he reached the sanctuary. He tested the springs, sitting on the still-warm bed. 'You're nicely set up here!' He suddenly noticed a photograph pinned to one of the boards of the partition, and nodded to it: 'What a beautiful lady, and dressed so finely . . . '

'Yes' murmured Nicolas.

'That's a beautiful house behind her too, is that where she lives?'

Nicolas nodded in confirmation but his eyes grew steely.

'Tell why left!' he commanded.

'Well, you see . . . ' began Paul.

He reached the point where the doctor had made him take

some sugar with mint when he suddenly collapsed into sleep. So the tall man with white hair bent over him, slid him between the sheets, straightened the blankets and the plump eiderdown, and furtively, with the back of his hand, stroked the downy cheek of the sleeping child. Then he seated himself on a stool, took out his snuff-horn and settled down for a sleepless night.

'But, good God, man, I don't understand a thing you're telling me!' moaned Léon, passing his hand through the opening of his nightshirt.

He scratched energetically, yawned and stretched. He had just got up when Nicolas irrupted into his kitchen.

'Me knowing you always first up in village,' Nicolas had apologised, then embarked on an improbable tale which totally baffled Léon, in his sleepy state.

Léon went to the stove, poked it, pushed three logs into the grate and put a pan of coffee on the top plate.

'Go on, tell me while the coffee's warming,' he urged as he took out two bowls.

'Little fellow here, leaving the town, boss not happy for sure!'

'Bloody hell, if I didn't know that you only drank milk I'd think . . . Which little fellow?'

'Paul!'

'My God!' Léon started. 'You mean to say my nephew has run away from school?'

'That's right!'

'Well, what a turn up! And where is the hooligan?'

'With me.'

'Dammit, there'll be trouble!' murmured Léon, nervously rubbing his stump. He grabbed his false arm and tied it on quickly, lacing the straps and pulling them tight with his teeth and good hand. 'Dear, oh dear,' he worried on, 'what's to be done? If it were only my sister it'd be all right, but Pierre-Edouard! He'll tan his backside with his belt! Okay,' he suddenly made a decision, 'it's not five o'clock yet, I've got plenty of time to take him back to Brive. Over there I'll sort things out with the priests, and when I come back I'll explain what happened to my brother-in-law, no one'll be any the wiser, and the kid will be out of his way! Go on, fetch that wretched Vialhe boy, hurry up, he must be here before his father gets out of bed.'

'Right!' said Nicolas as he went out.

He returned soon afterwards carrying the child, still asleep, in his arms.

'Devil of a boy, all the same!' whispered Léon. 'Since you've got him, follow me, we'll put him in the car.'

They laid him on the back seat and covered him up again with a rug. The child curled up, pursed his lips like a baby searching for its thumb, but remained asleep.

He woke as the car reached the suburbs of Brive, and sat up with a start.

'Hallo, young fellow me lad!' cried Léon.

'Oh, it's you, Uncle,' murmured Paul, without quite understanding the situation. Then he began to remember, and recalled all the adventures of the night. 'Where are we going?' he said at last.

'Where you should never have left, of course!'

'And Papa?'

'He's still asleep, I expect.'

'And he didn't say anything?'

'What should he have said? He didn't see you. Come on, don't worry, I'll explain it all to him gently.'

'You're taking me back to school . . . ' Paul realised. He had always known that it would end like this, that his father would not give in to blackmail. Thanks to his uncle – and he didn't quite understand how he had miraculously intervened – he was avoiding the worst thrashing in his life, for the time being.

'What time do you get up at this school of yours?'

'Seven o'clock.'

'Well, we're in time . . . ' murmured Léon, 'it's just six.'

Now that he was almost there, he was not sure how to extricate himself from this bizarre situation. Basically, the principal of the school could misinterpret his intervention. Paul was only his nephew, not his son; it was not for him to bring him back, to explain, to plead his case.

He didn't even know this priest anyway! And apart from Father Verlhac he was not really very fond of priests; they were not straightforward people, they did not speak frankly to your face, but always used speeches or sermons or roundabout ways of saying things! So what was he going to say to them?

'So you really hate it in this school, eh?' he asked as he slowed down.

'Oh, yes!' sighed Paul. 'If you only knew, Uncle!'

'Come on, don't cry. Look, if you promise me that you won't leave again, I'll try to get your father to understand that you really are very unhappy, perhaps that'll make him reconsider the matter. You promise, no more running away, eh?'

'Promise,' stammered Paul, swallowing his tears, 'and you give me your word that you will explain to Papa? Oh, if you only knew, those walls are horrible, I . . . sometimes I wish I was dead.'

'Don't talk stupid,' interrupted Léon quickly. 'Come on, shake on it,' he said, holding out his hand. 'Word of a Dupeuch, if you're a good boy, I'll speak up for you, okay?'

'Shake, word of a Vialhe,' said the child, touching his uncle's huge palm with his little hand. And his gesture made it a binding pledge.

'By the way, how did you get out?' asked Léon casually.

'Over the back wall, it's easy.'

'If I could be certain . . . You say they wake you at seven o'clock?'

'Yes.'

'We've still got three-quarters of an hour . . . Really, if you manage to get back in without being seen, no one would be any the wiser, eh? You go back the way you came and there'll be no trouble . . . '

'Well, yes, but . . . but from this side I can't climb the wall, it's too high . . . '

'Huh, if that's all! And which way is it to the back of this blasted school?'

'Turn down there, into the lane, then we'll have to go on foot at the end and cross the gardens.'

'That'll be easy as pie . . . Come on, that's decided, we'll go that way. And make sure you don't get caught, otherwise I'll look a fool, won't I?'

Paul slipped into his bed at twenty to seven, his return accomplished as easily as his leaving. He could hardly believe his luck, and felt overwhelmed with gratitude towards the doctor, Nicolas, and most of all his uncle, who had saved him by giving him a leg up to climb back over the wall.

Pierre-Edouard was deeply disturbed by what Léon told him when he returned. He didn't lose his temper – what good would that do, anyway! But his disappointment, his sorrow even, was such that Léon was disarmed, at a loss. He had been prepared to argue fiercely against the cold anger which he thought would overwhelm his brother-in-law when he knew the whole story. Instead, he saw a worried man before him; Pierre-Edouard looked almost demoralised.

'What shall we do with that kid?' he muttered, nervously fiddling with his pipe. 'When I think that we're bleeding ourselves white to pay for his schooling, and he thanks us by jumping the wall! But why did he do it?'

'He hates it so.'

'Oh, I know that! And his mother, don't you think she hates it too! But we're doing it for him!'

'Well, yes . . . But it seems he's not the sort to study.'

'That's rich, coming from you! You who want your son to be a gentleman! He'll have to go away to school too, will your son! So what'll you do if you see *him* running off in the middle of the night?'

'I don't really know,' admitted Léon.

'Whatever happens, his mother mustn't find out about this, you hear, not a word! She couldn't live with it, she'd make me take him away.'

'So you're going to leave him there in spite of this?'

'At least for this year, yes; after that I'll see. But for the time being, he has to make the best of it at boarding-school; it will teach him that a Vialhe doesn't give up.'

'And if he bunks off again? The doctor won't always be around to pick him up, or Nicolas to tell me, and me to take him back! Have you thought of that?'

'He won't leave again. He gave you his word, he'll keep it; or else he's not a Vialhe.'

'Yes, but it's me who's not keeping mine; I promised him

I'd speak for him.'

'I'll talk to him. I've got the whole Christmas holidays to do it, he'll understand.'

'You must try to understand, as well. I think he's very unhappy, you know, it wasn't just an impulse.'

'That's why he must at least finish the year. If we give in to him, he'll be ruined; he'll think that running away is a good solution for the rest of his life.'

'You may be right, but it makes me very sorry for him.'

'Me too . . . Well, thank you for doing what you did last night, it was for the best.'

'I thought you'd fly off the handle and do something you'd regret.'

'Fly off the handle? Yes, probably, but you're wrong even so. Because, you know, after I'd calmed down, I don't know whether I'd have had the guts to take him back to Brive.'

Chapter 9

FACED with a constantly deteriorating economic and political situation, it was in a mood of despair close to fatalism that the inhabitants of Saint-Libéral began 1934.

Most of them had given up trying to understand the way the government people, up there in Paris, were managing affairs of State. Only the schoolmaster, encouraged by a few party faithful, tried to shake them out of their apathy and overall discouragement. Almost every evening he held forth in the main bar of the auberge, but his tirades fell flat; the drinkers shrugged their shoulders, preferring to pay court to Suzanne, who was still beautiful and kind.

They were fed up with all this politics, whether right or left; fed up with all the various movements, with the leagues which were supposed to be attacking each other in the towns. It would all come to no good; it smelt of corruption and scandal. And the price of wheat continued to fall.

Even Father Verlhac no longer took the trouble to challenge the vengeful suggestions made by the young teacher, content to shrug his shoulders when echoes of his new adversary's oratorical salvos reached his ears. Disheartened by the extremism that, whichever way he turned, was the norm amongst those purporting to be the saviours of the country; exasperated by the appeasement of some and the fanaticism of others, the priest wished to stand aside from the fray in the future. And, since the adults seemed to be quite beyond saving, he turned all his efforts towards the young people; at least they were not yet corrupted by politics.

Thanks to his Pathé-Baby film projector, he was in contact with most of the children in the village. Already he was in the process of forming a small group of adolescents inspired by the aims and ideals of the Young Christian Farmers movement. The results were concrete, obvious and refreshing. So the teacher could go on haranguing the bar customers, even try to discredit the Church by associating it with such contradictory movements as the royalist Camelots du Roi, the nationalist Croix de Feu, the new isolationism of Marcel Bucard – the priest did not care.

One evening at the beginning of January, when Dr Delpy had invited him to take an aperitif at Suzanne's, he contented himself with putting his lay rival in his place in public, by reminding him about the Stavisky swindle.

'Stavisky was closer to the ministers, government bigwigs and other politicians of the radical left than to any poor country priest.

'Besides,' he continued wickedly, '*we* don't encourage our friends to commit suicide . . . '

Luckily, Dr Delpy defused the situation and prevented imminent warfare. He grasped the two men and steered them towards the billiard table, placed a cue in one hand, a glass in the other, and rolled the balls into the middle of the table.

'Come on, settle the matter graciously on the green baize. Politics isn't worth fighting about, you don't see me getting mixed up in it! No indeed! So!'

It was a pleasure to see how happy he was. His wife had been away from Saint-Libéral since August, but had returned on Christmas Eve. She was in mourning for her mother, who had died on 20 December; had stayed at home since her return, and was quietly reintegrating into the community. She helped her husband, visited a few chronic invalids or new mothers. Via Marthe, the doctor's maid, everyone knew that the joy of their reunion was not feigned. And since nobody, apart from Léon and Pierre-Edouard, really knew what her movements had been during their long separation, they finally accepted that, when all was said and done, perhaps she really had been visiting her mother for years. The tittle-tattle, rumours and other whispering by the gossips did not completely stop straight away, but at least they became more sporadic and discreet; they cooled down for lack of fuel to fan the flames.

Only Léon knew the details of the story. He heard, from a horse-butcher in Limoges – who had it from a charcutier who was a neighbour of the admirer – that the gallant gentleman had simply abandoned the doctor's wife for a much younger mistress.

'What luck that her mother died just at the right time, how convenient for everyone!' Léon had whispered in his brother-in-law's ear.

'Yes, but the doctor can't be fooled by it!'

'Of course not, he's not crazy! Never mind, he doesn't go to Brive any more: I know that for a fact, too . . . '

'Of course!' continued Pierre-Edouard ironically. 'You and your sister are conspiring to keep people talking!'

'Did Mathilde know about the doctor?'

'No, I don't think so, it wasn't that I was thinking of . . . '

'What then?'

'Paul's running away – she found out about it almost at the same time as I did.'

'How the devil could she?'

'He dropped his hanky in the cowshed. You know all their clothes are marked, so when she found that hanky on her way to do the milking, she started to ask herself a few questions, then she asked Nicolas some more . . . He ended up spilling the beans. Anyway, I think he was relieved to tell her about it.'

'Poor Nicolas, you should have seen him, he was just as unhappy as your kid! And what are you doing about Paul?'

'What I told you. He understands that he has to finish this year and take his School Certificate. After that we'll see.'

It was still completely dark when Pierre-Edouard disappeared into the cowshed and carefully closed the door behind him. He shivered; this February morning was cold and sharp as a knife. A mean east wind brought flurries of snow and howled over the village; it rattled the shutters, lifted the slates and seared the faces of all who left the warmth of their beds to care for their animals.

'Good morning, Nicolas!' called Pierre-Edouard.

'Good morning, boss!' said Nicolas, coming out of his recess. He held a bowl of milk which he raised to his face as if to drink a toast.

'Your good health!' cried Pierre-Edouard, filling his first pipe of the day.

This way of starting the day had become a ritual for them. Nicolas got up at least an hour before his boss. He lifted the manure and renewed the cows' litter, then he drew a litre of milk for his breakfast, which he enjoyed while washing and dressing. Pierre-Edouard would arrive and set the calves to sucking, then feed the cows which Mathilde would later milk.

'Terribly cold this morning,' commented Pierre-Edouard lighting his pipe.

'Yes, outside dungheap quite hard.'

'We'll have fun trying to break the ice on the pond so that the stock can drink. Did you see how thick it was yesterday? I'm sure it'll be worse today!'

'Winter . . . ' observed Nicolas.

'That's right, I expect you've seen some! And so have I. Here, give me the halters for the calves.'

The door suddenly banged behind him, and he turned in surprise. Mathilde was usually quieter than that.

'Oh, it's you!' he said, seeing his brother-in-law. 'What brings you here?'

'My God! Do you know what I've just heard on the wireless?' shouted Léon. 'They're fighting like madmen up there, in Paris!'

'What's that you're saying?'

'I'm telling you! Seems there are twenty dead and more than six hundred injured! And you know what? Those bloody gendarmes fired on the ex-servicemen! Just imagine, they dared do that to us! And when I think that only yesterday I sent Auguste over to La Villette! He's such a fool, he may well have been dragged into all this.'

'Tell me what's happening, I don't understand!'

And Léon related what he had heard on the news. The demonstrations in Paris the day before, the crowds threatening the Chamber of Deputies, demanding the resignation of everyone they accused of being involved in the Stavisky affair and other scandals.

'They lost their nerve and fired into the crowd. The bastards!' he finished in an angry shout.

'*Crédiou*, they should all be hanged,' growled Pierre-Edouard. 'I've been saying that for a long time! It wasn't worth fighting a war for four years if this is what happens! But what's Auguste got to do with it?'

Auguste was one of Léon's workers, the most capable and

sensible of them.

'I had twelve steers to deliver, but I didn't want to leave because the child's got chickenpox; all right, it's getting better now, but you never know. So I sent Auguste with the animals. I bet he'll have stuck his nose into it up there, just for fun . . .'

'Come on, you know Paris; La Villette isn't the Place de la Concorde!'

'Okay, but I know my fellow Auguste, he's as curious as a magpie!'

'His sort don't put themselves in the front line,' Pierre-Edouard reassured him. He grasped the pitchfork and sighed: 'And you say there are twenty dead?'

'Yes, and six hundred injured.'

'It'll get worse before it gets better, that's for sure; something will have to give one way or the other. What a day, and there'll be worse to come.'

Auguste came back that same evening. The village was still in a state of shock and the men, especially the ex-servicemen, were growling and snarling. He was bombarded with questions and an audience surrounded him as he took his place at the bar of the inn.

But he had seen absolutely nothing, heard nothing, suspected nothing, for at the time of the fighting, he was happily sipping brandy in a bordello on the rue Blondel. He smilingly accepted the insults which this admission provoked.

'Old reprobate!' cried Léon. 'I don't send you to Paris to go to a brothel. You won't get back there for a long time!'

Auguste let them have their say, then held up one hand. True, he hadn't seen anything of the demonstrations: 'But I can do better than that!' he assured them, puffing out his chest. He had travelled all the way back with one of the demonstrators, a fellow from Toulouse.

'And do you know what really happened?' he began.

From him, the men of Saint-Libéral learned all about it. Their hearts pounded with the crowd which massed in the Place de la Concorde at six o'clock; they shook with rage when charged by the horses of the mounted police; their knuckles whitened when the first shots rang out. But they laughed when they learned that Edouard Herriot had only just escaped being thrown into the Seine!

They turned pale when Auguste described how the dignified column of veterans of the National Union of Ex-Servicemen, walking peacefully down the Champs-Elysées, their chests weighed down with medals and the 'Marseillaise' on their lips, were attacked by the forces of law and order.

'Then,' explained Auguste, 'came the great battle, that's when the blood really flowed. And it seems that's just the start of things.'

The men shook their heads, emptied their glasses and left the inn; they were angry and worried.

The death of the former solicitor, Maître Lardy, surprised no one. He was known to have been ill for a long time, a broken man since the death of his wife five years earlier. He had also been afflicted by the constant presence of his two daughters. They had both lost their fiancés, one after the other, during the war, and had never recovered from this ordeal, since when they had aged badly. They were so clouded by sorrow, so embittered by sadness, that life with them was a perpetual torture, a calvary.

Maître Lardy died on the morning of 30 April. Pierre-Edouard and Mathilde were the first to visit his bedside. For them it was more than a duty, it was a mark of recognition and respectful affection. All those who saw them go by, and push open the gateway to the garden of the former office, approved their action.

No one in the village had forgotten that the notary's wife had been Mathilde's godmother, or that Maître Lardy had been the one who, sixteen years earlier, had let the cottage at Coste-Roche to Pierre-Edouard for a peppercorn rent.

It was two days after the funeral, which was attended by a considerable crowd, that Maître Chardoux, the solicitor from Terrasson, summoned Pierre-Edouard and Mathilde. As executor of his dead colleague's will, he advised them that the latter had left his wife's god-daughter the tiny smallholding of Coste-Roche, its cottage and the two hectares of wasteland surrounding it.

'But you aren't obliged to accept it!' he added in honeyed tones.

Pierre-Edouard frowned. He did not like this solicitor, his cunning flattery and his shifty looks. 'And why should we not accept it?' he asked sharply.

'Oh well, according to what I hear the house and land are in such a state, they won't even be worth the expense involved in the inheritance! If you accept them, that is!'

'Of course we accept!' interrupted Pierre-Edouard. 'And I suggest you get in touch with my solicitor, Maître Lachaume of Ayen, to settle things properly and as quickly as possible.'

'I must remind you that this concerns Madame; it is her agreement I require,' insisted Monsieur Chardoux, as he pulled each finger in turn to make the joints crack.

'We both feel the same way,' replied Mathilde, 'so do as he says.'

'Very well, I will undertake what is necessary,' said the notary, getting up. 'I understand that you accept this . . . legacy, and the expenses it will bring! I admit that I find your attitude strange, but after all, that's your problem, isn't it?'

'Exactly,' said Pierre-Edouard before they left, 'but it isn't a problem at all, it's a gift – a very fine gift.'

'The notary couldn't understand, could he?' commented Mathilde with a smile.

Pierre-Edouard and she had just covered the three kilometres which separated Coste-Roche from Saint-Libéral. Now they were there, side by side, in front of the house, their house. It was almost a ruin, surrounded by brambles, nettles and bushes; even the little field which Pierre had cleared long ago was a pitiful sight. It was in the process of becoming a tangled thicket, an anarchic profusion of young ashes, elders, hornbeam and gorse; already honeysuckle and old man's beard had taken over, throwing their invasive tentacles in all directions.

'Well, well,' commented Pierre-Edouard, 'it is in a terrible state, but I'm still pleased to be here!'

'Me too,' murmured Mathilde, gripping his hand tightly.

This house, with its thatch slipping off on all sides, was theirs: the place which had welcomed them on their wedding night, that snowy evening in December 1918; which had seen the birth of Jacques and had sheltered them, happy and in love, for four years. Four often difficult years, when they were close to poverty; hard, tiring, testing times – but now, with hindsight, they seemed the richest, finest, happiest years of their life.

Pierre-Edouard slashed a path through the nettles and fool's parsley which blocked the entrance. He pushed open the door. The room smelled musty, damp and dusty. Mathilde hurried in, opening the window and the shutters.

'Look,' said Pierre-Edouard, pointing to the fireplace, 'our chimney hook is still there. It was a good thing we left it, it's been waiting for us.'

'You know you should never take down a pot-hanger, that brings bad luck,' said his wife, as she pushed open the door to the bedroom.

'Our room . . . ' she murmured, 'do you remember?'

'Of course.'

'It's a pity we can't live here. Here we'd have our own home, whereas in the village . . . '

'I know, I know,' he said, and put his arms around her shoulders, 'but you know we can't move house just because my father won't put the farm in our name!'

'Of course not. But promise me that we'll do this house up whatever happens. Then if one of the children wants it one day at least *he* will have some walls to call his own.'

'Agreed, we'll do that. But you know, the notary in Terrasson may be proved right. What with the fees on the inheritance, the roof to be repaired and all the rest, it'll cost us a lot, this present!'

'That doesn't matter,' she said. 'It's our house, we'll sort it out. That way we can come here for lunch, or even a siesta in the summer, when we're working on the plateau; it won't be so far as going right back down to the village.'

'The siesta's a good idea,' he joked, and kissed her on the neck. 'All the siestas you like, so long as we take them together, as we used to, eh!'

While replacing a joist in the loft of the small cowshed, Nicolas made a discovery which delighted him. For the past two months, Pierre-Edouard and he had got in the habit of going up to Coste-Roche every Sunday to effect whatever repairs they felt qualified to complete themselves.

The price demanded by the roofer to replace the thatch with a strong layer of slate had sent Pierre-Edouard reeling. The Ayen tiler asked for 3,840 francs, the price of a good pair of cows. It was much more than Pierre-Edouard could pay. So they had postponed this work until they had enough money, and made do with repairing what they could themselves.

Helped by Nicolas, who turned out to be an excellent craftsman, he had first patched up the thatch by blocking the holes with sheets of corrugated iron. It was not beautiful but it worked; it no longer rained into the house.

Now they were on to the roof of the barn. Pierre-Edouard was down in the yard, trimming a rafter with his axe, when he heard Nicolas's laugh, followed by a monologue in Serbian.

Fine, he thought, *now he's talking to himself!*

Then he noticed his companion leaning out of one of the holes in the roof and waving to him to come up and join him.

'What do you want?'

'Come, come! Good thing!' called Nicolas with a beaming smile.

Pierre-Edouard stuck his axe in the log and went over to the barn, pulled himself up into the loft, and almost poked his head into an enormous swarm of bees which, between midday and two o'clock had chosen to make their home in the old barn.

'*Miladiou*,' he gasped as he hurriedly dropped back down. 'Are you quite mad?' he called out, after retiring about ten metres. 'Does that amuse you? Wait while I fetch some sulphur matches, you'll see how I take care of those devils!'

'Not devils!' Nicolas corrected him. 'Nice creatures!'

'Come down!' Pierre-Edouard ordered. 'If they go for you, you won't even have time to run to the doctor's!'

'Not wicked! Me know!'

'Know or not, I'm telling you to come down!' he insisted. 'We can't go on with the work while they are there!'

He was frightened of bees, which he considered just as nasty and dangerous as wasps or hornets. He was going to smoke the swarm to sleep with sulphur, destroy it and make sure that none of the horrid beasts escaped punishment; they had given him such a fright.

'Well, are you coming?' he called out again.

'Yes.' Nicolas gave in, and his white head disappeared under the rotting straw of the roof.

Pierre-Edouard heard him humming gently; the man was definitely mad!

'Good thing,' said Nicolas, when he reappeared a few moments later. 'Me put them in . . . ' he searched for the word 'in box,' he explained with a smile, 'and after we have good honey, great!'

'You want to put them in a hive?'

'That's right, in a box.'

'And you know how to do it?' asked Pierre-Edouard with great scepticism.

'Of course! Me, over there,' explained Nicolas, with a jab of his thumb to the east, 'lots, lots of bees on the estate, all full of little boxes. So take that one and do same, easy!'

'Well, you'll have to do it without me, mate! I'm not setting foot in the barn while they're there! But how will you do it?'

'Easy! No one keep bees in village?'

'Oh, no! At one time, yes, the last teacher had a dozen hives, but since he left . . . We don't trust those beasts, you know, they're treacherous.'

'So no one? Damn nuisance, but I fix it all alone!' confirmed Nicolas, whose progress in the French language was picturesque. 'Madame will lend veil perhaps, like women at burials? And puffer too?' asked the tall fellow; his vocabulary was also enriched by dialect words.

'You mean a mourning veil and the bellows? Yes, we'll find those for you; is that all you need?'

Nicolas nodded, and consulted the big watch which filled his waistcoat pocket.

'Too late this evening, me come tomorrow, all right?'

'Well, yes. We would have wasted the morning anyway trying to kill them, horrid things! But you manage it yourself, and too bad if they sting you; you can't count on me to help you.'

Despite this resolve, Pierre-Edouard did accompany Nicolas back to Coste-Roche. He was curious to see how Nicolas set about it, and at the same time he did not want to be considered cowardly in the eyes of this man whose confidence disconcerted him.

He had watched with interest on the previous evening as Nicolas prepared his equipment and hive. Now they were climbing up to Coste-Roche. On his shoulder Nicolas carried a large hollow log of chestnut wood. He had closed off the two ends of it with boards, leaving only a narrow opening at what was to be the bottom of the hive for the insects to pass through. Inside the trunk he had carefully arranged and firmly fixed slender rods of hazel wood on which the bees would build their combs, so he assured Pierre-Edouard.

Nicolas had improvised a smoke pump by adding an old tin can to the end of the bellows, and Pierre-Edouard was carrying this. They entered the little courtyard at Coste-Roche.

'Sh,' said Nicolas, after putting down the log. He listened, smiled, and pointed to one of the holes in the roof. 'Still there,' he said, 'already working!'

From where they were, they really could hear the buzzing of the thousands of insects busy up there. They went closer.

'Bloody hell!' muttered Pierre-Edouard, looking up at the bees who were pouring out of the opening. 'We'll be eaten alive!'

'No,' Nicolas reassured him, picking up the bellows.

He filled the smoke chamber with a mixture of nutshells, chestnut peelings and a few old scraps of jute sacking, and set the kindling alight with a spark from his tinder box. When the fire was crackling, he smothered it with a lid and activated the bellows. Thick white smoke poured from the hole he had punched in the tin.

'Good smoke,' he said, sending a plume of it on to his hand, 'not hot, just good, as it should be.'

'Yes,' replied a worried Pierre-Edouard.

'Put muslin,' said Nicolas. He took the mourning veil given to him by Mathilde, covered his hat with it, and tied it round his neck.

'Oh, you look magnificent with that on!' Pierre-Edouard teased him.

'You too put veil, boss.'

'You're joking, aren't you? Me, I'm staying here, or better still going a bit further away!'

'Me need you,' insisted Nicolas, 'to hold box . . . '

'No, no, you can go to damnation alone!' protested Pierre-Edouard. But he could see even through the black veil that Nicolas' eyes were mocking him; he angrily took out the second veil which he had stuffed in his pocket, and covered his head with it.

'You, my fine fellow, if I get a single sting, you'll hear from me!' he grumbled as he rigged himself out. He rolled down his shirt sleeves and did up the buttons. 'My God, if I'd known, I would at least have brought a coat! And you're going in with bare arms, are you?'

'That's right,' Nicolas smiled, 'and if the bees come and land there,' he said pointing to his hands, 'not be afraid, not touch, not squeeze, do nothing, they go away. Now we work?' he said, grasping the hive.

'Yes, but you go first . . . My word, you won't catch me doing this again! If anything goes wrong, I'm telling you, I'm off!'

Nicolas climbed the old ladder, hauled himself into the loft and began to laugh.

'And it makes you laugh!' groaned Pierre-Edouard, as he gingerly poked his head through the trap door.

A humming greeted him; he looked up fearfully at the swarm hanging behind a rafter.

'Well, you don't say! That's what you want to put in the box? I wish you luck!'

'Come here,' said Nicolas, paying no attention to the hundreds of insects which were already hovering around him.

My God, thought Pierre-Edouard, *I can't let it be said that this fellow saw me lose my nerve.* And he pulled himself into the loft.

Nicolas lifted the flap which covered the trunk, and held out the open hive.

'Hold just underneath,' he explained, 'me take down.'

Pierre-Edouard controlled himself, forced himself to keep calm, not to look at the myriad bees surrounding him, circling him in a maddening dance. Nicolas smoked the swarm, and the buzzing tone changed to a deep humming, whilst the thousands of insects collected around the queen suddenly began to quiver. Then he gently slid a lath the width of his hand along the underside of the rafter and pushed at the tip of the swarm, which broke off with a dry crack. The brown ball and the framework of combs which had been constructed since the previous day fell into the tree-trunk. *At least four kilos*, thought Pierre-Edouard.

'Hell and damnation!' he yelled suddenly, 'my hands are covered in them!' He tensed, expecting to be stung.

'Don't move,' said Nicolas, and directed a thick cloud of smoke towards him, 'they will go away, the queen calls,' he explained with a smile.

'You won't catch me doing this again,' cried Pierre-Edouard, anxiously watching the bees running over his fingers.

They left one by one, and made for the little slit in the hive. All the insects which had escaped when they dislodged the swarm were disappearing through it in a constant stream.

'That's it,' said Nicolas, 'wait a little for them all to come, and then we go away.'

'It's finished?' asked Pierre-Edouard, withdrawing towards the trapdoor.

'Yes, finished. Easy, eh?' called Nicolas with a smile.

'The bees weren't the only ones to be trapped,' grumbled Pierre-Edouard as he quickly climbed down.

He sighed with relief when he reached the courtyard and lifted his veil. At that moment, a bee caught in the material stung him on the ear. He howled like a muleteer, span round in a circle, jumped up and down and cursed Nicolas whose white head appeared through a hole in the roof laughing like a madman.

'Never again, do you hear! Go away, you idiot! You and your tricks, you won't catch me doing this again!'

But it was he who discovered a new swarm as he walked down from the peaks three days later, hanging from the branch of a flowering acacia.

'Hey,' he called to Nicolas as soon as he got back to the farm, 'I've found a new swarm by the path to the peaks, shall we go and get it? It would be a pity to let it go off again, wouldn't it? Come on, hurry, you told me they make off when the sun passes its highest point.'

'Good thing!' rejoiced Nicolas. 'Boss like bees too!'

'Like them? That's going a bit too far! But they are beginning to interest me all the same, those beasts of yours.'

In that season Nicolas and he gathered nine more swarms, and from then on Pierre-Edouard spoke of his hives with pride.

PART THREE

The Wind from the South

Chapter 10

PAUL groaned, turned over under the blankets, and tried to escape the hand which was energetically shaking him.

'Come on, get up! It's four o'clock!' whispered Jean-Edouard.

Paul opened one eye and regarded his grandfather grudgingly. He did not deserve any credit for getting up at such an unearthly hour! Wasn't he always telling the family that he was bored lying in bed after four o'clock! How could you be bored in a nice warm bed in the middle of the night!

'Come on!' insisted Jean-Edouard, 'you must get up, otherwise he'll have to come here to fetch you, and I don't want that to happen!'

The young boy sighed, sat up and rubbed his eyes. He was in a very bad mood and, as every time he was torn from his dreams at such an hour – that is, three or four times a week – he almost regretted that he had succeeded in convincing his parents that he was not the studious type. His obstinacy had displeased his father. However, he had given in. The teachers at Bossuet had testified that his son, like a caged lion at the beginning of the year, had become over the months as miserable and pitiful as a young badger on a chain.

'All right,' his father had decided, 'you have your School Certificate; I didn't go any further, so I won't make you. Besides, nobody can force a donkey to drink when he's not thirsty! But believe me, from the point of view of work you won't gain anything by changing! I'm going to put you through the mill, I am! You'll see what it's like, working on the land!'

'That's not what I want to do . . . '

'What? It seems to me that you don't have any choice! It's the farm or school, you decide!'

'I want to be like Uncle Léon . . . '

'Oh my God! That's all I need! Don't you think one stock-dealer in the family is enough? Tell me, don't you know that people like that live off our backs?'

'Not Uncle Léon!'

'He does, just like the others!'

'But he's your friend!'

'Well yes, but he was that before he became a shark.'

'You still care for him, even so. I want to be like him.'

'Well, well, that's all we needed,' his father had sighed, 'and that makes you laugh, of course!' he added as he looked at Mathilde.

'Why not? That for once the Dupeuch blood should prevail over the Vialhe . . . '

'Huh, that's really funny, what you're saying. So you don't mind if your son becomes one of those louts who earn their living off our backs!'

'Don't exaggerate. Anyway, we need them, stock-dealers.'

'Yes, more's the pity! All right, okay, I'll go and talk to Léon, and if he wants to accept you as his assistant, you won't find a better master than him. But believe me, with him you won't be laughing every day.'

Six months on, Paul had had plenty of time to realise how right his father was. With his uncle there was no question of idling around market stalls, or of balking at cleaning out the stable or grooming the animals. Added to that were three or four markets each week, when he had to leave his bed at impossible times.

On those mornings he envied his brother Jacques. At least he could sleep to his heart's content and, whatever he said, his studies were less tiring than this apprenticeship with Uncle Léon.

'Here,' said his grandfather, setting a bowl of milk on the table, 'have a quick breakfast, it'll be a long day. Where's that one going today?'

Jean-Edouard made it a point of honour never to say 'Léon' or even 'your uncle'. To him he would always be 'Dupeuch' or 'that one'.

'We're going to Dorat.'

'Dammit! You'll never get there! In my time, we would have set off the day before. Still, that one has his car! And what's he trading in, so far away?'

134

'Buying horses.'

Jean-Edouard shrugged. He had always rather despised those animals; he thought them too delicate, too sensitive and, whatever certain people might say, in his opinion not as good as a fine pair of oxen, or even a couple of working cows.

'Horses,' he grumbled, 'what an idea! Well, just listen to me, young fellow. Remember, those animals are vicious, mind you don't get kicked! Come on, eat your breakfast and get on, that one will be fed up waiting for you.'

Father Verlhac had known the news for a month, but he waited until Sunday, 10 January 1935, before communicating it to his parishioners.

What he announced threw them into consternation. It was during Mass, at the end of his sermon, that he revealed what he could no longer conceal. He ended his homily and made the sign of the Cross, but instead of climbing down from the pulpit, he grasped the rim and leaned towards his flock.

'Brethren, what I am about to tell you seems to me like one of those April showers which we shall soon see. They make you sad because they still smell of winter, of frost and cold; they cheer you up because with them spring is reborn. Today my heart is heavy, but my soul is joyful. It is joyful, for the Lord has judged me worthy to serve him further. But my heart is heavy, for the Lord's decision forces me to leave you . . .

'Do not complain, one does not grumble in the house of the Lord! Yes, brethren, I am going to have to leave you after twenty-five years of life together. One evening in April when I was thirty-one, I discovered my new parish, and this church dedicated to Saint Eutrope. Today, at the age of fifty-six, I must start a new life, launch out on a new mission. Monseigneur the Bishop has honoured me with the onerous task of serving at his side, as diocesan chaplain for Action Catholique. It is a weighty but uplifting responsibility.

'However, as I told you, if my soul is joyful, my heart is heavy. After twenty-five years you have all become my friends. Thanks to you, I have been a part of this extended family which is our parish, and I have felt at home here. You have all invited me into your homes. I have baptised your children, blessed your flocks and your fields, shared your joys and sorrows. You have given me a great deal.

'Now I must leave, but I did not want to part without receiving an assurance that my place would not remain empty. Next Sunday you will be introduced to your new priest, Father Delclos; I know that you will make him welcome, he deserves it. As for me, I must take up my new post on February the first. So you see, this still leaves me with almost a month in which to bid you farewell. And now, let us celebrate together the Holy Sacrament. I will pray for you; do you pray for me, I am in need of it.'

The news took off as soon as Mass ended. It spread rapidly through the whole parish, reaching the farthest farms and upsetting everyone, even the anti-clerical types, even the Reds, like Bernical, Tavet and Brousse.

Some of the women had eyes reddened by tears as they told their menfolk. In the bar at Suzanne's or Noémie Lamothe's the men were silent at first, dumbfounded over their aperitifs. Then came anger. This priest was theirs, even if he was pigheaded, made biting comments and gave sarcastic replies, even if he made a great fuss, with his *dominus vobiscum* and his *pater nosters* which some of them did not believe in, he was still a good priest, an honest and trustworthy man. 'They' had no right to take him away!

'Oh my God!' moaned one drinker. 'They've done away with the train and the shuttle, and now they're taking away our priest! Bloody hell, what'll be left here for us!'

'Better tell Léon, and fast! Better put a stop to it!' bellowed another customer.

'Okay, let's all go!'

They went to him, and found Léon just as distressed and at a loss as to what to do as they were. His wife attended church, and she had told him as soon as Mass ended.

Pierre-Edouard was informed by Mathilde, and he too felt the blow. He was not in the habit of attending church frequently, but he did go four or five times a year. Besides, Father Verlhac was a friend, a support, an occasional confidant: that was what saddened him. It was he who had married them, who had baptised all their children, and who several times a year accepted a seat at their table as one of the family.

'Come on,' he said to Mathilde, as he pulled her to him to comfort her, 'life goes on. You know, I think he was too good for us, that's why they're taking him away from us. If he'd been like some people, whose names I won't mention, they would have left him here! Now don't make a face like that, think of the children – all the children in the village, they'll be the greatest losers. We'll lose by it too, but we've known other priests. But still, they could have left him with us, a priest like that, they won't give us another like him in a hurry, you can be sure of that! And you say his replacement has already been named?'

'Yes, he'll be here next Sunday.'

'Well, well, he'll need to tread very carefully; it won't be easy to take over, and with the council elections in four months' time, he'll be walking on eggs . . .'

All the children and young people in the parish were heart-broken by the announcement of Father Verlhac's imminent departure. All those who could – that is to say those who were not at work with their parents – gathered in the presbytery, in its youth club room, that Sunday afternoon, but they were dispirited and almost embarrassed.

Already they felt less at home; the priest forced himself to make a few jokes, promised he would not forget them, he would even come back occasionally, but it did not do any good. They remained withdrawn, hardly touched the ball and gave affected laughs almost out of politeness, when the priest projected several spools on his Pathé projector. Neither *Félix the Cat* nor *Jack and the Beanstalk*, nor even a documentary about aviation really cheered them up; they felt betrayed.

Even Paul was quite distraught. For several months he had shown a certain reserve towards Father Verlhac and had pointedly kept his distance from religion; now he almost repented having avoided the presbytery and the club. He had missed the opportunity of a warm friendship freely offered, and now the offer was being withdrawn. So to mask his sadness, he tried to show off.

'Well then, when you're gone,' he carelessly commented, 'we'll be able to go dancing without any worries!'

'I never prevented you from going,' the priest reminded him

137

with a smile. 'If my information is correct, it was your father who forbade it! I don't think he'll change his mind just because I'm leaving, quite the opposite, I expect! You know, Paul, at your age you're still a bit young to go round the dances, to pretend to be a man! What you should do is take over these meetings. I'm sure you and your friends could liven them up. Would you like me to talk to my replacement?'

'Certainly not! It's all just kid's stuff to me . . . '

'So why did you come today?'

'Well . . . ' Paul was embarrassed, 'to be with my friends, to see, you know! Yes,' he repeated it with a show of confidence, 'to come one last time. Say what you like, the new priest, he'll never be able to get us all together!'

'And why not?'

'Because he's not from here! He's a stranger to the village, we don't know him! And I, I' – he controlled the trembling in his voice with difficulty – 'I don't want to get to know him at all! So you see, it'll never be the same again!'

Father Verlhac smiled but said nothing. Paul, taking such pains to hide his sorrow, Paul was right. A page was about to be turned. It was turning for him, a simple country priest who suddenly had to confront a new world; it was turning for all his parishioners, for the whole village. Paul saw it clearly; it would never be the same, for anyone.

The arrival of Father Delclos amazed everyone. One Saturday 16 January, towards midday, he appeared in Saint-Libéral at the wheel of a B2, which made a great impression on all the watchers even though it was wheezing and dilapidated. In the village no one was accustomed to seeing a priest who owned a motor-car; this ancient Citroën, despite its well-worn state, was an unmistakable sign: it represented wealth.

In Saint-Libéral, no one knew of a country priest rich enough to buy himself a motor-car.

The priest jumped down with a thump – he was stocky, almost squat, and extremely corpulent – opened the rear door, and helped an old lady to climb out.

'Bloody hell! A married priest!' whispered one joker, who was drinking his gentian-bitters at the inn. 'Yes, yes really, lads, come and see!' he said. 'Hey, look, look!' he insisted, as he pushed aside the red-and-white checked curtain which covered the glass in the door.

'Idiot! If that were his wife he'd certainly have chosen someone younger and plumper!' joked one of his friends. 'And look how he's helping her – it's his mother, I bet!'

Without letting go of the old lady's arm the priest climbed the few steps up to the presbytery; he was about to push open the door when the heavy portal swung open to reveal Father Verlhac.

From the inn the men took in every detail of the scene. So it was learned that the new incumbent had just arrived, with his car, his mother and a considerable load of suitcases. It was decided that he must be extremely rich for, early in the afternoon, a removal van stopped in front of the presbytery and unloaded a great deal of furniture: armchairs, beds, and even two woodburning stoves which were much admired by all the onlookers.

'That's not a priest, that's a bishop!' commented Martin Tavet sarcastically, as he helped the blacksmith to shoe two of his cows at the other end of the square.

'You'll always find a stone in the hoof,' replied the smith, placing the iron on the anvil. He formed it, put down his hammer and spat onto the hearth of the forge. 'Dammit, it'll be a change from Verlhac; he wasn't our sort, but at least he wasn't proud! Did you see him, when he looked at us just now? My God! A bishop, did you say? He thinks he's the Pope, he does!'

Father Verlhac took the offensive two days before he was due to leave. The day was drawing to an end when he knocked on the Vialhes' door and entered.

'So, it's your last visit?' Pierre-Edouard asked him. 'May I offer you a glass of white wine?'

'If you like.'

'Will you stay for supper?' suggested Mathilde. 'Look, we're just about to sit down, so if you'd like to . . .'

'Bless me, I suppose I should eat, and it would give me great pleasure to do it with you – though it may be a long evening,' added the priest in an enigmatic tone.

Pierre-Edouard frowned, but kept his counsel and filled the

glasses. It seemed that Father Verlhac had something important to tell him. Since he had come before the meal, he obviously wanted to be sure he would find them still up. He was long familiar with the customs of the village, and knew that the Vialhes went to bed early in the winter – as did everyone, unless they were going to spend the evening with neighbours, to help them make up bales of tobacco or play a game of cards.

'To your good health, all of you,' said the priest, raising his glass. 'I must talk to you after the meal,' he warned Pierre-Edouard. 'Is that possible?'

'Of course, start right now if you like.'

'No, it would take too long.'

It was a peculiar dinner; the atmosphere was strained and conversations stopped short. It was only at the end of the meal that old Jean-Edouard went onto the offensive, ignoring any pretence at diplomacy.

'Tell us, Father, who is this bird who's taking your place, eh? Where's he from, the old crow? You know what he said to me the other day in the square? – "At your age, Monsieur Vialhe, you should be in church every day, you have nothing else to do, think on it, you must prepare yourself, nobody lives for ever!" – And his turkey of a mother nodding her head in approval! We don't say things like that around here. He'll have to change his tune. Dammit, he won't be seeing me in his church! I'll go and take communion in Perpezac or Yssandon at Easter, in Ayen even, if need be, but certainly not here!'

'Come, come, Monsieur Vialhe, he said that as a joke! He's not a bad man! It's just that he's not accustomed to country people, you know, he's always been a town vicar, you must understand that.'

'Well, I shall be going to Perpezac as well,' said Mathilde suddenly, 'and that will be every Sunday too!'

'Now, now! You as well?' sighed the priest. 'And what has he done to you?'

'That's my business!' she said, collecting up the plates. 'But believe you me, he won't be seeing me again in a hurry!'

The priest looked at Pierre-Edouard, but he only made a face indicating ignorance, and shrugged his shoulders. Mathilde had told him a week ago that Father Delclos was an old cabbage-face, but she had not said any more.

She had not spoken to anyone and was not about to do so, she was so ashamed at what the priest had suggested. He had the audacity to say that he hoped a good Christian woman like her, still young too, would not be content to bring only four children into the world. Especially as her last little one, if his information was correct, was already three years old!

'Three years, my child! He is weaned now! So I hope that you will soon be welcoming another little angel, for I have no doubt that you love your husband and he loves you!'

Mathilde had gasped in surprise and turned her back on the priest, swearing to avoid him like the plague from that moment.

'And what about you, Nicolas,' joked Father Verlhac, 'has he said anything to you?'

'No, no,' Nicolas smiled as he rose, 'people don't speak to me unless I want, and that fat pope, I don't want he speak to me.'

'Well, *we* must have got on with each other,' said the priest, 'because we often talked to each other.'

'For you, it's not the same,' said Nicolas, making for the door. He bade them all goodnight with a nod of his head, and went out.

'All right,' said Jean-Edouard, 'I'm going to bed as well.' He held out his hand to the priest. 'We shall miss you, you must come back to see us.'

'Of course, Monsieur Vialhe, and above all, keep your faith!'

'Come on, children, time for bed!' called Pierre-Edouard. 'Paul, you'd better go and sleep in our room with the little ones. You see,' he explained to the priest, pointing to the bed at the end of the room, 'he usually sleeps there, but as you wish to speak to me and it seems to be a serious matter . . . '

'I'll leave you to it,' announced Mathilde in her turn.

'Oh no,' said Father Verlhac, 'I need you, and your brother too. He'll be coming at nine o'clock, I've arranged it with him.'

'He's coming here? What if my father-in-law hears him?'

'And what if he does? I'm here to keep the peace, aren't I?'

*

Nine o'clock was striking on the long-case clock as Léon pushed open the door.

'Have you explained to them?' he asked the priest.

'No, I was waiting for you.'

'What is going on, you conspirators! This is beginning to irritate me!' said Pierre-Edouard, bringing out the bottle of plum brandy. 'Now are we allowed to know what it's all about?'

'Yes,' said the priest. 'In three months' time there will be council elections. Martin Tavet will offer a list of Red candidates and it will be accepted!'

'Bloody hell!' exclaimed Pierre-Edouard with a laugh. 'And that's why you're making all this fuss? Really, it's not worth it. Besides, Tavet won't be elected, he's too stupid.'

'He will be elected! The teacher is behind them and believe me, he's a worker, that one! He's already begun to canvass door to door . . .'

'Well, I thought he was a radical!' Pierre-Edouard was astonished.

'You're behind the times, my friend,' said the priest, 'he took his party card after last year's disturbances.'

'All right, so what?'

'So if we let them agitate, Léon will be beaten, and you too, and all the others like you who wait around without doing anything!'

'Don't exaggerate,' interrupted Léon, 'our council *does* work!'

'Yes, but Tavet has got the credit for what you have achieved so far, because he's a council member at the moment. He's already telling everyone that the water and electricity are thanks to him, and they have you to blame for the loss of the trains!'

'People aren't that stupid!' said Pierre-Edouard. He was not worried, but he was annoyed. If, as the priest assured him, the Reds took control in the town hall, life would not be much fun in St Libéral; as for the farmers' co-operative, he would have to hand over the presidency to one of those second-rate admirers of Stalin.

'The reverend is right,' said Mathilde, 'something must be done, and I'm sure that he has an idea.'

'Yes,' said the priest. He rolled himself a cigarette, dipping into Pierre-Edouard's tobacco pouch. 'Our young people have no meeting-place, they don't know where to go any more; my colleague has installed his mother in the room which I had given them. So there it is, you have three months in which to build a village hall. It will be their club room, their library too, they could meet together there. I shall leave behind my projector and screen, my books and everything I can think of. That's what needs doing, and quickly, and all the while you'll be telling everyone that it's your idea, it's thanks to you moderates and those who'd like to vote for a sensible list of councillors.'

'Three months, that's not long,' said Léon. 'And then we need money, land, to vote for it in council, all that!'

'Right now, you're in the majority on the council; make the most of it. As for money and land, get a move on!'

'It would be in our interests to get a move on, it really would,' commented Pierre-Edouard. 'But tell me, Father, why are you bothering about all this when you'll be gone the day after tomorrow?'

'It's given me a new lease of life. You see, you weren't here when I arrived, you didn't follow the elections in 1911. I can tell you now that those elections were partly engineered by me, with Léon, and in opposition to your father. We got the squire elected and he was a very fine mayor; and so was your father, later on. Now that I'm going away, I want to leave everything in good order. I want the people of Saint-Libéral to continue to live in some sort of peace. Most of all, I don't want the young people to be let down. You must be elected; that will be my leaving present.'

Father Verlhac had got it right. Two days were enough to convince Pierre-Edouard that the opposition were losing no time. Almost every evening Jacques Sourzac, the teacher, with Tavet, Brousse and friends alongside, held the stage at the auberge; and his remarks carried weight, made an impression, sowed doubts. He spoke of the flight from the land, caused by poverty, and his statistics, which were undeniable, impressed everybody.

'Don't forget, my friends, and consider this well. Less than a century ago the rural population, the wealth of the nation, represented seventy-five per cent of the total population of France. In 1926 it was no more than fifty per cent; this year, it won't reach forty-eight per cent! More than thirty-five thousand workers have left their land every year since 1931! And, look at this, in a region neighbouring ours, in the Creuse, there are eleven thousand two hundred and sixty-six miserable souls who have had to seek refuge elsewhere between 1921 and 1931!

'It is essential that we act. This government has been corrupted by the Jews, and it's vital that we convince them that the people of France no longer recognise their own kind among the elected, up their in Paris and in our town halls, stuffing themselves and growing fat on the sweat of the proletariat. From now on we must act to take over the positions which have been held for too long by unworthy men – by stock-dealers! Then next year, we shall win the general election!'

All these arguments and figures, which he declaimed clearly and passionately, produced a substantial effect on people who were inclined to admire and follow a man who could speak so definitively.

It was therefore essential to counter-attack as soon as possible; to destroy by one means or another this fascination, almost infatuation, felt by the electors when they listened to the teacher's commanding discourses. In order to triumph they had to gain the upper hand.

There was no time to lose. It was not for nothing that Léon was a stock-dealer, Pierre-Edouard a worthy representative of the Vialhes and Dr Delpy a liar, as was fitting.

The first problem to be resolved was of the administrative kind. It was essential that the vote for the construction of the youth club should be carried only by those associated with Léon. Better still would be if their adversaries pronounced themselves totally opposed to the project. There was no doubt that they would vote against it, unless . . . unless they felt they were in the minority. In that case they would join the bandwagon and later on take all the credit.

The framework of the conspiracy was to make them believe

that the majority would not agree to the project, then there would be a vote. At the very next council meeting Pierre-Edouard launched the attack.

'You know, I've been thinking . . . Our young people have no room for their youth club now. Here, in the mairie it's much too small, we should build them a shelter . . .'

'Have you gone mad?' said Léon, shrugging his shoulders.

'What do you mean?' insisted Pierre-Edouard. 'It's no big deal: four walls, a roof and they'll be happy!'

'They don't need that to keep entertained, there's plenty of space out in the country!'

'Besides,' slipped in the doctor, 'those film shows the priest organised weren't very healthy – I mean for their eyes, of course. The faculty of medicine is unanimous in the opinion that the light from cinema projectors strains the retina, over-stimulates the crystalline lens and contracts the pupil. Furthermore . . .'

'Yes,' interrupted Léon, who was afraid that the doctor was overdoing it, 'anyway if they want something to do, they can always work! Isn't that so?' he said, addressing Tavet.

'The idea of a non-religious youth club for the children is quite a good one, but we should see about that later,' proposed Tavet, who had already decided to revive the idea on his own account as soon as he was elected.

'That's it, we'll see later,' agreed Léon.

'And besides, we have no money,' the doctor reminded them.

With a glance, Pierre-Edouard reassured himself that his friends Maurice, Edouard, Jacques and Pierre Delpeyroux were playing their parts; they seemed as undecided as a cow who has found some chervil in a clump of clover.

'We only need to vote for or against the project,' he remarked. 'That's the best way. I'd like to know who agrees with me . . .'

'You've certainly got plenty of time to waste!' protested Léon.

'Considering that it's growing late already,' put in the doctor, consulting his pocket-watch.

'No, but seriously! I have the right to demand a vote on it!' interposed Pierre-Edouard.

'Yes, yes,' Léon soothed him, in a humouring tone. 'Come on then, we'll take a vote to please you, then we'll go home to bed.'

Even the teacher, who was present at the meeting, fell into the trap. He was convinced that neither Léon, nor the doctor, nor Maurice or Edouard would come down in favour of the project, so he acquiesced when Tavet quietly signalled 'no' to him with a flick of his finger.

'Results,' said Léon shortly afterwards: 'For the immediate construction of a youth club, eight votes.'

'Swine!' yelled Tavet, standing up with a great crash of his chair. 'Dungheap! You were against it, and so was the doctor!'

'Against the project,' announced Léon imperturbably, 'five votes. Project adopted.'

'It's a fiddle!' bellowed the teacher.

'Young man,' the doctor looked him up and down with a scornful eye, 'as for fiddling elections, go and ask your comrade Stalin how he feels about that, and you'll learn something!'

'You were against it,' grumbled Bernical. 'It was dishonest of you!'

'Me? Did I say I was against it? Did you hear me say that? I said that excessive film-watching was harmful to the eyes!'

'Yes, and it sounded as if you were against it!' Brousse reproached him. 'And Léon did the same!'

'I never said that I would vote against it!' protested Léon, in the offended tone of an honest man whose word has been questioned.

'All right,' groaned Tavet, 'you made fools of us. Build your club-thing, it won't stop us from beating you hollow at the next elections!'

'We'll talk about that later, my little fellow,' said Pierre-Edouard placing a hand on his shoulder, 'we'll talk about that later . . .'

Léon and his friends lost no time. A plot of land was found the very next day: it was common ground presently occupied by an old bakery which had been abandoned thirty years ago. Situated on the edge of the village, it was ideal for a youth club.

The excavations began three days later, and everything went very fast after that, for Léon let it be known that he would make a gift to the community of a barn which was threatening to collapse; the metal-work and a fair number of the slates were still usable. The people of St Libéral suddenly developed a great enthusiasm for this building which would be the pride of the village, for besides the youth club, it would serve as a village hall, and dances could be held there in the evenings after weddings.

Many electors who had been tempted by the teacher's fine words suddenly changed their minds about him. Of course he spoke well, was learned, had an answer for everything; but that was just it, he was a talker, and words are like the wind.

Léon and his friends were working on something tangible, concrete. A building, it was constructed, it was finished off, it was not described in fine sentences, nor in statistics, it was there for all to see! And in *what* there was to see, they were not disappointed.

They saw Léon, Pierre-Edouard and Nicolas, Maurice and the others, often many young people too, lending a hand with the work, mixing the cement, chiselling the stones into shape, fixing the laths, nailing on the slates. It was hard work, more honest and healthy than fine speeches, politics and all that rubbish! That really was proof that Léon was a good mayor, and that he and his friends were worthy to be chosen by the majority of the electors in the community.

The youth club was inaugurated with due solemnity two days before the first round of the elections, and Father Verlhac made a brief appearance in the village for the occasion. He made good use of his time by visiting several families, and even agreed to bless the smart little hall – only because he was pushed into it, and his colleague was taking an afternoon rest. 'Youth Club of Saint-Libéral-sur-Diamond, 1935' was inscribed in letters of gold on the front of the building for all to read.

Two days later, Léon and seven of his party were re-elected with a commanding lead. At the second round Martin Tavet and his comrades resumed their seats as well, mainly because nobody was particularly interested in the election any more.

'But,' as Léon commented when he offered a round of drinks to everyone at Suzanne's, 'with five against eight, my dear old Martin, you haven't got enough weight. Come on, your good health anyway, and no hard feelings.'

Chapter 11

'IT's incredible, the number of doves flying over!' cried Pierre-Edouard in delight, as he gazed after a huge flock of wood-pigeons which were skimming over the White Peak.

'I told you to bring your gun!' said Mathilde.

'Yes, but you know how it is; if I had carried it, I'd never have come away from up there,' he said, pointing to the peak rising 200 metres from the Peuch field where he and Mathilde were pulling beets, with the help of Nicolas. The crop was magnificent, and Pierre-Edouard was justifiably proud of it. This year he had given up growing the fodder variety 'Eckendorf' with its swollen, fat, round roots, more full of water than nourishment, and had planted only the 'Pink-collared White' sugar-beets, which were much richer and better for the animals.

Once again Jean-Edouard had raised his eyebrows when faced with this innovation; but Pierre-Edouard had not even attempted to explain his new choice – what good would it do! The old man would not have been convinced. Pierre-Edouard was constantly surprised by his father's reactions. Thirty years earlier he had been a pioneer, but as he grew older he had become just as conservative and stubborn as his friend Jeantout, which was saying something!

Pierre-Edouard did not understand this reactionary attitude – or maybe his father really believed that he held the key to the secrets of modern agriculture, and was content as things were. That was more worrying, for his agricultural methods had aged too. Pierre-Edouard was constantly aware of this; he only needed to read the professional journals which arrived at the farmers' co-operative. Everything was always changing, and at great speed. From one year to the next new products appeared – fertilisers, pesticides, graded seeds, tools, growing methods – and he was convinced that it was essential to move with the times, to innovate. He was a thoughtful man, and sometimes wondered whether he too would be capable of adapting to the new techniques applied by his successor, if one of his sons did take his place one day; he hoped he could.

'Hey, look!' he called out once more. 'What a flock coming over! Hundreds of them, and all within range!'

Mathilde lifted her head and admired the huge billowing blue cloud which beat by against the south-east wind. The wind had risen from the south on the morning of St Luke and had been blowing for four days; everyone knew that the autumn rains would start before it died away. This rainfall would be mild at first, almost summery, would green the pastures and bring out the mushrooms, if the moon were favourable; at first it was welcome, but it would soon turn cold, even freezing. Then one night, after a blast of wind from the north, the first frosts would attack and the fog would arrive. It was therefore important to get the crops in while there was no rain in the sky.

Mathilde looked at her husband and shrugged her shoulders with a smile. He was sorry to be in the fields, annoyed that he was not crouched behind a juniper bush up there on the White Peak, waiting with bated breath for the approaching flocks and aiming for them swiftly as they came within range.

The doves had been coming over since the beginning of the month. At first there were only a few isolated, scattered flocks which flew high because of the fine weather, putting them out of danger from bullets. But in the last four days there had been a real surge. The flocks followed one another with the regular rhythm of a pendulum, and it was torture for a huntsman without a gun, for they were flying low; the wind kept them close to the ground.

'Dammit, I'm going up for some pigeons tomorrow morning, beets or no beets!' Pierre-Edouard warned her as he tossed two roots into the cart.

'Do you want me to go and fetch the gun?' suggested Nicolas. His hands were covered in red earth, and he wiped them on his trousers.

'Oh, no, it's not worth it,' said Pierre-Edouard, taking out his pipe and tobacco.

For his part, Nicolas took out his snuff-horn and poured a portion on to the hollow which he formed on the back of his hand by lifting his forefinger and stretching out his thumb; he filled his nostrils.

'But just look! Look at that!' repeated Pierre-Edouard in great excitement, 'and they pass over there every year, on the dot, in the same place, in spite of the gunfire. And it may be thousands of years that they've been flying over that peak! I'd love to know why! It's probably a landmark for them, a signpost to the south . . . Where you come from, are there wood-pigeons flying over there too?'

Nicolas nodded his white head and sneezed.

'Yes, lots. And then there are geese, ducks and . . .'

He spread his arms to show the wingspan and indicated a lengthened nose, then he squealed comically. Although he had made enormous progress, his French still lacked certain words.

'Oh, I see,' said Pierre-Edouard, 'cranes! Do you hear that?' he asked, turning to Mathilde. 'They have flocks flying over there too!'

'Stupid!' she said with a laugh.

He had long ago related to her the anecdote which had made such an impression on him as a child: his grandmother and mother discussing the bad luck which Mathilde had brought with her when she was a baby, for she had been conceived one night when a flight was passing over. But at that time neither his mother or grandmother had wanted to accept the explanation of what it really was. It was the Wild Hunt, the souls of the damned crying out, not birds! They believed this quite sincerely! What was even more astonishing – it was, after all, 1936 – Pierre knew a certain number of old people – and young ones too – who still crossed themselves when a flock of birds flew over.

'Well, I'm very fond of flocks of birds,' continued Pierre-Edouard in a serious tone which was meant to fool Nicolas, 'they leave beautiful traces behind them . . .'

'Have you quite finished?' cried Mathilde, turning red, but her eyes sparkled with amusement and understanding.

This story of her birthmark, supposedly due to the Wild Hunt and therefore a sign of misfortune, was the subject of jokes each time Pierre-Edouard rediscovered his youth in the arms of his wife; she carried a tiny blemish in the shape of a crescent moon on her left breast, and he delighted in it. 'I could easily put up with it,' he would assure her as he kissed her, 'if bad luck only left this sort of reminder!'

'Come on,' Mathilde urged him, grasping the neck of an enormous beet, 'if you want to go after pigeons tomorrow, we'll have to finish pulling all these today!'

'Yes,' he agreed, getting down to work again. 'All the same, that Nicolas has been giving me ideas . . .'

'What ideas?' asked Mathilde, fooled by his serious and measured tone.

'Well,' he said, telling the most incredible lie, 'it was he who started talking about the Wild Hunt, wasn't it?'

They worked all morning and afternoon. In the evening, when the mist was settling in the hollows and the beet field was nothing but bare earth, Mathilde suddenly noticed little Mauricette at the edge of the plateau, calling as she ran towards them.

'What's happened?' she wondered anxiously. She lifted her skirts and ran towards her daughter.

'What's the matter?' murmured Pierre-Edouard, frowning. Mauricette had no business to be up on the plateau at that time! Something really unusual must have happened for her grandfather to have sent her like that, with night about to fall. He watched his daughter with concern as she met Mathilde, and tried to hear what they were saying; he felt reassured as they hurried back towards him.

'Well, what's the matter?' he called out.

'Tell him,' said Mathilde, stroking her daughter's cheek.

'Pépé told me to come,' explained Mauricette. 'There's a tall gentleman and a beautiful lady who arrived on the evening bus. They're at our house, waiting in the yard. Pépé didn't want to let them in without you there.'

'What's all this about? And you don't know who this gentleman is?'

'No.'

'And Pépé doesn't either?'

'I don't know.'

that the majority would not agree to the project, then there would be a vote. At the very next council meeting Pierre-Edouard launched the attack.

'You know, I've been thinking . . . Our young people have no room for their youth club now. Here, in the mairie it's much too small, we should build them a shelter . . . '

'Have you gone mad?' said Léon, shrugging his shoulders.

'What do you mean?' insisted Pierre-Edouard. 'It's no big deal: four walls, a roof and they'll be happy!'

'They don't need that to keep entertained, there's plenty of space out in the country!'

'Besides,' slipped in the doctor, 'those film shows the priest organised weren't very healthy – I mean for their eyes, of course. The faculty of medicine is unanimous in the opinion that the light from cinema projectors strains the retina, over-stimulates the crystalline lens and contracts the pupil. Furthermore . . . '

'Yes,' interrupted Léon, who was afraid that the doctor was overdoing it, 'anyway if they want something to do, they can always work! Isn't that so?' he said, addressing Tavet.

'The idea of a non-religious youth club for the children is quite a good one, but we should see about that later,' proposed Tavet, who had already decided to revive the idea on his own account as soon as he was elected.

'That's it, we'll see later,' agreed Léon.

'And besides, we have no money,' the doctor reminded them.

With a glance, Pierre-Edouard reassured himself that his friends Maurice, Edouard, Jacques and Pierre Delpeyroux were playing their parts; they seemed as undecided as a cow who has found some chervil in a clump of clover.

'We only need to vote for or against the project,' he remarked. 'That's the best way. I'd like to know who agrees with me . . . '

'You've certainly got plenty of time to waste!' protested Léon.

'Considering that it's growing late already,' put in the doctor, consulting his pocket-watch.

'No, but seriously! I have the right to demand a vote on it!' interposed Pierre-Edouard.

145

come on, don't worry about your grandfather, he puts on a fierce act, but it's not serious.'

They were climbing the steps to the front door when it suddenly opened to reveal Jean-Edouard ensconced on the threshold. He stood in silence, hands in pockets, legs firmly planted, and regarded them, his gaze resting longest on Félix. Then he nodded his head.

'Good,' he said at last. 'I see that I wasn't dreaming, you really are Louise's son? It's Félix, isn't it? I didn't want to let you in before because I thought my head was playing tricks with me. I'm seventy-six now, you know, so . . . Now that I'm sure I wasn't dreaming, you may come in.' His voice broke a little, and trembled. He cleared his throat and stood aside to let them pass.

'Come in,' he repeated, 'after all, you belong here. Even though,' he whispered as he turned away, 'I swore that you would never come in here, but we're not savages! And then, it's all so old now, so long ago . . .' He paused a moment and considered. 'Twenty-seven years! It would be inhuman to harbour a grudge over such a timespan, especially for no more than childish mischief . . .'

'I believed in this Popular Front too,' agreed Pierre-Edouard, 'as did almost everyone else around here as well. Only Léon predicted disasters ahead, and he wasn't entirely wrong, because since then . . .'

They had been seated by the fire since finishing their meal. Paul and Mauricette, exhausted, had very soon followed their little brother, who had been asleep for a long time; Pierre-Edouard, Mathilde, Félix and his wife were chatting like old friends.

First they had talked of Louise, who was still governess at the château in Indre where Félix was now a forester. Then Pierre-Edouard had spoken of Berthe, and brought out her latest postcard, from London this time – and this was in front of his father, who had always condemned the life she had chosen.

The old man had spoken very little. It made him happy just to watch this grandson whom he had previously rejected; he was delighted to discover the build of the Vialhes in this man, the character, too, and the vitality. And Pierre-Edouard watched his father surreptitiously and realised how moved he was, how affected by this unexpected reunion.

Jean-Edouard had said nothing since his first words of welcome, but to anyone who knew him those were astonishing, revolutionary even. For despite their simplicity, not to say roughness, they marked the end of a long period of disagreement and half-hearted forgiveness. Now, after twenty-seven years, came reconciliation. Then Jean-Edouard rose:

'I must go to bed. Tell me, will you be staying a few days?' he asked Félix and his wife.

'Yes, until Sunday, if you don't mind,' explained Félix, rising as well.

'Don't get up. In that case, you should know that my other grandchildren, who are only kids compared to you, well, they say "tu" to me. You must do the same — and you too, *petite*,' he added, looking at Thérèse. 'Right then, until tomorrow.'

He went into his room but came out again shortly afterwards, carrying a bottle which he placed in the middle of the table. 'It's plum brandy from 1910, the year of your birth. It should be good!'

'There's no doubt about it,' Pierre-Edouard commented a little later, 'Father is just like this brandy, he's mellowed with age . . .'

'Yes, when I tell my mother about it she won't believe me, after all the stories she's told me,' murmured Félix, as he savoured the smell of the brandy.

'That's understandable. It wasn't always much fun for her, you know!'

'I know . . .'

Then the conversation moved on, and now they were discussing politics, the war in Ethiopia and the more worrying one which had rocked Spain for the last two months, followed by the May elections and the success of the Popular Front.

'For us there's at least one good thing: the Wheat Office,' said Pierre-Edouard, filling his pipe. 'With that we're protected from those grasping grain merchants. Those scoundrels have almost ruined us, it's time it was stopped! But apart from that I think Léon was right; I don't believe this Popular Front will work miracles.'

'The situation was so complicated,' Félix attempted to explain. 'Blum did what he could.'

'I know, but that was no excuse for devaluing our money! What are we left with now? And then all these strikes, all the unemployed! What are they thinking of? A forty-hour week, paid holidays! My God, let them come and do a turn here, they'll soon see whether we only work forty hours. Me, I do their forty hours in three days, and your aunt does too! And we're not asking for holidays on top of it! Oh, don't think I begrudge them their holidays. That's not it, but what I don't understand is that they're all demanding more money for less work. If I want to earn more it's always the other way round; I have to work longer hours to earn more. And that's not likely to change!'

'It's not so simple,' repeated Félix. 'You see . . . Thérèse will explain it to you better than I can,' he said, turning to his young wife.

She blushed and agreed. Everything in this house was very alarming, except Mathilde, who seemed to be so gentle. But the men! She could not say which of the two was the more intimidating!

'Until we were married, Thérèse worked in a shirt factory at Châteauroux – that was no joke, you know,' explained Félix, placing his hand over his wife's.

'I'd agree with that,' said Pierre-Edouard. 'It's never a joke to have to work for someone else, I know a thing or two about that too. I've taken it easy, too, occasionally. And with my workmates, we even had a sort of strike – oh, yes we did! But when we'd got what we wanted, we didn't go on asking for the moon! Whereas nowadays the more that's given, the more some people want! It's no wonder that prices go shooting up as a result. In the end it'll all finish with a crash, I've been saying that for five years and more!'

'Paying the workers better won't cause a crash!' insisted Félix.

'No doubt. Besides, it doesn't worry me if they *are* paid more, all the better for them. Mark you, we can discuss these things, but it's all political manœuvering and that kind of stuff! All through history, we peasants and workers have never been anything but the losers, it's always the same everywhere!

here, have another drop of brandy and tell me a bit more about what you do up there in your forest; that's more interesting than talking about all this rubbish!'

Félix and his wife stayed two days in Saint-Libéral. They slept at the inn, and on the first evening Pierre-Edouard accompanied them there feeling quite nostalgic.

'Did you know that your father had lodgings here?' he asked, as they entered the saloon bar of the auberge.

'Yes, it seems that he and my mother met each other here.'

'Here and elsewhere, yes ... Good evening, Suzanne, I'm sure you've been waiting for these young people? Here they are, now you can shut up shop.'

'May I get you something? It's on the house,' she suggested, as her eyes slid fondly towards Félix.

Pierre-Edouard smiled: really, good old Suzanne never gave up. Despite her forty-one years, she was still just as greedy for men!

'No, not for me. We've seen the bottom of enough glasses this evening,' Pierre-Edouard thanked her. 'So which room are you giving them?'

'As many as they like, if it makes them happy! No one comes here any more, you know. I often wonder why I stay on, I'd do better to close down!'

'Come, come, don't complain; I'm bringing you some customers, you look after them well. All right,' he said, turning towards Félix, 'you can have all the rooms you want, but if I were you I'd take number seven.'

'Why number seven?' asked Félix, although he was sure he knew the answer.

'That was your father's room. Come on, I'll take you up, I haven't been up there for almost thirty years!'

When he came down again a few moments later, he found a melancholy Suzanne sipping at a huge glass of curaçao.

'Youth is beautiful,' she commented, with a nod in the direction of the stairs. 'They're both good-looking, especially him, and so young . . .'

'All right,' Pierre-Edouard cut in, 'you look after them; they'll be here until Sunday. When they leave, don't give them the bill, eh? Even if they insist on it, I'll come by on Monday and settle with you, okay?'

'I understand, but . . . Who are they really?'

'Oh, that's right, you weren't here then. He's my nephew – and from tomorrow on, I bet you'll hear talk of his father and my sister too! I'd be very surprised if the over-forties had forgotten them!'

For two days Pierre-Edouard and Félix strode over the Vialhe lands. Félix wanted to see everything.

'And the Caput, which hill is that? And the mine-cutting, how do we get there? And the source of the Diamond, where is it? Oh, I'd like to go to Combes-Nègres, too. You see, my mother talked to me so often of these places, I feel I know them by heart. That's why I want to see them all. When I was a kid, I hoped for a long time that we'd come back and live here one day! So now I'm catching up with my dreams.'

'Your mother came back once, you know, at the beginning of this month sixteen years ago.'

'Yes, for Grandmother's burial. But she didn't want me to come with her.'

'And why hasn't she been back since then? No one was stopping her!'

'I think she was afraid – of people, the neighbours, Grandfather too, of course. And then she had no work here, because you know her pension as a war widow . . . '

'Never mind that, she could come and spend a few days!'

'Yes, but she was afraid of doing that as well. Afraid that she might not have the courage to leave again. If you knew how she loves this land! I think she must have talked to me about it every day. So I've learned to love it too, almost as much as her. And when I was coming here, I was worried that I'd be disappointed. You know very well how rarely the reality is as beautiful as what you imagined. Now I'll be able to tell her that her country is even more beautiful than she told me. Christ! Up here on this peak, it's as if we're right up in the sky. You don't need to raise your eyes to look at the clouds, you don't feel them hanging over you like you do at home. Here, you are their master. You're master of everything, up here! That's what's made you so strong. You Vialhes have grown used to seeing everything from above, even the sky, right from when you were little.'

'You are a funny fellow,' murmured Pierre-Edouard. 'Listening to you, I understand why my sister fell in love with your father — he must have talked the way you do, she couldn't have resisted that. Come on, we should go down, Léon's expecting us for lunch; you'll see, he's an original too! Your mother must have spoken of him, I'm sure!'

When the time came for Félix and his wife to leave, Jean-Edouard planted himself on the threshold as he had done when they arrived, and looked at his grandson.

'You should come back,' he said to him, 'now you know the way. I ought to tell you something else. When you were born I didn't want to recognise you as a Vialhe grandson; now that I've seen you, and I've heard you, I know I was wrong. You have the Vialhe blood. There, that's all. Oh, and if, when you see your mother . . . tomorrow, you say? Right, well tomorrow then, you simply say this to her: "Your father would like to remind you that he is now seventy-six." She'll understand . . . And then you tell her as well: "The stones in the Diamond are just the same as when you were here, but the water and the sand have worn them down a bit, they're less cutting than they were, so since time has succeeded in smoothing down the stones . . . " All right, off you go now, both of you, and when you have a son bring him here as soon as possible. But remember, I'm seventy-six . . . '

Chapter 12

IT had become a habit. For four years, Jacques Vialhe's class-
mates had resigned themselves to watching him run off with
almost all the top prizes. So, at the end of 1936, the day before
the Christmas holidays began, when the headmaster strode
into the class to announce the results of the end-of-term
exams, all eyes turned to Jacques. Some were admiring, some
disheartened, others jealous.

There were actually, among the other serious contenders,
the sons of a lawyer and of a surgeon from Brive, two youths
who literally worked themselves up into a rage at having to
cede first place to that bloody country bumpkin, that
strapping lout, who not only beat them in physics, chemistry,
French and maths, but also overwhelmed them with his size,
his strength and his self-confidence. It was abnormal,
unnatural almost, that it should be this peasant and not one of
them taking the lion's share.

They were from well-established families, with a good
education and breeding. They already had their positions in
the little clique of Brive society. He was nothing but a yokel,
with mud on his boots; logically he should never have left the
plough or the cow's backside! Instead of which, he always
passed them at the post and, despite his background, would
almost certainly earn a distinction when he sat for the
baccalauréat exams in six months' time.

The headmaster cleared his throat and began to read out
the prize-winners. And the marks rang out: French 16 out of
20, first Jacques Vialhe, English 17 out of 20, first Jacques
Vialhe . . .

Jacques was standing to hear the results, and his face shone
with pleasure and pride. His parents would be happy again,
very happy. And even his grandfather would celebrate! The
old man had eventually accepted his choice of studying in
preference to farming. Besides, the path chosen by Paul was a

great comfort to him; at least he was staying close to the land. Thanks to him there would be no break; some day or other, when he grew tired of running around the market-places, he would return to take up the position which was his. Reassured about the future of the farm, Jean-Edouard no longer had any reason to criticise the path chosen by his grandson Jacques. On the contrary, for there was another Vialhe coming to the forefront in a completely different manner, in a new sphere!

'Total average: sixteen out of twenty, first Jacques Vialhe,' the headmaster finally announced. 'We can wish you at least a good holiday; you've earned it. Which isn't the case for everyone in this class . . . '

Jacques sat down and his thoughts flew towards Saint-Libéral where he would return that same evening. His holidays — he knew already how he would spend them. First of all he would work with his father and Nicolas — and he was not put off at this thought, quite the opposite. He used up his energy by chopping wood; it was a healthy job which gave him an appetite, developed his muscles, allowed him to use all his strength, testing it to the limit when he used the sledge hammer to split the thick logs of oak or the knotted trunks of chestnut trees.

Then he would go hunting as well; it was a matter of proving to his godfather that the gun he had given him on his sixteenth birthday — a twelve-calibre Darne — was in good hands. Finally, in the evening, he would meet his little group of friends in the youth club.

Gathered there, happily reunited, they would discuss things, sort out the world, build the fairer, finer and more honest future they all wanted. They would comment on the articles in *La Jeunesse Agricole*. Best of all, Jacques would find Marie-Louise there, the daughter of Pierre Labrousse. Like him, she would soon be seventeen and was a boarder in Brive, at the Notre Dame school. Like him, she was taking her baccalauréat at the end of the year. She too was a farmer's daughter and not ashamed of it; everything fitted.

They had gone to school together in Saint-Libéral, sat and passed their school certificates on the same day. Then they had lost sight of each other, for Jacques had remained a child, small in stature and young-looking in comparison to others, whereas in a few months Marie-Louise grew attractive and graceful, with the mind of a young lady. Jacques had been rather annoyed. He was acutely aware of the difference in height which separated them and made him look ridiculous; he did not want to be taken for Marie-Louise's little brother! So he restrained himself from meeting her for two years.

Everything had changed in the last year. Now it was his turn to grow taller and stronger, and Jacques had become, not quite a man, but still a fine-looking youth. He was already a head taller than the girl; he now found her charmingly fragile, and felt ready to protect her.

They were glad to meet again, to exchange opinions on Shakespeare, Barrès, Victor Hugo. They amused themselves by conspiring together in a display of erudition, to enjoy the admiration of their friends in St Libéral who had only achieved School Certificate.

At this stage, neither she nor Jacques had yet confessed that they nurtured plans for a common future. But both felt that the time was fast approaching when their mutual feelings would force them to exchange the serious promises that knot the first ties of love.

Although Jacques felt big and strong, sure of himself, he was aware that his age was against him, even if he thought it quite respectable. Furthermore in Saint-Libéral, and in his family too, although it was quite acceptable for a man of twenty-five to go out with a girl of seventeen with marriage in prospect, nobody seriously considered that a boy of his age could suffer more than mild, passing fancies. Whereas he *was* serious, in everything. So, to avoid his attraction to Marie-Louise becoming the subject of teasing, he preferred to remain silent and wait. This did not prevent him from dreaming about the girl every day, and gazing with feeling at the tiny passport photo which she had given him six months earlier.

'And this one, what do you think of him?' Léon asked his nephew. 'First of all, how old is he?'

Paul walked around the horse, examined it, opened its mouth. 'He doesn't look bad,' he said at last, 'and he's getting on for eight years old, roughly . . . '

'You don't know a thing,' sighed Léon. 'It's a sorry nag, with every vice, and your eight years are more like twelve! Didn't you see that all his teeth were worn down! Good God! When I think that your father could still teach me a thing or two about horses! He knows about them, does your father! But you – away from cows, you're lost in a fog!'

Paul accepted the rebuke in silence, but shrugged his shoulders. He had no affection for horses; they were not to be trusted, too quick to respond with a kick or even a bite. And according to his uncle, they were more often than not riddled with hidden faults, which were to be avoided like the plague!

'Let's go and see him in the ring,' suggested Léon.

Paul stuffed his hands in his pockets and followed. It was cold enough for wolves on that Tuesday, 5 January 1937, and on the market field at Dorat a freezing wind blew straight from the Auvergne, burning your ears and making it hard to breathe.

Paul would have gladly avoided this chore of going to buy horses for his uncle to sell again two days later at the Kings' Market in Brive. With all these markets sending him to the far corners of the region, he had not been able to enjoy the time his brother was spending at home as he would have liked. That lucky devil Jacques was on holiday, and he was probably stalking woodcock in the acacia thickets by the château at this very moment.

For the last two weeks the woods of St Libéral had been swarming with woodcock. Paul was not yet old enough for a firearms licence, but he liked to accompany his father or brother when they went to scour the woods. Sadly he only had the pleasure of taking the role of beater when Léon gave him some free time, which was to say, not very often. He did not resent his uncle's strictness at work; he would just have liked to stay with his brother, especially during the Christmas holidays.

The two boys still got on very well together, although their relationship had changed. Jacques now took the role of elder brother; it was he who decided how they spent their time. There was no longer any question of dragging him into escapades, or rowdiness at the inn. He said no and it meant no. And Paul obeyed him, not ashamed to admit that his brother impressed him, intimidated him almost. He would be taking the baccalauréat; knew English and maths, talked about everything with ease and confidence, had his own opinions about politics, the war in Spain, Italian Fascism, the phenomenal resurgence of Germany. And to cap it all, Jacques would discuss all this with his father, seriously, with the newspaper on hand to analyse some situation or other.

Paul had his own opinions too, but they were still vague, blurred and difficult to express. The respect he felt for Jacques was increased when his brother confided in him that he wanted to continue his studies and become a veterinary surgeon, eventually setting up a practice in Saint-Libéral. Veterinarian – that was the height of ambition, and Paul never for a moment considered that his brother might fail. He would succeed, just as he had succeeded in conquering his depression earlier at Bossuet, as he succeeded in always being at the top of the class!

Naturally, in comparison to him, Paul felt a little over-shadowed, rather mediocre. Jacques did not do anything to draw attention to himself; he did not show off. It was just that, at the moment, he was preparing to obtain outstanding marks in his exams.

Meanwhile Paul was nothing but an apprentice stock-dealer. Even if he earned a good wage – for Léon was generous – he felt the gap widening between himself and Jacques. He now knew that he would not be a stock-dealer all his life, but he kept this to himself. One day he would have to escape; to find an exciting, stimulating job. And it would not be on the farm, as his grandfather believed, nor with his Uncle Léon. Both occupations lacked appeal, romance. One day, when he was stronger and more secure, he would go out into the world. For the time being he remained silent and waited, and gave his parents and uncle every satisfaction – apart from the matter of his relationship with horses.

'Well, are you coming!' Léon called to him from the edge of the ring where the sellers were trotting their horses at the request of prospective buyers. 'Look,' his uncle explained to him, 'I asked the fellow holding the bay to show me his paces; we'll be able to judge him.'

The dealer handed the animal to a groom, who moved up

towards them from the end of the ring; he held the animal by the halter and trotted beside it.

'Stop!' Léon called to him when he had covered fifteen metres. 'I don't want your old nanny-goat! She's limping on her left fore! Did you see his technique?' he asked his nephew. 'No? . . . Oh,' he called to the groom, 'go on, perhaps I made a mistake. Look, watch the devil,' he whispered to Paul, 'just look at it, my God! Can't you see how the groom is limping too, and with the same timing! That way, it gives the impression that the man and the animal are both normal. We call that the limping-horse trot. Hah, the fool, to try that on me! Good God, there's no one alive who can teach me how to doctor a nag, I know all their tricks! That'll do,' he said to the groom who had just stopped opposite him, 'you can go on with the circus, but you'll have to find a different stool-pigeon! Come on, let's go,' he said to Paul, 'we'll go and look at that lot of cart-horses; from a distance they look good, but we'll have to check them out from close to. Remember, you can never check anything too much. Come on, tell me what you think of this one, for instance. If you give me a good answer I'll let you lead the bidding and you can have that one. Come on, kid, talk like a man.'

The inhabitants of Saint-Libéral would probably not have reacted at all to the fall of the Blum government if it had not been for the opinions expressed by Father Delclos.

Everybody in the village had better things to do than bother about politics on 22 June 1937; many of the men were disappointed to see the fine dreams inspired by the Popular Front end so sadly, but the seasonal work left them no time to hold a post mortem on what was, after all, an everyday occurrence. They had become accustomed to seeing governments succeed one another for some time. It was not worth losing precious moments discussing Blum when the hay-making demanded fifteen hours work a day. The weather was fine, warm, just right for cutting hay; they had to make the most of it. Hard work made the week fly by.

The bomb exploded on Sunday, 27 June. The sky had been dangerously overcast as the last quarter of the moon approached. The wind had veered, and the swallows swept up the main street in a constant stream, skimming the ground with their russet throats. Faced with these portents, it was not wise to do any mowing, so a number of men were taking advantage of the respite from work to take a little rest and enjoy an aperitif at Suzanne's.

Even Pierre-Edouard and Léon were sitting on the terrace of the inn, in the sweet-smelling, cool shade of the old lime trees. Pierre-Edouard was the first to realise that something unusual was happening in the church.

High Mass had begun almost half an hour before the heavy clang of the church door echoed all around the square, swinging shut behind the doctor and his wife.

Since her return to the fold, the doctor's wife had attended services punctiliously, behaviour that contributed greatly to her rehabilitation in the eyes of the village women. Sometimes she was even accompanied by her husband, an indisputable sign of perfect conjugal harmony.

The couple had not yet reached the bottom of the steps before the door banged once more and Pierre-Edouard was amazed to see Mathilde also emerge. She had in fact continued to visit the church in Saint-Libéral, despite what she thought of the priest; it was after all much more practical than going to Perpezac-le-Blanc every Sunday. She only went over there for confession, a move which was extremely vexing to Father Delclos, but which she had no intention of changing for any reason.

'Now what?' said Pierre-Edouard, putting down his glass and getting up. 'What's going on over there? Hey! Mathilde, I'm here! Has Mass finished already?'

The doctor suggested that his wife and Mathilde go home, and marched towards the inn. He was red with anger, but smiling all the same.

'What's going on?' asked Pierre-Edouard again.

'Oh, my dear fellow, I've never heard such rubbish, it was more than I could bear! Nor could your wife. Really, I think that poor priest has gone mad, or he's an idiot from birth — both, probably! Suzanne, a cherry brandy!'

'He wanted you to serve Mass, perhaps?' suggested Léon ironically.

'If that were all! Listen to this! I don't expect you know that

166

we're celebrating the sixth Sunday after Pentecost; I didn't until twenty minutes ago. I have nothing against the day's reading from the Gospel, I quite like it actually. Well, you and the Gospel . . . But Pierre-Edouard will remember it, I'm sure; it's the loaves and the fishes. You see what I'm saying? Five thousand hungry people, five loaves and two fish for everyone, and despite that the whole crowd eat their fill and there are even left-overs! Well, you could argue about that, make allowances for poetic licence, but that's not the problem. Just imagine, this miserable priest thought it good to draw a parallel between this parable and the fall of Blum, I ask you! Yes, he did! Basically, he explained to us that God had no need for social reform, for forty-hour weeks or paid holidays to feed his people! That the previous government's materialism was an insult to the faith; in short, we should thank the Lord for having relieved us of it and pray that he install a regime devoted to order and morality! It was laughable, sad but laughable!'

'That's why you walked out, and Mathilde too?' questioned Pierre-Edouard.

'Oh, no, that was simply stupid. It was after that he went beyond the limit, when he announced quite boldly that all those who voted for the Popular Front last year were virtually public sinners! Well, that was too much. I made off, and he won't see me again in a long time!'

'So that's how it is!' grumbled Louis Brousse unexpectedly; he and other customers had drawn nearer while the doctor was holding forth. 'He's all right, the bastard! He's so fat himself, he doesn't give a damn if the people die of hunger!'

And suddenly, shouts rang out. At a stroke all these men felt the shame of their defeat. They had previously accepted the failure of policies they believed in, but if the priest was rejoicing, that was proof that the reactionaries were gaining ground.

In no time at all the group found their numbers swelled by new arrivals, and the shouts redoubled. In the heart of the crowd factions were attacking each other, opinions and insults exploded.

'Don't do anything stupid!' called Léon suddenly. 'You're not going to fight about rubbish like that!'

'If you're on the priest's side, you'd better say so straight away!' Martin Tavet shouted at him, his face blue with rage. 'That wouldn't surprise me anyway, you've always chosen the strongest side, where the money is! Perhaps you're one of the top two hundred families?'

'If you go on like that you'll get my hook in your face!' threatened Léon, brandishing his false hand.

'Stop it,' said the doctor. 'Let them bellyache, it'll blow over – and they're half right anyway! Look, there's our teacher, that's all we need.'

Jacques Sourzac quickly found out what was going on, and was happy to joke about it at first. Then he exploited the occasion by giving the radicals and other socialists – never mind the reactionaries – a piece of his mind; they were all responsible for the failure of the Popular Front, being too lukewarm and flabby to surmount a crisis.

'But history will judge their mistakes and their weaknesses! Today the important thing is to respond to the attacks of the bourgeois clergy. Let us defend ourselves! Mass is being sung, it seems; well, let *us* sing, we, the proletariat!' he cried, climbing up the steps of the church. And he intoned the 'Internationale'.

'The priest isn't the only one who's mad!' said Pierre-Edouard, shrugging his shoulders. 'I suppose it's because there's a storm brewing, it taxes the brain! Leave them, Léon, let them bawl, the lot of them; they'll calm down soon enough! I'm going to see my little Mathilde, I must congratulate her. She knows how I voted, that's why she walked out.'

As Pierre-Edouard predicted, the demonstration did not last long, mainly because very few men knew the words to the 'Internationale', and many people did not want to get mixed up with the band of hot-heads led by the teacher. That did not prevent the priest from being shouted down when he felt obliged to come out and curse the blasphemers who were disturbing the sacred Mass. Then everything returned to a peaceful torpor in the expectation of the warm showers all the signs indicated.

Curiously enough, Father Delclos emerged from this incident with enhanced stature, at least in the eyes of those who shared his ideas on the subject of moral codes – and there were more of them than the anti-clericals thought. The priest was reinforced in his position, sure of his adherents, and he made the most of it by asserting his authority and leading his flock along the path to salvation.

As, once, had done his predecessor Father Feix – but he had been a saintly man, all those who had known him agreed, for he at least lived frugally – Father Delclos marked out and condemned everything which could weaken Christian moral values: dancing, of course, but also the cinema, the wireless and the reading of novels, which, he said, excited the imagination of young people and might lead them into depraved acts. Uncompromising with regard to the respect which he felt was his due, he never forgave the doctor, nor his wife, and still less Mathilde, for the insult they had inflicted on him. As a result he never spoke to them again.

In July, Jacques passed his baccalauréat with very good marks. The whole Vialhe family took great pride in his success, and even old Jean-Edouard did not deny himself the pleasure of remarking that only his grandson had managed to survive the test – without in any way gloating over the failure of the other candidate from the village. No one dared to remind him that a short while ago he had fiercely opposed Jacques continuing with his studies. He himself seemed to have forgotten completely his previous position on the subject.

What was remarkable was his action the day after the results appeared, after he had read and re-read twenty times the name of Jacques Vialhe inscribed near the top of the list printed in the newspaper. All alone, despite his seventy-seven years, he took the bus which stopped every day except Sundays in the main square, and went all the way to Brive.

There he strolled slowly, stick in hand, black felt hat jammed tightly on his skull, along the streets Puy-Blanc, Toulzac, Carnot and Hôtel-de-Ville. Indecisively he retraced his route, sauntered around St Martin's Square, and stopped once more in front of a shopkeeper's display window.

In order to consider his problem carefully, he went as far as Chez Pierre and ordered a dozen snails and a half-bottle of white wine. When he had wiped his plate clean, emptied his glass and rolled a cigarette, he finally made a decision, and shortly afterwards he pushed open the door of Maigne the jeweller.

He had hesitated for a long time, not over the present he wished to give, just its shape. He preferred big watches, round, solid and long-lasting, those plump fob watches which slip into your waistcoat pocket when you are twenty and your grandchildren are pleased to inherit sixty years later. But Jacques was young, progressive, he had his baccalauréat; so a wrist-watch was what he needed.

The business was quickly concluded, since Jean-Edouard did not quibble over the price. He pushed away the little things made of steel which the jeweller first offered, even refused a silver-plated watch with a shrug of the shoulders.

'It's that one I want!' he said, pointing his calloused forefinger towards a Zenith. He examined it, turned it between his fingers, held it up to his ear. 'It's not working!' he protested.

'Of course not, it needs to be wound up.'

'Well, yes . . . Fine, I'd like it gift-wrapped. It's for my grandson, he's just passed his baccalauréat with very good marks. And it's even printed in the newspaper!' he explained, as he took out his wallet and counted the 1,750 francs which the Zenith cost. It was a superb piece of engineering, in a rectangular gold case; a watch which could even be read at night, with a tiny hand to count the seconds and a crocodile-leather strap which made it look very superior.

'There you are,' he said that evening, holding out the box to Jacques, 'it's for you. Now that you're a scholar and have your name in the newspaper, that will remind you of your grandfather. Come on, give me a kiss, or even two. You know, my boy, on days like this, I wish your grandmother were still here, she'd be so happy. Well, I'm happy for both of us . . .'

'Bloody hell!' exclaimed Pierre-Edouard when he saw the gift. 'Your grandfather is really doing you proud! That's worth thousands, a jewel like that!'

'Yes, indeed, Father,' said Mathilde, 'you shouldn't have, it's too fine, it's embarrassing.'

'Get away with you, both of you, it's not your money I've spent, it's mine! Come on, my boy, put it on quickly, I want to see it on your wrist. Yes,' he gave his opinion when Jacques had complied, 'there's no doubt about it, that's the latest thing, it's fine. But you know, to me, a contraption like that around my arm would get in the way of work.'

Léon learned of his godson's success when he returned from Lyons, where he had been negotiating over a large number of army reject horses. He too was as proud of Jacques' success as if he had been his own son. Furthermore, as soon as he was informed of the magnificent present given by Jean-Edouard, he determined to go one better: a matter of marking the occasion and of annoying that old relative who stubbornly refused to address one word to him and kept his door closed to him.

First of all he bought a beautiful wallet in fine leather with the initials of his godson on it. Having done that, and enhanced it with the neat sum of a thousand francs, he slipped a note into it – which he got his wife to write, conscious that his own writing was too basic and rough to satisfy a baccalauréat.

Towards evening, when he was sure that all the Vialhes would have returned to the farm – the harvest of winter barley was at its peak and required all hands – he went up to the Vialhes' and found the whole family in the process of unloading a cart full of sheaves. Even old Jean-Edouard was there, sitting in front of the house and regarding the grain-laden sheaves with evident satisfaction. He gave Léon a dirty look but remained silent; the yard was not the house, it was almost neutral territory.

'Hey!' called Léon to his godson. 'Put down your fork and come over here a minute! Here,' he said, when Jacques had greeted him, 'this is for you. Go on, open it quickly,' he suggested, lowering his voice and smiling. 'A wallet is like a woman, not to be judged just by the outside! In my time I always used to check by feeling . . .'

'What are you telling him?' asked Mathilde, coming closer. She knew her brother well, and suspected that his whispering would be to conceal something risqué. 'Oh my! You must be mad to give presents like that!' she said when she saw the wad of notes. 'What's he supposed to think now, that money like that grows on trees!'

'Well, so what,' said Léon, 'he earned it with his work! Anyway, it's not very much for that. I can prove that, because even if I put in a thousand times as much, they wouldn't give the baccalauréat to *me* in exchange for it, so there!'

'And this, what's this? asked Jacques, taking out the sheet of paper.

'Read it, read it out, nice and loud, so that everyone can hear!' suggested Léon, glancing mischievously towards Jean-Edouard.

'Voucher for a trip to Paris,' Jacques announced clearly, and as soon as he had read the note he flung his arms around his godfather's neck. 'Oh my, is it really true? To Paris? And I could see the International Exhibition? And everything?'

'You bet! Why do you think I'm sending you up there? To run after the girls? You'd better not, your mother would have a fit!'

'It's too much,' said Pierre-Edouard, leaning on the handle of his fork. 'You and Father, my word, you've really gone too far. Really, you're treating him like a prince!'

'Showing us up, us and our present!' said Mathilde, putting her arms around her son's shoulders.

But she was smiling, and everyone knew that she was only joking; that she was happy and proud to see him so well rewarded.

'You,' said Léon, 'you've paid for his studies, that's worth more than any present! Isn't that enough for them, have they given you something else as well?' he asked Jacques.

'Yes, a bicycle, a Saint-Etienne, with pneumatic tyres, a lamp and three gears!'

'I knew it,' said Léon, giving him a friendly cuff.

'But we haven't even had time to go and fetch it,' bemoaned Pierre-Edouard, 'what with the haymaking and the harvest, and everything, you know! Well, as soon as we can, we'll go and buy that bicycle! Well, well, you'll be going to Paris!' he said to his son, 'you'll see, it's beautiful. One day I must take your mother there. But even so, will you wait until we have finished harvest before you go?'

'Of course,' promised Jacques, 'but ... Look,' he continued, turning to his uncle and shaking the wad of notes, 'with this I could pay for Paul's ticket, if you'd give him a few days off. I'd like him to come with me, because all alone, it wouldn't be so good as if I had his company. You'll give him some leave, won't you?'

'Of course I will,' said Léon, moved. 'You really are a fine lad, and your brother too. And he deserves this trip as well, because you know he works, and hard! Oh, I know he's not like you, but believe me, it's still work and it's not much fun some days.'

For the whole month of July Jacques remained at his post, helping with the harvest. He was strong and capable now, and had the stamina to make his help valuable in getting it all in.

The yield was beautiful, even abundant, and for the first time in years Pierre-Edouard was not in agony waiting to know what income he would derive from his grain, since the Wheat Office had come into operation.

He had been cautious, and only sown one hectare of 'Dattel' wheat, preferring to plant the other fields with barley, oats, rye and maize, for although those cereals sold less well than wheat, they could always serve as fodder for the animals. If wheat stayed at a good price – as the new Chautemps government assured him it would – then he resolved to sow at least three hectares the following autumn. This news cheered old Jean-Edouard, bucked him up no end; three hectares of wheat, that was proof that the farm was still hale and hearty.

So Jacques worked through all the harvest, and gladly. He was happy to have his bac, happy to have his presents. He rode up to the plateau on his bicycle, and was madly excited at the prospect of exploring Paris with Paul.

Only one shadow clouded his horizon and almost gave him a guilty conscience about feeling so cheerful: Marie-Louise Labrousse had failed. He felt really sorry for her. However, she had the right to retake in September, and so he used every opportunity to go to her house to help her revise the syllabus.

The two young people worked diligently under the eye of an ancient grandmother, who could neither read nor write and who gloried in their knowledge, emitting little cries of delight when they juggled with logarithms. Already there was talk in the village that the Vialhes' son and the Labrousse girl were really made for each other.

Chapter 13

JACQUES and Paul were driven to the station at Brive by their uncle, accompanied by Pierre-Edouard and Mathilde; weighed down with advice, food and luggage, they climbed into the third-class carriage which would take them to the capital in less than eight hours.

'I hope you haven't forgotten anything,' repeated Mathilde, worried to see them launched into the unknown in this way. 'And if your aunt isn't at the station, get someone to show you the way properly so that you can walk to her house!'

'Of course, of course,' Jacques reassured her, 'she lives in the Faubourg Saint-Honoré, it's not complicated!'

'And tell her the eggs are fresh, she can eat them soft-boiled!' insisted Mathilde; besides two chickens trussed ready to roast, four jars of duck confit, three pots of goose liver and two kilos of honey, she had added three dozen eggs at the last moment. In her eyes this was the least she could do to thank her sister-in-law Berthe, who had said she would be delighted to welcome her unknown nephews when they had written asking.

'And tell your aunt that we'd like to see her,' suggested Pierre-Edouard. 'It's true,' he said, turning to Léon. 'She's always got one foot on the aeroplane, ready to go to America, and it's nearly twenty years since she's been back to see us!'

'And above all,' said Léon, winking at his nephews, 'don't run after those little Parisian girls; they're dreadful, and your mother will blame me afterwards!'

'I'd like to see them chasing girls!' protested Mathilde. 'Especially Paul, at his age!'

'Well, at his age, I, I tell you . . .'

'We know,' interrupted Pierre-Edouard with a laugh. 'Go on then, children, we'll leave you now, the train's about to leave.'

'I've put some napkins in for your midday snack,' Mathilde told them as she kissed them, 'put them on your laps so that you don't make a mess. And in the bottle it's a mixture, the wine's already diluted, don't add any water when you don't know where it's come from! And most important of all, don't lose your aunt's address, and be very polite to her,' she repeated, before jumping on to the platform.

'Tell me,' slipped in Pierre-Edouard as he put his arm around her, 'Jacques is going on eighteen and Paul sixteen; don't you think they're big enough to look after themselves?'

'Yes, of course, but . . . Well, just so long as everything is all right. It's so far away, Paris!'

Jacques and Paul regarded their Aunt Berthe, whom they knew to be forty-three years old, as almost an old lady. So when they arrived at the Gare d'Austerlitz they scanned the crowd to try to find an elderly lady who resembled their father. In her letter Berthe had written: 'I will wait for them at the barrier, and I will recognise them.' The two boys remembered this sentence well, but it did not prevent a little worry creeping in. There were so many women with greying hair!

'Anyway, if we don't find her, we'll go to her place,' decided Jacques, grasping his case and marching towards the ticket-collector.

They handed in their tickets and plunged into the crowd at the exit.

'Well, I suppose so,' said Paul. 'It's all very well Aunty saying it, but she hasn't recognised us, or else she hasn't come! What shall we do?'

'We can always look at the map of Paris, there's one over there. I'd be surprised if we couldn't find our own way!' said Jacques making for the display board. They were absorbed in careful study of the map when a voice, clear but with a sardonic lilt, made them jump.

'Disia mé, dronles, ont'vol anar? Chas mé béleu? Ané, vene mé far lou poutou!'

They turned round quickly and tried to see who had just addressed them in pure Saint-Libéral dialect. Two metres away an elegant lady was smiling at them; she was blonde and shapely, so refined and well dressed that Paul could hardly believe that such a vision could speak patois. So he instinctively asked in return: '*Que setz-vos*? *Tanta Berthe*?' without daring to look at the smiling lady.

'Well of course!' she exclaimed, holding out her arms, 'who else would speak Corrèze dialect here! You must be Jacques, the oldest,' she said as she kissed him, 'and you are Paul. Well, well, you really do look like Pierre-Edouard, don't you?'

She smelled deliciously fragrant, and her cheeks were as soft as a peach fresh off the tree.

'Is that why you were sure that you'd recognise us?' asked Jacques nervously.

'Yes,' she said with a smile, 'but by this too,' she added, tugging at her nephew's jacket. 'Oh, don't worry, you're both very, very well dressed, and I'm sure you are the most elegant young men in Saint-Libéral, but for here . . . Come on, let's go, we'll remedy that straight away. You shall see, my dears; I am going to show you Paris, and soon you'll wish you could stay for ever.'

Jacques and Paul experienced a week of perpetual amazement. At first they felt very intimidated, both by Berthe and by the luxury of her flat in the Faubourg Saint-Honoré – it lay above her couture house – but they very quickly fell in step with her and adopted this life, a bit crazy in their eyes, of seductive comfort.

For her everything seemed simple, easy, natural; so the boys were delighted to be carried along by the events which she organised, apparently with immense pleasure. She had been very touched by the provisions Jacques presented to her from his mother.

'That's truly kind,' she murmured, gently fingering the eggs and chickens. 'They're beautiful, they smell of the farm . . . Oh, confit de canard! The real thing, from home! You tell your mother that she is very, very kind. Yes, yes, you wouldn't understand . . . Now, you talk to me for a change; tell me everything, what's happening in Saint-Libéral?'

They had talked until midnight, for she wanted to know everything, to hear about everything, as if, beneath her effervescent gaiety, she was concealing deep down a few nostalgic tears.

The whirl of activity began the very next morning. Berthe first conducted her nephews to the Boulevard des Capucines and pushed them into the shop at number twelve, called 'Old England'. There, despite their feeble protests, she kitted them out from head to foot, and went into raptures when the two brothers emerged from the fitting rooms, dressed in comfortable golfing clothes and blushing with embarrassment.

'That's exactly what you need! Before, you looked like little boys dressed as grandfathers; now you're young men. You look magnificent!' she exclaimed, walking around them. 'Ah, a little alteration needed here!' she said, taking a tuck in Paul's jacket. 'It can be done right away. Here, pass me the pins.'

'Certainly, Madame Diamond,' said the salesman dancing attendance. He waited for her to mark the place, helped Paul take off the jacket, and went off to the workroom.

'What did he call you?' whispered Paul. 'The Diamond, that's our stream, at home!'

'Well, yes,' she explained, as she tried a tie on him, 'didn't you know that it's the name of my couture house?'

'Oh no, we didn't know,' chorused the boys.

To tell the truth, they knew next to nothing about her. They strongly suspected that she led a life which their parents would regard as less than exemplary, as the few allusions which their father occasionally made to her eccentric life-style were unmistakable in tone. Nobody in the family had ever mentioned that her unmarried life might nevertheless be filled with masculine company. At the Vialhes' it was not the sort of subject you touched on, especially in front of the children. Although Jacques and Paul were young, they were sufficiently aware to understand, for instance, that the elegant gentleman who had driven them from the station to the Faubourg Saint-Honoré in his 11 CV Citroën the evening before, was more than a friend to their aunt.

'Or if he is her friend,' Paul murmured in his brother's ear just before falling asleep, 'he's a close friend . . .'

'Yes, that's obvious. Anyway his photo is all over the place here – but, after all, we don't care, do we? I think it would be better not to tell our parents about him though, okay?'

'Of course not! They wouldn't understand!'

Apart from this discovery, their aunt's life remained a closed book to them.

'There, I think that will be better,' said the salesman, returning with Paul's jacket, 'if the gentleman would like to try it.'

'Perfect,' said Berthe, taking out her chequebook. 'Good, I'll take these four shirts and these ties as well, and don't forget the caps! Your berets don't go with these clothes at all,' she explained with a smile.

She made out a cheque, and Jacques happened to see the amount; it seemed to him so exorbitant that he protested.

'Really, Aunt,' he tried, genuinely embarrassed, 'it's . . . it's much too much, you shouldn't! Maman won't be at all happy, you know, and Papa even less so!'

'Now you be quiet,' she said, taking his arm, 'I have every right to give myself a treat, haven't I? Anyway, it's not as expensive as you think! And now, let's go and conquer Paris!'

In one week of Parisian life, Berthe dragged them along at such a pace that they lost all sense of time. They saw everything, or almost everything, and they were so full of enthusiasm that it was a joy for Berthe to help them discover new marvels.

For the first three days they made their way around the International Exhibition. Everything delighted them; they wanted to see it all, to visit every pavilion which stood on the banks of the Seine from Les Invalides to L'Île de Cygnes.

The foreign pavilions were grouped around the Chaillot Palace and at the foot of the Eiffel Tower, which stretched towards the sky like a sparkling arrow in a blaze of floodlights every night. Like everyone else, they were very impressed by the imposing construction crowned with a black eagle which was the German pavilion. But to their great astonishment, this was the only place where their aunt tried to hurry them through their visit.

'Don't let's linger there,' she said, 'it doesn't smell good. Believe me, my dears, I know that country well. I used to go there often at one time, and I did very good business there. But that's all over. Come on, let's go on to the island to see the Colonial Centre, it's much jollier!'

'You don't like the Germans, either! You're like Papa, then?' teased Paul.

She smiled and shook her head.

'The Germans? Yes I do, but not all of them.' She ruffled his hair. 'Come on now, and if you like, before we go to the colonies we'll take in Great Britain; it's over there, on the other side of the bridge.'

Three days at the Exhibition then, during which they also visited the Palace of Discovery, the planetarium and the upper platforms of the Eiffel Tower as well as the foreign and French creations, including all the regional exhibits. For Jacques' sake they sauntered through the Museum of Modern Art on the quai de New York. Finally, as a relaxation, they strolled slowly in the amusement park set up on the esplanade in front of Les Invalides. And every evening, although they were very tired, their aunt dragged them to the cinema. So they saw Pagnol's trilogy and also *Lost Horizon* and *The Story of a Cardsharp*.

When they had had their fill of the Exhibition, Berthe next led them round Paris. They saw everything, or at least believed they did: the Louvre, Saint-Chapelle, Notre-Dame and the Arc de Triomphe; also the Jardin des Plantes and les Halles, which made a great impression on them.

On Sunday morning Berthe did not have the heart to shock them by missing church, so she took them to eleven o'clock Mass at the Madeleine, where they were amazed by the pomp and ceremony of the High Mass.

Then came the eve of their departure. Jacques and his brother had grown so fond of their aunt that they wanted to show their appreciation in some concrete way; they clubbed together to give her a present. But what should they choose? Her flat was already full of pictures, vases and knick-knacks.

'Must be something to keep,' said Paul.

'Yes, but what?'

'Uncle Léon says that all women love jewellery.'

'Huh! Do you see yourself going and buying something like that? All alone? You'd look a right fool!'

Their aunt had accompanied them to help them choose the other presents for the family; she was so self-assured! So they had acquired a tobacco pouch decorated with views of Paris for their grandfather, a liqueur flask in the shape of the Arc de Triomphe for their parents, and also a fine scarf for their mother. There was a penholder with pictures on it for Mauricette, a big pencil box showing the Eiffel Tower for Guy, the Sacré-Coeur Church in a globe for Uncle Léon and his wife. Not forgetting Nicolas, they found a frame for the photo which was turning yellow on the wall of his room. But in this last case, they would have to manage without their aunt if the gift were to be appreciated. Where would be the surprise and delight if she helped them to choose and knew the price!

'Can you see yourself going into a jewellery shop?' repeated Jacques.

'Bah, the people in there can't be any worse than the butchers I meet with Uncle! Whatever we do we mustn't try around here; you heard what Aunt Berthe said: this is the most expensive area. You'll come with me, won't you?'

Eventually they set off on foot together for a jeweller's in a street in the St Martin district, and bought a small brooch in Limoges enamel. It was a modest gift, but they realised that their aunt's pleasure when they gave it to her was in no way feigned.

'But why? Why? You shouldn't have!' she said, pinning the brooch to her bodice. 'Oh, you remind me of your father, he always had a way of making thoughtful gestures. You have made me very happy. Now you are going to promise me that you'll come back, won't you?'

'Well, we'd love to,' said Paul, 'but what about you, why don't you ever come to see us?'

'Oh,' she replied, 'it's not so simple as all that, but I'll get organised one day, that's a promise, I . . . Listen, tell your father that I may be getting married soon . . . to a colleague. Or better still, don't say anything to him, I'll write to him.'

'Is it by any chance the gentleman who drove us in his car?' asked Jacques.

'That's right.'

'He seemed very nice, I'm sure Papa would like him.'

'I'd be very surprised if he did! But that isn't the problem,' she added quietly.

*

Jacques and Paul could not stop singing Berthe's praises and talking of the wonderful holiday they had spent with her, right up to the start of the school year which was to see the departure of Mauricette, whose turn it was to be sent to board in Brive. Furthermore they talked of her in such affectionate terms that even their grandfather, who was inclined to judge her severely, finished by simply shrugging his shoulders whenever the conversation returned to his daughter. He made do with mumbling the same response each time: 'Really! I never knew that plonk could turn into fine wine as it aged, unless it were a special plonk in a magic barrel!'

However, everyone knew that his surly comments masked the pride he felt in knowing that his daughter had succeeded so brilliantly; she was, after all, a Vialhe. She was now a true Parisienne, rich and famous — even the shopkeepers addressed her by name, that proved it! So Pierre-Edouard and Mathilde only smiled when the old man himself brought the conversation round to his daughter again, all the while looking as if butter would not melt in his mouth.

'And you say she calls herself Diamond? What an idea! Why not Vialhe!'

Pierre-Edouard had to bite his tongue in the effort not to remind him that twenty-three years earlier, if he could have, Jean-Edouard would have erased his daughter's name from the civil register without blinking an eyelid!

Nobody in the Vialhe family ever forgot that Monday, 25 October 1937; and for many years afterwards Pierre-Edouard recalled all the details of the events each time he strode over the Coste-Roche field which he had been sowing that day.

With the help of Nicolas, he had succeeded in clearing the plots surrounding the tumbledown cottage of Coste-Roche for the second time — that land which he and Mathilde had cultivated sixteen years earlier and which had been turned to scrub by fifteen years of neglect. He had energetically rooted out this invasion, and was planting oats on the reclaimed ground when Mathilde's call halted his work. Instead of flying out in a fine spray, the fistful of grain he was holding fell onto the ploughed earth in an awkward heap.

'What's happened?' He put down the seed sack which hung round his waist. Then he caught sight of Mathilde running up the rough track which climbed to Coste-Roche, despite the steep gradient and the stones.

'Bloody hell!' He rushed towards her. 'It has to be a catastrophe! What is it?' he called from a distance as soon as he thought she would hear him. 'Father? The children? Léon? What?'

'No,' Mathilde stopped, and used her apron to wipe the beads of sweat from her forehead.

'Well what then?' he demanded as he reached her.

'Louise telephoned . . .'

'Yes?'

'Oh, it's not fair! It's not fair!' she blurted out, suddenly throwing herself against him and beginning to cry. 'It's not fair,' she repeated.

'Tell me!' he ordered, shaking her.

'Thérèse, Félix's little Thérèse, she had her baby in the night . . .'

'Oh,' he murmured, 'and it didn't live?'

'It's not that, it's she who died, it's her, you see . . .'

'God be damned! What harm have they ever done, in heaven's name? It always strikes them! Always! But why?' he cried suddenly. 'First Octave! Then Jean! And now this young girl! Bloody hell, why?'

'Calm down,' she wiped her tears, 'it does no good to curse heaven about it.'

'Who did she call to tell us?'

'The Post Office.'

'What else did she say?'

'Don't you think that's enough? She said the mother died of a haemorrhage, the baby is beautiful, but Félix is beside himself. That's all she said.'

'All right,' he decided immediately, 'I'm going there. I should be up there – Félix will need me, and Louise too, I'm sure. I'll leave right away.'

'But . . . how?'

'Is your brother at home today?'

'Yes, I saw him an hour ago.'

'Well, he'll take me. I know him, he won't refuse. I'll

183

manage on my own for getting back, and Nicolas will deal with things here. Come on, don't let's waste any time!'

Léon did not hesitate for a second.

'Of course I'll drive you there,' he said, as soon as he was put in the picture. 'We mustn't leave Félix all alone, nor your sister, if it turns out they don't have any close friends up there. Pack your case, I'll come for you in ten minutes.'

'Have you told Father?' Pierre-Edouard asked Mathilde before they went into the house.

'No, I didn't have time.'

'But you think we should . . .'

'How can we avoid it?'

'You're right.' He pushed open the door.

His father was on the settle, fashioning a basket from willow wands; he looked up at his son.

'What are you doing here at this time of day? Have you finished sowing up there already?'

'No. Listen, Father, we've just heard a, a . . .'

'Who's died?' Jean-Edouard demanded fiercely. 'Come on, tell me, tell me right out!'

'Félix's wife. She had her baby and she's dead. So I'm going there right away.'

'Poor kid,' murmured the old man, twisting a willow shoot in his hands without noticing it, 'and I told them to bring the baby as soon as they could . . . You're right to go. Go and take care of them, go on! Your wife and I will look after the farm, with Nicolas.'

A quarter of an hour later, Pierre-Edouard and Léon were on the road to Limoges. At first they travelled without saying anything; then, gradually, since they could not spend the whole journey brooding over their sorrow, a dialogue was established.

'We should be there in three and a half hours, but of course it'll be dark by then,' said Léon, glancing at the clock on the dashboard.

'Yes, I hope I remember the way! Well, we can always ask. She goes well, your car.'

'She should do! But she's still running in.'

'What is it, what make?' asked Pierre-Edouard, who was

quite ignorant when it came to cars.

'I told you when I bought it,' Léon reproached him cheerfully. 'I've had it less than a month and you've already forgotten. It's a Renault, six cylinders, six-seater, a hundred and thirty-five kilometres an hour! Okay, it cost me 46,000 francs and it swallows fifteen litres every hundred kilometres, but at least we're sitting in comfort!'

'That's true . . . But still, 46,000 francs! I'd prefer to put the money into something else!'

'Bah! Money is for using! Not for when you're dead. Oh, sorry . . .'

'Well, no, you're right.' Pierre-Edouard lit his pipe. 'I don't really know what I'm going to say to poor Félix, nor to Louise either . . .'

'Nothing. You must just be with them, that's all. Words have never comforted anyone, but being there does.'

Pierre-Edouard had left the Château of Cannepetière on 2 August 1914, the day of the general call-up; he had never returned since then. In broad daylight he would have found the way, but night fell even before they arrived in Châteauroux. They were therefore forced to stop several times to ask directions.

It was nine o'clock before they finally reached the château. The caretaker explained to them that Félix did not live there, but in his forester's cottage, more than six kilometres away.

'Oh yes, that's right,' Pierre-Edouard remembered, 'Louise and Jean moved there when they got married. We have to take the lane just past the outbuildings and turn left down the forest track, is that the one?'

'Well yes, that's just about right,' said the man, surprised at his accuracy.

'Let's go,' said Pierre-Edouard, 'and don't worry about your car; if it hasn't rained too much, we'll make it.'

It took them almost twenty minutes to reach the keeper's cottage, because the road was pitted with deep ruts and Léon was obliged to drive at walking pace.

'As you said, it's a good thing it hasn't been raining; if it had, we'd be in a mess!' he grumbled. 'My God, what an idea to live this far off the beaten track!'

They eventually perceived a faint light, which twinkled from a hollow in the forest.

'It's over there,' said Pierre-Edouard.

The nearer they drew, the more depressed he felt at the idea of seeing his sister again under such circumstances. Once before in their lives their reunion had taken place beside a death-bed, in a pitiful attic, in Orléans. And that time too, there had been a baby sleeping on one side of the room; Félix had been that baby. As Mathilde had said, it was not fair.

Léon stopped in front of the house and turned off the engine; a dog yapped faintly.

'Right, I must go in . . . ' murmured Pierre-Edouard.

'I'll come with you, unless you prefer to go alone.'

'No, come on.'

He knocked on the door and, when nobody responded, pushed it open and went in.

What shocked him immediately was the sight of an old woman asleep, sitting huddled in a corner by the kitchen range. An old woman with white hair whose eyes were closed, the rims reddened with tears, the lids a network of fine blue veins; her hands were clasped instinctively on her stomach, gripping a useless rosary. As he drew near he recognised her.

'It can't be Louise?' whispered Léon behind him.

'Yes it is!'

Then he noticed the cradle, in a corner of the room dimly lit by a little paraffin lamp. He leaned over the baby, quite pink but still wrinkled; sleeping with its mouth half open.

'And Félix? He should be here!' Pierre-Edouard said in surprise.

'With, well, with his wife, next door perhaps?' suggested Léon.

Pierre-Edouard picked up a candle, lit it, and pushed open the door. Thérèse was there, alone. On the bedside table, next to a saucer of holy water with a sliver of box-wood soaking in it, a small candle-end was alight; a tiny flame, but still enough to show the pretty, child-like features of the young woman, only her dreadful pallor betraying her true state.

'He's not there,' said Pierre-Edouard, turning back towards Louise.

He gently placed his hand on her shoulder, and his fingers

186

felt the bones through lean flesh. She lifted her head.

'Oh, it's you . . .' she said. 'I was sure you would come.' Then she noticed Léon. 'You came too; thank you.'

'Where is Félix?' asked Pierre-Edouard.

'Félix? Oh, poor boy, he went out into the forest a little while ago.'

'But good heavens! This isn't the time to be going out into the forest!' protested Pierre-Edouard, 'especially with . . . Well it's not, anyway!'

'You don't understand,' she said. 'The little one, we were up with her for two whole nights, but she was alive then. Two nights of labour, it was long, too long, especially when you're all alone. So she finally fell asleep, that's all. She couldn't go on, you see? And nor could we. That's why you found me asleep and Félix out in the forest, to revive ourselves a bit, and because to be there with her, when she looks as if she's just fallen asleep, it's . . . it's enough to drive you mad.'

'Which way did he go?'

She shrugged her shoulders.

'Into the forest, it's big . . . Or maybe he's by the pool.'

'But my God! He shouldn't be left alone! He could . . . Well! In the name of God, Louise, stir yourself! First things first, where's this pool?'

'That way, about five hundred metres, at the end of the path which goes to the right at the bottom of the garden.'

'Stay here,' said Pierre-Edouard to Léon. 'I'm going to see if I can find him.'

As ill luck would have it, the moon was in its last quarter and gave only a feeble light. However, Pierre-Edouard gradually became accustomed to the darkness. He knew before he reached it that he was close to the pool; he could smell the mud and hear the rustling of the cat's-tails and reeds in the breeze.

He drew nearer, climbed the embankment, and jumped when a pair of teal flew off with a great clatter of wings and water. It took him another five minutes of searching to find Félix. He was there, leaning back against the pillar of an old shooting butt; he hardly turned his head as his uncle approached him.

Pierre-Edouard waited without moving. He did not know what to do or to say, convinced that he would blurt out something stupid if he spoke, or make an awkward gesture if he moved. So he waited patiently. Since his back was aching from the strain of the journey, he sat down beside his nephew, filled his pipe and lit it.

By the flickering light of the flame he saw that Félix was crying. Like a man, without a sound, without a sob, just an abundance of tears which had been held back for too long and now flowed over, rolled down and disappeared into the stubble of a two-day-old beard.

Ten minutes passed, and soon the grebes and coots reappeared from the shelter of the irises and rushes where they had hidden in fear at the sound of footsteps.

'You've got a fag?' Félix asked at last.

Pierre-Edouard held out his pouch and his papers, and clicked his lighter when his nephew stuck a cigarette between his lips.

'Why?' asked Félix, after the first few puffs. 'Why her? We loved each other so much! You know, she was . . . Oh, how can I say it? . . . She was me. You can't understand, you can't know. We two were, were like a tree and its bark! You know very well that a tree can't live without the bark! And that the oak dies if the lightning burns its skin! You know that! So! And now there's nothing for me but to die! Answer me that!'

'Well, I've seen a young walnut tree,' said Pierre-Edouard after a pause, 'which should have died when the goats ate its bark. But it's still standing. Oh, it suffered, and more than that; yes, it suffered, but it began to grow again despite that. Of course I helped as best I could. I made a plaster of clay and dung and tied it all on with an old sack. It didn't prevent the tree from weeping, but at least it stopped the sun from burning it and killing it. That walnut tree still bears the scars. In May, when the sap rises, it still weeps a bit, but it doesn't want to die and every year it gives its portion of nuts.'

'But I couldn't do that. Without her, it can't be done. You understand, to go back into the house and not see her ever again, not hear her, nothing, emptiness, it can't be done!'

'You know,' Pierre-Edouard spoke after a very long silence, 'I knew a young woman, still a child, and one day the house was empty for her too. She wanted someone again and once more the day came when she found the house empty . . . '

'Yes,' murmured Félix, 'yes, but it's not the same!'

'It's always the same. If you really love someone it's always the same, for everyone, in every case! But you think you're the only one because it's so overwhelming, so unbearable, that you think another case like yours can't possibly exist. You see, one night, I too felt the anguish of losing Mathilde. I was with an old doctor who said to me, speaking of us, believe me I remember it well, "You two are like the eyes in a face, one doesn't turn without the other." He was right. But since then I've also learned that a face can still live even if it has lost an eye. And believe me, a child doesn't give a damn if his father or mother is blind in one eye, especially if that's all he's ever known. That's not to say that the kid isn't missing anything, but it's just that to him, the most beautiful face is the one that bends over him and smiles at him, even if it only has one eye. You know that better than I do, after all you didn't know your father . . . '

Félix remained silent, then he rolled himself another cigarette.

'You've seen it, the baby?' he asked eventually.

'Yes, is it a boy?'

'Of course; she always said to me it would be a boy.'

'And what are you going to call him?'

'Pierre.'

'That's good,' said Pierre-Edouard, getting up. 'Now I'd like to go in, because I'm cold. Are you staying here?'

Félix drew on his cigarette and got up too. 'Perhaps I'd have stayed if you hadn't come, but now . . . '

'Come on then; you'll see Léon, he's there as well.'

'I didn't think you'd come so quickly,' Félix admitted as he gazed at the pool. 'If I'd known, I would have waited for you at the house. No, I would never have thought . . . '

'Well, that's because you don't know me very well. Your mother was certain that I would come.'

'Why?'

'Because she learned earlier than any of us that a burden is borne more easily when there are plenty to carry it. And because she knows that with us, the Vialhes, the living always gather around the dead. To make a united front, you understand. When there are several of you, you can keep each other company. Even if it doesn't ease the pain, at least it gives you the feeling that you're doing something.'

That night Pierre-Edouard and Léon kept the vigil over the dead body; that allowed Louise and Félix to sleep for several hours. In the small hours Léon had to leave for Saint-Libéral; Pierre-Edouard went out to the car with him.

'I'll come back the day after tomorrow,' promised Léon, 'and if Mathilde would like it, I'll bring her for the funeral, and I think Yvette will come too. That way they'll be a bit less lonely.' He nodded towards the house.

'Safe journey, and thank you.' Pierre-Edouard stifled a yawn. 'Oh, now I think of it, tell Nicolas to begin ploughing the Malides field, then we can plant it when I get back. And tell Mathilde that the baby is a big boy and he's called Pierre. Off you go, cheers!'

Louise had risen and was making coffee when he returned to the house. It seemed to him that his sister looked less old and worn now that she had rested. Even so, with her white hair and lined face she looked almost sixty. *And yet she's only forty-seven*, he calculated, *it's not such a great age, after all!*

'Léon has gone back?' she asked.

'Yes, he's got some work to do, but he'll be back the day after tomorrow.'

'I was sure you would come,' she said, as she slowly poured the boiling water into the earthenware filter. She lowered her voice. 'What do you think about Félix?'

He made an evasive gesture.

'I can't say really. Last night he was too tired for me to tell; we'll see soon enough, when he wakes. And you, how are you? I'm not talking about what's just happened, but in general?'

'Oh, me . . . ' She made a dismissive movement of her shoulders. He saw that she was crying, without a sound, without even changing her expression; only a slight trembling of her lips, and the blinking of her eyelids as the tears escaped, betrayed her vast sorrow.

He moved towards her, pulled her to him and held her

against his shoulder.

'Go on,' he said as he gently stroked her hair, 'cry as much as you like, there's no shame in that. Cry as much as you can, but afterwards — afterwards you'll go and tidy yourself up, comb your hair properly and dress in your Sunday best. That's what you have to do, for Félix, and for the baby too, and for your own sake even.'

'First I must go and milk the goat for the baby; a good thing she's there, that nanny-goat!'

'I'll take care of her; you drink your coffee and after that, go and make yourself beautiful. You're good at that, I know; you just have to have the will.'

For two days, Pierre-Edouard watched over his sister and his nephew. When Félix saw his mother rejuvenated by a change of clothing and a little make-up, he became aware of his own miserable appearance — his cheeks blue with stubble, his clothes crumpled, he looked like a tramp going downhill. He felt obliged to react.

Once he was clean and changed, it was towards the forest that he turned his steps, and his uncle was at his side. Pierre-Edouard listened for hours, hardly saying anything himself, to all the confidences which were retold loudly and disjoint-edly. The confidences, secrets even, all centred on the dead young woman. In this way Félix gradually poured out his sorrow. Instead of burying it within himself like a cancer, he scratched the wound until it bled and squeezed out his misery, drop by drop. His distress was very little diminished, but discouragement and depression gave way initially to resigna-tion, and then later to stoicism.

Two days later, Félix and his mother were surrounded by the Vialhe and Dupeuch families as they accompanied the coffin to the little cemetery of Mézières-en-Brenne. Even Jacques and Paul were there, on either side of Mathilde. Only Berthe was missing — she was out of the country, and so Pierre-Edouard had not been able to tell her — and old Jean-Edouard, who was too old to make the journey.

He was at least represented by an enormous wreath which trembled on the side of the hearse and on which could be read:

To the grand-daughter whom I would have liked to have got to know better.

Everyone appreciated this nice touch, but only Louise knew its real worth. This wreath was a discreet thank-you from her father to her after twenty-eight years; one day in January 1909 she had been newly married, banished from her family, and had not been able to attend her grandmother's funeral, so she had expressed her feelings via her modest offering of flowers. Today, Jean-Edouard remembered.

Chapter 14

PIERRE-EDOUARD made use of a fine crop of walnuts, which realised a decent price, to execute a plan which he had cherished for several years. When winter came he undertook the modernisation of all the farm buildings with the help of Nicolas; they were sorely in need of it.

First of all he attacked the cowshed. It was old, dark and impractical, with wooden stalls and uneven flagstones which made cleaning difficult. He wanted it functional, airy, modern.

He enlarged the access, removed the wooden mangers and replaced them with low cement feeding troughs. He concreted the floor and rendered the walls. He even installed a tap, and was sorry he could not afford to buy those automatic drinking troughs he had seen in advertisements sent to the syndicate.

Despite this drawback and his father's criticisms – that the new building was too light, the cement too cold and the animals too cramped – he could now line up eight cows on each side; his shed was the finest and most modern in the village. Over the years other farmers frequently came to him to use his as a model when they were trying to renovate their cowsheds.

After that he went on to the sheepfold, which he refitted likewise from top to bottom. Then he passed on to the pigsties, which his father had built to undertake pig breeding when the railway line was being constructed. Here again, he demolished the ancient wooden boxes which had been chewed by the sows and rotted by dung, and were only held together by extensive and frequent reinforcement with chestnut planks. He built concrete sties fitted with troughs which were easy to fill, and provided ventilation by replacing the tiny skylights with wide frame windows which could be opened.

'Well, well,' remarked Mathilde when everything was

finished, 'the animals and Nicolas are better accommodated than we are . . . Nicholas's room may still be in the cowshed, but it's almost nicer than ours!'

Pierre-Edouard noticed her rather injured air, and sighed.

'I know, even the pigs are more comfortable than we are, but how do you think I can undertake alterations in a house which doesn't belong to me? It would be stupid. Besides, if I know him, my father would never let anyone touch his walls.'

'You're right,' she said, 'but you know there are days when I'd almost like to go up to Coste-Roche and set up house there again, be at home, in our own place. But I know that's impossible. Never mind; when you've got a bit of money, promise me you'll get the roof fixed up there. We must think of our own children – one day they'll get married, and we wouldn't want them to have to live with us, that's not good for anyone.'

'Have you had words with Father?'

'Oh, no, not at all. But you know how it is; he has his little fads, his own set ways and times of doing things and his ideas too, and he still doesn't want to accept Léon, which is pure spite when all's said and done.'

Pierre Edouard regarded the annexation of Austria with a very jaundiced eye. He kept himself sufficiently well informed about current affairs to realise that a crisis was looming, quite apart from the deplorable vacillations of the French politicians. Already the franc was worth almost nothing and prices rose unremittingly; but it had been the same old story for several years now.

What worried him, and Léon too, was the power and consequence being assumed by a nation which had been beaten and vanquished twenty years ago. Pierre-Edouard did not like the shows of force in Germany, nor the Italian's bravado and least of all that Franco fellow's fascism, for there was no longer any doubt that he was going to win the war. There was no need to be a first-class politician to predict that. Léon was already employing two Republican Spaniards who had fled from reprisals and had recently arrived in Saint-Libéral. According to them, terrible atrocities and frightful massacres were taking place in their home country, and that was thanks to help from those Germans who were as proud as ganders, and those Italians who were as arrogant as peacocks.

'Mark you,' Léon said to him one night in April, when they were taking an aperitif at Suzanne's, 'for the time being they're leaving us in peace: after all, Ethiopia, Spain, Austria and Czechoslovakia, it's none of our business. All right, it has a nasty smell about it, but it's a long way off!'

'You're damn right it's a long way off!' said Delpeyroux, joining in the conversation. 'To me their Cze-losco-vakia, I don't even know where it is! I'm not in a hurry to fight for people when I don't even know where they live!'

'Yes,' said Pierre-Edouard, 'it's a long way off, but Hitler and Mussolini are our neighbours, both of them. I don't trust neighbours who move the boundary markers to gain a few furrows.'

'Neither do I,' said Léon, 'but just so long as it's not round here.'

'That's right, it never does any good to mind other people's business; all the same, those neighbours, I don't trust them.'

'Neither do I if it comes to that,' agreed Léon. 'Shall I tell you something? Well, in 1918, with the Huns, we stopped too soon; we should have given them a real hammering! It's true that I couldn't have gone on and neither could you, but . . . ' He finished by banging his metal hook on the zinc of the bar.

Thinking that he was calling for another round of drinks, Suzanne filled their glasses and then smiled at Léon.

'You're into politics again, are you? I've heard that's all you're interested in nowadays; that's not much fun for us women!'

'Mm, yes.' Pierre-Edouard ignored the interruption. 'We weren't exactly fit in 1918, but I'm not so sure that we are today either!'

'I wouldn't go so far as to say that,' protested Delpeyroux. 'We've got the Maginot line, and that's the real thing! It's unbreachable – that's what my wife's cousin told me, and he spent four months of his service on it. Unbreachable! And then we've got aeroplanes too!'

'Yes,' added Léon, 'it's true what he says, we're prepared.'

'Listen, you two,' said Pierre-Edouard in a grave tone: 'in 1914 I found myself on the front without knowing a thing; I didn't even believe there would *be* a war on the thirty-first of July, the day before German mobilisation! So you can imagine what a fool I felt on the first of August! But this time I want to be able to see it coming, if the balloon goes up. It won't stop it happening, but at least I won't look so stupid.'

That year, the 'Ice Saints Days' lived up to their name and their cruel reputation. On 11 May Saint Mamert arrived with a white frost; on the twelfth Saint Pancras did the same, and on the thirteenth, a Friday to boot, Saint Servais succeeded in destroying the few flowers which had escaped his colleagues' attentions.

In Saint-Libéral it was a bitter blow for those who made a profit from plums, cherries and spring vegetables. A year without fruit would mean less money, and nothing could replace that loss.

It was hard for the Vialhes. Pierre-Edouard had drawn heavily on his savings to modernise the farm buildings, and he had hoped that five or six tons of plums would replenish his nest-egg. But what could you do against Heaven's will? So he shrugged his shoulders over the blackened petals and twisted pistils and even tried to comfort Nicolas, who was concerned for the bees which were hampered by the cold.

'Well, old fellow, that's the way it is. You should know that, considering how long you've been here. One year it's all right, the next it isn't. If the nuts yield well, the plums freeze, and if the tobacco is good, it's the wheat that's poor! Come on, let's go, we mustn't let it stop us from going to spray the potatoes; they're just pushing through and the Colorado beetles are gobbling them up already. The frost doesn't kill those filthy pests, that would be too easy!'

The weather remained dreadful until the middle of June, as if it had been set off course by the late frosts. Torrential showers, which washed everything away and drowned the crops, were followed by low temperatures which stopped the grass from growing and delayed the development of the cereals and vegetables.

Towards 15 June warmer weather arrived, and Pierre-Edouard began haymaking, relying on the fact that there were still two weeks left until the change of moon. It was a good thing that he seized the opportunity, for those who delayed setting to work then had to wait until the end of July to bring home any dry hay.

In the midst of all these anxieties, only Jacques' success in his second baccalauréat exams brought a ray of happiness into the Vialhe household; and it brought pride too, for as soon as he had the results Jacques announced to his parents that he intended to sit the entrance exams for the Veterinary College, either at Maisons-Alfort or at Toulouse – always providing that they could pay for his studies.

'Blimey,' muttered Pierre-Edouard, happy with his choice but worried about the cost of it all, 'you're aiming high. Well, I hope we'll be able to pay for it.'

'We will!' decided Mathilde.

'We will! We will! We'll have to see! It certainly won't be with what we've made out of plums this year!'

'Oh, I know,' she said, 'but I also know what I myself have managed to put aside over the years. What did you expect?' she asked her husband with a smile. '*I* was never in the habit of throwing thrushes to the wolves!'

'That's enough,' he interrupted. 'You're not going to bring out your brother's hoary old tale, are you?'

That was exactly what she did every time she wanted to tease him, and both of them really enjoyed the banter; it brought back their youth.

'Joking apart,' she said, 'you must find out, dear, exactly what it will cost us. We'll do all we can, but it shouldn't be to the detriment of your brothers and sisters, you understand?'

'Absolutely.'

'And how many years will it go on?' asked Pierre-Edouard.

'Four.'

'Really! Your mother was very well advised when she saved them, her . . . her thrushes! Four years of study, that'll cost a pretty penny! Especially if every year is ruined like this one!'

'We'll manage!' cut in Mathilde.

'All right, all right, we'll manage . . . In the meanwhile, you must understand that this year we can't give you a big present for your bac like we did last year. Before we had that frost I was thinking of buying you a wireless set. Oh, not a big one, but still a set that we could all have enjoyed. Well, we'll see later on, maybe.'

'Don't worry about that! Uncle Léon is going to get me one next time he goes to Brive . . . '

'There you are!' cried Pierre-Edouard triumphantly, laughing, 'and afterwards your mother will say that I'm the one who throws money out of the window! Well, I see that you've started smoking a pipe, so you can have this.' He took a box from his pocket. 'I bought you this, it's a strong one, a real briar. By the way, did the Labrousse girl get her bac too?'

'Yes, and with a good grade.'

'That's great. Well, you must ask her to come to our house one day. I think she's rather sweet, don't you?'

After his sixteenth birthday, Paul felt that he was a man at last. He had put on weight and grown taller in the last few months, was strong and well proportioned; he had to shave at least twice a week, and was very proud of the fact. He was also very proud of the lingering looks he attracted from the village girls.

Where they were concerned he assumed an air of self-confidence which he by no means felt; he pretended to be blasé, almost cynical, all the better to conceal a sort of instinctive reserve which held him back and prevented him from going the whole way. They saw in him the reliability, high standards and honesty of the Vialhes together with his uncle's imagination, and the dissolute, disreputable, un-scrupulous streak which Léon used to his own advantage – although he had settled down since his marriage.

Some evenings Paul was burning to respond without further ado to the advances he provoked from, among others, the tantalising Suzanne, but he banished the wicked idea by reminding himself that the landlady of the inn was old enough to be his mother. Besides, he was secretly dreaming of a *grand amour*, and he didn't want to do anything which might spoil the way he pictured it would happen. He was torn by these conflicting emotions, but it was a point of honour to him that he should never let his state of mind show.

Only Jacques guessed the extent of his inner torment, but he knew that his brother's pride and sense of propriety prevented any exchange of confidences. The only secret Paul was willing to discuss was the plan which he had nurtured since their wonderful trip to Paris.

'You know,' Paul had confessed to him six months earlier, 'I don't want to be a stock-dealer all my life.'

'That's what Papa's counting on; he's hoping you'll come back to farming. That would be better really.'

'Well, he's wrong there, I don't want anything to do with the farm!'

'But why not?' Jacques had protested. 'Someone's got to take it on!'

'It's up to you then! But you want to be a vet instead!'

'Yes, but I can make that choice!'

'All right, we all know you're very clever! But if you think I've got to stay here because I haven't passed exams, that's where you're wrong!'

'But you don't have any choice!'

'We'll see, but let me tell you, I shall be off to Paris just as soon as I can. Up there, that's really living! Look at Tante Berthe, do you think she passed any exams?'

'Maybe not,' grumbled Jacques. 'One piece of advice though; don't tell Papa any of this rubbish, or he'll soon make you think otherwise!'

'I know, but that won't stop it happening. I'll wait, and one day I'll do it, you'll see. We'll talk about it another time . . .'

And he really did talk about it; he built his castles in Spain, cherished his project, nurtured it. Jacques listened patiently, but he felt so much more mature than his brother that he had to control himself so as not to demonstrate to Paul that his idea was just childish nonsense, a dream. For him, a brilliant scholar, life did not depend on daydreams; it had firm foundations and was to be lived in reality. Already he was methodically organising his life, with persistence and effort; he loved Paul's imagination and spirit, but he did not consider it a sensible line to conduct.

Old memories were awakened amongst the veterans and those who remembered 1914 when the call-up came for the reservists and soldiers on leave to join the Maginot Line. The news came on Sunday 4 September and led to a lot of talk, but taken altogether things were quite reassuring – it was a far cry from total mobilistion – and as nobody in the village was directly affected by it, the conversations turned on ways of preserving the peace rather than making war.

Nobody felt particularly belligerent, especially not those who had left twenty-five years earlier, shouting like men possessed, that they would not stop until they reached Berlin. They knew what war was really like and, although they enjoyed the chance to talk about their four years in the trenches yet again, what they said about it did not encourage anyone to plunge into such a hell on earth.

Thus everyone tried to reassure themselves, and the many men who got out their guns were only doing so in preparation for the opening of the hunting season. Despite that the worry ate at them, because the news was so alarming, especially to those who were the right age to bear arms.

On Friday, 23 September came the announcement of partial mobilisation; it affected about a million men and this time several reservists in the village had to leave. All those with a number 2 or 3 on their military records had to report to their barracks.

Nevertheless, many people in Saint-Libéral continued to believe that a war was impossible, as if it were enough to deny the evidence to render it null and void. Besides, the veterans of 1914 confirmed that real conflict did not begin like this. This mobilisation was more like a grand army exercise; simply a warning, a deployment of forces intended to impress any possible adversary, to prove that they were ready to defend themselves, but equally ready to discuss the matter and do everything to avoid a fight which nobody wanted.

Despite this rather forced optimism, there was a crowd that night in the church in response to Father Delclos' exhortations; during the afternoon he had called on all his parishioners to come and pray for peace, and it was best to have all the winning cards in your hand at times like these. Everyone believed that peace had been preserved when they learned, a week later, that Chamberlain, Daladier and Hitler had met in Munich and arrived at a lasting and fair agreement.

Although they were reassured about the future, Pierre-

Edouard and Mathilde were not happy to see Jacques leave for the Veterinary College at Maisons-Alfort. After his departure, which came immediately after Mauricette had returned to her boarding-school in Brive, the house seemed even emptier and the table looked bigger, for Paul was also often away. The first days were the worst and Guy, feeling lost between his parents, grandfather and Nicolas, never stopped demanding that his brother come back, and also the sister whom he adored.

'They'll come back in the holidays,' Mathilde reassured him during supper.

'It's a long time until the holidays.'

'Don't complain! You're not unhappy at school, and you only have to walk down the main street to get there!'

'Well yes, but I liked it better when Mauricette was here to go with me. When I'm big, do I have to go away too?'

'You're eight years old; you've still got time to think about it, haven't you? Finish your dinner and get to bed quickly.'

'But you'll leave the door open so that I can listen to the wireless?'

'All right.'

That had become the custom at the Vialhes'. Ever since Léon had given Jacques a radio, the whole family gathered around the receiver every evening. Old Jean-Edouard was absolutely captivated by it. To him this musical box was a constant source of wonderment, and the fact that his old enemy Léon was indirectly the architect of this miracle did not diminish his admiration of it one jot. He who had previously gone to bed as soon as he had swallowed his soup now settled down comfortably by the fireside, placed his packet of coarse tobacco and his old pipe on the little hollow in the andirons, and blissfully appreciated the programmes from Radio-Paris and Poste-Parisien. Often Pierre-Edouard and Mathilde retired to bed before him, exhausted by their day's work.

'You won't forget to turn off, eh?' Pierre-Edouard advised him each time.

The reminder was unnecessary. The old man never forgot to pull out the plug before going to bed; he considered that much less complicated than turning all those knobs.

'A good thing Jacques didn't take away his wireless, with

that here at least we're not bored,' declared Guy as he got up from the table.

He kissed his parents, grandfather and Nicolas, and retired to bed.

'You see, that's how you know you're getting old,' whispered Pierre-Edouard in Mathilde's ear a little later, 'when the children go away and the last one is bored with you! It's a good thing we've got the wireless, as he said!'

They had just gone to bed in their turn, and were curled up together waiting for sleep to come.

'Do you feel old, then?' teased Mathilde, stroking his chest.

'That depends on the night . . . All the same, I do miss the kids. I hope it was right for Jacques to enter that college, and I hope most of all that we can pay for his four years of study.'

'But of course we'll be able to. Oh, I know it bothers you, it does me too, but you'll see, we'll get there. That's not what's worrying me.'

'What's wrong?'

'Paul.'

'What about Paul?'

'Léon tells me that he's changed, he's less cheerful. He works hard, but according to Léon he's not really interested in what he's doing.'

'That's all we need!' groaned Pierre-Edouard. 'Bloody hell, he was the one who chose the job!'

'Perhaps he's realised that he's made a mistake,' she defended him.

'It's a fine time to think of it! Well, if he wants to come back to the farm he could be useful. Deep down, I always thought it would end up like that.'

'You'll have to talk to him,' she insisted. 'I've noticed myself that he's changed recently.'

'It's his age, it'll pass. Or he's got a crush on some girl . . . '

'Don't talk about things like that, he's still too young! Anyway, he's sensible, I know he is!'

'Do you think he'd come and tell you!' he teased, and wound his arms around her.

'You will speak to him, promise?'

'All right, and if he wants to work with me, there's no shame in that, quite the opposite. Now come on, we must go 'to sleep.'

He kissed her and turned over.

'Basically that was true, what you said just now,' she sighed after a moment's silence.

'What did I say?'

'That you were getting old! Well, as the child said, it's a good thing we have a wireless,' she said with a laugh.

'That's enough of that!' He embraced her fiercely. 'And I'll prove to you that you get the best shafts from old ash trees!'

From a distance Pierre-Edouard indicated to Paul to move forward a few steps then, with a wave of the arm, showed the direction in which he thought the bird would move. He waited for his son to take up his position in the right place, and then advanced into the huge bushes of box and broom which clung to the slopes of the Caput Peak.

On this chilly Sunday morning in November, he and Paul had been tracking the same woodcock for almost two hours. They had flushed it at the other end of the plateau, in the acacia wood by the château. They greeted it with two useless volleys and it zigzagged between the trunks before heading towards the chestnut grove, to go to ground in the heart of a huge sloe bush, just before reaching the chestnuts.

When they put it up again it had surprised the hunters by flitting like a butterfly – never leaving the shelter of the brushwood – as far as the Vialhes' chestnut copse. From there it took flight again, this time as straight as a die, and flew swiftly towards the Caput, where Pierre-Edouard believed it was hiding in the thickest broom bushes.

Methodically Pierre-Edouard began to beat the undergrowth, always ready to raise his gun. He was forced to hunt without a dog, for the one he owned, a fine mongrel with a trace of griffon in him, was excellent when hunting mammals but a disaster area when it came to birds. He tracked partridge, quail, rail and woodcock as if they were hares or rabbits, with much bounding and barking; the lovable idiot simply tried to catch the birds by the tail as soon as he spied them! He was such a loudmouth that it was no use hoping to shoot a woodcock; he flushed them all before they were within range of the guns.

Pierre-Edouard slipped behind a clump of broom and then a gentle whirr of wings alerted him to the escaping woodcock, invisible behind a curtain of branches but heading straight for Paul. He did not even have time to warn his son before he heard the dry crack of a 16-bore gun.

'Did you get it?'

'Yes!' cried Paul triumphantly. 'Direct hit! It dropped like a stone. I nearly missed seeing it; good thing I heard it getting up!'

'Bravo!' Pierre-Edouard joined him. 'It's a fine one!' he cried appreciatively, as Paul waved the golden bird at arm's length.

He took the woodcock, weighed it in his hands and ruffled its warm feathers. A drop of cherry-red blood hung like a pearl from the end of its long beak, and splashed on to the white pebbles which were scattered on the ground.

'Poor beast,' he murmured. 'You see, now we've had the hunt and got it, we should be able to bring it back to life, don't you think?'

'Well . . . yes,' Paul hesitated, 'but they're delicious to eat as well. So . . . '

'That's true,' Pierre-Edouard admitted. 'They are very good and your mother cooks them marvellously; all the same, that's what cost him his life, nothing is perfect. Come on, it's time we were getting back.'

A little later, as they were walking down to the village, he asked: 'By the way, it seems your work with Léon isn't really to your liking, is that right?'

'Did Jacques tell you that?' demanded Paul with a scowl.

'Jacques? Oh no, it was your mother.'

'So Uncle Léon has been complaining about me?'

'Not that either – just the opposite, he's very pleased with you. But he thinks you seem to be bored, is that right?'

Paul shrugged his shoulders but remained silent.

'All right,' continued Pierre-Edouard, 'we'll assume you mean yes. So, listen to what I suggest, then at least you'll be able to choose. Here it is: if you like you can come back to the farm. We'll work together and we won't talk about running around the markets any more, okay?'

Paul stopped, stared at the ground and kicked a stone.

'It's not that,' he said seriously. 'The markets — it's true, I am fed up with them, but . . . Oh, bloody hell, it's not easy to say! . . . I don't want the farm either, you've got to understand that as well.'

Pierre-Edouard gazed at him and shook his head. He was terribly disappointed. He had thought Paul would accept his offer with pleasure; was looking forward to initiating him in his profession, to teaching him all the secrets, to sharing the happiness it brought.

'*Miladiou*,' he murmured at last, 'I didn't expect that, and neither did your mother.' He took out his tobacco pouch and nervously filled his pipe. 'But good God, what do you want to do then? Eh? It's not as if you've got any diplomas! Well, answer me then, have you any idea?'

'Not yet,' confessed Paul.

And it wasn't really a lie; although he knew very well that he wanted to go to Paris, he still did not know what he would be doing there. He was annoyed with his father, for catching him unawares, for forcing him to reveal part of his plan, for it was still vague and incomplete. He sensed that he was still too young to embark on his own venture, yet he was not so naïve as to believe that it would be easy to make it happen.

'So, if I understand you correctly,' said Pierre-Edouard bitterly, 'you know what you *don't* want, but you don't know what you *do* want?'

Paul shrugged his shoulders once more and lowered his head. Despite his disappointment, turning gradually into anger, Pierre-Edouard restrained himself: he pictured himself at the same age, or almost, and remembered how brutally his father had kept control of the family at that time. Above all he remembered the results of this, and he softened his approach.

'All right,' he sighed, 'we won't beat you for that. I won't hide the fact that I was counting on you to help me with the farm and to take it over later; your mother was hoping you would too, and your grandfather as well. You tell me you don't want to, and I can't force you. Anyway, it wouldn't do any good; to work on the land, you have to love it, because if you love it, you forgive it all the tricks it plays on you. So if it doesn't appeal to you, leave well alone. Besides, you're still young, you may change your mind; so, before you embark on anything else, think about it a bit, wait a bit. And above all don't be in a hurry to destroy things; you'll find out that it's easy to break something and afterwards it takes a long time to mend it. Believe me, I know that.'

'I'd like to go and work in Paris,' said Paul suddenly.

'In Paris? And what would you do there? Don't you think there are enough unemployed up there? And why Paris! Your stay with Berthe must have turned your head!'

'It's not the town which attracts me,' protested Paul, 'but Paris itself. You know, it's big, it's all happening, it's exciting. It's full of new ideas, you can do anything there!'

'Huh, any sort of mischief!' Pierre-Edouard was disconcerted by his line of argument. 'Anyway,' he cried angrily, 'you didn't think your mother and I would let you leave, did you?'

'Well, no,' admitted Paul. He continued to scratch the ground with the toe of his boot, then he lifted his head and took a chance: 'And when I'm eighteen, may I leave then?'

The question stung Pierre-Edouard.

'Leave! Leave! Are you unhappy here? Don't you like your family? Are you bored? Come on, tell me, now we've got this far!'

'It's not that.' Paul felt his courage evaporating. 'It's not that at all!' he repeated furiously. 'But here! Here it's always the same, always the same work, the seasons and the days go by and nothing changes! Here there's no . . . no life! That's how it is! I want to live where there's something happening!'

'Well,' sighed Pierre-Edouard, 'after all, each to his own. You asked me if you could leave when you are eighteen, and I'll tell you – yes. But I'll make one condition: that you at least know what you are going to do in your bloody Paris!'

'I'll find something, I'll manage!' Paul suddenly felt cheerful again.

'You'd better!' grumbled his father. 'But while you're waiting, in the next two years, will you stay with Léon or come to us?'

'I think I'll stay with Uncle Léon. You know with him I can save a bit of money that'll be useful to me in two years' time.'

'Seen like that, of course, I can't give you what he gives you, what with the cost of your brother and sister . . . '

'If you like, I could help you out.'

'No, no, we're not that badly off.' Pierre-Edouard put a hand on his shoulder, and gazed at him at length. 'You really are a strange one. You see, I thought I knew you, but I was wrong. When you know someone, you understand, and I don't understand you. But it doesn't matter, it isn't important. So we'll do it like that, all right?'

'All right.'

'But don't talk about any of this to your grandfather. I can take it on board, it's fine by me, but it might kill him. He was counting on you for the land . . . And don't say anything to your mother either; I'll tell her. And now let's go home; she'll be getting worried about us by now.'

PART FOUR

The Hour of Decision

Chapter 15

THE thermometer fell to minus ten after several sharp frosts at the beginning of December, and then winter arrived with snow. Unfortunately it did not lie long, so that there was nothing to protect the cereal crops, already weakened by those early frosts, from the terrible cold of January 1939.

On the plateau which overlooked Saint-Libéral, huge stretches of wheat froze, only the strips protected by curtains of trees or hedges managing to survive. On the Vialhes' land seventy per cent of the wheat and oats perished, and four walnut trees on the Long Field cracked open one terrible night, split to the heart-wood by the biting cold. Four superb trees, luxuriant, gloriously strong and healthy – they were still young, only thirty-eight years old; they should have lasted two hundred years. One night was enough to kill them.

'Done for,' murmured Pierre-Edouard a month later, as he stroked the rough bark of one of them. 'Poor old thing, just like the wheat! We're in trouble!'

He had just surveyed the extent of the losses on the cereal fields, and he knew already that he would have to sow spring wheat and oats in March. To set his mind at rest he had gone to check the walnut trees – a sad surprise.

'Well?' asked Mathilde when he returned to the house.

He moved to the fire and held his hands out to the flames.

'We'll be resowing, that's all – oats, wheat, maize, doesn't matter what it is, we'll be sowing it again! But that's not the worst.'

'Oh?' she breathed a sigh.

'Four walnut trees, the ones at the bottom of the field, split like old turnips.'

'Like in 1917. The frost killed three of them in the same place . . .'

'I know,' he said, 'that sort of hollow is as cold as death. So that's it, four nut trees less. We planted thirty-one, we've got twenty-four still. At this rate our grandchildren won't need to quarrel over how to divide them up, there won't be any left . . . But by God, I'll plant more, as often as it takes!'

He felt weary and discouraged. It was easy to proclaim that he would resow, but he remembered all the work, all the effort expended the previous autumn, and to no avail.

'Well, we can't do anything about it, that's life,' he said, slipping down onto the settle. He looked at Nicolas, who was opposite him. 'And the bees? I bet they're all dead too?'

'No, no,' said Nicolas with a smile, 'they're humming, all humming!'

'Are you sure?'

'Sure! I put my ear to the hives and I tap with my finger, they are purring away!' Nicolas assured him very proudly.

He had a right to be proud, for it was he who had covered the twenty-five hives with a huge straw hood long before the first cold spell; thanks to his precautions the swarms had triumphed over the frost.

'Well, that's one good thing; the state we're in, I thought they'd all have died. Where's Father?' he asked Mathilde.

'He's resting.'

'Oh, again . . . '

For several months now, old Jean-Edouard had taken to lying down for a rest at ten o'clock in the morning, and this habit worried Pierre-Edouard and Dr Delpy as well. Both of them were relying on the spring to help the old man give up this dangerous practice. As the doctor had said: 'At that age, when you take to your bed you're finished. Young people who stay awake and old ones who sleep already have one foot in the grave . . . '

Jean-Edouard was not ill, but from month to month he was shrinking, growing weaker and more bent. And, much more alarming, he grew a little confused; he rambled, was not always sure whether it was 1939 or 1919, and called for his wife. Luckily these episodes did not last long, but they were distressing for everyone.

'It's not worth telling him about the wheat and the walnut trees,' said Pierre-Edouard. 'He won't go up to the plateau to check anyway.'

'He knows about the wheat already,' announced Mathilde.

'Pierre Delpeyroux came by just now to borrow your wedges for splitting wood, he doesn't know where he's put his. Your father was there and Pierre explained to him that the whole plateau was frosted.'

'What did Father say?'

'The same as you: we'll resow.'

During the month of February, the bell never seemed to cease tolling in Saint-Libéral. It rang first to announce to everyone that Pope Pius XI had begun his eternal life. Father Delclos organised a service attended by the usual female parishioners and a few kids from the confirmation class. Nobody noticed that he prayed very little for the deceased and a great deal for his successor, whom the Conclave was soon to elect. He implored the Holy Ghost that the next inheritor of Saint Peter's key should not attack the wrong enemy, and above all, would recognise the true perils which menaced the Church.

Nobody in Saint-Libéral knew that Father Delclos, an active supporter of the nationalist *Action Française*, had been heart-broken when it was condemned; he hoped that this change of Pope would restore the disciples of Maurras to their rightful position – he considered them the true defenders of the Faith and of France.

After Pius XI, four old people succumbed in less than ten days; although they had succeeded in surviving the rigours of winter, they had no defence against the damp, penetrating cold which permeated everything. So they faded away: old Germaine Meyjonade from the hamlet Fonts-Perdus, then Célestin Pouch from the locality of Ligneyroux, and then Jeantout, whose death affected the whole Vialhe family, for he had always been their friend and was their nearest neighbour.

Finally, on Saturday, the squire's wife died. Everyone in the village was sad, for she represented a wealth of memories and with her death a whole era disappeared; the great and good era of the château, of wealth and display, and the pride which everyone felt in it. For the château was the jewel of the village, even if its inhabitants did not belong to the same world as everyone else in Saint-Libéral; the association honoured and benefited them all.

So they all thronged to the funeral of Madame Duroux, firstly out of politeness, then for friendship's sake, and finally out of respect. It was no secret that she and her daughter had lived in straitened circumstances, close to poverty, for several years. But they did not attempt to hide their indigence and nobody considered them to have fallen in rank; even when ruined, the lady of the manor inspired respect to her dying day.

'And what will her daughter do?' asked Mathilde, on the way home from the funeral.

'What do you expect her to do,' said Pierre-Edouard. 'She'll stay there, probably.'

'The American could at least have helped them!' said Mathilde, referring to the second daughter who had emigrated to the USA in 1918.

'It's a long way off, America,' he explained, pushing open the door. 'Look, the postman's been.' He noticed a letter which had been pushed under the door.

'Is it from Jacques?'

'No,' he said, turning over the envelope, 'it's from Berthe, and not a postcard, a letter! What a surprise, that must have taken some effort.'

'She's mad, I tell you!' groaned Pierre-Edouard, shaking the sheet of blue paper which he had just read, 'raving mad! No, but I ask you, at her age, it's almost embarrassing!'

'That remains to be seen,' said Mathilde, joining him on the settle. 'For twenty years I've listened to you saying she runs around too much, she needs a good hiding; today she announces that she's getting married and you make a fuss about that?'

'But bloody hell! You don't get married at forty-five! And especially not to a German!'

That was what was really making him angry. It was bad enough to have a sister whom you were not always proud to know, but a German brother-in-law! That was the limit, the end of the world!

'Anyway, I don't want to see them, either of them! She hasn't been here for over twenty years, she might as well keep up the record,' he decided. He read the letter again and shrugged his shoulders. 'And she wants Jacques and Paul to attend the wedding! No, I swear, she's cracked. Why are you laughing?'

'Well, you don't want me to cry, do you?' She pushed a few twigs into the fire. 'You sound so like your father when you talk like that, that I wonder whether it wouldn't be better to cry!'

'Don't exaggerate,' he grumbled. 'All I am saying is . . . Anyway, she doesn't need my permission, does she?'

'Fat chance she'd have! You'd refuse it!'

He filled his pipe, sat down again, and read the letter once more.

'Come on, admit it, she must be a bit crazy!' he repeated in a quieter tone. 'And then, this marrying business, why doesn't she do it straight away? You'll tell me there can't be any hurry, considering how old she is, but why wait till October, what's that all about?'

'She explains it all there; she has her winter collection to show in America. And then you can see, from what she says, that he has business to settle beforehand as well.'

'Well, why does she tell us so soon? Just to annoy us?'

'Listen,' she smiled at him, 'don't try to look more stupid than you really are, and stop questioning everything she does. You know perfectly well why she's written to you.'

'Well, I suppose so. Okay, she'd like to come and show us her chap, but I'd like to know why? Twenty years without showing her nose around here and all of a sudden, hey presto here I am, and with a Boche into the bargain! Can you fathom it?'

'Yes; she's happy and she wants everyone to share it.'

'Oh?'

'That must be the reason.'

'But what are we going to tell Father?' he asked, with a nod towards the bedroom.

'The truth, that's all.'

'And the children?'

'The same. After all, there's nothing to be ashamed of in getting married.'

'That depends on how old you are and who you marry . . .' he muttered again.

'Come on.' She got up and stroked her fingers through his hair. 'Don't play at being Grandpa Vialhe; I can cope with one, but two is beyond a joke. You'll write to your sister and tell her that we're all very happy to hear her news.'

'Happy! Happy! We'll see about that!'

'Yes we are. And then if they come, you'll be very nice to them, especially him.'

'It's easy to talk,' he said with a smile. 'What if he's one I missed in 1914! Mind you, he may have missed me too, so I suppose we're quits!'

'That's right,' she approved. 'Look, here's the paper. Come on, write to your sister, I know you're dying to really.'

As soon as it was possible to get back on to the land – that is to say, as soon as the March wind and sun had dried the soil – Pierre-Edouard attached his Canadian cultivator, urged on his oxen, and began to remedy the damage done by the winter.

He had bought this lightweight plough three years earlier, and did not regret having paid 435 francs for it. Thanks to this, with the nine triangular tines which smoothed over the furrow ridges, it was possible to resow without a complete reploughing. Nevertheless this extra working of the soil, plus the sowing, the harrowing, and of course all the other normal seasonal work, filled his days and those of all his farming neighbours. None of them paid much attention to the election of the new Pope. So it was Pius XII; good for Pius XII! As for the re-election of President Lebrun, it was scarcely mentioned in Saint-Libéral.

From March to July, Pierre-Edouard worked without a break to try to recoup the losses caused by the frost. As he could no longer count on any help from his father, nor afford to engage any seasonal workers, he threw himself into the fray with only Nicolas to support him. Whenever she could, Mathilde came to his aid. She was there to plant the potatoes and the beets, to thin out the tobacco seedlings, sow the maize and to hoe. But her own burden of work was so onerous that she could not help him as often as she would have wished.

She had been very disappointed to learn that Paul would not be returning to work on the farm, but she felt, like Pierre-

Edouard, that it would be pointless to force him. Besides, he was doing everything he could to make up for his rejection of the land. He was a good son, he gave his father practical help whenever he had the time. He was kind, respectful and hardworking, but he had no enthusiasm for the work of caring for the land.

Pierre-Edouard and Mathilde had no more illusions. The day would come, and soon, when Paul would politely apologise, perhaps even with some embarrassment at having to break the bonds which held him despite himself, and would ask: 'And now, may I go?' And since there was nothing they could do to persuade him to stay, they would watch him on his way and wish him good luck.

'But you'll see,' Pierre-Edouard had said to comfort Mathilde. 'I don't know what he'll do, but he'll make a success of it. And as for the farm, it'll be Guy who takes it on, that's how it'll be. We'll wait patiently until then, all right?'

'And what if he doesn't want it either?'

'Well, if he doesn't, that will be the end of the Vialhes,' he murmured, shocked at this unexpected realisation. 'Yes, the end of the Vialhes.'

Berthe had twice fixed a date to visit Saint-Libéral since she had informed them of her engagement, and twice cancelled it on the eve of her arrival. She pleaded pressure of work, business affairs in need of delicate negotiations, and other problems which her fiancé Helmut was having great difficulty in resolving. So Pierre-Edouard shrugged his shoulders when a card posted in New York arrived at the end of August and informed him that his sister would be passing through Saint-Libéral in the first week of October. Just before her wedding, which was to be on the tenth.

'You'll see, something else will get in the way,' he predicted, holding out the card to Mathilde.

'Jacques will have gone back by then,' she said. 'He'll be sorry, he was so looking forward to seeing her again.'

Pierre-Edouard and she had been amazed when they saw how happy Jacques and Paul were to hear that their aunt was engaged.

'And you'll see,' cried Paul, 'her fiancé is a great chap! Now we can tell you, she warned us about this two years ago!'

'It gets better and better!' grumbled Pierre-Edouard. 'So you both knew about it and I, her brother, don't have any right to hear first!'

'Well . . . She told us that you might not agree with what she's doing.'

'And she was right! Well, don't let's talk about that any more. But if she comes, and him too, it won't stop me asking this German what he thinks of the German-Soviet Pact. It's not a girl from the Corrèze he should be marrying, he needs a Cossack!'

'Come, come,' Mathilde soothed him, laughing, 'it's nothing to do with him!'

'Of course it is! Everybody is concerned in this treachery! That's what Tavet and his gang were trying to tell me the other night at Suzanne's! That little teacher doesn't look too happy at the moment; I can tell you, your brother gave him a piece of his mind, they almost came to blows!'

'I know, but I don't think it helps anyone to quarrel about that sort of thing!'

'Yes it does! They got us all in a stew about the Nazi peril, and now they're buddy-buddy with Hitler! Well, right now, the Russians and the Germans and all that lot, I've had them up to here! And I'm not changing my opinions just because my sister has gone and got herself one of them! Just the opposite! All this will lead to no good, you'll see, as I shall enjoy telling my sister's Boche to his face!'

The inhabitants of Saint-Libéral fell asleep one evening, deafened and dead tired amidst the dust raised by the mechanical thresher, which had been working its way around the farms of the village for a fortnight, and awoke to find themselves in the middle of a war.

On the morning of 1 September, they were catapulted from their beds by the announcement that German troops had entered Poland. Then, at 10.30 a.m., whilst many were still trying to play it down and reassure themselves, the second piece of news reached them. It was a direct hit and shocked everyone: general mobilisation.

'This time,' said Pierre-Edouard, 'this time I knew it would come, it couldn't end any other way, but what a mess! Right, we've got to beat them back again!'

'But this call-up doesn't affect you? You're not going to leave, are you?' Mathilde was suddenly worried.

'Me? No, I'm too old. Besides, with four kids and my wound . . .'

'And Jacques? He's not twenty yet!'

'Oh, him . . .' Pierre-Edouard turned to his son. They looked at each other, then exchanged a conspiratorial smile.

'I'm going to enlist,' said Jacques. 'It's the only thing I can do.'

'I absolutely agree,' said Pierre-Edouard.

'But . . . What about the college?' Mathilde protested feebly.

But she knew already that his decision was not rash, nor a thoughtless impulse following the recent events; it was considered and irreversible.

'College can wait. Anyway, the exemptions from call-up are bound to be cancelled, so sooner or later . . .'

'Of course,' she said, and turned away.

Two days later, when the village was empty of men and the threshing machine lay abandoned in Delpeyroux's yard, silent for lack of hands to get it working, came the dreaded news of the declaration of war.

Bewildered, overwhelmed, taken unawares, the villagers drifted in a haze of silence for several days. There were now so few men left that it seemed impossible to start anything without them; their support, their strength, their knowledge. But the work was there to be done, decisions had to be made.

They came from Léon, who as mayor was forced to act. He had experienced the call-up in 1914 and had admired — without ever admitting it — the role played by Jean-Edouard Vialhe at that time; so he, Pierre-Edouard and a few of the widows from the Great War were the first to shake themselves and banish the dangerous stupor which was paralysing the village and would have gradually stifled it. Without considering what old Jean-Edouard might say, Léon flung open the Vialhes' door on the evening of 6 September, at supper-time.

Finding the whole family seated at the table, he ignored the old man's mumbling and came straight to the point.

'We can't go on like this!'

'I was counting on you,' said Pierre-Edouard. 'Have you eaten?'

'No, no time.'

'Well, come on, sit down,' said Pierre-Edouard, pushing a plate to the end of the table. 'I thought you might come,' he repeated, when Léon was seated, 'so, what shall we do?'

'I've already counted all the farms without men; there are too bloody many!'

'I thought as much.'

'Now, you weren't here in August 1914, but your father's probably told you that he organised support teams, and that worked well; we'll have to do the same again. Just think, we haven't even finished threshing and at the end of the month we should start ploughing, not to mention the grapes! In my opinion the old men like us should get together and go from farm to farm to get through the heaviest work, and I'm damned if we won't manage to clear a bit of ground with the help of the women!'

'You can count on all of us,' said Pierre-Edouard. 'Jacques as well, he's here for some days yet. They're in such a muddle at Brive that they told him to go away and wait! With Nicolas and me that makes a few hands already; we'll get the urgent tasks done, starting with the threshing.'

'Excellent, and I'll tell Paul to join your team, because the markets, at the moment . . . So I can count on four men from here.'

'Not four, five!' cried old Jean-Edouard, 'I can work too!'

'Listen, Father . . . ' began Pierre-Edouard.

'Shut up, I told you I could work and I will work. What do you think, I'm not an invalid!'

'All right, you come with us, but I thought you'd be useful here to help Mathilde . . . '

'Mauricette will take my place,' the old man interrupted him. 'Where's the threshing machine at the moment?'

'Still at Delpeyroux's,' said Léon.

'Have you warned them that we'll be threshing there?' the old man interrogated him.

'No, not yet, we needed to get organised first,' explained Léon.

'Well, what are you playing at, eating our soup instead of going to see them? Good God, in 1914 I was often up for two whole days, that's how we made a success of it!'

Léon, annoyed, pushed away his plate and got up.

'I know,' he said, 'you, you always did better than everyone else, but I just do what I can! I know you gave up your time in 1914. I only gave up a hand!' he rapped out, banging his hook on the table.

'Sit down and eat,' Pierre-Edouard cut in, 'it's not 1914 now. Today you're the mayor, and it's up to you to decide how we do things, not to worry about what others may say. And we Vialhes are going to help you. Besides, you've already heard it,' he continued in an amused tone, 'even my father has said he'll lend a hand! Come on, finish your dinner and afterwards we'll go together and tell the rest that we'll have to join forces.'

One cool morning at the end of November, Mathilde was alone in the house when the postman called. Besides the newspaper he delivered two letters. The first was from Berthe, but it was addressed to Pierre-Edouard so she didn't open it. Happy to know that she would shortly have some explanation for her sister-in-law's silence – they had heard nothing from her since the beginning of August – she put the letter on the sideboard, and hurried to open the second envelope, which came from Jacques.

Overjoyed to have some news of her son, who had been in the army for more than a month, she rested on the settle and began to read it with a smile. And her contentment increased as she took in the words. Jacques was getting on well, was in rude health, not eating too badly and had made some good friends. She felt reassured and placed the letter beside Berthe's before continuing her work with a song; the war was a long way off and seemed to have gone off the boil. It hit her in the face, however, when Pierre-Edouard came in at midday, and turned pale as he held out Berthe's missive to her.

'Read it,' he said.

'No, tell me,' she gasped, disturbed by his sudden pallor.

'Her fiancé, her German, they've arrested him.'

'What? Who has?'

'Them – the Germans, those bloody Nazis!'

'But I thought he was a German too!'

'Yes, but apparently he didn't like the government. According to Berthe he hasn't lived in Germany for the last four years; he went back in August to settle some business, and they arrested him.'

'And what about Berthe?'

'She's in Switzerland, trying to find out where he is.'

'So they haven't managed to get married,' she murmured, 'poor Berthe. What can we do?'

'Nothing, nothing,' he raged. 'We were thinking it wasn't a real war, and now you can see we're right in the middle of it!'

Up till then, Pierre-Edouard and Mathilde had been little affected by the conflict. Jacques had gone, some horses had been requisitioned, and there were a few difficulties with supplies, but otherwise it was developing in a strange way, just festering quietly. Pierre-Edouard himself admitted that he didn't understand a situation which was nothing like what he'd known in 1914. Surely the war wasn't going to peter out for lack of fighting?

What was more, several soldiers had already returned to the village on leave, which really surprised the veterans. They were brief visits, naturally, perhaps without permission, but still they had the time to give their point of view, in particular to explain that they weren't fighting, had never seen the enemy, and were bored.

Then, reinforcing the idea that the conflict was not serious, it was rumoured everywhere that lots of the soldiers who had been called up were returning to their homes and taking up their old jobs, designated as being on 'special assignment'; it seemed that the arms factory in Tulle was welcoming back workers every day. Really, the general state of mind was not geared towards war.

Pierre-Edouard folded his sister's letter and contemplated the fire.

'She finishes by saying that as you believe in God, you should say your prayers; she knows the Germans, and this war will be dreadful.' He pushed a corner of a log towards the flames. 'Dreadful,' he repeated forcefully. 'I'd like someone to explain to me why we're still not bloody doing anything! It's three months since this damned war started!'

Chapter 16

PAUL had so often imagined exactly what he would do on the day of his eighteenth birthday that he was quite disconcerted when the date finally came round in April. All his plans and ideas, his enthusiasm, had been reduced to nothing by the war. He had pictured himself taking the train to Paris and embarking on new ventures; for the time being that was impossible. Paris at war held no attractions.

So instead of being able to realise his dream, he was forced to wait patiently. He was amazed to discover that this decision was no burden; it was almost a relief. One year earlier he could have left with few regrets, but today the situation had changed; there was such a need for men in the village, even though a few had been able to return briefly on farming leave, and Paul was aware that he had become a valued companion to his father and a comfort to his mother.

With Jacques gone he had naturally taken his place as the eldest, and nobody begrudged him it, especially not his brother, who had encouraged him in his letters not to leave the farm and above all not to anticipate his call-up, when Paul had enquired about this.

'I thought I would be of some use,' he had written. 'I wanted to fight, and the only battles I'm engaged in are gin rummy contests! Don't do what I did, one idiot in the family is enough.'

Jacques' bitterness and disappointment made a strong impression on him, so he abandoned the idea of going to enlist on his eighteenth birthday. Even without the disillusioned advice from his brother, he had understood from some of the soldiers on leave that this phoney war was not worth supporting, even with the modest gesture of voluntary enlistment as a private.

Everybody seemed to be indifferent, disheartened, even his father and Léon. They who had been so full of energy now drifted slowly into despondency; each day saw them more taciturn and bitter. Pierre-Edouard had already stopped listening to the wireless so as not to be disheartened by the communiqués and the pitiful babbling of the politicians. Only old Jean-Edouard was still an enthusiast, and persisted in searching the air-waves in the evenings. And Paul, in his bed in the corner of the room, fell asleep every evening to the sound of music.

The people of Saint-Libéral completed the spring work without any enthusiasm, locked in a disillusioned apathy; their hearts were not in it, nor their strength, too many men were away. So a great many plots of land, even whole fields, received none of that attention which transforms sad fallow lands into ploughed acres full of promise. Dock, henbane, blue thistle and other weeds multiplied in the abandoned patches, preparing the way for the bracken and broom which were always ready to spring up on bare ground. And all this land forgotten by man gradually returned to nature, to scrub, and added to the areas which had been inexorably engulfing Saint-Libéral since the last war – the Great War – choking it with a tight collar of brushwood.

Only the Vialhe property remained as it should be; Pierre-Edouard made sure that nothing affected the beauty and wealth of his farm, despite his disillusionment. With the help of Nicolas and Paul he plunged into the work to deaden his senses; it became his sole aim and occupation. Thanks to it he was dead tired each evening and fell asleep in a trice, as if felled by a knock-out blow, without having to struggle against the sombre thoughts which lurked in his subconscious and would have kept him awake half the night.

However, his refusal to reflect on the events which were shaking the whole country did not prevent the war from developing. In the space of a fortnight, when he thought he had already plumbed the depths of discouragement, the news from the front undermined his morale and brought him to his knees.

First of all there was the invasion of Belgium, Holland and Luxembourg and the pathetic convulsions of those unhappy countries, already beaten and in the throes of death. Then, on

18 May, Léon returned from Brive and informed them that the town had already suffered two air raid warnings and was collapsing beneath a ceaselessly growing flood of refugees from the east and north: children, women, old people, who could no longer find house-room anywhere and hunkered down in cinemas, even the theatre and the station.

And with the passing days came the certain knowledge that everything was collapsing, cracking up, crumbling beneath the formidable thrust of an enemy who seemed invincible, and so swift! There was worry too, for no letter had arrived from Jacques to reassure his family since the beginning of the month, and finally anger, at the impotence of governments and the vacillations of the military command. The only hope amidst this anguish came with the announcement that Marshal Pétain had accepted the Vice-Presidency of the Council of Ministers.

'At last!' sighed Pierre-Edouard when he learned this news. 'With him there things are bound to change; he'll be able to turn the tables on them, like he did in 1917. But why did they wait so long to call on him!'

'You know, he's not so young any more,' suggested Léon. 'Perhaps he would have preferred not to be bothered!'

'Probably. Never mind, he's there and that's good news. He's a soldier, not a politician!'

'If that's all that's needed, he's sure to get these spongers moving, but let's hope he hurries up! Oh, I think they've wasted too much time, messed around too long.'

'We can still halt them, it only takes the will. We did it before, didn't we? So what's to stop us doing it again?'

For seven months, Jacques had passively let himself be carried along by events. One week in the army was enough to teach him that there was no point in trying to understand any of the orders, counter-orders or wild decisions which governed his life as a soldier.

He had been dumbfounded right at the start by his posting, which bore no relation to his request. With his baccalauréat, he had opted for the Officers College of the Army Reserves and he had found himself a private in the 15th Regiment of Algerian Infantry in Périgueux. There he voiced his astonishment and made mild protests, and heard the reply of an old captain who was completely dessicated by the sun of the Atlas Mountains and also, probably mainly, by anisette:

'Certificates, we wipe our bums with those, they've never made good soldiers! And the *petits-bourgeois* who have them – here's where we lick them into shape!'

He remained silent, disconcerted by such a wealth of stupidity, all his illusions destroyed. Because he wanted to fight – and the rank hardly mattered to him – he completed the classes and stages to become corporal and sergeant without saying anything. He champed at the bit and got bored all winter whilst regretting that Périgueux was so far from the front; however lifeless that was, in his eyes it was the only place worthy of interest.

He was therefore happy to learn, at the beginning of April, that he was to be posted to the 22nd Border Regiment of Foreign Volunteers stationed in Dannemarie. He arrived in Alsace on 11 April and realised bitterly that, as at Périgueux, the only enemy to be killed was time. One month later torpor gave way to feverish activity, when the German breakthrough tore Jacques and his comrades from their siestas and gin rummy and hurled them into battle.

The 22nd Border Regiment returned to France in great haste, and disembarked in the middle of the night at Isle-Adam on the River Oise; they then squeezed into Paris buses which attempted, despite the incredible congestion on roads flooded with refugees, to clear a route in the direction of the Somme and the Weygand Line. Obstructed by the confusion and the accumulation of incongruous vehicles which jammed every tiny path, the convoy was forced to stop shortly after Pont-Sainte-Maxence.

So it was on foot and proceeding along the ditches – the roadway was too cluttered by the fleeing crowds – that Jacques and his comrades covered the seventy kilometres which separated them from the front.

Two days later, when he was in position in the woods close to Fonches, Jacques found the war. Suddenly. It bore no resemblance to what he thought he knew from his father's accounts. God knows, he had heard talk of the hideous rain of shells and the terror they inspired! But Jacques as a child had never imagined that fear could reach such a level; that it could be so paralysing, hellish, unbearable. And like his father before him under shelling, he wanted to be swallowed up by the earth, for it to open up and shelter him; but also like his father, he knew how to leap to it when the orders rang out, pushing the men forward, throwing them into attacks, withdrawals, counter-attacks and advances over a period of days as they moved towards the villages of Marchélepot, Saint-Christ and its bridge over the Somme, Villers-Carbonne, Briost.

They were equipped with single-loading guns, the old Hotchkiss rifle, and 25mm cannons, never enough of them – and they were instructed to be sparing with the shells – and before them appeared the huge rumbling armoured cars of von Kleist's 4th Panzer Division, the 15-ton KW3s with their 37 mm cannon and the MG34 with 7.92 mm guns. The light infantrymen following them, as jackals follow the lions, were lively and flexible: formidable enemies, for they were not encumbered with rucksacks, backpacks or other gear; they did not catch their feet in their puttees or the hem of their greatcoats; when faced with the strong but slow MAS36 handgun, they deployed the terrifyingly rapid fire of the automatic pistol, the MP40 . . .

Entrenched in the village and château of Misery on 1 June, surrounded on all sides, cut off from the world, out of breath, out of reinforcements, out of ammunition, the 22nd Border Regiment surrendered to the enemy after destroying their weapons, as recommended in the regulations.

Paul never forgot the pain and ensuing anger he felt when he saw how his father was consumed with shame and sorrow. To him, Pierre-Edouard had always represented strength, trust and honour. He was a model of energy and honesty, he was invulnerable; so Paul was wounded to the heart when he perceived that his father, once so admired for his reassuring aura of power, was sliding day by day into a lethargic and agonising melancholia.

Every bulletin, every communiqué, tortured him anew and left him pale, with clenched teeth and fists, deep in the depression which seemingly nothing could relieve. He no longer talked any more, but enclosed himself in a distant silence, only interrupted when it was time for the news by: 'The swine! The swine, they're selling us down the river!' And he no longer smiled, even when Mathilde placed her hand on his arm to calm him, with that familiar gesture which showed that she understood and sympathised.

Amidst this gloomy atmosphere old Jean-Edouard seemed quite serene, as if he had no worries for the future; he even went so far as to say that all this was not a bad lesson for those who had, for a quarter of a century, constantly demeaned themselves and defied morals and traditions. Pierre-Edouard looked at him so fiercely that he was quickly constrained into silence. His glare was so hard and ferocious that Paul felt encouraged and comforted when he noticed it; in these fleeting moments, he recognised the father he loved.

The rest of the time he hated the whole world, for its spinelessness had succeeded in transforming Pierre-Edouard into an old man full of shame and grief. For a long time this memory of his father's humiliation burned in him; the eyes, empty of hope, reflecting such a heart-breaking mental anguish.

It was two o'clock in the morning, on the night of 15 June, when the sound of an engine followed by the barking of the dogs dragged Pierre-Edouard from his slumber. The evening before, he had gone to bed, still devastated and demoralised by the announcement that the Germans had entered Paris. Now there was nothing that could be done, nothing further to hope for.

'There's someone coming, put on the light,' whispered Mathilde, who was now also awake.

'No, let's have a look first,' he said as he got up. He slipped on his trousers and shirt, slid over to the window and looked through one of the vents in the shutter. The moon was almost full, and lit up the courtyard.

'What's that thing?' he murmured as he made out a dark humped shape in front of the gateway; several people were grouped around it.

'Who is it?' asked Mathilde.

'I've no idea; refugees probably, their car's loaded up like a carrier's cart.'

'We'll have to go out.'

'Of course,' he said, but without leaving his look-out post. He frowned as he watched a woman enter the yard. 'My God!' he cried. 'It's Louise, put on the light!'

He pushed open the shutters and called to his sister. It was not until after he had opened the door to her that he saw she was carrying little Pierre asleep in her arms.

'Tell me what's happened!' he demanded a few moments later.

'What do you want me to tell you!' Her voice was exhausted. 'We left yesterday morning with them,' she explained, pointing to the four adults and three children whom Mathilde was hurrying to comfort. 'Everyone is leaving, you see, everyone! Oh, if you could only see the roads! It's crazy, crazy!' she repeated with a sigh. 'It's dreadful too, it took us a whole day to reach Limoges! It was a good thing I made them take to the lanes after that. But if you could see the main roads! And all the children crying . . . '

'I know, Léon was in Brive yesterday, it seems it's far worse than anything we've ever imagined. Just think, there are almost seventy thousand refugees in the town! And even here the inn is full! But these people,' he lowered his voice to ask her, 'who are they?'

'The steward of the château with his wife and children, and the cook and her husband. The steward was kind enough to bring us –he wants to go on to Spain and the cook wants to go to Toulouse, so as Saint-Libéral was on the way . . . '

'Yes. So everyone is running away, from what I can see! That lot will be able to move in, there'll be plenty of room for them!' he said bitterly. 'Aren't you hungry?' he asked after a moment's silence.

'Yes, but first I must put the child to bed,' she said, pointing to the baby whom she had lain on Paul's bed.

'Put him in there, Paul can spend the rest of the night in the hay. By the way, do you have any news of Félix?'

'No. And you, what about Jacques?'

'Nothing either . . . '

'And Berthe?'

'Not a word. You knew about her . . . her fiancé?'

'Yes, it's terrible.'

'Are you going to stay here?' asked old Jean-Edouard, coming nearer.

'Of course,' Pierre-Edouard cut in before she could reply, 'where else would she go?'

'Oh! I just wanted to know,' said the old man, 'because you could put the child in my room,' he pointed to Pierre. 'There's space and it's quiet . . . '

'We'll sort it out tomorrow,' decided Pierre-Edouard. 'For tonight he'll stay in Paul's bed, Louise will sleep in ours, and her friends can use the barn. I'll tell Nicolas to spread some straw.'

'I've done that,' said the old man. 'I sent him to see to it as soon as they arrived; we weren't going to leave them outside!'

Despite the hunger and thirst torturing him, and the over-whelming fatigue which made him want to stay lying in that meadow where they had been dumped like animals, Jacques got up once more and observed the little wood which lay about two hundred feet away, just beyond the field of wheat where the sentries paced.

For the two days that he had been marching – one wretched figure drowning in the sea of tramps – Jacques had been looking for a chance to escape, to flee from this apathetic flock of beaten men who were being pushed towards the north-east by a handful of guards.

Once already, on the previous day, as the column passed through the village of Nurlu a little after Péronne, he had dashed into a gutted house. He was spotted immediately, recaptured and beaten up; he had fallen into line again without for one second abandoning his plan to escape.

He took several steps and bent over a corporal who was stretched out on the clover.

'Got any tobacco left?' he asked, taking out his pipe.

'No, none at all,' replied the other, chewing a grass-haulm.

The young corporal observed him, and a ghost of a tired smile appeared. 'You,' he said, 'as far as I can see you're still trying to get out of this!'

'Dead right.'

'It's stupid, they'll catch you! Besides, I bet they won't keep us, they're too many of us!'

'Maybe, but I'm going to slip away anyway. Look, there's nothing to stop us, just a few sentries . . . Let's go together!'

'Nothing doing! I'd rather stay alive!'

Jacques shrugged and moved away to lie down and await nightfall.

He contained himself until eleven in the evening, and then crawled on his belly into the wheatfield. A quarter of an hour later he was in the wood. He took his direction from the stars, and marched due south.

It was as he tried to skirt round the little village of Avesnes-le-Sec that he ran into a German camp. A great burst of gunfire stopped him in his tracks, and was still ringing in his ears when a blow from a rifle butt knocked him out.

Under heavy guard, he rejoined his comrades in the early hours of the morning, and endured another beating before the convoy moved off in the direction of Valenciennes.

Conquering his despair he scribbled a brief note to his parents, and as they passed through Douchy-les-Mines, he took the opportunity to throw it towards an old woman sitting in front of her ruined house.

Louise's friends camped at the Vialhes' for two days; the driver's experience on their first journey made him fear the moment when he would again have to join the flood of vehicles fleeing southwards.

Huge groups of refugees now poured along the road through Saint-Libéral itself; they came from Limoges, from Châteauroux, from everywhere. They all had the wild eyes of hunted animals, and rushed to the wash-house fountain as soon as they saw it. Many also crowded into the mairie to beg for the shelter of a roof, be it only for one night. Léon, inundated with work, called for help from all the members of the town council.

To Pierre-Edouard and Maurice fell the job of feeding those who were hungry, and they were all hungry. So Pierre-Edouard found himself obliged to combat his depression, to fulfil his allotted task. That saved him. He got back on his feet, found new reserves of energy, and although the news – ever more disastrous – continued to torture him, at least he no longer greeted it with despondency and submission, but with anger and violence.

However, he succumbed to despair again when, on 17 June at 12.30 p.m., whilst the whole Vialhe family were sitting down for lunch, the trembling voice of the Marshal was heard on the wireless. Pierre-Edouard listened attentively and nodded vigorously at the end of the first sentence of the announcement, even murmured: 'Bravo, it's high time he took the reins!' Then gradually his expression changed, and suddenly his face crumpled.

Until that moment he had placed his trust, all his trust, in the old soldier, and if the Marshal had asked him to take up arms he would have resumed his place at the head of a battery of 75mm guns without hesitation. All the hope and faith which he had entrusted to this man as guardian and saviour collapsed in a few seconds.

Paul saw him turn pale, then his face tensed. He noticed the quickened breathing and trembling lips and was appalled to think he might see him cry. He did control himself eventually and his eyes stayed dry but, when he put down the spoon he had been gripping, Paul noticed that it was twisted like a single strand of wire. Then he rose, briskly turned the knob of the radio, and sat down again.

'Why did you turn it off?' asked old Jean-Edouard. 'We would have had the other news!'

'Not interesting!' he cut him short.

'I think,' his father continued, 'I think the Marshal couldn't have done anything else. Now the war will stop, and that's better for everyone.'

'Listen,' said Pierre-Edouard sharply, 'you're free to think and say what you like, but don't do it in front of me!' he shouted, banging his fist on the table.

'Well, but what's the matter with you?' protested the old man. 'I thought you were all for Marshal Pétain, like me!'

'Not so that he could surrender, the lump of shit!' He was yelling again. 'He's just sold us out, the old swine! And he dares talk of honour? My God! Even if he put a pistol to his head at the end of it, that speech wouldn't be honourable, the bastard!'

'Calm down,' begged Mathilde. 'As your father says, he

probably couldn't do anything else. I believe we should put our trust in him.'

'It was obvious,' interrupted Louise, 'if you'd seen the refugees, like I saw them . . . It had to stop! Besides, we couldn't hold out!'

'You shut up!' shouted Pierre-Edouard, getting up. 'If you'd seen war as I saw it, you wouldn't talk of defeat! War is for fighting, not for turning tail! And we've just turned tail!' he sneered, as he opened the door.

He slammed it brusquely behind him and set off towards the peaks.

He walked for two hours, and ranged over all his land but did not really see it, such was the anger burning in his heart.

Then he climbed the White Peak and sat down at the foot of a juniper bush, took out his pipe and lit it. Gradually he calmed down, even reasoned with himself, compelled himself to find some hope, recalled Pétain's speech and tried to detect a sentence, a word, from which he might draw fresh courage. It was no use.

It was with a heavy heart that he later knocked out his pipe on the heel of his clog and walked back down to the village. There he immediately noticed that others had reacted in the same way as him, were now just as despairing, miserable and distraught; faced with a fait accompli and forced to accept it.

'Now what?' asked Léon as soon as he saw him.

'Now nothing.'

'Are you thinking what I'm thinking?'

'What are you thinking?'

'That we've been betrayed.'

'Yes.'

'But I don't know,' murmured Léon, 'whether the old fellow could have done any different. Of course I feel sick at heart, but there it is, the Boche are in Paris, so . . . '

'We should have fought! *We* fought them, and you know a thing or two about it!'

'Yes, well, maybe it's only a trick. The old man's cunning, perhaps he has a plan . . . '

'Perhaps,' admitted Pierre-Edouard, 'but he's hiding it well. At the moment all I can see is that he's telling people to lay down their arms!'

'We'll have to wait,' said Léon, 'wait and see.'

'I think we've waited too long and now we *are* seeing, and it's not a pretty sight.'

'You should go home. Mathilde came by just now to see if you were here; seems you were bleating like a calf and bawled them all out! Oh, there's nothing wrong with that; I haven't anyone to bawl out, so I broke the radio with this,' he said, waving his hook. 'All of a sudden I felt so depressed listening to it, that I wanted it to stop, I turned the knob a bit too hard . . . And now, after thinking it over, I tell myself that maybe we don't understand it all; they can't tell us everything, can they?'

'It's possible,' Pierre-Edouard admitted, 'perhaps we don't understand it all. That's what we have to hang on to, it's the only thing that gives a bit of hope.'

During an exhausting journey which took him from Valenciennes to the southern part of East Prussia, Jacques never found another chance to give his guards the slip.

After twelve days of travelling across the whole breadth of Germany, he and his companions were unloaded in a terrible state at the station of the little village of Hohenstein, then herded under close escort towards Stalag 1B where thousands of prisoners were already milling about, where every evening they were supposed to fit five hundred men into huts designed for two hundred.

For a week Jacques endured the camp régime. Like everyone else – lest he die of hunger – he had to rise at four in the morning and queue, sometimes until two in the afternoon, to get that vital mess-tin full of soup.

Weakened, undernourished, sometimes beaten, he gradually lost all hope of escaping. Besides, where would he go? And how would he cover the two thousand kilometres which separated him from Saint-Libéral?

On the night of 29 June, Jacques and about a hundred of his colleagues were wakened by the shouts and blows of the guards and escorted to the station.

'Perhaps they're going to set us free?' suggested an optimist as the train set off.

'Don't count on it, we've got our backs towards France,' grumbled Jacques, after he had peered through the tiny slit in their cattle truck.

'And how do you know?'

'Blockhead! Look at the sun, we're heading straight for it. Have you ever seen it rising in the west?'

They arrived at Lützen during the morning and it was in lorries that they eventually reached the hamlet of Reichensee, where they were lined up in the main square.

'Labourers and peasants over here, students and office-workers over there!' bellowed the interpreter who was with several officers and NCOs.

Jacques did not hesitate for a second. He took the arm of his friend André, whom he had lost sight of at the time of the battles on the Somme and found again during their journey, and marched towards the group of manual workers.

'You're mad!' protested André. 'I'm a chartered accountant, I'll have you know!'

'Shut your face!' whispered Jacques, who guessed instinctively that the peasants' camp would be the lesser evil, perhaps influenced by the memory of the captain in Périgueux and his contempt for intellectuals.

Soon afterwards they were examined, and he felt the weight of suspicious looks directed at him by the soldiers and civilians who were there to choose the best recruits.

'You, not from land! Not earthy!' yelled the interpreter suddenly. 'Hands too white, not earthy! Nor him, him and him! Fat French toads!'

'That's a joke for a start,' said Jacques, 'it's ten months we've been hanging around doing nothing!'

'Not from land!' insisted the other man.

'Yes I am,' said Jacques. He suddenly spied an old peasant with his scythe on his shoulder, passively watching the scene as he walked towards them. 'Me, farmer,' Jacques addressed the interpreter again, 'look, watch this – bear's bum,' he added in a murmur as he held out his hand for the scythe.

The other man hesitated, then handed over his implement. Jacques passed his forefinger along the blade, made a face, drew the whetstone from the sheath hanging from the mower's belt and briskly sharpened the scythe. And his technique demonstrated such long practice that it was enough to convince the old peasant.

'*Schön, schön*!' he told the interpreter, 'good, good!'

'See, it wasn't a joke!' Jacques was triumphant.

'Well, he not from land!' decided the German, pointing to André.

'Yes he is!' protested Jacques. 'Look, he's going to mow that bed,' he suggested, pointing to a superb display of tulips.

The man looked at him in alarm, then shrugged and muttered, '*Ja*, you two from land!' and took no further interest in their fate. That same evening Jacques and André discovered the village of Kleinkrösten, situated on the other side of Lake Jagodner, where they joined old Karl's farm as agricultural labourers.

Despite his discouragement, and the additional work created by the presence of the refugees whom they had to take in, lodge and occasionally watch – some of them had an annoying tendency to pilfer the farmyard fowl, fruit and vegetables – Pierre-Edouard decided to begin cutting his hay. He was already more than a fortnight behind and now felt cross with himself: nervous exhaustion had paralysed him until then, reinforcing his deplorable inertia. He was ashamed of this weakness, and did not try to excuse it by saying that everybody in Saint-Libéral had sunk into the same depression; you could count on the fingers of one hand the men who had the courage, or the insensitivity, to throw themselves into the haymaking as if nothing had happened.

So on the morning of 20 June, helped by Paul, Nicolas, Mathilde and Louise – who assured him that it would rejuvenate her – he began to mow. It was high time: the grass was over-ripe and had a tendency to flatten, and in places the white clover was already growing mouldy.

In two weeks of unremitting work he made up the lost time and, helped by weariness, forgot a little of the shame and anger of 17 June. Nobody had talked about it again at home anyway, and the only conversations arising from the situation were concerned exclusively with the fate of the prisoners, and above all the date of their liberation. Although everyone was optimistic about this – it seemed unlikely that the Germans would want to be encumbered with two million captives – Mathilde and Louise were in a state of pitiful anxiety. Without news of either Jacques or Félix, they watched feverishly for the postman, then, when he sadly shook his head, they turned to each other for mutual support, trying to find a glimmer of hope in each other's arguments.

Once the haymaking was completed, Pierre-Edouard immediately began to harvest the grain. Then the news broke about the bombardment of Mers el-Kébir by the English fleet and the massacre, by these supposed allies, of 1,300 French sailors.

Pierre-Edouard, already completely disorientated by the political strategy being pursued since the defeat, now lost his balance; did not know where or to whom to turn, and ended up thinking that all things being equal, Marshal Pétain was the lesser of two evils; but he still did not forgive him. To him, Pétain would always be the architect of the surrender.

The note scribbled by Jacques took more than a month to arrive in Saint-Libéral. It was short and out of date, but still brought a little joy to the Vialhe household.

Comforted, but aware that her happiness was distressing to her sister-in-law, Mathilde hastened to reassure Louise that the message she awaited was probably already on its way, that patience was all that was needed. And the letter did arrive, on 27 July. It had been posted in Marseilles.

At first Louise could not understand at all and, convinced that her son was a prisoner too, wondered what right the English had to keep him there. For Félix was writing from London. It was only gradually that she came to understand. Trapped in Dunkirk, he had been lucky enough to get aboard a ship for England. 'And now,' he explained, 'I have the pleasure of being able to continue to fight, under the orders of General de Gaulle . . . '

'But what's all this about?' wailed Louise. 'And who is this general? And why the postmark from Marseilles?'

On reading the postscript, she understood: Félix had entrusted his message to a friend who was returning to France. Not knowing whether to laugh or cry, she hesitantly proffered the letter to Pierre-Edouard.

'Here, see if you understand it!'

He read it in his turn, and first frowned, then smiled.

'So this Legaule really exists! No, de Gaulle,' he corrected himself after checking what Félix had written. 'Damn Léon, he's always so well informed! Yes,' he explained, 'he mentioned something about this a week ago, but I didn't pay much attention to it because it seemed impossible. It seems de Gaulle said in an English broadcast that he wants to go on fighting.'

'But the war's over!' protested Louise.

'Obviously he doesn't think so! Really,' he added, feeling suddenly quite happy, 'I'm very glad that there's at least one general who's ready to stuff the Boche! That at least is good news!'

'But what's to become of Félix?' insisted Louise.

'How should I know! Anyway, he's not a prisoner, not him, that's one good thing. Come on, no need to worry any more; now you know where he is, that's the main thing, isn't it?'

'Well, of course,' she agreed, 'but in the end I'd still have preferred him to come back. We could have gone back home, instead of me getting in your way here and taking your bedroom!'

'But this is your home!' he protested.

'Maybe, but I'm a nuisance.'

'Not at all,' Mathilde intervened. 'In the first place you're helping us, and little Pierre is as good as gold! And what's more, Father is crazy about him!'

'That's right,' added Pierre-Edouard, 'don't worry, you can stay here just as long as you need to. After all, we can squash up a bit, can't we? There's a war on. That's what Félix seems to think anyway.'

Absorbed in his work, Pierre-Edouard had turned his back on the current events which so disheartened him, but Paul had heard talk of the appeal from London on 25 June. One of his friends in Perpezac had been lucky enough to receive the signal, and had explained to him what this mysterious general had said.

Paul had been immediately captivated by this opportunity for adventure. To leave, to reach London, and there to fight,

fight like a dog to wash away the shame which had almost made his father cry, and to forget the humiliation he had felt when he realised that he too was among the vanquished.

For a month, because he still doubted whether it was possible to continue the struggle, he kept himself informed and discreetly questioned those whom he thought might know of this momentous event. One evening he even managed to listen to the BBC, when his grandfather, feeling tired, had gone to his room much earlier than usual. He was overwhelmed. So it really was true! There were still Frenchmen who said that the war was not over; that it had only just begun, and must be continued by all those who refused to submit to the German jackboot.

He almost ran to tell his father, to get him out of bed and announce the good news to him, that very evening. But he thought better of it. His father was so bitter, so sad, that he was capable, quite unintentionally, of destroying all his arguments one by one, of banishing all his hopes and dampening his spirits. So, because he needed to pour out his feelings, to declare his enthusiasm, to hear himself say that he was right to want to go, he went to see Nicolas.

'And why are you telling me this?' asked Nicolas a little later. 'Me, I'm not French, not Italian, not German; my country is not at war. So . . . '

'But you fought for it, in your time, Papa told me that. And that's why you're here, after all!'

'That's true,' admitted Nicolas, 'I fought and I lost.' He took out his snuff-horn, poured himself a pinch, and ingested it in two sniffs. 'I lost,' he repeated, 'but I was still right to fight. One should always fight for one's country.'

'Ah, you see!' Paul exulted. 'So I have to go, don't I?'

'That's not for me to say.'

'And do you think Papa will understand if I go away?'

Nicolas shrugged.

'He's unhappy, very unhappy, he didn't even come to visit the hives with me, so . . . '

'Do you think I should tell him beforehand?'

'You're not going to make off like a thief in the night, are you? And your mother, what would she think?'

'That's true,' murmured Paul, suddenly aware of the

seriousness of the decision he was about to take. 'All right, I'll tell them.'

The letter from Félix arrived the next day, and Paul saw it as a sign from heaven. That same evening, when the three beautiful stars, Vega, Altaïr and Deneb, already glowed in a triangle in the summer sky, Paul was just finishing the harvest in the Perrier field with his father; he placed the thirteenth sheaf, the one that protects the stook, then turned to his father.

'I'm going to leave,' he announced.

'Ah, *bon*,' said Pierre-Edouard, who immediately thought he understood. He pulled a stalk of wheat from a sheaf, rubbed the husks off the ear in his hand, and quietly munched the grains one by one. 'It's true,' he continued, 'you've been eighteen for quite a time now, but I had thought with all these things happening . . . And what are you going to get up to in Paris now? It's quite likely that the Boche won't even let you go there!'

'I don't want to go to Paris, I want to go to London, with de Gaulle, like Félix!'

'Oh well, that's different,' murmured Pierre-Edouard, 'that's quite different.'

And despite the darkness, Paul saw that he was smiling.

'Well, can I go?' he persisted.

'I told you I wouldn't stop you,' his father reminded him. 'But how will you get there, it's a long way to England!'

'I don't know; I'll manage.'

'That's right, you must manage it, at all costs. You must succeed! Listen, I wouldn't ever say this to your mother, because she, she's sort of happy that your brother is a prisoner. To her he's safe now, do you see? She's content, that's natural. Mothers like all their young to be in safe places. But it makes me ashamed to think of him in their clutches – yes, I'm ashamed! A prisoner, a prisoner should escape, or at least try to. I'm afraid your brother doesn't know how to get himself out of it. So *you* must succeed, for the honour of the Vialhes! Then no one will be able to say that my sons were just pushed around, like so many silly sheep. Remember, we Vialhes have always been shepherds, for centuries, never sheep. With this war lost and your brother a prisoner, I was afraid I'd find myself in with the flock; now I feel better. Well, in some ways, because . . . You know, I'm still frightened about you going . . . Look, if you like, rather than plunging into the unknown, let's try to get some leads for you. You must win, Paul my boy, you must . . . '

Chapter 17

PIERRE-EDOUARD tentatively stretched out his hand and felt for Mathilde; his calloused fingers touched her shoulder as she lay close to him and then wandered up to her face and stroked her damp cheek.

He had been right: she was crying — silently, perhaps because of Louise tossing in her bed not two metres from them, or not to arouse the curiosity of Mauricette and Guy, who were probably not asleep either. It was seldom that Mathilde succumbed to her misery, but when it did happen it was always with great self-control, with a pathetic discretion which disarmed and demoralised him. And tonight she was crying, and he could neither do nor say anything to comfort her.

He had expected the announcement that Paul was leaving would upset her, that she would protest and try to prevent it; he guessed right as to her first reaction, but what came next surprised him. Mathilde simply said: 'That's right, that's what he should do,' but he knew she had done such violence to her feelings in uttering this short sentence, had so suppressed her true wishes, that he suffered for her. She, who already endured in silence and without complaint Jacques' absence, would now carry a double burden of uncertainty, anguish, and at times despair.

He slid towards her, pulled her to him, cuddled her on his shoulder and with his roughened hands stroked away the tears which rolled down for a long, long time.

'Your father's right,' said Léon, 'if you leave just like that, without doing your homework, you won't get very far!'

They were all three of them in the Dupeuch kitchen, and Pierre- Edouard was glad that his sister-in-law had disappeared when Léon simply said: 'It's something we have to sort out quietly . . . '

Now they had studied the map thoroughly, and always came back to the same point. Getting to the Spanish border was no problem, but crossing it illegally was another matter, and it would take a miracle to spirit him right across Spain to Portugal without getting caught, especially as the country had barely recovered from civil war.

'I've got an idea,' said Léon, 'but I can't tell you this evening whether it'll work. The best way is for me to go and see for myself, that's more reliable. At the moment I don't trust letters, let alone the telephone!'

'What's this idea of yours?' asked Pierre-Edouard.

'Quite simple,' said Léon, filling the glasses, 'I have a colleague who covers all the markets in the south-west. He sells Spanish horses as far north as Toulouse. He's a rogue — he has a whole team of pals on the other side of the border, and these blokes smuggle the horses across in great droves, at the gallop, miles from anywhere; so for the customs officers it's catch me if you can!' he said with a laugh. 'And he brings over some fine horses; I know, I've bought some from him . . . It's more than ten years since he started doing it. The war in Spain restricted him a bit, but now I've heard he's got his little business going again, which shows he knows the area and the Spaniards!'

'Well then,' Pierre-Edouard said with a smile, 'it's a comfort to me to know that you're not the only incorrigible swindler! And where does this smuggler of yours live?'

'Near Saint-Girons, but if I want to see him, I only have to go down to Auch. He usually works around that way, and I'm sure to find him there on a market day.'

'And you think he'll get Paul across?'

'Him, no; he's not crazy, it's not his way to cross the border on the quiet. But his Spanish friends will, certainly. Dammit, they've got to go back home when they've delivered a drove . . . So if you give them a little something, I'm sure they'll look after this young colt. How do you feel about that?' he asked Paul.

'Oh, that's great, but I'd rather not hang about too long; I'd really like to be off now!'

'But you could wait a couple of weeks, eh?' said Léon, toying with his empty glass.

'Yes of course,' said Pierre-Edouard, 'but how does he get to Portugal?'

'As for that, old chap, I've no idea,' Léon apologised. 'Mind you, once he's on the other side, if he gets on with the fellows who got him across, perhaps they'll help him. Because they go a long way into Spain to look for those horses, so if he sticks with them . . . But listen, my boy, if this is to work, tell them you're in the business too, and prove it to them. You'll see, they'll help you. People always moan about us dealers, but so long as it doesn't hurt us in any way – that's to say, so long as we don't lose money by it – we know how to help our own.'

Paul arrived in London four months later, in the middle of the Blitz, on 12 December 1940. When he left Saint-Libéral one morning in September, he had naïvely imagined that his journey to England would be over within a month, even by the longest estimate.

He had been quickly disillusioned by Léon's colleague, one Antoine Puylebec, who laughed to see him so disconcerted when he explained that his Spanish friends never organised their expeditions in the summer; the nights were too short and too light.

'But they don't go over in winter either, there's too much snow. So I expect you'll see them towards the middle of October, or a bit earlier if it begins to turn cold.'

Paul had to grin and bear it. He had worked with Puylebec, running round the farms and markets as he had done previously with his uncle. And it was on one of these tours, during an evening stop over at a little auberge in Payssous, that he chanced to catch the eye of a young woman from whom Puylebec had just bought thirty lambs; if he wanted it, a bed was waiting for him not two kilometres away.

The first night of manhood, in the arms of a woman of whom he knew nothing but her first name: Marguerite. A long-awaited, long-imagined discovery: joy. And then disappointment and even remorse in the morning, when she told him with a laugh, as he pulled him to her again, that it was the first time she had deceived her husband, who had been a prisoner since June, and she was not disappointed. Paul had cherished different ideas about marital fidelity.

Then, on 20 October, when it had been raining for two days and low cloud capped the Pyrenees, Puylebec announced that they would be leaving together that very evening. They drove part of the night and arrived at the foot of the mountain in the early hours, at the head of a bare valley which already had a wintry look about it. The horses were there; Paul counted about forty of them.

They were medium-sized animals, soundly built, with strong well-muscled backs and loins and prominent withers; their muddy grey coats merged cleverly into the rocks.

'I'd say Barbary horses crossed with a bit of Arab,' said Paul.

'You've a good eye, boy, that's right,' agreed Puylebec.

Léon had always taught his nephew that it's better not to ask too many questions about the provenance of an animal, but he risked it.

'Tell me, I thought people were dying of starvation in Spain. So why don't they keep their horses?'

'They've got no money left, they can't pay a decent price for them; that's why these fellows take the risk of crossing the border. Here we pay well, especially since the war,' explained Puylebec cynically, as he walked to meet the group of men who had just emerged from a mountain shelter.

'Right,' he said to Paul shortly afterwards, 'it's agreed; you'll go over with them tonight. They don't even want any money, I told them you're a colleague; you only have to help them carry their stuff.'

'Ah, *bon*? We're taking things back over?'

'You might as well . . . '

'But not horses, then?'

'Are you mad? With stockings, silk stockings and panties too, a whole heap of women's knick-knacks. Are you surprised? It's true they're dying of starvation over there and they've no money, but not all of them, my boy, not all! When nearly everyone is poor, there'll always be a few people making money out of it . . . So if the rich want their tarts to ponce around in silk with their boobs covered in lace, we'll have to give them what they want! The trouble is, with this war on we can't find enough fancy goods any more!'

'Of course,' said Paul, rather disgusted. 'Where are we

now?'

'On my land, in a corner of the Neste d'Aure. Right, I'm off now. Good luck, lad, I'll tell your uncle that you're a good fellow, you've got a good eye and know how to buy. He taught you your trade well, he'll be glad to know that.'

'Sure,' murmured Paul nervously, for with Puylebec's departure, his last link with France was severed.

They crossed the frontier the following night, not far from Pic Lia, by an incredible pass where only a goat could have followed them. In the morning, after an exhausting forced march, they reached the Cinca river, crossed it, and plunged into the forest, heading for Parzân.

In a month Paul traversed the six hundred-odd kilometres which separated him from Portugal, thanks to the help of three horse-rustlers who had to return to the Salamanca area. He very quickly realised that his guides were also terrified of falling into the hands of the civil guards. So they avoided the large towns, and never entered any unfamiliar villages.

They therefore passed around Taffala, Logroño and Lerma. They avoided Palencia and Zamora too, and pointed Paul in the direction of the River Douro, advising him to follow its course downstream but at a distance, then they slipped away to the south.

A week later Paul arrived at Mata de Lobos. From there he reached Porto, where he waited over a month before getting passage on a cargo boat flying the Turkish flag which was heading for Newport. Four times he had refused to take up a place on one of the ships returning to North Africa. Neither Tangier, Oran nor Algiers held any attractions. To him these towns were no more than dots on a map, and the Frenchmen who broadcast each evening to France were not calling from there. So why go and waste time in North Africa when it was all happening in England?

He learned – from a major, no less – when he disembarked in Newport that his persistence had probably saved him several months in some French colonial jail.

'And now, my boy,' smiled the Englishman, placing a hand on his shoulder, 'I'm arresting you, instead. Come on, little Frenchie, follow me. Your story's . . . very beautiful, but who's to say it's true? Britain's swarming with spies at the moment!'

It took the English police a full week to find a certain Félix Flaviens – apparently with de Gaulle – to whom Paul vigorously referred them. It was Félix himself who came to identify him, and finally got him out of his cell.

Since 24 October 1940 and Marshal Pétain's meeting with Hitler at Montoire, the population of Saint-Libéral had divided into several factions.

First of all there were those who idolised the Marshal. To them the old man was the reassuring incarnation of a long-awaited leader, the saviour who exalted work, honoured the family and defended the nation. And his every move – even his shaking hands with the Nazi Chancellor – his every word, was welcomed with a fervour bordering on fanaticism. Father Delclos had immediately taken the lead amongst these new found zealots and he made sure that they were led to the worship of God via their faith in the Marshal. His pious activism, far from dividing him from his flock, actually swelled their numbers; they were mainly women and old men to start with, but also former soldiers such as Delpeyroux or Duverger.

Confronting them were a minority, the little group of floating undecideds, the wait-and-sees, the almost convinced – after all, the Marshal had some good ideas – and the sceptics too. Delpy lined up with the latter, and sneered as he shrugged his shoulders:

'The priest would have us believe we're being led by a second Saint Philippe. He'll soon be telling us he's a virgin! Bloody hell, as far as I can see he's more like a damn good prostitute, that old man!'

Finally there were the Communists, like Brousse, Bouyssoux and Tavet, who were fierce opponents once they knew that the Vichy government was attacking them. As for Pierre-Edouard, Léon, Maurice and a few others, they remained silent. To them the Marshal was an enigma: good because he promised to work to free the prisoners-of-war, because he got rid of the dreadful Laval and preached the virtues of labouring on the land, but patently bad when he signed the armistice, shook Hitler's hand, and recommended collaborating with the enemy.

All these twists and turns, these contradictions, inclined Pierre-Edouard and Léon to think that he was playing a cunning double game, and this idea pleased them. All they knew was that the only true enemies were the Germans.

Without really believing in it, Pierre-Edouard listened to the English broadcasts every evening after Paul left. Paul had asked him to, assuring him that once in England he would get a message to him.

'All right,' Pierre-Edouard had said after a moment's thought. 'You mustn't on any account say our name, so all you have to say is: "My name is Paul from the Corrèze in Limousin; I'm well and I send my love to you all." We'll understand.'

Then Paul left, and the months passed. Mathilde, in agony following his departure, never stopped worrying for a single day; but there again she controlled herself, and succeeded in presenting a smiling face to little Guy, and to Mauricette whenever she came home from boarding-school. As for Pierre-Edouard, he was also gripped with anxiety, and each passing week reinforced his conviction that Paul had failed. He had learned from Léon how long he had had to wait before crossing into Spain, but now Christmas was approaching, and Paul had given no sign of life.

Everything else was going badly at the Vialhes'. First there was Father, who was losing all notion of time and place for longer periods, and more frequently too. He emerged from these attacks quite dazed, as if embarrassed, and resumed a state of complete lucidity for a while.

Pierre-Edouard had never understood how he knew that his grandson had left for London, but he did know, and was very proud of it – all the while criticising an action that ran contrary to what the Marshal said.

To add to Father and his wanderings, Berthe gave the Vialhes cause for worry. She had not written for more than a year, and Pierre-Edouard was beginning to believe that, like Paul, she had disappeared. To cap it all, neither Jacques nor Félix had made any further contact.

On 24 December 1940, Léon, Yvette and their son came to

pass the evening at the Vialhes', as they had done almost daily for several months. It was a long time now since Jean-Edouard had last muttered when he saw Léon; he had reconciled himself to seeing his old enemy seated at the table. Besides, for the sake of listening to the wireless he could put up with anything!

'It's time,' said Léon, looking at the big clock.

'Don't worry, I haven't forgotten,' Pierre-Edouard reassured him, turning on the set.

Silence fell, reverently: they leaned towards the receiver the better to hear the messages which filtered through dreadful interference. The messages were not yet incomprehensible, as they would later become, and at the moment they simply spoke of Jean, André or Edmond who sent his love to Thérèse, Raymonde or Charlotte.

'It's funny,' whispered Léon, 'you get better reception, you must be in a better position than us; I'll have to extend my aerial.'

'Sh!' old Jean-Edouard frowned.

' "This is Pierre, from Saint-Ouen. My love to Jeanine and my parents. *Vive la France!*" '

'They say the same as the Marshal, don't they?' suggested Guy.

'Shh . . . ' said his father.

' "My name is Paul, from the Corrèze in Limousin. I am well and so is my cousin Félix; we send our love." '

They remained frozen, not daring to believe what they had just heard.

' "I repeat," ' grated the voice: ' "My name is Paul, from the Corrèze in Limousin. I am well and so is my cousin Félix; we send our love." '

'That's it!' cried Pierre-Edouard, hugging Mathilde. 'That's it, dammit! He's done it, and he's even found Félix! Oh, the devil!'

They all hugged and kissed each other, and the men clapped each other on the back with shouts of laughter while the women wept for joy.

'Did you hear, Father?' called Pierre-Edouard. 'Paul's in London with Félix! Well, you've got some damn fine grandsons after all, that's the Vialhes for you!'

The old man nodded, and they all saw that he too was weeping with happiness.

'Bloody hell, we must drink to it!' ordered Léon. 'It's Christmas Eve anyway, the champagne's on me!'

'Yes,' said Mathilde, raising her voice to make herself heard, 'but we'll have a drink in a little while. First of all we're going to Midnight Mass, here, in the parish church.'

'Here?' Pierre-Edouard could not believe his ears. 'But we'd decided to go to Perpezac! You know very well that we've all fallen out with this priest!'

'Here,' she repeated, 'even if the priest is a . . .' She swallowed the word for the sake of the children, and continued: 'Even though the priest is not of the same opinion as us, even if it's donkey's years since he's seen us. For me it's the church where I was christened, where I took my first Communion, where we were married; *that's* where I want to thank the Good Lord, and not anywhere else. Even if it costs me something – especially if it cost me something we owe it to Him.'

'I agree, you're right,' said Pierre-Edouard. 'We'll all come with you. Well, those who want to, of course . . .'

'I'll come,' said Léon, who had not set foot in a church since his wedding. 'I'll come, to let everyone in the village know that we're happy tonight!'

'I'll come too,' said Nicolas, 'if you like.'

'You mustn't feel obliged to!' said Mathilde in embarrassment. He shook his white head and smiled.

'I don't mind, I was christened too and . . . and all that. And sometimes, madame . . .' He hesitated as his accent hindered him. 'Yes, madame is right, sometimes we should think to say thank you to Him!' he finished, pointing a finger skywards.

Shortly after midnight, they pushed their way through a crowded church to the chairs in the front row which were reserved for the Vialhe family at all times. They were empty, for the old chair-woman watched carefully to make sure that all the parishioners found their own places for the services, even if they only came once a year. It gave her added satisfaction to see that the truly faithful could work out who was missing at a glance, their empty chairs betraying them . . .

When he saw the Vialhes Father Delclos could hardly

believe his eyes, and was overjoyed to think that this family had finally seen the light. He secretly vowed to go and visit them as soon as he could, and made the mistake of keeping this promise. Two days later, after ten short minutes of political and theological discussion with old Jean-Edouard and Mathilde, he was firmly shown the door by the lady of the house.

'Really,' she reproached him, 'you're always interfering in things which don't concern you! But try to remember, here we don't ask Him to meddle in our private lives, nor do we mix God with politics!'

Paul swallowed his saliva with difficulty, contemplated the little hollow filled with sand which awaited him thirty metres below at the foot of the tower, and jumped. All very well for the instructor to explain that the FAM system was absolutely foolproof and that the big spring – to which his harness was attached by a cable – would break his fall; the ground was still a long way off . . .

He landed heavily, but still managed a very good roll, and got up feeling like cock of the walk.

'Good,' commented the instructor, 'but keep your legs together next time! My God! Think of a virgin and act like one!'

Paul nodded, unbuckled his harness and rejoined his comrades. He was happy, full of spirit and enthusiasm, despite the rigours of training; each day spent in the Ringway camp brought him fresh proof that he was made for this job.

Already he was experienced in hand-to-hand fighting, with guns, with explosives; he knew how to use a 303 Bren gun as well as a Thompson 45 or a Lewis machine-gun. Soon he would be making his first real jumps. First he would throw himself from a barrage balloon, which was fixed in the sky. Those who had experienced it assured him that this was more frightening and dizzying than jumping from aeroplanes; firstly because of the slow ascent in the balloon, and then because you had to launch yourself through a narrow hatch which opened in the middle of the gondola; there was the added danger of slicing off half your face if you were not careful.

Then, one day soon, he would finally clamber into the old Wittley, hook his static-line to the attachment bar and then watch the hangars and the landing-strip grow smaller below him. Once they were high in the sky, at the cry of 'Go!' from the dispatcher, he would plunge towards the ground. After six jumps during the daytime and one at night he would have his certificate in his pocket, and could go proudly on to test the value of his red beret amongst the little English girls of Manchester.

After he had finished getting in a supply of wood for the following winter, there were still two good months until the spring hoeing should begin, so Pierre-Edouard decided to give Mathilde a treat. She really needed it, for after the happiness of Christmas Eve had come the sadness of days, then weeks and months, with no letter from Paul.

Only Jacques had finally managed to send news, short but good. He was working on a farm, seemed to like it, and was eating well. Despite that, since she had his address, his mother made up a huge parcel of food and sent it to him every month. Pierre-Edouard was almost certain that none of these arrived at their destination but let her do it; it gave Mathilde such pleasure, and he guessed that she was pining for her sons.

So, because he had promised her several years earlier, and since he had put by a good supply of poplar laths and some solid chestnut rafters, seasoned for five years, and could buy slates at an unbeatable price – he went to find and select them himself in the quarries at Allassac – he undertook to redo the whole roof of the house at Coste-Roche.

The biggest problem was to find the nails for the slates, because in this time of shortages copper nails were almost unobtainable. It was Léon who tracked down several kilos of them at an old ironmonger's in Terrasson, who demanded an exorbitant price and in addition four hens, six dozen eggs and a bottle of brandy. Pierre-Edouard gave him what he wanted and set to on the rotten roof.

He had to take the whole thing down and renew the rafters. But thanks to Nicolas, who was really capable of doing anything, and seemed to know the tricks of every trade, it was almost child's play. When the roof timbers were raised, the tie-beams, braces, struts and ridge-pole firmly jointed, they tacked on the laths and, row by row, nailed on the slates in perfect alignment.

'There it is,' he said, when all was complete and Mathilde came to admire his work towards the middle of April. 'That was worth waiting for, wasn't it?'

'It's magnificent!' enthused the delighted Mathilde. 'When I think that you wanted to employ a roofer! You've done it just as well and more cheaply! Our house is beautiful!'

'Very beautiful, and even if it's no use to anyone at least it isn't being rained into.'

'It will be used,' she assured him. 'It will be used, one day, by . . . by one of the children, or perhaps by us, who knows?'

A week later, during the midday meal, a car stopped outside the Vialhes'. Immediately, even before Pierre-Edouard had time to look out of the window, someone pushed open the door and a woman came in. She held the hand of a boy of about ten, who smiled as the dog came to sniff at his legs.

For a few seconds Pierre-Edouard remained silent, examining the new arrival; noting her refinement, her make-up, her light-blonde hair, but also and above all, her family resemblance, which he still recognised after twenty years.

'It's you, Berthe,' he said at last, and it was not a question.

Louise also rose, ran to her sister and embraced her.

'You're here at last!' murmured old Jean-Edouard after staring at her for a few seconds, but he did not leave his chair and waited for his daughter to approach him. 'Is this your son?' he asked, pointing to the child.

'No; I'll explain,' she said, leaning over him.

He hugged her.

'You took your time,' he reproached her. 'Oh, I was always expecting you to come, but I didn't bank on it . . . '

'I would have liked to,' she said, 'and Pierre-Edouard knows that, but . . . ' Her voice broke. Then she straightened up and cleared her throat: 'But I couldn't, that's all there is to it!' she said briskly.

'Maybe you're hungry? And the boy too,' asked Mathide.

'What's your name?' she bent to ask the child.

'He doesn't speak French, not yet,' said Berthe, stroking his cheek. 'Well, you see,' she explained with an apologetic smile, 'he's a German . . . '

Mathilde started slightly, looked at Pierre-Edouard, and smiled back.

'Well, first and foremost,' she said, 'he's a little boy, and if he's hungry he must eat.'

That evening, when the children and Jean-Edouard had gone to bed and Nicolas returned to the barn, Berthe talked, explained, told them everything. And often she stopped, as if to gather her strength, to control her suffering and to preserve at all costs her neutral tone; she sounded almost detached, as if what she was saying did not concern her. It was, however, horrifying.

First there was Helmut, the man she was supposed to marry, the German who, after his divorce in 1933, had fled a regime which he knew to be appalling. But he had not fled far enough, nor cut the ties to his country sufficiently, for he had kept two couture houses, although only by appointing managers.

'And that's how we got to know each other,' explained Berthe, 'that was in '34. And during the summer of '39, when the bad smell over there had begun to grow stronger, he wanted to go back to see to the sale of his businesses. That's when they arrested him . . . He wanted us to go and set up in America after we were married. Yes, he knew this war was going to be terrible . . . '

She fell silent and took out her cigarette-case.

'And now what?' asked Pierre-Edouard.

'He's dead, I heard two weeks ago . . . ' she said, lighting a cigarette.

And her brother was filled with compassion for he saw that her hands were shaking.

'Are you sure?' he persisted.

'Yes; I found out from his sister, who still lives over there. I was writing to him every week. They put him in a camp, I don't know where, but not far from Munich it seems, and he's dead. His sister even received his ashes in a little wooden box, an old cigar box.'

'I see . . . ' murmured Pierre-Edouard, 'but why were you in Switzerland?'

'Because of the boy, Gérard; he was at a boarding-school in Zurich since his father's divorce. Helmut asked me to look after him if anything happened to him, he had custody of him. So, now I know there's nothing else I can do, rather than leave the kid all alone over there, I thought he'd be better off here, in a family.'

'You're right,' he said. 'It was the right thing to do, and we'll manage, but . . . ' He hesitated.

'Yes?' continued Berthe.

'We'd better not say he's a German; the people in the village wouldn't understand, and we don't need to explain the whole thing to them, do we? It's none of their business. We'll say he's a little orphan from Alsace whom you picked up during the evacuation. That way no one will bother us with stupid questions. And then he'll have to learn French, that's the most important thing. That way it'll be easier for everyone.'

'There's another thing,' said Berthe. 'As soon as he's settled in, I'll have to leave you, because I can't spend my life here, I've got things to do in Paris.'

'You want to go back up there?' protested Pierre-Edouard.

'Yes; even during the war women like to dress up — well, some of them do. I know, my assistant has written to me that the business is running along very nicely, but I must still go back. Of course if the boy is an embarrassment to you, I'll take him with me.'

'No, we'll look after him,' said Mathilde.

'If you like,' intervened Louise, who had remained silent until then, 'I'll take care of him. I thought I could move into Coste-Roche with little Pierre, we'd be nice and quiet up there. I'd love to have Gérard, he'd be company for me. And then it would give you a bit more room.'

'I've already told you that you're not in the way!' protested her brother.

'I know,' she said, 'but all the same, with Berthe and the child, we'll be eight of us for two bedrooms, and nine when Mauricette comes back in the holidays!'

'Fine,' continued Pierre-Edouard after a moment's reflection. 'I hadn't thought of that, but it's a good idea; we'll do that. And we'll get the kitchen garden sorted out at Coste-Roche straight away, then you'll have some vegetables handy. But there's still a problem! There's not a stick of furniture up there!'

'If that's all it is, I'll take care of that,' said Berthe, 'I'll buy everything that's needed.'

A week later Louise, her grandson, Berthe and Gérard were able to move into Coste-Roche, where they lacked for nothing, except electricity.

Berthe allowed herself three weeks' rest, then she returned to Paris by train. She knew that petrol was almost impossible to find in the occupied zone, and anyway her car would probably be requisitioned if she made the mistake of attracting attention to it. She therefore stored her little white Peugeot at the back of the barn, where Pierre-Edouard and Nicolas placed it on blocks, spread a tarpaulin over it and covered that with straw.

'I'll come back as soon as I can,' said Berthe to her brother, before boarding the bus which would take her to the station at la Rivière de Mansac.

'Whenever you like, you know the way.'

'I entrust the boy to you.'

'Don't worry about him. You've seen how it is already, he and Guy make a fine pair!'

'Well, see you soon.' She kissed him, and then hesitated a moment. 'By the way,' she said, lowering her voice, 'I've been here a month and I've seen that you don't really know which way to go. On the one hand you listen to the English radio and you encouraged Paul to leave for London, and yet you think that the Marshal will manage to get us out of this, is that right?'

'And so what?' he asked, rather aggressively, for he felt he didn't need any advice.

'Well, the two don't go together. You'll have to take sides one day; I'm sure you'll choose the right one!'

'That may not be the one you're thinking of !' he said drily, irritated to hear her raising a subject which he thought was of no concern to women.

'Don't get annoyed,' she said, smiling. She climbed into the bus which had just arrived, then turned round: 'Forget what I just said; now I know that you've already chosen!'

PART FIVE

The Silence of Screams

Chapter 18

MAURICETTE was just as brilliant a pupil as her elder brother had been, and easily passed her baccalauréat in June 1942. Her success was the only event which gave the Vialhes a little happiness.

For more than a year, depression and sadness had prevailed in their household as everywhere else. Pierre-Edouard and Mathilde had tried in vain to encourage each other, for the absence of any news from Paul was torturing them, as Louise was tortured by Félix's silence. And the letters which Jacques sent, although they gave a little comfort, also proved to them that their son was not about to return, despite the promises of the Vichy government.

Added to these trials was the now certain knowledge that this war would be long and pitiless. It was now world-wide, and if it was slightly reassuring to know from the English radio that the Germans were running out of steam in Russia, it was not encouraging to learn from Radio-Paris that the Americans were making pathetically little progress in the Pacific.

But all this news, which was more or less partisan and biased according to which camp you listened to, affected Pierre-Edouard and Mathilde less than what Berthe told them on each of her visits.

She came roughly quarterly, spending a week or ten days in Saint-Libéral and then disappearing for three months. And what she related of life in the occupied zone did not restore their confidence. She spoke of the hunger and poverty raging in the capital, and of the occupying forces becoming daily more oppressive and demanding.

'Here, it's paradise! You eat your fill, the rationing doesn't affect you, but in Paris . . . '

It was true, Pierre-Edouard freely admitted it. They did not know what hunger was. They had bread, chickens, eggs and when they needed it – while they were waiting for the piglets to fatten, for example – Pierre-Edouard would sacrifice a lamb or two. Besides, when it came to meat, Léon had connections, and he made sure that his brother-in-law benefited from them. In return Pierre-Edouard supplied him with excellent honey – which conveniently replaced the rationed sugar – and with tobacco, which had also become scarce.

In 1941 Pierre-Edouard had begun to cultivate tobacco for himself. It was against the law, but he didn't care. Anyway, who would know that the little field of maize behind Coste-Roche concealed, in its centre, some luxuriant tobacco plants; they weren't visible until you were right on top of them, and nobody except the Vialhes ever went up there!

'And you're making money as never before as well!' continued Berthe.

That was true too, and Pierre-Edouard was not ashamed of it. It was not his fault if everything was selling, and selling well! Some people in the village had an annoying tendency to take advantage of the situation, and demand exorbitant prices for produce which would have been used to feed pigs before the war. Pierre-Edouard was not among them. It was one thing to cultivate illicit tobacco, to slaughter stock illegally, or even to poach shamelessly on the plateau and the hills in collusion with Léon, who loved that sort of outing – since hunting had been forbidden, game was abundant – but to exploit the hunger of townspeople by raising prices, that was a step he would never take; he had always been honest and intended to remain so.

The surprising fact was that Léon also disdainfully refused to do business in this way, and Pierre-Edouard resolved to ask him one day if he did so on moral grounds or quite simply because it was much too easy to cheat like that. Almost too crude, and certainly not exciting enough, for a man who had spent forty years in his profession earning a reputation as the most formidable stock-dealer ever, to lower himself to the sort of sharp practice which any idiot could commit by coining it in with a little bunch of carrots!

'No,' insisted Berthe, 'you eat well, you're making money, you've no right to complain!'

'We're not complaining about all that, but about the boys who've gone away and show no sign of coming back!' retorted Pierre-Edouard. 'And anyway, you look as if you're getting enough grub!'

'That's true. What can I do, the Germans like their women to wear beautiful dresses, so . . . '

'And so you sell them to those bastards!'

'Wouldn't you sell them your calves if they wanted to buy them?'

'First of all I'd have to have some available when they came, and I don't think that's likely to happen . . . All right, let's talk about something else.'

All these conversations ended with him in a fury. He had difficulty in understanding how his sister could reconcile her business sense with her hatred of the enemy. Because she did hate them; it was obvious. She also made use of them, for it was through them that she so easily obtained her permits to enter the free zone, whence she set off on each journey back loaded like a mule with all the provisions given to her by Mathilde.

'Basically, she's conning them all the same,' Mathilde told him in an attempt to pacify him, for she knew that he considered her attitude dubious.

'Maybe, but I wouldn't like to do that and I don't like her doing it!'

'I don't expect she's got any choice.'

'I hope not! That's all it needs, if she's doing it without being forced to! Because that's what you call collaboration, and it's not a word I like to hear around here! Yes, you're right, all things considered; every time she leaves again with her kilos of meat and butter, her dozens of eggs and her honey, when it's forbidden, then she's making fools of them!'

The visit of the Head of State to the Corrèze presented Léon with a very delicate problem. The orders from the préfecture were definite; the mayors of all the communities had a duty to recruit the largest possible number of supporters and conduct them to Brive – they would be collected by buses supplied for the occasion – to cheer the august personage.

It was energetically recommended that veterans should

display all their medals and bring out their flags, that women and children should equip themselves with flowers and baskets full of rose-petals, which should be scattered over the official procession at the appropriate moment.

Everyone should be in position on the afternoon of 8 July to welcome the Marshal as he deserved. Coming from Tulle, he would arrive at Brive station by the 18.07 train, and the entire population of the *cité Galliarde* and its hinterland should prove to him that it deserved its name of Happy Gateway to the Midi!

Fifteen months earlier, Léon would doubtless have complied with the directives from the préfecture and, whilst considering this sort of demonstration rather childish, taken his place at the head of his people and led them to Brive. But too many things had happened since June 1940.

Now Léon no longer believed that Pétain would be their deliverer, for every concession he made to the Nazis just proved that he was incapable of resisting them. His behaviour was not a façade for a game of clever double-dealing, but the pitiful, grotesque indolence of an old man whom fate had passed by and who was, above all, extremely badly advised by his entourage.

Léon had therefore no wish to go and cheer for a man in whom he no longer had faith. He still respected him, because of Verdun, but not to the point of running to applaud him. What annoyed him was not so much the Marshal, as all the hangers-on who crowded around him. Those were the ones who were really responsible for the situation, and it was obviously in their interests that the head of state should be hailed as the Messiah; the enthusiasm he aroused gave them a free hand to act in his name.

As he knew that Pierre-Edouard shared his feelings, he sought advice from him. It was obviously impossible to hide the Marshal's impending visit from the villagers. Everyone had been forewarned; the newspapers talked of it ad nauseam. Already Father Delclos was making the children in his catechism class practise a song he had composed, with five rhymed couplets to the tune of 'Chez nous soyez Reine':

'Le Maréchal sauve la France
Il fut vainqueur à Verdun
Il guérira nos souffrances
Nous sommes en de bonnes mains . . . '

'And you'll see,' prophesied Pierre-Edouard, 'there'll be plenty of people there, Mathilde even wants to take the children. Mind you, that's to be expected; it isn't every day they'll see a Marshal!'

'Yvette wants to go too, with the boy; she's right. But I don't want to set foot anywhere near it, because it's all just a load of rubbish!'

'You only have to be ill that day,' suggested Pierre-Edouard.

'I've never been ill in my life!'

'Then now's exactly the time!'

'That's right,' smiled Léon, 'and I'll arrange for my place to be taken by the first deputy, that's you . . . '

'There's no chance of that; I can't possibly leave the house, on account of my father. He's been completely off his trolley for the last two weeks.'

Old Jean-Edouard's mind really was wandering, recalling snippets of memories from here and there and trotting them out repetitively.

'That's true,' admitted Léon, 'it's a good excuse. All right, so it's Maurice who'll replace me.'

'Don't count on it, he's at a wedding that day, at la Bachellerie.'

'You're all leaving me in the lurch, eh!'

'No, no, Delpeyroux will be delighted to take your place, he's already polishing his medals! So if you make him your representative as well, he'll probably burst with pride!'

'He's just the man!' Léon gloated. 'I'll get everything ready, and then at the last minute I'll cry off.'

That was what he did and nobody, not even the priest, suspected him for a moment of antipétainism. When 8 July came, he waited for the special bus to arrive and then called Delpeyroux.

'Right, you'll have to take my place.'

'Aren't you coming?'

'Uh, no . . . '

'But why not?'

'I'm ill,' said Léon, sliding his right hand into his waistcoat pocket. 'A twinge there, near the heart.'

'Oh, all right,' said Delpeyroux, perplexed but delighted. 'Okay, I'll be in charge.'

'That's right,' said Léon, lighting a cigarette, 'you take charge; with you there our people will be well represented!'

He watched the gas-powered bus depart, returned home, called his two workers and set off to the fields to reap.

Pierre-Edouard and he learned from their wives that it had been an imposing spectacle: Brive was beautiful with be-ribboned triumphal arches and had given the Marshal a magnificent welcome. They even recounted how one woman, one of those who had been able to get a place in the station, had thrown herself in a craze of rejoicing on to the track at platform number three, to kiss the rails over which the train carrying the Marshal had just passed.

The circular from the préfecture, announcing an agricultural survey which would require personal declarations, arrived on 29 September 1942 at the mairie in Saint-Libéral and aroused a general outcry amongst the farmers; even the most fervent supporters of the Marshal grumbled. Father Delclos tried to convince them that civic duty demanded they comply with the Marshal's orders – which were after all always for the common good – to no avail.

This survey was a bitter blow; it was an intolerable intrusion into people's private lives, an attack on their freedom and rights of ownership. Furthermore, it stank of an inquisition and boded ill.

Nobody was fooled. If every farmer had to declare, almost to the square metre, the size of his farm and the use he made of his land, to declare also the exact number of all his animals, including hens, ducks and rabbits, it was either to increase the taxes or to prepare for requisitioning; the rise in one did not in any way prevent the implementation of the other!

'I'm not going to declare anything!' cried Martin Tavet that same evening during the council meeting.

'Just as you please,' said Léon, holding out the circular to him, 'but it's compulsory, according to the law of 20 February 1942. If you refuse they'll stick you with a fine of 800 to 10,000 francs, it's written here . . .'

'All right, then mine will be false!' warned Tavet.

'Idiot,' Pierre-Edouard whispered to him so as not to be heard by Delpeyroux, 'there's no need to say it out loud, when everyone's going to be doing it quietly.'

'Oh, I see,' said Tavet. 'So it's like that; okay.'

'Yes, but watch out,' warned Léon after the meeting, when Delpeyroux had left, 'we'll have to play it very carefully. Those fellows in the préfecture may come and check up, so I want declarations that look truer than the truth! And keep a good note of the numbers you put down, because next year it'll all start up again, I bet. No fooling around, eh? If you write down two hectares of fallow or scrubland out of ten, then make sure beforehand that you've got at least one hectare classed as grade five land on the register! Those bastards from the préfecture aren't idiots, after all; they'll compare the two, they've got nothing else to do! And the same with the stock; if you have four hectares of pasture, don't say that you've only got one cow and two goats, they won't believe you. I'm telling you, they'll be watching!'

The announcement of the American landings in Algeria made some people smile whilst others were deeply shocked; immediately afterwards came the cruel news of the invasion of the southern zone. It was a hard blow for all those who, since June 1940, had grown accustomed to living on the good side of a divided France; who had known of the war only by its shortages and by the prisoners taken. Now they would be under the same flag as those who had been subject to the occupying forces since the armistice.

'And those bastards did it today!' said Léon bitterly, on the evening of 11 November 1942.

'Of course,' murmured Pierre-Edouard, 'it's to try to live down the hammering they got in '18!'

'Well, I'm the mayor – am I going to be under their orders? Bloody hell, I resign!'

'No, no,' Pierre-Edouard calmed him, 'we've already been under their orders for two years, only we pretended not to see it. And if you resign, they'll do the same as they did in 1940 in the villages with over 2000 inhabitants; the prefect will appoint a mayor, and you can be sure he'll foist that ass Delpeyroux on us! By the way, is it true that the imbecile has signed up in the Vichy militia?'

'Yes, just this week,' replied Léon. 'It seems he's the area commander.'

'Better be even more careful what we say, now, because he'll have his eye on us.'

'It's not him who worries me,' said Léon with a shrug, 'he's not a bad fellow — but the Boche, that's a different matter! Do you think they're going to come this far?'

'Why not, it's all their country, now.'

Vigorously encouraged by his father the Delpeyroux boy was the first to leave for the Compulsory Work Service. The unanimous opinion was that the father was a good deal more enthusiastic than the son when he accompanied him to Brive in December 1942.

Two other young people from the village copied young Delpeyroux, but there were many more who, from the spring of 1943, began to disappear and lose themselves in the countryside. A rumour ran around Saint-Libéral that they had sought refuge in the woods near Cublac or even further away, fifty kilometres from there, towards Noailhac, Meyssac or Lagleygeole; in short, they had gone underground.

Father Delclos did not hesitate to label them deserters, and recommended that parents of boys who were of an age to go and work in Germany do everything to ensure that their offspring remained deaf to the call of the forest. He was wasting his time. In the course of a few months the community lost all its young people and the village, which had already been weakened since the men were in prison camps, fell into lethargy.

That year the thickets and scrubwood strengthened their encirclement, overwhelmed all the isolated plots which were difficult to reach or maintain, and clung to the previously well-kept slopes in green patches of cancerous growth.

Pierre-Edouard and Nicolas tried to struggle against nature, but from the beginning of the year they also had to battle against requisition orders.

In 1943 Pierre-Edouard was ordered to provide one cow, minimum live weight 440 kilos, five calves of at least 85 kilos, six lambs at 18 kilos, 275 kilos of potatoes, 125 kilos of wheat, 165 kilos of buckwheat, 120 kilos of rye and 23 kilos of dried beans, not forgetting 325 kilos of hay, 8 cubic metres of firewood and 224 eggs.

Of course they were offered compensation for these deliveries, but it was ridiculous, very much lower than the prices in the discreetly operated unofficial market everyone used. So for example, in April 1943 Mathilde was selling her eggs, without cheating anyone, at 33 francs a dozen. They were traded at 70 francs or more on the black market and, Berthe assured them in one of her letters, were worth 110 francs in Paris! But the Board of Supply set them at 21 francs for sixty, next to nothing. And all the official tariffs were in keeping with this, for they were based on 1939 prices!

So Pierre-Edouard did all he could to reduce these ruinous compulsory levies, arguing now that a calf and three lambs had died of diarrhoea, then that frost or drought had spoilt the crops, or again that his war-wound prevented him from cutting firewood.

In spite of this he did have to concede a few bits and pieces, if only to avoid the fines which threatened those who resisted, and which could reach twenty times the value of the undelivered goods – the price of a fine cow, for instance, if 224 eggs were not supplied! But it was with a heart full of rage that he did it. Luckily, thanks to Léon's co-operation, he did not have to draw on his cattle herd, and his Limousin cows escaped the massacre.

'It's easy,' Léon told him when the first requisition appeared, 'they're demanding a cow from you? Fine, I'll let you have one, at cost price, you pass it on to them, and I bet you'll profit by it!'

'But you won't get me to believe you paid the official

price for that animal!' Pierre-Edouard was worried. 'So you'll be wasting money! They'll pay me less than you bought it for!'

'Don't talk stupid; the day's yet to come when I lose money on a cow,' Léon reassured him with a smile. 'You don't understand the system?'

'No.'

'You wouldn't have made your fortune in this job! It's quite simple. I buy the animals at the official price, if you really want to know, but only from idiots like Delpeyroux and Duverger, and I know a few others like them! You don't imagine I'm bothered about them? Anyway, if I paid the current price they're quite capable of denouncing me for economic sabotage! So I don't mess about with them, believe you me!'

'Oh, I see,' said Pierre-Edouard, laughing.

'But that's not all,' continued Léon. 'Look here, these mugs in the préfecture,' he said, pushing the official notice over to his brother-in-law, 'they really don't know a thing. They specify animals which provide at least 45 per cent meat to live weight – that's nothing, 45 per cent! But now that's the measure I use to buy from all the fools like Delpeyroux in the area! They're quite content to believe me, because it's written there!' he said with a sneer. 'Since I've been walking around with this paper in my pocket, none of the cows I've bought from them has been over 47 per cent,' he exulted. 'In fact they're all at least 52 per cent! Do you see, I'm making five per cent every time, that's how you'll make a profit!'

Actually, the cow Léon obtained, which he had bought for 6,230 francs from a notorious collaborator, netted 6,541.50 francs for Pierre-Edouard, who once again marvelled at his brother-in-law's infallible eye; the 311.50 francs difference represented exactly five per cent.

But he did not wish to keep this money, and hurried to return it to Léon.

'I don't want it,' replied the latter, 'it's your profit. You don't want it either? Fine, well, put it in poor old Jacques' savings account, that'll be fair, won't it? For once, a collaborator is giving him something!'

Chapter 19

WHEN Pierre-Edouard came to renovate his haymaking equipment, during the month of May 1943, he was dismayed to realise that his old reaper was absolutely unusable. He had known for years that it would not last for ever and the day would come when he would have to change it; it had been working since 1905, rattling on all sides and making a horrible grinding noise. But up until then it had always done its job properly.

In order to oil the gears more easily, tighten the block on the cutting-bar and check the teeth, he brought it out into the middle of the yard, where it collapsed all of a sudden, with an ominous squeal of the drive-wheel as the axle snapped right through; the cogs, thus released, rolled to the ground.

'Bloody hell!' groaned Pierre-Edouard, seeing that the damage was irreparable.

'Busted,' commented Nicolas, passing his fingers over the worn metal.

'Yes, and it has been for a long time, that crack didn't appear today. All right, well, we didn't reckon on it, but we'll be making hay with a new reaper. It'll cost me an arm and a leg, but it's just too bad, we can't do it all with a scythe!'

Two days later, accompanied by a delighted Guy, Pierre-Edouard caught the train at la Rivière de Mansac and went as far as Brive. He made a face as soon as he emerged into the station yard.

'Look at those bastards!' he muttered, glancing towards the balconies of the Terminus Hotel, where German officers with naked torsos sprawled on chaises-longues in the sun. This sight put him in a bad mood, and the price demanded by the agricultural machinery dealer a little later did not improve matters.

'What?' he protested, '5,500 francs for a reaper? Are you ill or what?'

'Look,' the salesman defended himself, 'you are selecting our premier model, the number fifteen, you must realise. This Dollé brand is really something, with a covered gear-casing and integral sump! But if you want the old-fashioned type with the gears exposed . . . '

'When I think that the other one cost us 365 francs,' murmured Pierre-Edouard, 'and it was expensive!'

'Pardon?' said the man, thinking he had misheard.

'Yes, 365 francs!'

The dealer thought it was a joke, and laughed.

'For that price, I'll throw in two good blades, genuine pre-war Swedish steel, plus two shafts and I'll add rakes, how's that for you?'

Pierre-Edouard shrugged and walked around the machine.

'I hope that at that price you'll deliver it, with the harvester?'

'Yes.'

'It's beautiful, isn't it?' Guy was in raptures as he climbed into the seat.

Pierre-Edouard watched him, smiled, and felt thirty-eight years younger. Then it was he who had accompanied his father to buy the reaper; his father who had struggled grimly to obtain a few concessions, and who had finally succeeded. He should do the same. He took out his pipe and filled it slowly.

'Fine,' he decided, as he used his fat copper lighter, '5,500 is a deal of money, so you'll need to knock a bit off . . . '

'No, no!' The salesman stood firm.

'Oh yes! You're not going to tell me you get customers like me every day . . . Look, I can still go to one of your colleagues. You say it's a Dollé? It's not a big name, that!'

'Yes it is, monsieur!' protested the sales rep, 'Dollé of Vesoul, everyone knows them!'

'I don't,' Pierre-Edouard assured him. 'Now if it was a MacCormick . . . '

'How are you going to find one of those with a war on!' sneered the other man.

'Or even a Puzenat, or an Amouroux,' he continued smoothly, 'but a Dollé . . . '

'It has gears with helicoid teeth of sharpened steel, fixed in an enclosed chamber and then tempered,' the salesman tried.

'And so what? So do the others!' said Pierre-Edouard, who had studied the brochures he sometimes received at the syndicate before coming. 'All right, you take off 350 francs and you deliver it to me, agreed?'

'Certainly not!'

'Well, too bad then,' he said, moving towards the door. 'Look,' he said, turning round, 'you could take away the old one, let's say for 300 francs, couldn't you?'

'Listen,' the salesman kept him there, 'I'll take the old one for, let's say . . . 250, okay?'

'That's not a lot per kilo for scrap iron, when you think metal's in great demand at the moment . . . ' Pierre-Edouard stepped back towards him and picked up a big tin of grease. 'All right then,' he decided, 'and you add this in for me.'

'Oh! Hey! That tin costs 45 francs!'

'Come on,' Pierre-Edouard persisted. 'Tell me, is it you who'll be delivering? Good,' he continued, lowering his voice, 'well, I'll put a chicken, a few eggs and some butter on one side, just this once, okay?'

On 8 July 1943, in the evening, shortly before eleven o'clock – but because of keeping German time it was still almost light – the whole Vialhe family was seated at the table when the dog barked in the yard. Pierre-Edouard immediately switched off the radio and went to look out of the door at what had caused the animal to sound the alarm.

'Oh it's you, Doctor,' he said, recognising the visitor. 'What brings you here at this time of night?'

'Is your father all right at the moment?' enquired Dr Delpy.

'Fine, he's in good form.'

'Yes,' murmured the doctor, 'he has an iron constitution, pity about his brain, from time to time, well . . . Tell me, can I speak to you quietly somewhere?'

'Of course, but won't you come in? We're having dinner.'

'I'd prefer to stay outside, but I'd like your wife to be with us too . . . '

'I'll call her. But what's happened, is it something serious?'

'No – well, not yet, but . . . Come on, better go behind the barn,' suggested the doctor, when a worried but intrigued

Mathilde had joined them. 'It's this,' he explained, 'I don't know how to say it . . . Well, anyway, I know you tend to my way of thinking.'

'Which way?' asked Pierre-Edouard prudently.

'Still not the way of the Boche, if I'm not mistaken?'

'Maybe not . . . Go on.'

'I have a problem, I'll give it to you straight. I have some friends who are looking after two kids, that lot mustn't find them, do you understand?'

'No,' said Pierre-Edouard.

'What? Yes, you do. These kids are Jews, and you know very well that the Germans are searching for them!'

'Of course,' Pierre-Edouard remembered. 'I've heard talk of it, like everyone else. But I didn't know they were looking for kids too, what do they want with them?'

'But dammit all, Pierre-Edouard, we're at war! They're arresting all of them! Bloody hell, Berthe must have talked to you about it!'

'Yes, but she never told me they were arresting children. Anyway, my sister, we haven't seen her since the Boche have been in the southern zone! That's almost nine months, and she doesn't send cards any more!'

'And these children, where are they?' asked Mathilde.

'On a farm, not very far from Varetz, but the people looking after them are afraid they may have been denounced, so the children need to disappear as quickly as possible!'

'So they're even arresting kids,' murmured Pierre-Edouard, who could not come to terms with such infamy.

Until that day, he had never concerned himself with the Jewish problem. First of all he didn't know any, had nothing against them and didn't understand why some people swore such hatred for them, and he believed, in all good faith, that the hunt for Jews was aimed solely at expelling them from France. And he was not the only one to think like that in Saint-Libéral!

'Are you in the Resistance?' he asked abruptly.

'No, not exactly. Well yes, like you, like lots of people,' explained the doctor. 'From time to time it happens that I help those who are really fighting, but no more than that; you'd do the same.'

'Yes, perhaps. Well, let's get it straight – these kids, you want us to hide them, is that it? What do you think?' he asked, looking at Mathilde.

'The same as you.'

'Well, bring them over,' said Pierre-Edouard, 'we'll trust Louise to take care of them. Up there, at Coste-Roche, they'll be safe.'

'It's because of that isolated house that I thought of you. And also because I knew you wouldn't refuse.'

'When will you bring them? We'll need to know that at least.'

'Tomorrow, probably, and quietly. On that subject, I suggest you take every possible precaution. Sheltering Jews could mean a very stiff penalty, so complete silence, all right?'

'As to that,' said Pierre-Edouard with a smile, 'I hope it won't upset them to be with a Kraut?'

'What?'

'Oh yes, the kid Berthe brought to us, little Gérard . . . '

'I thought he was from Alsace!' The doctor gave a muffled exclamation.

'Well, you go on thinking it, but now you know that the Vialhes know how to keep quiet.'

The two children arrived the next day; two brothers of eight and six. It was the doctor who went to fetch them, with the horse and cart which he had taken to again since petrol had become so scarce. To avoid any inquisitive eyes, he did not drive into the village, but turned off immediately up one of the tracks which climbed to the plateau.

Pierre-Edouard, Mathilde and Nicolas were waiting for him while loading a cart with wheat. As for Mauricette and Guy, they were already at Coste-Roche with their aunt Louise.

'So that's what they're arresting!' said Pierre-Edouard with a nod. 'My God, we need to shoot people who attack kids!'

'Come here,' said Mathilde, holding out her hand to them. 'What's your name?' she asked the older one.

'Louis Duval,' recited the boy without lowering his eyes, 'and my brother's called Jean, we're refugees from Lorraine and . . . '

'And you lost your parents during the exodus?' sighed Pierre-Edouard. 'Is that it?'

'Yes, sir.'

'I'm called Pierre-Edouard,' he said, squatting down to be at their height, 'and she's Mathilde, my wife. She's very kind and she's going to take you up to the house. You'll be fine up there. Come on, give me a kiss.'

'They've learnt it well,' said the doctor shortly afterwards, as he watched them walk away. 'In fact they're called David and Benjamin Salomon.'

'What does that matter to me! They're kids, that's enough,' said Pierre-Edouard forcibly, for he needed to mask the sorrow which had overwhelmed him at the sight of the two children. 'Excuse me.' He recovered himself and picked up the pitchfork to go back to Nicolas and the team.

'No offence taken, old fellow, I understand,' the doctor assured him as he climbed into his cart. 'By the way, have you heard talk of the maquis who've formed a group near Terrasson?'

'Vaguely,' said Pierre-Edouard evasively, 'but I don't think much of these young tearaways playing at war you know, it's not serious.'

'That depends,' asserted the doctor, 'if they're well trained . . . '

'That's exactly what I'm saying! Listen, Doctor, I did four years in the war, like you; I saw what an army is, a real one. I finished up as warrant officer – believe me, it's something to command fifty twenty-year-old kids! So when I'm told they've just got hunting rifles and no real leader . . . ! If it wasn't such a serious matter, it'd make me laugh!'

'I share your point of view, but it seems that in some areas they're getting organised like a proper army.'

'Well, if it's an army, a real one, that's different.'

'And there are some Communist maquis too, I've been told.'

'I'm not getting myself worked up about them, they know what they're doing! But the others, they won't work any miracles. No, I'm telling you, I don't have much faith in them.'

'Between ourselves,' asked the doctor with a smile, 'Paul

isn't in Paris, is he? He's with the maquis somewhere and that's why you're so critical of them, because he went off with them; is that it?'

'That's it exactly,' said Pierre-Edouard sarcastically, 'Paul went off with the maquis, just like the boy brought by Berthe is from the Alsace!'

'How wrong can you be . . . ' murmured the doctor. 'From what I know of him, I could have sworn he'd have been one of the first to leave!'

'That's about right . . . '

'Uh-huh,' said the doctor, observing him, 'you won't be saying any more about it, eh? You're right; the way things are going now, you can't be too careful.'

'Don't take it amiss. Anyway now, with these kids you've brought, we're all for the gallows together. Paul left for London, three years ago last September,' admitted Pierre-Edouard, not without pride.

'The devil!' said the doctor, jumping to the ground and clasping his hand. 'The devil! And you haven't said a thing to anyone since then? Well I never! So there's a boy from Saint-Libéral with de Gaulle! Look here, this is fantastic news! Now I know why you didn't want to talk about Paul – oh, the lucky blighter!'

'Oh yes,' said Pierre-Edouard as he filled his pipe, 'we're like that, we Vialhes. We know it's a waste of energy to talk while you're working, so when we're working we keep quiet.'

After three years of captivity, Jacques had abandoned any idea of escape across a countryside surrounded by vast lakes and treacherous peat bogs; how could he find his way through all those thick forests? Convinced that attempts to flee were destined to fail, Jacques finally resigned himself to captivity.

It made him angry to admit it, but he sometimes felt a sort of satisfaction, not in being a prisoner, but in the work he was doing. A work which pleased him, for old Karl's farm was beautiful: rich, with twenty-four hectares of good land for potatoes and rye, with forty-five milch cows, with its big half-diesel Lanz tractor which he had very quickly learned to drive. Just as he had learned to milk the cows with the milking machines in the spacious modern cowshed.

And on this magnificent farm, he was at least the foreman, if not the boss, for since the last of the four sons of the family had returned to the front – where one of his brothers had already died – old Karl depended on him. He had complete confidence in Jacques, for he had seen immediately that he was of his own tribe: a farmer, who considered the land, wherever it lay, worthy of the best possible care.

And Jacques, working each day with André – who ended up knowing how to hold a scythe – and working well, did not have any sense of betrayal, or of labouring indirectly for the Third Reich. It was not to feed the German troops that he hoed and earthed up the long rows of potatoes, watched the rations for each cow; it was out of honesty, towards Karl, and above all towards the land.

At the beginning he had thrown himself into the work to stifle his mourning for his lost freedom, his abandoned studies, for his parents, for Marie-Louise. And the remedy did him good, for even if he was still quite often besieged by black thoughts, at least he had the daily satisfaction of completing a task which he enjoyed.

However, in the past three months he had increasing difficulty in controlling the anxiety aroused by his fiancée's last two letters. They were unclear, full of ambiguities and innuendos, almost empty of love. Enough to make you think that back there in Saint-Libéral, young Marie-Louise was no longer missing him.

It was not without some difficult that Mauricette gained entry to the teachers' training college established at Brive, since the one at Tulle had been closed by order of the Vichy government. To achieve her aim she needed to exercise all the strength and will of the Vialhes, and the obstinacy and persuasiveness inherited from her mother.

Like Pierre-Edouard she went straight to the point, but like Mathilde, she used her charm and her smile to defeat the final obstacles. A little taller than her mother, she was, at eighteen, just as sweet and graceful as Mathilde had been at the same age and, like her, she knew how to persuade those whom she wished to win over.

Nevertheless, she had to do battle with Pierre-Edouard to

extract his authorisation to attend the training college. He instinctively mistrusted this sort of establishment and feared that his daughter would become just as sectarian, secular, not to say self-opiniated as, for instance, was the teacher's wife, who had taken full charge of the school since her husband had been captured.

In addition, he still had bad memories of the quarrels which had set the Church against the State at the beginning of the century, and feared that the atmosphere in the training college would be just as stupidly anti-religious as it had been then. Without being a pillar of the Church – to Father Delclos he was actually a complete infidel – he thought it had a role and a place in society, and he did not love those who wished to destroy it.

Despite all this he gave his daughter the authorisation she required, for he understood that her vocation as a teacher was sound, considered and final. He realised very soon that his worries on the subject of partisan attitudes fostered by some were not unjustified; that ostracism was still practised in the teaching profession, and that the doors were difficult to open for those who, like Mauricette, had done all their studying at independent Catholic schools; that was considered a defect.

This discovery made him furious, but far from depressing him, it spurred him on; stimulated his natural pugnacity and pushed him into action.

'So they want to play stupid games? Fine, if it comes to that, I know a few tricks,' he said when Mauricette, in tears, had recounted the scornful rebuffs she had suffered when she had presented her request to register, and above all for a grant. 'I'm going to see Léon,' he said as he went out.

He found him at the mairie, and explained the matter to him.

'With people like that, you need to go at it sideways,' decided Léon, as soon as he was informed.

'That's what I thought.'

'But I don't know anyone there.'

'Well!' Pierre-Edouard reproached him. 'You're forgetting our mutual brother-in-law, that idiot who's so proud to have become one of the pillars of the préfecture and an officer of the Vichy Militia in the Corrèze. But he hasn't forgotten us, not him, the bastard!'

Indeed, as if by chance, since the beginning of rationing, Léon's sister had remembered that her brother lived in Saint-Libéral and was a stock-dealer; that her sister Mathilde existed, and that Pierre-Edouard owned a fine farm . . .

With initial discretion, she and her husband had renewed contact; then, spurred on by hunger, they had established a firm if not sincere relationship. From then on, they came every fortnight. When they arrived on Saturday the trailer attached to their tandem jumped about behind the machine, because it was empty. But when they set off again on Sunday afternoon, the cart was weighed down with varied provisions and had a decided tendency to collapse.

Neither Léon nor Pierre-Edouard liked these two parasites, and if it were not for Yvette and Mathilde, who made it a point of honour to feed them, would happily have left them with their tongues hanging out; for they were not satisfied with being given free two-thirds of the provisions they came to fetch; they even paid for the other third at the official rate! Léon shrugged, Pierre-Edouard grumbled, but both of them let it pass.

There was only one point on which Pierre-Edouard had not given in: supplying his brother-in-law with tobacco. He knew he was a heavy smoker, and took a malicious pleasure in filling his pipe in front of him, after placing his pouch on the table, overflowing with the coarse, pungent, black tobacco which he prepared himself.

The skinflint from the préfecture drooled over it and his nostrils twitched as he saw Pierre-Edouard pulling on his pipe.

'Ah,' Pierre-Edouard would say at this point, 'I always forget that you smoke too; here, roll one,' he offered, pushing the pouch towards his brother-in-law.

The latter would roll himself an enormous cigarette, and his hand trembled as he lit it. He coughed for five minutes afterwards, for the mixture was rougher than iron filings, and as corrosive and suffocating as a sulphur match for fumigating casks!

'Aah!' he finally exhaled, his eyes full of tears. 'Your tobacco is marvellous! Could you get me a little bit?'

'No way,' Pierre-Edward then said, as he put the pouch in his pocket, 'you can see that I've hardly enough for myself!'

'I'm prepared to pay a good price for it!' begged the addict.

'Impossible, my supplier won't do it. You understand, he grows it himself, and I don't have to tell you that that's forbidden, like the black market as well . . . So you can imagine how he's on his guard!'

They would need to play on this weakness. Léon considered for a moment, scratched his head.

'Yes,' he agreed at last, 'perhaps he could intervene, but we'll have to induce him to do it. And then, does he have enough pull?'

'Don't forget that he succeeded in getting his son repatriated. And as for inducement – if he refuses, I'll kick him out, he can go and get his supplies somewhere else!'

'That wouldn't be a bad thing.' Léon was amused. 'I'm beginning to get really fed up with him, and especially as you have to be careful what you say in front of him!'

'We'll have a go at him on Saturday?' suggested Pierre-Edouard.

'Saturday, all right. But come to my house; I'll send Yvette and my sister to keep Mathilde company, that way we can discuss it man to man.'

Jacques twisted round on his seat and checked that the self-binding reaper he was towing behind the Lanz was functioning properly. The fine line of fat bales reassured him that he had everything correctly adjusted. At the beginning of the work he had experienced some difficulties with the knotting mechanism; it had really been devised to work with string made from vegetable fibre, not with this sort of paper thread which old Karl had brought back from Reichensee.

'How are you doing?' he asked André, as he passed close to him.

His friend, who was stacking the sheaves, shrugged his shoulders. He did not complain about his work – infinitely preferable to employment in a factory or at peat cutting – but he, unlike Jacques, found nothing exciting in it; he endured it while awaiting better days.

Jacques reached the end of the field, turned, and saw the

owner's wife coming towards him. Every day at ten o'clock she brought them a snack, and it was not a meagre one. Since the death two weeks earlier of another of her sons, killed on the Russian Front, the little old woman was a pitiful sight, quite shrivelled up with sorrow, and silent. She gazed at things and people without seeing them and her stare, now dry from having cried too much, touched the hearts of all those who met it.

Jacques put the Lanz into neutral, jumped to the ground and thanked the old lady who held out the basket to him. Marie-Louise's letter had been slipped in between the cob loaf – made of rye and potatoes – and the cheese. He opened it, deciphered the few lines, and turned pale.

'Are you fagged out?' joked André as he came up. Then he saw the letter gripped in his friend's fingers. 'Oh,' he murmured, 'I understand . . . '

In three years of living with Jacques he had learned everything about him, and Jacques had done likewise. For several months he had suspected that all was not well with Marie-Louise.

'Right,' he tried to help, 'you'll have to fight on, my old mate.'

'She's getting engaged . . . '

'Well, you don't say . . . ' whistled André.

'Big trouble?' the old woman asked quietly.

Jacques stared at her, understood that his pallor had not escaped her notice, and was moved by her solicitude.

'Mother? Father? Dead?' she continued.

He guessed she was quite prepared to comfort him, as his grandmother would have done.

'No, nobody's dead, thank you,' he said, summoning a semblance of a smile. Then he turned and strode to the tractor. 'It's only my dreams that are dead,' he hurled out as he crumpled the letter.

He climbed on to the Lanz and drove it into the rye.

As soon as he was aware of the plot, their brother-in-law protested, assuring them that he, an ordinary official, had no power to act in a realm so impenetrable as that of education.

'Don't spin me that yarn,' Pierre-Edouard interrupted.

'Official you may be, but this as well . . . ' he said, placing his finger on the badge of the militia which his brother-in-law sported in his buttonhole.

'You wouldn't want me to take advantage of this . . . this responsibility, to get preferential treatment! The Marshal's Militia consists of honest people and . . . '

'Oh yes, we know that,' cut in Léon, 'but I like to come straight to the point in my business dealings, so I suggest a deal: either you get the girl into training college and get a grant for her, or tighten your belt!'

'What do you mean, my belt?'

'No more tatties, no more butter, no more chickens, nothing. You could come without your trailer, then, if you still want to come . . . '

'Well, you lousy rotten swine! That's blackmail!'

'No, no,' Pierre-Eduard calmed him down, 'we're just talking, that's all. Come on, if you look after Mauricette, on my word, I'll give you a ham.'

'You're asking too much, you two,' their brother-in-law protested feebly.

'And look here, on the day college opens, that is, if she's one of the students I'll put aside a packet of tobacco for you . . . '

'A big one?' asked the official, licking his lips.

'Er . . . Two kilos, will that do you?' asked Pierre-Edouard carelessly. 'No? All right, I'll go to four; after all, if we can't help each other within the family . . . So, a ham, four kilos of tobacco and your other provisions, as usual; is it on?'

'It's on. But tell me, if I get a favourable response early on, will you give me a bit of tobacco in advance?'

'Naturally,' said Pierre-Edouard magnanimously. He took out his pouch and drew from it enough to roll three or four small cigarettes. 'Here,' he said, 'that will help you to consider the best way to get Mauricette registered and to get her a grant.'

The young lady began her first year at teacher training college in September 1943.

The Germans entered Saint-Libéral for the first time on the morning of 14 November. Until that day the village had never entertained any occupying forces, and there were even some old people – amongst those who had not left their house or garden for years – who had never in their lives seen a single German, except in a photograph after the Great War, and who demanded to be accompanied to the Church Square to appreciate that they were really there.

One of the first to be aware of their arrival that Sunday morning was Pierre-Edouard, who was taking the opportunity while Guy was out – he was at Mass with his mother – to check that his guns were still in good condition. He was worried about the damp in the stable where he had been hiding them since the beginning of the war, and he examined them periodically to see that no spots of rust were attacking the barrels or locks.

When the order to deposit all hunting rifles at the mairie had arrived, he had not for an instant considered obeying this command. He had meticulously greased his Hamerless, likewise Jacques' Darne and Paul's Robust, wrapped the guns in oily rags and had slid them on top of a wide beam in the cowshed.

Then, without batting an eyelid, he had carried his father's old Lefaucheux to the mairie; it was an unusable gun, eaten up with rust, and its exposed hammers had rattled about ever since their mainspring had broken, some fifteen years earlier.

'Are you sure you can manage without it?' Léon had asked, straight-faced.

'Hey, what can one do; I obey orders, I do!'

But since that time he liked to get out the guns three or four times a year; to polish them, to feel their weight, even bring them to the shoulder, for the pleasure of it.

He was about to take aim at an imaginary hare which had just bolted between the cows' hooves, right beside Nicolas' room, when he heard the deep rumble of the armoured car which preceded four lorries loaded with men.

'They're all we need!' he murmured, realising immediately what it was.

He hurried to slip the guns into their hiding place, went out into the yard, and anxiously awaited the arrival of the Germans.

The five vehicles filed past the house shortly afterwards, went up the main street and stopped in the square; the men jumped out of the lorries.

Better go and fetch Mathilde, he thought; she'll have a heart attack if she bumps into them coming out of Mass. He endeavoured to remain calm, trying to banish the memories which besieged him; to chase from his mind the crazy vision, which projected a picture of a battery of 75s, there, in the courtyard, nicely lined up between the sheepfold and the house, and himself, as in days gone by, giving the order to fire!

'From here, set to zero, with shrapnel shells, I won't let one of them get away, not one!' he thought, as he marched towards the church.

When he reached the square he saw Léon parleying with an officer. He approached them, his hands in his pockets, and waited for the Obersturmführer to move away.

'What do they want, those horrors?' he asked.

'Nothing, they're passing through, that's all. I think they have a rendezvous with another convoy . . .'

'Are you sure that's all?' insisted Pierre-Edouard, noticing his brother-in-law's worried expression.

'No,' admitted Léon. 'They've been told there were some maquis around here, so it's my guess they're swaggering about a bit, a matter of letting themselves be seen. But the other young fool over there,' he added with a nod, 'also warned me that they were shooting people who were helping the terrorists. My God, I hope they go quickly: we'd have a job explaining if the kids who came through the other day appeared just now!'

A week earlier, in fact, a dozen young people had come to the village. They just paraded about a bit, kicking up a rumpus at Suzanne's, proving that they weren't frightened of anything or anybody. They had no weapons but nobody was deceived; they were certainly the maquis. Besides, they had left an hour later bellowing the 'Marseillaise'.

'I know they're a bit excitable,' Pierre-Edouard reassured him, 'but if they are around here, they must have seen them arrive, those vermin!'

'Let's hope so . . .'

'And now look, see those fine warriors, there they all are at Suzanne's!'

'You're right, but really I can't wait for them to get out of here.'

They did not leave until late afternoon, about four o'clock. After having settled in at the inn to consume their tins of rations, they then spent the afternoon nosing around the village; but without any real determination, without even going into the houses, except at Deplat's and Froidefond's, where they bought some eggs, chickens and real farmhouse bread.

Then, on the orders of the young Obersturmführer and to the shouts of the junior officers, they climbed back into the lorries and left the village.

Chapter 20

BERTHE Vialhe was arrested on Thursday, 2 March 1944 at seven o'clock in the morning, at her home in the Faubourg Saint-Honoré.

Before taking her away, but after having put handcuffs on her, the men from the Gestapo ransacked her apartment, emptying the drawers, overturning the writing desk and cupboards, searching in vain for papers which would permit them to start hauling in other people, or compromising documents which would confirm their prisoner's guilt.

They had no need of proof to condemn her – the charges laid against her were quite weighty enough – but they liked the work well done and the dossiers watertight.

After dealing with the apartment they went down to the shop, where again, with methodical fury but great cunning – fruit of long experience – they combed through everything which might possibly hide a piece of evidence.

Leaning against the wall, her eyes closed, Berthe was at last at rest. Now she had finally reached the end of that exhausting, secret journey which had begun in September 1940 and was drawing to a close on this spring morning. Almost four years of double-dealing and contacts, of alternating between clandestine meetings and fashionable soirées, between wanted men and the lords who ruled France.

A demanding, exhausting life, full of hopes and discouragements, of occasional joy and constant fear. The life of a hunted creature which doubles back, bolts along the edge of a field, crouches, sets off again, runs out of breath, stumbles and falls.

She opened her eyes and smiled quietly to see the worried expressions of the henchmen who were in the process of leafing through her files. Files which featured the names of generals, colonels, lofty German dignitaries, not to mention the insignificant ones like commandants!

She had always known that her only defence would be there, in those notebooks, those orders, those bills, and that if she were capable of denying the charges, the others would never provide the slightest proof against her. Suspicions, yes, as many as they wanted, but certainties, no. She noted with satisfaction that the men from the Gestapo piled all the papers into a case, and hoped that they would hurry up and examine them to find there, on every page, the great names of her Nazi patrons; patrons whom she was going to exploit further.

Two men hastily grasped her, pushed her outside, and propelled her into a black 11 CV Citroën, which moved off down the deserted street.

Two hours later, the concierge of the block of flats opposite the shop with the sign Claire Diamond, left with her shopping bag under her arm, in the direction of the Rue de Monceau, where a shopkeeper had promised the previous day that he might perhaps be able to supply her with half a pound of turnips – not swedes, real turnips.

It was on the way back, after an hour of queuing, that she dropped in on one of her colleagues in the Rue de la Boétie. She announced to her that there were no more turnips, but that she had nevertheless found several very fine artichokes, and slipped her, as she left, a letter entrusted to her by Berthe eighteen months earlier, which she had undertaken to carry to the Rue de la Boétie should anything happen.

After many a detour, pause and change of bearer, the letter arrived in Saint-Libéral two weeks later. It had been posted two days earlier in Saint-Yrieix.

Pierre-Edouard, helped by Nicolas, was in the process of shearing his ewes when Mathilde called him.

'Yes!' he said, without stopping his manipulation of the shears. 'I'm here, you know where, don't you?'

He was annoyed because the implement was cutting badly, pulling the wool and carving steps in the fleece, a rotten piece of work.

'Come here!' repeated Mathilde from the house.

'Dammit!' he grumbled, tossing the shears to Nicolas. 'You finish it if you can!' .

He wiped his sticky hands on an old sack to get rid of the woolgrease, and set off for the house, convinced that yet again his father must be calling for him at the top of his voice; then he would forbid him, as he had done long ago, to speak to that little arsehole of a surveyor who was sniffing around Louise! It was distressing, upsetting, especially when Louise was present; her little surveyor and first husband had been dead for thirty-five years! But there was nothing to be done about it, except wait patiently until the crises passed.

'Well, has he started up again?' he asked, as soon as he saw Mathilde on the steps of the house.

She shook her head and held out the letter to him; she had opened it because it was addressed to Monsieur and Madame P.-E. Vialhe.

'What's happened?' he murmured.

'Read.'

'I haven't got my glasses.'

'Here,' she said, holding them out to him.

'Oh, it's Berthe!' he said straight away. He read, and turned pale.

Dear Brother, dear Mathilde,

If one day you receive this message, it will be because I have been arrested by the Germans. I do not know why, but I have the impression that they have been watching me for some time, though as you know, I have never concerned myself with anything but fashion. Despite that, since I returned to Paris it seems that they mistrust me. It is true that I was obliged to buy material on the black market, perhaps that's the reason. Anyway, don't worry, they'll release me quickly I think. They know very well that, like you, my dear brother, I chose which side, once and for all.

Most important of all, look after the children. Guy must be a big boy now; as for Gérard, he must be able to take care of his little brother Pierre. See you soon. Kiss Louise, Father, Léon, Yvette and Louis, not forgetting Mauricette. Greetings to Nicolas and the neighbours as well. Love to you both.

Berthe.

'What's that supposed to mean?' stammered Pierre-Edouard in dismay. 'And then, when was this letter written?'

'It's not dated . . . '

'So, they've arrested her,' he said, fumbling around to find his pipe. 'Poor little thing, and she was worried whether I'd chosen the right side.'

'She was in the Resistance, wasn't she?' asked Mathilde, who needed to have confirmation of her guesswork.

'By God yes, and she'd thought of everything, even that this letter might fall into the hands of some other bastards! My, she's strong, Berthe, she's really something!'

He was so sad he could have cried, but he was proud of his sister. Proud that she had known how to do battle according to her ideals and in her own way, and above all in silence, not letting a word of these activities escape to anyone; even breaking off with her family, to prevent that lot following the trail to Saint-Libéral.

'Do you think they'll release her?' questioned Mathilde.

'No; they've got her, they'll keep her, that's the rule.'

'And what can we do?' begged Mathilde. Since the beginning of the war she had complained of not being able to *do* anything. Nothing for Jacques, or very little, and nothing for Paul either, who had been silent since Christmas 1940.

'Nothing,' he said, 'except watch over her lad, and the two others as well. That must have been written somewhere, that our job would be to look after other people's kids.'

'But what about her, can't we try anything? Through the préfecture, maybe.'

'You must be joking! Your brother-in-law, we don't see him any more, he's much too scared of being picked up by the maquis if he comes here! Believe me, in view of what's happening, he must be thinking of how to keep his backside covered, and he's not the only one!'

He pulled her to him and stroked her hair.

'Come on, it'll soon be over. They'll come back, all of them, Jacques, Paul, Berthe, Félix; the war won't last. Or else it'll kill us all.'

*

Scream yes, talk no. Scream like a madwoman, without restraint, because that gave some relief and most of all because you couldn't do anything else.

Because the foul water in the bathtub stifles you, drowns you until thousands of stars explode in your skull, searing your brain, and the water full of vomit and blood seeps into your lungs, corroding and crushing them.

Scream then, scream all the time, but not talk, never, say nothing. Turn each minute gained into a century of victory, each second of biting your lips into a battle won.

Say nothing, except: I am Claire Diamond, the fashion designer; you know that, your leaders know me! And repeat that ad infinitum, until the soothing mists envelop you and you float in them, to draw strength and gain fresh energy to scream anew.

But be silent, be absolutely silent, all the time, to the end, to the finish. And so prove to yourself and prove to them, that you are the braver, the stronger, the better. And that they will never succeed in breaking down that wall, that dumb citadel where screams are only silence.

Despite the shock they felt at Berthe's arrest, Pierre-Edouard and Mathilde overcame this new ordeal by reacting with that surge of energy and courage which spurred them on and inspired them to defend themselves each time misfortune struck.

They rejected the morbid temptation to passivity and despair and faced up to it, not only by throwing themselves into their work, but also by not attempting to conceal this fateful blow which had once again struck the Vialhe family. Instead of suppressing the news Pierre-Edouard broadcast it, not out of misplaced defiance or boastfulness, but because he reckoned that with one son a prisoner, another God knows where, a sister in the hands of the Gestapo and a nephew who had disappeared, it was his duty to show everyone that he supported these four members of his family.

A year earlier, some people in the village would have sneered when they learned that Berthe was behind bars, because prison was shameful, even when the deed was Resistance. But everything had changed in a few months.

There was more and more talk of the imminent landings and the few, select resistance workers of the early days were augmented by a constantly growing wave of patriots, the more boastful and noisy for being new converts.

Already the Marshal's most fervent supporters were becoming discreet, humble, careful. For them an ill wind was blowing, and they dreaded the storm which they heard rumbling all around. Even Father Delclos was tacking between two currents. He spoke no more of politics, nor did he rant against the maquis, who now often came down to fetch provisions in the village.

They also requisitioned shamelessly. In Saint-Libéral, those who came were content to make a few restitute their ill-gotten gains: they targeted the specialists in the black market and the collaborators – Delpeyroux and his friends were their favourite suppliers, and that was only fair – but rumours abounded of real sharks who were plundering the countryside. Taking advantage of the protection afforded by their supposed membership of the French Interior Forces, they held to ransom, even tortured, and mercilessly pillaged the unfortunates who were suspected of owning anything of the slightest value.

Luckily, these predators had not yet swept down on the village. Certainly it was cowardice rather than caution, for Léon, as soon as he got wind of their extortion, had no worries about announcing good and loud at Suzanne's one evening, that anyone who didn't know the difference between the Resistance and robbery would get the worst of a hunting rifle. As for Pierre-Edouard, he had recalled that his guns were in excellent condition; that he, and Nicolas too, knew how to use them, and that even Mathilde and Guy, if need be, would know how to slide a pair of triple-o cartridges into a 12-bore.

But all these stories, all these rumours, and also the difficulty of distinguishing at first glance between the real fighters and the scum, created a climate full of suspicion and uncertainty.

This changed to terror when the news surfaced, on 31 March, that sections of Vlassov's army – a formidable horde of Germans and Georgians who had just plundered the

Dordogne — were now moving towards the lower Corrèze. They arrived in a terrifying flood.

Pillaging, raping, killing, laying waste to everything, the vast cohort first shed blood in villages quite close to Saint-Libéral —Villac, Ayen, Juillac — then went on to carry death, fire and horror to Brive, Noailles, Vigeois, Tulle.

Still in despair at all these atrocities, the inhabitants of Saint-Libéral received another terrible shock when they learned, on 7 April, that Father Verlhac, who had been in the Resistance from the first moment, had been shot two days earlier, in a ditch not far from Uzerche.

On the morning of 6 June, during the maths lesson, Mauricette made sure that the lecturer wasn't watching her and quietly opened the history book balanced on her knees to re-read for the tenth time the letters she had received an hour earlier. A long and beautiful love letter, which had filled her with joy and tenderness.

Jean-Pierre was well, he loved her more and more, and when this foul war was over — partly thanks to him, of course — nothing would be able to prevent their marrying.

It was during a meeting of the Young Christian Students that Mauricette and he had bumped into each other at the beginning of the school year. The two young people, though meeting for the very first time, immediately identified with each other and very quickly loved each other. Everything drew them together and bound them closer: the same ideas about life, family and ideals in general, and the teaching vocation which they both shared.

At the end of the first term the two young people already considered themselves engaged, and both of them had told their parents, without immediately revealing quite the extent of their feelings for each other and the promises they had made.

Pierre-Edouard had frowned at first. He had only one daughter, and had no intention of letting her leave on the arm of the first young whippersnapper to turn up. Then he had tried to find out more; he was not fooled and neither was Mathilde, for the way in which Mauricette talked to them about this boy proved that she did not think of him as an ordinary friend by any means.

'And where's he from, this remarkable fellow?' he had asked with quiet amusement.

'From Uzerche, his parents keep a small shop. You'll see, he's very nice . . . '

'Oh, I see, so he's going to come here?'

'Well, I thought that perhaps during the Carnival holiday, at Shrovetide . . . he could come, well, if it's all right by you . . . '

'Of course,' Mathilde had said, 'he must come and see us. I only hope that we won't feel ashamed of our house, because, you know, town people are used to fine accommodation!'

But he had never come. Between Christmas and Carnival the rumour had spread that nineteen-year-old students, too, would have to leave for the Compulsory Work Service. Perhaps it was only a schoolboy joke, a nasty hoax, but it had hit home. Three days later Jean-Pierre joined the maquis, and disappeared into the woods near Argentat.

For Mauricette the ordeal had been cruel, and the days were sadly depressing until at last the first letter arrived. So on 6 June and for the tenth time she re-read the fourteenth letter which Jean-Pierre had sent to her since his departure.

The joy which surged through Saint-Libéral at the announcement of the landings was short-lived. It lasted four days, then was shattered when the terrible news broke on the morning of the tenth.

It was the driver of a gas-powered bus who revealed the tragedy that had taken place in Tulle the day before. He did not know many details, but maintained that the Germans of the Third Reich Division had hanged one hundred and twenty hostages, and imprisoned more than three hundred. It was not until after the Liberation that the exact number of victims in Tulle became known: ninety-nine.

Pierre-Edouard was helping the wheelwright to shoe his oxen when he learned of the tragedy. Devastated, he abandoned his team, ran home and found Mathilde hanging out the washing.

'Tell me,' he called to her, 'Mauricette's young boy-friend, which maquis did he join?'

'Somewhere near Argentat.'

'Are you sure?'

'Yes, that's what she told me, but why?' She was worried to see his defeated expression.

'Towards Argentat, that's the secret army, I think, so he couldn't have been at Tulle. Well, I hope . . . '

'What's happened?' she asked again.

'An atrocity,' he whispered, 'a real atrocity. You know, I always said those young fools would cause some disaster; they think they're strong because they've got sub-machine guns and now look what happens. No,' he said, shaking his head, 'that's not the way to make war!'

'But what's going on? Tell me!'

'They wanted to liberate Tulle, all alone like big boys; it failed, of course, and the Germans came. With their tanks against those kids, it was screwed up before it started! So that lot, the Nazis, in revenge for having lost a few men and especially for having got a fright, they hanged a hundred and twenty hostages from the balconies and the lamp-posts . . . '

He saw Mathilde devastated, shook his head in despair, then clenched his fists and went off to fetch his oxen.

By the evening, they knew that the Third Reich Division was leaving a trail of fire and blood behind it along the whole length of the main roads: arson and death on the Routes Nationales 20 and 89.

But that was not all, and the inhabitants of Saint-Libéral, who thought that the peak of horror had been reached, did not believe their ears when they heard of the martyrdom of Oradour-sur-Glane. That same night, at 2 a.m., a grenade exploded in the garden of the presbytery, a blast from a Sten gun peppered the front of Delpeyroux's house, and two shots from a hunting rifle were aimed at his brother-in-law's farm. No one was injured, and nobody ever knew who was the instigator of these reprisals. But because of them, fear gripped Saint-Libéral for several months.

Berthe would not talk, ever. They could return to fetch her from her cell, take her to 84 Avenue Foch, restart the interrogation, beat her, torture her again; she would not talk.

They believed she was physically broken and morally annihilated, but they were deluded. Her body was shattered but her will remained intact. That will of iron; she drew immense power and strength from it. She had patiently forged and tempered it long ago, during her youth in Saint-Libéral, when she was forced to submit meekly to her father's relentless authority. So they could give her another beating, but they would not get anything out of her.

Besides, whatever they might do, even if they were to shoot her, they were beaten. The Allies had been there, in France, for nearly three weeks now, and nobody was going to throw them back into the water. And nobody would force her to say what she wanted to conceal, either.

She turned over on her pallet and could not suppress her moans, her body was so sore; it was one mass of cuts, contusions and bruises. With the end of her fingers she gently felt the deep gashes opened by the jaws of the handcuffs; between two interrogations the wounds had no time to close, and the pain sawed at her wrists.

But because she knew that lack of action is often quickly followed by an inability to act, she forced herself to move her hands, to shift her arms and legs, to react against the suffering which tempted her into soothing but dangerous inertia, a numb lethargy. She got up, as every morning since her incarceration, then washed herself carefully. Next she began to quarter her cell, counting the paces as she went.

She took 1,850 to cover a kilometre; then would come the time for a drink of coffee. Later, if she were allowed the time – that's to say, if there were no interrogation to disturb her day – she would resume her march. In the evening she would add up 9,250 paces, then would strive to reach a total of 10,000 before finally lying down, proud to have covered at least 5 kilometres, to have conquered her weaknesses and the terrible stabbing pains which every moment provoked.

The lock clicked and the door opened, well before the usual time. Berthe thought that she would have difficulty in completing her daily five kilometres, and allowed herself to be dragged off on a long, very long, journey: Compiègne, Strasbourg, Magdebourg, Ravensbrück.

*

After the delight inspired by the landings, then the brutal shock of the enemy's response in the Corrèze and elsewhere, Saint-Libéral relapsed into worry, depression and pain as they waited. It was more and more difficult to know whether the war was really coming to an end, as maintained by the growing numbers of maquis in the vicinity of the village, or whether it was going to continue for a long time yet, as the occupiers were trying to prove.

The atmosphere was murky and unwholesome, like a pond in August; exhausting too, a strain on the nerves, the result of constant, depressing instability, a disagreeable mixture of hot and cold, of optimism and despair.

It was now impossible to get to Terrasson, Objat or Brive, to sell produce there, without coming upon road-blocks, one after another. At the first, manned by the maquis, you had to prove your patriotism and sometimes, depending on the men questioning you, to give up, whether you would or no, a crate of plums, a couple of chickens or a basket of peas.

At the other road-blocks, those held by the Germans on the outskirts of the towns, you needed to prove that you had no ties with the terrorists who held sway in the countryside; that was not always easy, for the Germans mistrusted anyone who looked like a farmer. They were reputed to be assassins to a man.

To avoid these constant interrogations, which infuriated him, Pierre-Edouard no longer left the parish. Despite that, simply by climbing onto the plateau to go and work there, he had been stopped several times by these armed lads. Some were polite, friendly, and some even helped him bring in the lucerne from Léon's Letters field. But others had the suspicious air and untrustworthy look of those inclined to robbery and rape.

It was their presence which made him take the decision to bring Louise and the children back down to the village. Coste-Roche was really too isolated. It was easy prey for the bandits, and what could Louise do against them? Neither Gérard, who was now going on fourteen, nor the other children, who were younger still, could prevent the house being raided.

Louise protested. At Coste-Roche she was fine; it was

quiet, and the four children she cared for loved her as a mother.

'Yes,' she confessed to her brother, 'you know, I'm happy here, and if I weren't so worried about Félix . . . And then, you, Nicolas or Mathilde, you come nearly every day, so it's all right!'

'The evil doesn't strike during the day, it comes at night!'

'But I barricade myself in at night!'

'And so what? You're three kilometres from the village, they'd have the whole night to break down your door.'

'You're exaggerating,' she said with a shrug.

'Oh, you think so? Well, those bastards have made themselves felt recently, over by Perpezac and elsewhere too. Come on, don't argue; put your things in the cart and get going!'

'And the children? What about them?' she said, nodding towards the two brothers whom the doctor had entrusted to her.

'Bah – now, you know, I don't think anyone in Saint-Libéral will be informing.'

He saw that she was not convinced, and he placed his hand on her shoulder.

'Believe me,' he said, 'you can't stay here, it's too dangerous.'

'It's a pity,' she murmured. 'Here, with the four children around me, I nearly manage to forget that we're at war. And then,' she said suddenly, 'if I come back down, how will you fit us in?'

'Don't worry about that, we've worked it out. We'll put the four kids in the main room, Mauricette with Father, and you in our bedroom. Yes, it'll be a bit of a squash, but we began the war like that, we're not going to die of it now! And then, it won't be for as long as it was before!'

July passed, and with it the harvests. In the village the dark and depressing atmosphere still prevailed, that mixture of hope and joy stifled at birth by the fear of what the morrow might bring.

Already everyone was aware that certain people – whose political orientation was well known – were using their role in the Resistance as justification, and making preparations to sweep out all those who had opposed them in the past on the town councils; it was plain and unmistakable. Moreover, Tavet, Brousse and Bernical boldly asserted that Léon, and reactionaries like him, had had their day and would soon have to go, whether they would or no.

At first Léon let them talk; then, as the sneers and even threats continued to grow, he went into action on the evening of 13 August. Surrounded by Pierre-Edouard, Maurice, Edouard Lapeyre and also Delpy, he walked into Suzanne's, where he knew that Tavet and his supporters, plus several armed maquis, were holding a meeting.

'Right,' said Léon, after ordering a bottle of wine, 'so it seems someone wants to settle some old scores?' He filled his friends' glasses, turned round and gazed deliberately at the dozen or so youths who were joking and fingering their machine-guns and their grenades.

'Tell me, Tavet,' he asked quietly and with a smile, 'I didn't know that you had friends amongst the collaborators!'

'What?' growled Tavet, getting up.

'Hey!' said Léon, shrugging. 'Him, there, the little redhead, isn't he Feix's son from Meyssac? And the other one, over there, with his beret over his eyes, that must be Jeannot, Louisette's brother from La Roche-Canillac? Yes? Oh, I knew that by touring all the markets I'd end up knowing a bit about the world around me . . . '

'And so what?' cried Louis Brousse.

'Oh, nothing,' Léon reassured him. He drank a mouthful and put down his glass. 'Nothing, except that the little redhead's father has been trading with the Jerries right through the war, didn't you know that? Ask him then, the boy, why he only joined the maquis three months ago and more than fifty kilometres away from his home . . . Because from what I'm told, there are plenty of real maquis around Meyssac and Chauffour! And you, Jeannot! Don't hang your head like that! Have you told these fine pillars of the law that your sister is a whore in Brive, sometimes with the Boche, sometimes with the militia – it's so convenient, one night in the Terminus Hotel, the next at the Hotel du Parc, she only has to cross the Avenue de la Gare . . . '

'My God!' yelled Jeannot, getting up, 'I'll kill you for that!'

'Oh yes,' said Léon without moving, 'but you'd better shoot me in the back, because if I see you I won't miss.'

'In any case, they're not responsible for what their families do!' protested Martin Tavet.

'That's true,' admitted Léon, 'but it could cause a lot of gossip eh?'

'And what about you, what did you do during the war?' called out Louis Brousse.

'The same as you, old fellow, nothing, so we're quits!' He turned his back, filled his glass once more, then quickly faced them again. 'Right,' he cried, 'now we've got to know each other, the joke's over. You choose your friends where you like, that's your business. But don't muck around with us, because we could turn nasty too. You can't teach us any lessons; if anything it'd be the other way round!'

'Calm down, Léon,' the doctor intervened with a smile, 'you're not going to teach these gentlemen what all the honest people in the village already know! You're not going to tell them, for example, that your nephew Paul was one of the first to reach London, nor that Félix, Pierre-Edouard's godson, did the same thing, and least of all that Berthe is in the hands of the Gestapo . . . '

'That's true,' confirmed Pierre-Edouard, joining in the game, 'you're not going to tell them that the doctor spends more time treating the maquis than his own patients; you can be sure that Tavet knows all that!'

'Dammit,' agreed Léon, 'he also knows very well that Maurice's son has been in the maquis for a year over Terrasson way; isn't it true you know that?'

'And so what?' called a youth, brandishing his gun. 'What's that to us?'

'Nothing,' conceded the doctor, 'but you're young; if we say all this, it's so that you know that others besides your friends have fought and are still fighting!'

'And so that you know as well, and your mates too, that in Saint-Libéral we're not used to being pushed around by just anyone, even if he's wearing a fine armband, even if he has a machine-gun! Here we choose the ones we want to elect, understand, Tavet?' added Léon drily.

'We'll talk about this some other time,' promised Tavet.

'But of course,' agreed the doctor. 'As soon as the war is over we'll need to vote again, so we'll see. But meanwhile, the urgent matter is to kick out the Boche, isn't it? While we're on that subject, my children,' he said turning to the young people, 'I wonder what you're doing still here. As far as I know, all your comrades in this sector are busy encircling Brive; perhaps there's some useful work to be done over there, eh?'

'We haven't received any orders,' cried one of the youths, 'and it's not for you to give us any!'

'But I'm not giving you any, don't worry. It's just that if I were you, I'd be a bit embarrassed to be drinking shots here when my mates were exchanging shots with the enemy thirty kilometres away . . .'

'Those poor young things,' sighed Suzanne suddenly, 'they're so sweet!'

Without realising it, she broke the dangerous tension which was building up in the bar, for all the men, whatever their opinions, burst into laughter.

'Bless you, Suzanne!' spluttered the doctor. 'You're a real mother to them, a real mother hen!'

And the laughter intensified, for they all knew that Suzanne, despite her forty-eight years, had been indulging her fancies – beyond her wildest hopes – ever since the maquis had been roving the area.

'So what?' she said blushing. 'It's better than making war or politics!'

'Yes, yes,' shouted the youths.

'Vote for Suzanne!' yelled one of them.

'In the nude!' suggested another.

The doctor leaned towards Léon and Pierre-Edouard.

'That's better,' he whispered. 'Just now I was afraid that one of these crazy young men would shoot us point-blank!'

'No, no,' Léon reassured him while continuing to laugh, 'there was no danger, we were just in front of Suzanne, they were much too afraid of hitting her! You don't imagine that it's Tavet's beautiful eyes that keeps them here till this hour!'

One morning three days later, the village learned to its joy that Brive had been liberated. But the bells did not ring in Saint-Libéral, for when Léon and the members of the council went to the presbytery determined to demand — firmly if necessary — that the priest pull on his bells to announce the event properly, they found only a poor red-eyed man with a terrified expression, who announced to them between sobs that his old mother had given up her soul on the previous evening, on the Feast of the Assumption.

And the poor man was so pitiful, so helpless, that no one had the courage to celebrate in front of him for he was the very image of defeat.

Chapter 21

AFTER Brive, the first town in France to liberate itself independently, Tulle and Ussel were next to rid themselves of their occupiers. Now at last the Corrèze was free, and neither the bombardment of Brive nor the few sporadic attempts by the enemy to recapture the place succeeded in marring the happiness of the Corrèziens.

This joy increased, the following week, with the announcement of the liberation of Paris; many then thought that the war was over. At the Vialhes', as everywhere, the events were properly celebrated. However, neither Pierre-Edouard, nor Mathilde, nor Louise were fooled by the rather forced enthusiasm which they tried to show; during these days of jubilation the absence of Berthe, Félix, Jacques and Paul weighed heavily.

And suddenly on 30 August, during the siesta, when Mathilde, Louise and Mauricette were doing the washing-up, when Pierre-Edouard and his father were sleeping and the children had gone off to hunt for crayfish in the Diamond, Léon's shout echoed round the yard. A cry of delight, followed by the sound of running and the crash of a door being flung open.

'The boy's in Paris! He's in Paris!'

'Paul? Félix?' said Mathilde and Louise simultaneously.

'Paul!' cried Léon, hugging his sister. 'He's just telephoned me! The boy's in Paris!' he repeated to Pierre-Edouard, who had just come out of the bedroom.

'I heard,' murmured Pierre-Edouard, stuffing his shirt tails into his trousers. 'Explain,' he said.

He was so agitated that he stuck his pipe between his teeth and tried to light it, although he had omitted to fill it. He became aware of his absent-mindedness and smiled apologetically.

'Explain,' he said again.

'He's been in Paris since yesterday. He telephoned as soon as he could, it hasn't been easy. But he'll call our house again this evening, at seven o'clock so you can be there, and then we were cut off . . . '

'And . . . And is he all right?' asked Mathilde.

'Of course! Just imagine,' Léon shouted to his brother-in-law, 'he's a second-lieutenant!'

'Damnation!' swore Pierre-Edouard. 'He's been made an officer, the devil!'

To him, who had ended the 1914 war with the rank of sergeant-major, his son's stripes had a symbolic significance. Paul had outstripped him, had done better than him; it was fantastic. He felt himself brimming with pride, pulled Mathilde to him and kissed her.

'Did you hear that,' he said to her, 'your son's an officer!'

'And that's not all,' continued Léon. 'Do you know which branch he's in? In the parachute corps!'

'My God,' said Mathilde, 'he must be mad!'

She was suddenly paralysed with fear and trembled in retrospect, to imagine that he had thrown himself from an aeroplane, and that he was perhaps going to do it again.

'He must be mad!' she repeated weakly.

'No, no!' Pierre-Edouard reassured her, as he grew prouder every moment. Then he looked at Louise, who was standing a little to one side and listening without saying anything. He saw that she was sad and smiled at her: 'We'll hear from Félix soon too, you'll see. I'm sure of it, we're on to a run of luck!'

She nodded, but turned away so that neither her brother nor Mathilde or Léon should have their pleasure spoiled by seeing her so downcast, still in such anguish. She was happy that Paul was safe, naturally, but Paul was her nephew, not her son.

In the evening, she nevertheless went to Léon's house with the others to await the promised telephone call. But they all waited in vain; the phone remained dumb.

'Well, that's it,' said Pierre-Edouard towards eleven o'clock, 'he hasn't been able to ring . . . '

He was disappointed and sorry for Mathilde; she had been so happy to think she would be able to hear her son's voice after four years of silence.

'You know,' explained Léon, 'the telephone, at the moment, works when it feels like it. Perhaps he'll call tomorrow, and then I'll come and fetch you.'

Paul did not call again, but wrote a long letter which arrived two days later. A letter which Pierre-Edouard first read out loud so that the whole family could appreciate it, and which Mathilde read and re-read alone to herself. She was now overflowing with happiness and, if it had not been for the postscript, she too was ready to believe that the war really had ended and that her sons would soon be returning; but Paul's last lines were unambiguous:

'We're setting off again this very evening, I don't know where to, but it's certainly not for a rest . . .'

Félix did not write, did not telephone; he came. He arrived by the morning bus. Dead tired, for he had journeyed through the night, he was a little disappointed to find no one at the farm but two unknown children and his grandfather, who obviously did not recognise him. The old man was sitting in front of the house and mumbling endlessly as he played with an old stick, which he turned to and fro between his hands.

'Who are you?' Félix asked the older of the two boys.

'Me, I'm called David, and he's my brother Benjamin,' explained the child, making no attempt to hide how much he admired the visitor's uniform. 'Say, you're not Paul, are you?' he asked suddenly.

'Oh no, I'm Félix.'

'Hey, it's Uncle Félix!' exclaimed the younger boy.

'But . . . I don't know you!' said Félix with furrowed brow.

'Granny Louise told us about you!' explained the little lad ecstatically.

Félix, completely at sea, decided to leave any requests for explanation until later.

'Where's all the family?'

'On the plateau,' pointed David, 'they're harvesting the buckwheat. We're staying here to keep Grandpa Jean-Edouard company – and to look after him, too,' he added with a serious air.

'As if that explains everything,' murmured Félix. 'And are they well, at least?'

'Yes, yes!'

'All of them?' he insisted.

'Oh yes!'

'I'm going up there.'

It was just before he reached the plateau, while he was still under the chestnut trees which lined the track, that he noticed the child twenty paces from him, stalking blue tits in the bushes, his catapult in his hand.

The boy, knee-high to a grass-hopper and bronzed like a sun-ripened apricot, watched him warily as he approached. A thick fringe of chestnut hair fell over his eyes; he tossed it back with a quick flick and observed the stranger coming towards him.

Félix stopped, gazed at him, and then crouched down to be at his height. He caught his breath and bit his lips, almost surprised that the lad did not hear the wild beating of his heart, the heavy thumps booming out his happiness.

'Is it you, Pierre?' he whispered at last. 'Yes, it's you, you look so much like your mother!'

The lad frowned, and cautiously withdrew a step. Félix smiled at him and held out his hand.

'Don't be scared, please don't be scared. Nobody should be scared of their papa.'

'Papa?' the little fellow asked faintly. He hesitated again; seemed to make a huge effort, perhaps to try to remember the large silhouette which had loomed over him one morning in February 1940. Then he pronounced it again: papa, as if to get used to the word, to make it his own. And suddenly, he jumped. Félix almost fell over backwards when his son threw his arms round his neck.

Félix had to leave again the next day; but his visit, despite being so short, brought a huge measure of happiness to the Vialhe house, restoring courage and optimism in everyone. As for Louise, she looked ten years younger.

They all gathered in the evening to listen to Félix's extraordinary epic journey. He had left Dunkirk as a staff sergeant and returned a lieutenant, after having reconquered parts of Africa, Italy and Corsica.

'And now what?' asked Louise.

'Towards Germany, of course.'

'And make sure you don't do it like in 1918,' suggested Léon. 'This time, give them a good thrashing, once and for all. That way, we might avoid seeing them here again in twenty years' time!'.

'We'll make sure of it.'

Three days after his departure Mauricette returned from Tulle, in tears. She had set off for the prefecture, ostensibly to attend to her registration at the training college for the following year, but in reality to meet Jean-Pierre there.

A sad meeting, for her fiancé, without trying to soften an announcement which he knew was painful, and even before reassuring her that she was and would remain his only love, had revealed to her his enlistment in the regular army, for the duration of the war. He was proud of it; she was too, of course, but so sad as well, so torn. For her, the agony was beginning.

'I've been through it, too,' Mathilde told her. 'I know that's no comfort to you, but if you want the time to pass more quickly, be brave and strong. Cry if you need to, but don't get in the habit of it, or you won't be able to do anything else and the days will seem twice as long.'

'And you know,' Pierre-Edouard tried to help, 'at least it proves he's a man, a real man, who does what has to be done, even if it costs him something; that's good. I'm glad he's not a weakling or a shirker. I'm sure he'll make a fine son-in-law.'

'But you don't even know him!' sobbed the girl.

'Yes I do,' said Pierre-Edouard, 'you've been talking to us about him for months! Oh, that's not the same, I know, and it's true we've never seen him. But if I say he'll make a good son-in-law, it's because a man who can leave a beautiful girl like you and take up his gun, now, when he doesn't have to, must be made of the right stuff. That's why I've no worries.'

The gradual liberation of France did not bring the great economic changes which everyone was hoping for. There were shortages of everything everywhere, ration coupons were necessary for the slightest requirement, inflation was spiralling upwards.

Everything was scarce, if not unobtainable, and Pierre-Edouard, who still ran the farmers' buying syndicate, could envisage a time when business would have to stop altogether.

One September morning in 1944, he was re-reading, and grumbling over, the reply from Supply Services to his request for 2 tons of chalk nitrate – he had been allocated 220 kilos, which would allow him to give about 14 kilos each to the customers who had ordered some – when his nephew Louis, Léon's son, interrupted his work.

'Hey, Uncle!' called the boy, 'Papa needs you right away, he's at Delpeyroux's.'

'At Delpeyroux's? What's he up to at that idiot's place?'

But the boy had already turned on his heel. Pierre-Edouard hurried towards the alleyway where his neighbour's farm lay and frowned on seeing the gathering in the yard and hearing Léon's remonstrations. A black Citroën was parked in front of the house.

'What's going on?' he asked.

'These fellows want to arrest him,' Léon explained to him, pointing at three young men already surrounding Delpeyroux, who was white with fear.

'Arrest him? What the devil for?'

'Well, this is nice!' sneered one of the youths. 'Another one who wants to protect a collaborator! My word, it's the whole village that needs banging in the nick, we were well informed!'

'D'you want a thump?' Pierre-Edouard hurled at him, warning him off with a wave of his fist and sliding in beside Léon.

'These are the boys from the Liberation Committee in this département,' his brother-in-law explained, 'they've shown me their cards.'

'And that gives them the right to arrest people?'

'Well yes, so it seems. I telephoned the gendarmerie at Ayen, they told me it's legal.'

'Well now,' commented Pierre-Edouard, 'if you have to

arrest all the suckers who bawled "Long live the Marshal", there won't be many people left in France!'

The young man shrugged, and pushed Delpeyroux into the car.

'We're going to have a word with your priest too,' he warned as he got in behind the steering wheel. 'He's been identified as a collaborator as well. Luckily there are some true patriots in this dump.'

Léon was shaking with anger. God knows that he held Delpeyroux in very low esteem and considered Father Delclos an old mule, but to know that one or more of his electors had been informing made him furious; he was ashamed of them. He went briskly up to the driver and grasped him by the collar with the fearsome hook of his artificial hand.

'Listen carefully, little bastard,' he cried, 'I am the mayor, and those are the town councillors, and the others there, all the ones around the car, these are the people of Saint-Libéral. We don't like informers, and we've always settled things between ourselves. All right, you've got Delpeyroux on board, okay. He's a right bastard, but we'll still come and speak for him because he's one of our own. But if by any chance you go to the presbytery, you'll see – there are about twenty of us here; well, in five minutes you'll get twenty shots in your mug. We'll keep our priest and nobody in the Corrèze needs to know that he's been behaving like a fool; we know it, and that's enough.'

'Leave me alone! Or you'll be sorry for it!' protested the man.

'One more word,' growled Léon, without letting go. 'You can see, I've only got one hand left, but watch out, my lad; my other arm is bloody long, and his too!' he said, pointing to Pierre-Edouard. 'Remember, in the village we keep things in the family. Now get out, and I advise you not to stop at the presbytery, and not to set foot here again either!'

He finally released the man, who saw his chance and drove off like a maniac. The car took the road to Brive and disappeared.

Delpeyroux spent several months in prison, then was released. As he had promised, Léon went to testify; Pierre-

Edouard, Maurice and Edouard Lapeyre accompanied him. And even Tavet and Bernical went along as well, to explain that their neighbour had at least never denounced anyone nor done any great harm, although they all condemned his political decisions.

Tavet and Bernical's testimony, inspired by sixty years of neighbourliness and friendship with the accused, got them into trouble with their party officials; besides this partiality for a man who, in the eyes of the revolutionaries, deserved a dozen bullets under his skin, they were blamed for not being able to oust Léon and his friends from the mairie.

Their expulsion from the party grieved the two men deeply, but did not stop them getting themselves re-elected on the socialist ticket when the municipal elections came round a few months later. These elections gave Léon and Pierre-Edouard an equal number of votes. Léon played fair and offered the mayor's sash to his brother-in-law, who declined it. The older he grew, the less he felt attracted to politics. And the struggles which were already dividing France again, strengthened his scepticism and his condemnation of all those who, on the pretext of serving the public good, defended their own interests before all else.

A week after the arrest of Delpeyroux, a grey Peugeot stopped outside the Vialhe house, and Pierre-Edouard immediately thought that the youths of the Liberation Committee had not disbanded. He prepared to receive them coolly, but it was a woman who got out of the vehicle.

'I'm looking for Monsieur Vialhe,' she said, seeing him on the doorstep. 'Monsieur Pierre-Edouard Vialhe.'

'That's me,' he said.

'Oh, good,' she said, as she came nearer. She fumbled in her briefcase, consulted a list: 'Ah, here it is . . . Is it you who's looking after the children David and Benjamin Salomon? Is that you?'

'Maybe,' he admitted.

'Well, I've got good news; we're going to take them off your hands.'

'Who told you they were in our way?' he growled. 'And before you go any further, who are you?'

She held out a card embossed with the Red Cross.

'The two children have cousins living in Morocco, who asked us to make enquiries. It took a long time! They're ready to take in the boys. Where are they, the kids?'

'I don't know about all that,' he said brusquely. 'I only know one thing; someone entrusted the children to us, and I won't let them leave until that person has confirmed your story!'

'But, sir! I'm from the Red Cross!'

'What's that to me! I've been protecting these children for fourteen months, you don't think I'm going to let them leave with any old person!'

He was furious with this woman, who had dared to say she was going to take the children off his hands, just as coldly as a butcher coming to take delivery of a consignment of lambs! Mathilde and he had become attached to these children; they were well behaved, didn't make a fuss, and got on well with Gérard and Pierre; they were part of the family. Of course they couldn't stay in Saint-Libéral for ever, but there was a difference between that and loading them up like livestock!

'Where are they?' insisted the woman. 'I have the right to see them at least!''

'No, until I've checked up on your story, you've no rights.'

'Oh, I see,' she said, 'you probably want to be repaid the cost of their board. I should have expected it, with peasants . . . '

'Get out!' he shouted, advancing a step. 'I've never hit a woman, but it won't be long before I do!'

She took fright and ran to her car. He watched her go and shrugged. Then he smiled and thanked heaven that Mathilde had not been present at the interview. She was picking nuts with Mauricette, Louise and the children.

'She would have scratched out her eyes!' he murmured with a laugh. 'Yes, my girl, you were lucky that she wasn't here, my little Mathilde! She'd certainly have made you pay for their board, with a slap round the face probably!'

But he was worried, and set off immediately to tell Dr Delpy what had happened.

*

It was not until three months later, shortly before Christmas, that David and Benjamin left the Vialhe family. Beforehand, to make sure that the children would be happy in their new family, Pierre-Edouard and Mathilde had insisted that Deply get in touch with these cousins; they themselves had then written to finalise the details of the journey. The two boys were to take the train to Marseilles, where the organisation would receive them and accompany them as far as Rabat, where their cousins lived.

'So that's that,' said Pierre-Edouard when he discussed it all with the doctor. 'I'll be going with them as far as Marseilles, we're leaving the day after tomorrow.'

'You know,' commented the doctor, 'I think that you and Mathilde have done everything you could possibly have done. It's a long way, Marseilles, that's true, but I think the kids are old enough to take the train alone.'

'Possibly, but if they were my children, I'd really like someone to be there to hold their hands until they get on the boat.'

Three days later, it was with a heavy heart that he left the children in the middle of a bunch of kids who were also joining some distant cousin, ancient aunt or uncle, across the sea.

'It wasn't very nice,' he confessed to Mathilde on his return. 'They were like a litter of puppies abandoned beside a pond. Well, at least over there they'll be in their own family, that's one consolation.'

'Tell me, Uncle,' asked little Pierre during the evening meal, 'are you going to take Gérard to the boat as well?'

'And why should I take him?'

The boy shrugged.

'That's what he told me,' he explained.

Pierre-Edouard looked at the older boy, who was hiding his face and blushing.

'Gérard was just having a joke with you,' he reassured him.

'Well, why was he crying, then, when he said it?' insisted the child.

'Huh, you're imagining it! Anyway, Gérard's fourteen now, who cries at that age?'

'Well, nobody.' Pierre accepted this. But he was confused, looking first at his grandmother, then his uncle and his aunt, then at Guy, and finally at Gérard, who had now stopped eating.

'Don't worry,' Mathilde reassured him, 'Gérard will stay here until Aunt Berthe comes back, soon I'm sure. He'll be staying because he's one of the family, like a cousin, you know!'

'Ah, you see!' crowed the boy looking at Gérard. 'I knew we were cousins really!'

'But of course!' interrupted Louise. 'Now eat up if you want to grow as big as Gérard – as your cousin,' she added with a smile.

Jacques and André ran away on 20 January 1945. They had learned, the previous day, that the evacuation of Stalag 1B, to which they were still administratively attached, had begun, and that the prisoners were leaving on foot for an unknown destination.

So, instead of waiting passively for someone to come and collect them from the farm, they gathered up their modest belongings, dressed themselves as warmly as possible, and in the night left the tiny bedroom adjoining the cowshed where they had slept for almost five years.

They walked through the long byre, where they knew each cow, and emerged into the darkness. Jacques nevertheless felt some remorse as he broke open the lock to the cellar where old Karl matured his cheeses; Karl and his wife had always been good to them. What was more, with all four of their sons now killed on the Russian front, they too had suffered terribly in this ghastly war. But that was just what war was like. So Jacques and André filled their haversacks with cheeses, grabbed several kilos of onions and two bottles of schnapps, wedged the door shut again behind him, and left.

They marched in the direction of the muffled sound of cannon fire, which for weeks had indicated the position and progress of the Russian front. It was minus 30° and the snow came up to their knees; so the farm dog, who had watched their thieving with wagging tail, gave up following them as soon as they entered the forest.

Three days later, when they were at the end of their strength, dying of cold, hidden in the corner of a shed ripped open by a shell, the first Russian tank suddenly appeared. Five minutes later, hardly daring to believe that they were free at last, they fell into the arms of some huge fellows in fur hats, who not only thumped them heartily on the back but also kissed them on the lips.

The scarcity of foodstuffs still prevailing in France encouraged Pierre-Edouard to increase all his vegetable crops. He directed his efforts towards the production of quick-growing varieties, and in spring 1945 laid down big beds of potatoes, cabbages, turnips, carrots and haricot beans. At the same time he took particular care of his cattle stock, for meat was also fetching astronomical prices.

All the market rates had gone mad anyway, and Pierre-Edouard had difficulty in remembering the time, not so long ago, when he had taken on Nicolas for the sum of 8 francs a day, or 240 a month; now he paid him 1,100 francs and was not complaining.

Confronted with spiralling prices which showed no signs of abating, he was sometimes seized with panic when he considered the family settlement which he saw growing daily more imminent.

He had to be realistic. His father, although still strong, was declining fast now, and the moments were few and far between when he seemed to recapture a flash of comprehension. He was a heavy burden for Mathilde and Louise, who cared for him like a child; got him up, fed him, washed him. They looked after him without complaint, and Mathilde had even cut Delpy short when he had suggested finding the old man a room in a hospital in Brive. Pierre-Edouard had been proud of his wife's reply; it was exactly what he himself would have said.

'No, Doctor, here we don't turn old people out of their homes; we never have, and while I'm alive we never will. If he were a baby we'd gladly look after him, wouldn't we? Well then! Father's just the same. He has the right to remain under his own roof and the younger ones must look after him; that's how it is and ther 's no other way!'

Despite that, and in spite of all the care which his daughter-in-law and daughter lavished on him, Jean-Edouard was sinking fast. In addition to the sadness caused by his father's condition, Pierre-Edouard felt deeply worried at the thought of all the problems which would arise when he disappeared.

But there were much worse things than material worries. April arrived, and there had been no news of Jacques since December. As for Berthe, the lack of communication was agonising.

Berthe rose before her companions, as she had done every morning since arriving in the camp, slipped on her clogs and glided between the rows of three-tiered bunks on which hundreds of bodies were crammed. And, as every morning, it was with dread that she gently touched the shoulder of the one she came to waken; a shoulder as dry and thin as a juniper twig which she always feared would feel cold and stiff. She put out her hand, and sighed as she noted the warmth of the body.

'It's time,' she whispered.

So in the darkness the skeleton arose: a thin silhouette, puny and frail, of a girl of eighteen whom Berthe had been tirelessly willing to live, every day, every hour, for seven months. A life which wanted to flee, to escape, finally to leave the thirty-two miserable kilos of bones, and grant little Marie the rest she was seeking.

Berthe and she had travelled in the same convoy, suffered the same blows, and, in their accursed railway wagon, the same torture by thirst. Then they had experienced identical horror on discovering the world of the Ravensbrück camp: eleven huge blocks and sixteen small ones, populated by twenty thousand ghosts of women who were constantly urged to work twelve hours a day by other women — other plump women.

Very quickly, Berthe had sensed that Marie wanted to die; that she was letting herself slip away and that, if not supported, she would drift away before long, like the fine ash in the stinking, black smoke streaming out of the crematoria.

So, because she was inspired by a fierce will to live and to win, a will so strong that she had to share it, she had immediately taken Marie under her wing. She never left the young girl, constantly encouraged her, sometimes treating her harshly to force her to live and, against all logic, to make her believe that one day soon the nightmare would end.

And until now, Marie had survived. In some crazy way, incredibly, beginning with this duty imposed by Berthe of getting up each day before their companions, to enable them to wash in peace, before the mass of detainees surged around the tiny water taps, jostled and knocked about by the Kapos, those other women whose rags were adorned with a green triangle.

'Here,' Berthe had told her, 'everything is compulsory, we're ordered and dictated to on every side, so we must invent our own duties. They are what will save us, because we fulfil them of our own volition and when it pleases us!'

To wash at the time decided by Berthe was one of these deliberately chosen duties, and to do it despite exhaustion, cold or mortal danger. There were other principles like these: not to throw yourself like an animal at your mess-tin, for example, but to force yourself to eat slowly, despite the terrible hunger which knotted your stomach and confused your mind. Finally, the craziest perhaps, but the most subtle too, was to recite to each other long accounts of their past lives. Not tender memories – that encouraged nostalgia – but more demanding recollections, more factual.

'I will give you,' Berthe had said, 'the names of all my suppliers and their addresses, also of my clients. I will talk to you about the price of material, choosing it, the quality, the cut and how it's made up. I'll quote you all the measurements of my regular customers and explain to you how a model gown is created. You'll see, I have an excellent memory. And you, since you should have taken your bac last year, will recite to me all your lessons – all of them, you hear, I'm sure you remember them!'

And young Marie, a child lost in this hell, had acquiesced. Thus she survived, led by Berthe Vialhe's steadfast character; she rose each day a quarter of an hour before the others to wash herself, compelled herself to eat and not to guzzle, and recited her lessons in physics, maths, chemistry, Latin and Greek – Berthe understood none of it, but that was not the point.

'Come on,' whispered Berthe, holding out her hand and guiding her, 'we're going to win another day and they're going to lose it. They won't turn us into animals today either. Come on, dear Marie, you'll see, soon it'll be spring.'

Although the bells of Saint-Libéral had remained silent following the liberation of Brive, they pealed at full force on 8 May 1945. This time it really was Victory, the moment which history and mankind would remember as marking the downfall of a detestable regime and a Reich which was supposed to last a thousand years.

They danced that night in Saint-Libéral, at Suzanne's and on the main square; the prisoners were going to come back, and with their imminent return, life would begin again. Even Louise waltzed with Léon who, hugging her waist with one arm, waved a bottle of champagne in the other by jamming it in his hook – the froth spurted out in a serpentine stream.

Pierre-Edouard and Mathilde danced too. Now, they were sure, Jacques and Paul were going to come back, and even Berthe; she would return, it was not conceivable that she should not return.

Yes, she'll come back, thought Pierre-Edouard, smiling at Mathilde, *she'll come back, like Jacques.*

Sometimes Jacques wondered whether he had been right to escape. Since he and his companion had been found by the Russians and taken to a camp where other prisoners were kicking their heels, they were certainly not getting any nearer to France; they were actually moving further away!

Besides, the Soviet soldiers surrounding them, and the three daily roll-calls they were compelled to endure, had the familiar appearance of something extremely unpleasant. They were not prisoners, of course – not quite.

After a long detour across Prussia, interrupted by stops at Osterode and the camp at Zoldau, they had finally returned to Poland and the village of Hurle, not far from Warsaw.

Then they waited. They celebrated the Victory fittingly, noticed bitterly on the following day that there was no question of repatriation, and resumed their wait.

Marie could barely walk. However, she managed to get out of the hut, leant her back against the planks and stretched out her emaciated hands towards the sun.

Free, she was free and alive. But she could not believe it yet; her mind was a turmoil of dreadful memories, horrifying sights. Whatever she did, and despite the French and allied flags waving above the camp, the nightmare persisted; it was engrained, it sapped her strength. She closed her eyes, thought of what Berthe had said.

'Now we must be reborn. You, dear Marie, will be reborn when you can at last cry again; then I'll be sure you'll live!'

But she could not yet cry, and in the sunken hollows no tears formed; she felt herself as dry and stiff as a corpse.

A figure sat down beside her, and Berthe's hand gripped hers.

'Good news, Marie dear; we're leaving the day after tomorrow. We'll see France again at last; you're pleased, I hope?'

The girl nodded, but no smile enlivened her expressionless face. Then, because she knew that Marie could still fade away, like a flame at the lightest breath of air, Berthe continued her tireless struggle. Although she, too, was exhausted, almost finished.

'Come on,' she said, 'we'll have to resume our old habits again, we were wrong to give them up when the camp was liberated. Recite that poem for me, the one I love so much. Thanks to you I know it by heart but I like to hear it. Come on, Marie dear! Come on! All right, you want me to begin?' In a voice broken with weariness she murmured:

> 'Ma petite espérance est celle
> qui s'endort tous les soirs
> dans son lit d'enfant . . . '[1]

She fell silent and clasped the girl's hand.

'Go on, I've forgotten what comes next,' she lied.

Then, at first with short gasps, slowly, gradually growing stronger and finally in a clear voice, young Marie continued:

> 'après avoir bien fair sa prière
> et qui tous les matins se réveille et se lève
> et fait sa prière avec un regard nouveau.'[2]

She stopped, moved her translucent fingers to her cheeks, and was astonished to feel tears rolling down. Then, with a rediscovered smile, she threw herself on Berthe's neck and sobbed with happiness.

[1] My little hope
sleeps each night in its
childish bed . . .

[2] having said its prayers
each morning it
wakes and rises
and says its prayers with
eager eyes

PART SIX

The Late Spring

Chapter 22

GUY and Gérard shot out of the mairie like two missiles, and dashed towards home calling out the news Léon had just received on the telephone.

'Aunt Berthe's coming! Aunt Berthe's coming!'

The shout rolled down the main street and penetrated the seven alleyways of the village, announcing to everyone that Berthe Vialhe was at last returning.

For three weeks they had all known that she was alive, but from the newspapers they also knew what she had suffered in that camp. So, without anyone saying a word, but maybe because of Léon, who was seen to set off in the direction of the Vialhes', everyone in the village in the late afternoon of 25 May gathered together and, without even discussing it, they too marched towards the Vialhes'.

They all came; even Father Delclos – such a quiet, pathetic figure since the death of his mother – and old Léonie Lacroix, one of the doyennes of the community. Gathered in front of the doorstep, they offered Pierre-Edouard, Mathilde and Louise the gift of their presence. At first no one spoke, for there was nothing to say, but the happiness shone in their eyes.

'Thank you,' said Pierre-Edouard after a while, 'thank you for coming.' Then he turned to his brother-in-law: 'When exactly is she arriving?'

'Tomorrow in Brive, by the two o'clock train.'

'Thank you,' repeated Pierre-Edouard.

'We'll all go to meet her,' decided Léon suddenly. 'Well, if you'd like us to come with you.'

'Of course!'

'And we'll organise a reception at the mairie. The whole village must remember this homecoming!'

'Yes, you're right,' said Pierre-Edouard, 'and also . . .' He hesitated, placed one hand on Gérard's shoulder: 'And also,' he continued with emotion, 'believe me, Berthe is worthy of a fine welcome . . . Berthe, you know, is a great lady.'

The people of Saint-Libéral had all heard talk of the concentration camps, and everyone had been horrified by the photos shown in the papers, but no one had envisaged the sight which Berthe presented as she stepped down from the train.

The hurrahs and bravos, which they had all intended to shout when she appeared, died on their lips, as a tiny emaciated old lady, resembling Jean-Edouard, climbed laboriously out of the carriage. Thirty-four kilos of bones, rattling in a too-large dress, were topped by a gaunt little face with a halo of white hair, so short that you could see her scalp.

She gazed at them and shrugged slightly as if to say: 'Yes, that's how it is!' Then she finally spoke.

'What a lot of people!' she said in a clear voice.

And the sound of her voice, which they recognised, comforted them. Then, as Pierre-Edouard ran towards her, the clapping started. And it was in triumph, on the shoulders of her brother and Léon, that Berthe was carried out of Brive station.

Much later, when darkness fell over the village, when Berthe was being talked of in every house, and at the Vialhes' the broken ties of kinship were being reforged, then, with a slight note of reproach in his voice, Pierre-Edouard said to his sister:

'You could have told us right from the beginning, you knew very well we were on your side!'

'Yes,' she smiled, 'I knew that, but I didn't want you to get too involved, because of your children – and him too,' she said, placing a hand on Gérard's shoulder. 'And if you were hiding Jews as well! I know you, you'd have approached the Resistance like your work, to be done thoroughly, without concealment. They would have caught you straight away. Look, they got me, and I was careful! So don't worry about it; we did what we had to do, each in our own way, and I think we did it well. And that's all that matters.'

*

After an incredible journey which took him, via Bialystock, Brest-Litovsk, Kovel, Rovno, as far as Berdichev in the Ukraine, where he had spent over a month in a camp packed with 50,000 refugees, Jacques arrived in Paris on 1 August 1945. His return journey had lasted three weeks, a long peregrination across a Poland bled white and a ravaged Germany. And then, finally, France.

After almost six years away, he was dreading the reunion with his family, for he knew that his father and mother would not be able to recognise the youth of other days in the hardened, bitter man he had become. But he was going to have to resume a normal life, although he felt morally broken; without enthusiasm, will or hope. The war and his captivity had destroyed everything which had given his life meaning before the hostilities: his studies, his vocation, Marie-Louise.

He arrived in Saint-Libéral the following evening, and was surprised to notice immediately the dilapidation of the village buildings, their obvious lack of comfort, the untidiness in all the yards, the messy dung-heaps with pools of stinking brown manure flowing out, swarming with flies.

He realised then that the five years spent on old Karl's farm had changed him. There everything was clean, orderly and convenient. He walked slowly towards the Vialhe house, and guessed from people's looks that nobody recognised him. With his old torn uniform, his bag slung across his shoulder, his hollow cheeks and wild eyes, he looked like a tramp.

Jean-Edouard Vialhe died on 10 December 1945, aged eighty-five. Existing in a cloudy world of his own for years, he had not been aware of the end of the war, nor of Berthe's or Jacques' return. He had not even recognised Paul when he visited on leave, and did not realise that Louise and little Pierre had rejoined Félix, now finally discharged, to live with him again in his forester's cottage by the Château of Cannepetière. He did not know, either, that his granddaughter's marriage was planned for Saturday, 13 July 1946.

The day before his death, Berthe helped Mathilde as usual

to straighten out her father's immobile body in the bed which he now never left. The two women arranged the covers, smoothed the sheets, beat the pillow and plumped up the eiderdown, then they kissed the old man's warm forehead, wished him good night and left the room.

According to Dr Delpy, Jean-Edouard succumbed without pain, without suffering or sound, towards two o'clock in the morning. It was Berthe, sleeping in the same room as him, who realised at first light that he was no longer alive.

During the two days before the funeral, almost all the villagers made their way to the Vialhes' to pay a last visit to someone who had done so much for the community in the past. And cousins many times removed, who had not been in contact with the family for years, also came, for Jean-Edouard Vialhe was known and respected for thirty kilometres around.

Then, uniquely, all his descendants were gathered around him simultaneously: Pierre-Edouard and Mathilde, Jacques, Paul, Mauricette and her fiancé, and Guy. Also Louise, Félix and Pierre, and lastly Berthe, who at the church and in the cortège which followed the hearse to the cemetery, placed Gérard at her side and took his arm.

As for Nicolas, it was Pierre-Edouard who invited him to walk just behind them – in front of Léon, his wife and son, in front of the distant relations, in front of the neighbours. And nobody took offence at this. Furthermore, when they met again in the evening at Suzanne's to share the customary meal together, everyone considered it quite natural for Nicolas to join in.

He had the right, like the close neighbours and friends – those who had carried the pall, the coffin and the cross – like all those who during the dinner were to reminisce, sadly at first, about the old man, then to cheer up and search their memories for a reassuring anecdote, perhaps an amusing one, of which Jean-Edouard would be the focus. And none was shocked if smiles resulted. Thanks to this meal, and for its duration, Jean-Edouard lived again, and only his virtues were mentioned.

'Now, we must come to some arrangement,' said Pierre-

Edouard to his sisters the following evening. He looked at Louise and Berthe, then noticed that Jacques was moving towards the door. 'Stay here!' he said to him, 'a settlement isn't a secret. Sit down – and believe me, I would have said the same to Paul and Félix, if they'd had the time to stay, and to Mauricette and Guy if they hadn't had to go back to school. The Vialhe land concerns all the Vialhes.'

Jacques took his place on the settle, where he was soon joined by his mother and Gérard. Whatever Pierre-Edouard had said, only the direct beneficiaries were left sitting at the table.

'Don't you think we should have waited a bit?' said Louise.

'No, things need to be tidied up and no one should feel disadvantaged,' Pierre-Edouard assured her.

'Bah,' said Berthe, 'all that really doesn't matter. It's you who's working it; the farm comes to you. That's quite normal.'

'Yes,' he acknowledged, 'but there has to be compensation; that's quite normal too.'

'Compensation – you gave me that in looking after Gérard and letting me stay since my return, we're quits. Besides, you know, my business is still going well, I had good managers, so your money . . .'

'No,' he interrupted, 'if I listened to you I would feel that it wasn't my property!'

'That's stupid,' stated Berthe, lighting a cigarette. 'And you, what do you say?' she asked her sister.

Louise hesitated, looked at Pierre-Edouard.

'Listen,' she said in a rush, 'I know that it will be difficult for you, but if you like, you could keep all your cash and I'll take the Combes-Nègres meadow. That's all I ask. It represents about what you'd have given me in money, doesn't it?'

He almost protested; explained that this field of more than two hectares was as necessary to him as the others, that the land should never be divided, and this pasture was excellent for stock. What was more, it contained several superb chestnut trees, and also some magnificent oaks along the edge.

Then he suddenly realised why Louise wanted this field. It

was down there, right at the foot of those chestnut trees, that she and Octave had built their plans for the future forty years earlier; a pathetic future!

'Don't worry,' continued Louise, 'you could still pasture your cows there – after all, what does it matter to the animals whether the grass is yours or mine? You see, Combes-Nègres, that's . . .'

'Yes,' he broke in, 'I understand.' He looked over to Mathilde, seeking her help, but she was absorbed in contemplation of the fire and did not lift her head. 'Right,' he agreed at last, 'you shall have Combes-Nègres.'

'Thank you,' she said, placing her hand on his. 'I know that costs you more than giving money.'

He shrugged and looked at Berthe.

'All right, that leaves you. Do you want land too?' he flung out, with a degree of aggression which he immmediately regretted.

'What do you want to do with Combes-Nègres?' Berthe asked Louise.

'Well, I thought one day perhaps, when I'm retired, I'd like to have a little house built there, if I can, that's all.'

'That's not so stupid,' agreed Berthe. She reflected and searched her memory: 'Tell me,' she questioned her brother, 'is the Teissonières paddock still in the same state?'

'Yes,' he admitted.

That was the only plot, of over half a hectare, which several generations of Vialhes had never been able to cultivate. It lay next to the track which climbed up to the peaks and was therefore easy to reach, but the incline and the rocks clinging to its slope made it impossible to work, even by hand. The only consolation was that the land was worth nothing; it was chalky and heavy, rejecting tools and plants. Besides, as its name indicated, it was riddled with tunnels used by badgers.

'Well, give me the Teissonières and we'll be quits,' suggested Berthe.

'The Teissonnières? But that's worth nothing! You'll never build a house on that slope!'

'Come on now,' she said with a shrug, 'I've seen much worse in America, a house can be built wherever! So is that agreed?'

'You don't mean it,' he decided. 'Louise's bit, that's worth it, but the Teissonières! If the solicitor knows where it is he'll think we're making fun of him, or that I'm swindling you!'

'Don't get involved with a solicitor,' she interrupted. 'Or at least, if you let me draft the plan, you'll see, he'll have nothing to do but copy it out and everything will be in order. Good, that's settled,' she confirmed. 'You keep the farm, Louise takes Combes-Nègres and I have the Teissonières. There, the arrangement's been made, let's not talk about it any more!'

'But . . .' he attempted again, embarrassed at the imbalance in the division.

'Let's not talk about it,' she repeated. 'Louise is happy, you are too, and so am I.' She fell silent and thought for a moment: 'And you know what,' she continued, 'we have to face up to it; if Father had made the settlement while he was alive, Louise and I would have received nothing, not even a pocket handkerchief of land! You have to admit that!'

'Yes,' he concurred, 'but if he'd suspected that I would let you have land, he would definitely have made his own arrangements before going!'

But he was laughing quietly as he spoke, and they all understood that the succession was settled.

Despite the satisfaction which it gave him to know that he was at last sole owner of the land, Pierre-Edouard was not completely happy. Firstly, despite all the conflicts and quarrels which he had previously faced with his father, his death affected him. It marked the end of a long era, and reminded him that he too was moving towards old age, weariness and loss of energy. He would soon be fifty-seven, and should be thinking of giving way to someone younger.

There was the stumbling-block. Unlike his father, who had clung fiercely to his privileges as head of the family, Pierre-Edouard was ready to share his position and responsibilities. He understood that the impetus to improve the whole farm could no longer come from him; he did not lack for ideas about future progress, only for enthusiasm, spirit and courage. Already he felt too tired to throw himself into the struggle, as he had done thirty years earlier. But he was now forced to recognise that none of his sons was going to fulfil his expectations.

Paul was much too happy in the army to consider for a moment leaving it; it was his true vocation, his reason for living. He was ready to take on the whole world, and hoped that he would be given the chance to do so.

As for Guy, he loved his studies and shone at them as his eldest brother had. He was a boarder at the lycée in Brive and, although Mathilde had been a bit shocked at Pierre-Edouard's choice of the secular system, she had quickly admitted that her husband's opinion had a solid basis.

'The Catholic school? No thank you,' he had said. 'Remember the difficulties Mauricette experienced after leaving there!'

But Mathilde knew very well that this was not the only reason; the other one was more serious and fundamental. It hinged on the attitude of Father Delclos during the war. From that time Pierre-Edouard mistrusted the clergy, was suspicious of them and not at all sure that one could have complete confidence in them.

'But think of poor Father Verlhac,' Mathilde had argued, 'he fought, and that's why . . .'

'Exactly, I'm afraid that all the good priests may have been shot! Now if there are only the ones like Delclos left, I'm not handing my son over to them!'

So Guy was at the lycée with his cousin Louis, Léon's son, and both were doing well.

That left Jacques, and with him everything was difficult. Pierre-Edouard and Mathilde had immediately seen just how the war, captivity and the break with Marie-Louise had crushed him, but they had hoped that in time things would settle down; in vain. His bitterness was so painfully obvious that nobody dared question him about his plans for the future. Did he have any at all?

During the six months and more since his return, the only comments he occasionally let fall were marked by an aggressive pessimism which pained them. When Mathilde had asked him if he was considering continuing his studies, he had laughed in her face.

'After a six-year break, at my age and after what I've experienced! Can you see me getting down to learning how to treat verminous bronchitis or foot-and-mouth disease, amongst all those kids?'

When his Aunt Berthe retorted that age was of no importance; that she herself, at fifty-one and after what she had suffered, was preparing to start work again, he had drily revealed the heart of the matter.

'Yes, indeed! You can do whatever you want, you were in the Resistance. You have some fine medals now, and all doors are open to you, as they are to everyone who chose that route! Look at the way that it's enough for any young idiot to stick on a tricolour armband for all the girls to lie down on their backs! But we fools who enlisted in 1940, where's the glory in five years of captivity? We've done nothing, right? And everyone makes sure we know it!'

'Don't talk stupid,' Pierre-Edouard had interrupted, 'nobody's blaming you for anything!'

'Perhaps it would be better if they did, at least I'd be able to defend myself.' And he had terminated the conversation by leaving the room.

Since then he had lived at the farm and worked hard, but rather like someone uninterested in the results of his efforts, almost like a wage-earner who is content to fulfil the task without being concerned about the running of the business.

Nevertheless, Pierre-Edouard had soon become aware of his skill and knowledge, but the only time he had alluded to the future of the farm, Jacques had shrugged.

'The farm?' he had said. 'You think it's beautiful, don't you? It's miserable! You're working here like at the turn of the century. All of it needs to be changed, all of it!'

'Well then, do it, for God's sake! Let's see what you can do!' Pierre-Edouard had shouted at him, annoyed at the unfairness of such a judgement.

But Jacques had turned his back, muttering to himself. Since then neither Pierre-Edouard nor Mathilde knew how to take him, but to see him so deeply embittered clouded the atmosphere for everyone.

It was Mathilde who found the original impetus to help the

family out of the rut and escape the drowsiness which was engulfing the village. For despite the end of the war and the return of the prisoners, life was not going well in Saint-Libéral.

Jacques was not the only one for whom readaptation was painful; the other young people, whether they had suffered five years of captivity, two years of Compulsory Work Service, or had known the excitement of life with the maquis and the wild enthusiasm of the Liberation, could no longer accept life as it had been before the war. The routine had been interrupted, and for many the land no longer held any attraction; the work seemed so laborious to them, terribly monotonous and dull, and above all badly paid. So they succumbed to the lure of the towns.

There everything had to be rebuilt: there was no shortage of work, and even if the salaries were not as fantastic as some people said, they were secure, and so were the holidays. The young people therefore left, and the village suffered by this exodus.

It was obvious to everyone that the markets, for example, which had made the name of Saint-Libéral, were going to disappear, despite Léon's determination. Already they only attracted a few dozen sellers, and the stall-holders kept away. Like the Vialhe family, the community was not adapting well to the new-found peace.

Mathilde felt it was vital to act, and disclosed her plan. She had been nurturing it for more than twenty years, but before launching it she did the calculations, got the information, built up some practical evidence. Then, when she was confident of success, she enthusiastically revealed her project.

'Now,' she said one evening in February, having placed the soup tureen on the table, 'there's no need for us to live like animals any longer!'

'What are you talking about?' said Pierre-Edouard, surprised by her tone of voice.

'I'm saying that the settlement you made with your sisters spared you having to lay out any money. That money, if we save it, will lose value year by year, I'm sure of that.'

She poured herself two ladles of soup, waiting for her

words to take effect.

'And so?' asked Pierre-Edouard.

'So we're going to make this house comfortable, we're going to extend it. I've had enough of living in a hovel where we're all on top of one another when the children are at home, where I'm ashamed to receive your sisters, and even my brother!'

Pierre-Edouard observed her, touched to see her so resolute and determined. She was always like that when it came to making an important decision, and he honestly admitted that he had never regretted having listened to her and followed the paths she had chosen. But here was a grand design; a bit too grand.

'Mustn't overdo it,' he said after a while. 'All right, we can do a bit of work, but we're a long way from building a château!'

'There's no question of that,' she interrupted. 'I don't want a château, I want to live in a proper house at last, and for that we need to extend. We've got all the space we need on the garden side.'

'Maman's right,' declared Jacques suddenly.

His father had grown so accustomed to his silence that he was astonished; as for Mathilde, she saw that she was on the right track and pushed home her advantage.

'We must add at least three bedrooms and a dining-room.'

'Not forgetting a bathroom,' added Jacques.

'Are you two in league or what?' demanded Pierre-Edouard. 'I'm not a millionaire, you know!'

'Maman's right,' repeated Jacques, looking at his father. 'You know,' he said suddenly, 'on the farm up there in Prussia, the farmer's house was as comfortable as a house in town. Yes, they even had a bathroom with a shower! And the whole farm was just as modern, so when I compare it with here . . .'

Pierre-Edouard very nearly forgot himself and shouted: 'You should have stayed there if it was better than here,' but he controlled himself, recalling the occasional comments Jacques had made about the general condition of the farm. He remembered, too, that he himself had quarrelled with his father thirty-five years earlier, because the old man would not admit that someone could do better than him in a sphere where he considered himself an innovator.

'All right,' he said at last, 'it seems German farms are more modern than ours; I've been told that already, and not just by you. But what about the money?' He sighed as he rubbed forefinger and thumb together.

'No problem,' Mathilde assured him. 'We'll put in what you'd saved for your sisters and borrow the rest; that way we could still keep a little bit in reserve.'

'You've just been telling me that money's going to lose value!'

'If it's left idle, yes, but we won't leave ours . . .'

'Oh, I see! More investment schemes with your brother!'

'And why not?'

'Right, we'll consider the matter, but why think so big?'

'Because I hope that one day,' said Mathilde, without looking at Jacques, 'I hope that you'll need it to accommodate your grandchildren, and if you don't want to quarrel with your daughter-in-law, believe me, you'd better make some room!'

The work began in the spring of 1946, and proceeded at a good pace, for whenever possible Pierre-Edouard, Jacques and Nicolas helped the workmen.

Soon the new wing rose up, attached to the main body of the house; a solid construction of fine cut stone with a slate roof, a unit accessible from the old house by just one door. Mathilde had insisted on this, and opposed the demolition of the partition wall which would have enlarged the dining-room and made the new accommodation irrevocably part of the old.

'A door,' she had said, 'you can close it and be in your own place. Thanks to that you'll have two separate houses, if you need them; that's the best way.'

For a while, the extension of the Vialhe house provided the villagers with an interesting topic of conversation. Some found such an outlay completely senseless, others – the jealous ones – discreetly hinted that the Vialhes were investing the fruits of four years on the black market in their stonework. But no one believed those malicious tongues.

As for Pierre-Edouard, he let them talk, for he had no reply to the other argument, the only valid one, that reinforced all the criticisms: What was the use of all this outlay when Jacques remained as taciturn as ever and seemed to be retreating further into unsociable bachelordom? Neither would Paul, now in Indo-China, make use of it, nor Mauricette, who, after her marriage, would return with her husband to their small country school near Egletons. What about Guy? Nothing could be less likely: the land held little appeal for him and he did not hide the fact. So what was the good of this vast mansion? When he thought about it, Pierre-Edouard began to wonder whether, for the first time since they were married, Mathilde had been wrong.

As planned, and despite the recent bereavement which had touched the Vialhe family, Mauricette and Jean-Pierre Fleyssac were married on 13 July 1946. The celebration was joyful but quiet, for it would have been unacceptable if Pierre-Edouard and Mathilde had provided too ostentatious a wedding only eight months after Jean-Edouard's death. All the same, because the young people thought that you should do away with all the troublesome bits of tradition and only keep the pleasing customs — even Mathilde had taken the lead by wearing mourning for only three months — they cheered the newly-weds and danced late into the night in the square.

However, those over forty, out of decency and respect for their forebear, refrained from waltzing. So Pierre-Edouard and Mathilde, seated with friends and the parents-in-law in the main room of the inn, did not see that Jacques too made the most of the celebration.

His whole evening was spent at the side of a ravishing little brunette, a friend of his sister's from Perpezac-le-Blanc. Michèle was twenty-one, as fresh and pleasing as a wild rose, and she burst into peals of laughter at the jokes he whispered in her ear.

Towards eleven o'clock when the two accordion players took a break one of the guests who had brought his gramophone and some modern records made the square of

Saint-Libéral ring with unaccustomed music. All the young people shouted their delight and Michèle, who danced brilliantly, wanted at all costs to teach Jacques the frenetic steps to these newly arrived American dances which were all the rage in Paris.

Amused, he listened with good grace to his pretty partner's explanations, watched how the others were moving, and launched himself into a boisterous jive; for the first time in years, he was happy.

'You see, it's not difficult!' cried the girl triumphantly, when the record stopped with a nasty squeak of the needle.

'No, but it's tiring and loud. Look, wouldn't you like to take a walk somewhere quiet?' he asked, lighting a cigarette.

'Wait a bit, I know this record, the other side is a "slow", you'll see, it's easy. Slow, that's English for a quiet number,' she felt the need to explain.

'I know,' he said a little drily.

'Sorry,' she murmured with a blush, 'I forgot you had to give up your studies because of the war.'

The gramophone, duly wound-up by hand again, drawled out a slow rhythmic tune, a soothing melody, rather nostalgic.

'Come and dance,' invited Michèle. 'You'll see, it's quite simple.'

He embraced her, let himself be carried away by the music; felt the sweet pressure of the girl's breasts against his chest and the gentle touch of her fingers on his neck.

'You wanted to be a vet, didn't you?'

'That's right.'

She understood that he did not want to talk about it, and tried very clumsily to change the subject.

'I'd have liked to be a teacher,' she declared, 'but it was too difficult, I stopped in the third year. Still, it's better than nothing, isn't it?'

'Of course.'

'At that level, perhaps I could find a job in the town; I must find something to do, now I'm free. Yes,' she explained, 'my mother has been ill for two years, so I do her work at home. But now my father doesn't need me any more; my youngest brother is going to take up an apprenticeship in Brive.'

'The record's finished,' remarked Jacques, without for a moment letting go of the girl, 'shall we take a walk? All this noise makes me feel dizzy.'

Nobody noticed that they had disappeared. Jacques led her towards the track which climbed towards the peaks. At first he was silent, then, encouraged by the darkness and the girl holding his hand, he began to talk, rather as if he were alone; to express the burden weighing on his heart, which had grown heavier since the war had destroyed his dreams. He recounted all his heartbreak, disappointment and despair; talked of the emptiness which he saw before him and which he did not know how to fill.

'I thought you were supposed to take on the farm,' she said when he fell silent. 'Well, that's what everyone around here thinks.'

'The farm?' he said bitterly. 'I'd as soon be a bishop!'

'Don't you like it?'

'No, it's not that, but you know, working with my father . . . Oh, not that he's unpleasant, poor old thing! But it's just that he's old; he has his ideas and I have mine. On the farm, you'd need to be able to start it all again from scratch, which I'd certainly like to do, but with my father that's impossible.'

'So what are you going to do?'

He stopped walking, sighed, then turned towards her and smiled at the face shining with moonlight turned up to him.

'What am I going to do?' he said at last. 'I have no idea. Perhaps leave for the town, like the others. Unless . . .'

He put out his hand and stroked the dark fringe from the girl's forehead. 'It's amazing,' he continued, 'until this evening I thought that my father being there was stopping me from taking on the farm, but I was wrong. It wasn't his presence that put me off, but an *absence*. The most important thing was missing, do you understand?'

'Maybe.'

'Well, if you do, we'll see each other again?'

'Perpezac's not far, especially if you go over the top way . . .'

337

'That's right, I'll go the top way. Tomorrow then? It's Sunday. Tomorrow at two o'clock I'll be at the foot of the White Peak. Will you be there? Promise?'

She nodded and held out her hand to him.

Chapter 23

'So you still don't want a Boche or two?' asked Léon when he arrived at the Vialhes' one evening.

'I've already told you what I think of that; me, I've seen enough of those grey-green uniforms!' said Pierre-Edouard, inspecting the cleanliness of his gun barrels.

It was the eve of the hunting season, and on the table lay his Hamerless and Jacques' Darne, in pieces.

'It's no joke,' Léon assured him. 'Following our request, I've received the reply of the departmental Office of Works and Manpower; the commune will receive seven extra prisoners of war, so if you want one . . .'

'No,' insisted Pierre-Edouard, vigorously deploying the swab, 'prisoners, I don't want any of them. I'm no warder!'

'Well, since Mouly and the others have been using them they're not unhappy about it! And then, it's a good deal; bed and board doesn't even come to ten francs a day!' persisted Léon, who had enjoyed teasing his brother-in-law about this ever since the first prisoners of war arrived in the village six months earlier.

'*Miladiou*, I know!' grumbled Pierre-Edouard. 'Less than ten francs a day, okay, but what about the one who escaped from Maurice's and cost him a fine of fifteen hundred francs – not counting the pair of trousers, two shirts and the jacket he pinched when he left! Anyway, why don't you take some, eh?'

'Come on, I'm only joking,' said Léon, 'you know very well I feel the same as you. Prisoners, I'd rather tell them how and which way to get going! All the same, do you know who's asked me for one?'

Pierre-Edouard shrugged and began to reassemble his gun.

'That rascal Delpeyroux!' exclaimed Léon, laughing. 'Talk of a nerve! Well, I hope he gets a rogue who buggers off in a hurry! I'd really like it if Delpeyroux had to pay fifteen hundred francs for poor supervision! But that's not what brings me here,' he said, suddenly serious. 'Is Jacques around?'

'No, and I don't know where he is. For the last two months, as soon as work is finished, he's off!'

'I have my own ideas about that,' remarked Léon, lighting a cigarette.

'Me too, and Mathilde as well . . .'

'A girl, eh?'

'Of course, and I even know who!'

'Is she from the village?'

'No, it's the little Mas girl from Perpezac.'

'Mas?' Léon frowned. 'Oh yes, I know, it's little Michèle! The devil, he's got a good eye!'

'Yes, that's her. It was Ma Pouch, from Temple, who told Mathilde; she saw them together, over by the White Peak.'

'It doesn't sound as if you're very pleased, but she's pretty enough, that girl. He's got taste, has Jacques!'

'It's not that.' Pierre-Edouard was annoyed. 'The idiot never says anything, not a word! It's been a year since he came back, and I still have the feeling that he's just passing through!'

'That's why I'd have liked him to be here; what I've just learned might interest him. But it's you it really concerns. The squire's daughter is selling everything, even the château . . .'

'Everything?' murmured Pierre-Edouard, thinking immediately of the land on the plateau, not far from his own.

'All of it,' repeated Léon. 'She came to see me this afternoon. Yes, almost seventy hectares, thirty of them woodland – well, you know what there is!'

'Yes, yes. How much?'

'Expensive. She wants three million for the lot.'

'Bloody hell!'

'Well, yes,' said Léon, 'but I thought the land on the plateau would be just right for you. There are ten hectares up there; with those you'd have a nice little outfit.'

'Those . . .' admitted Pierre-Edouard. He thought for a moment, and continued: 'But what about you, what are you interested in? You're not going to tell me that you want to buy the château?'

'Well,' Léon looked a little embarrassed, 'I did think I might . . .'

'My God!' exclaimed Pierre-Edouard, 'but you're crazy! What do you want with that barracks?'

He was flabbergasted. All well and good that his brother-in-law should take the meadows and the woods, he could make use of them, but the château! Or perhaps it was simply to wipe out the memory of a poverty-stricken childhood: of his father hanging from the ridge beam of the barn – Léon had knocked against his legs one day in January 1900; of that sordid hovel where he'd lived, and all the humiliations he had been forced to endure, before becoming the rich and respected man he was today?

Yes, he thought, that must be it. He spent his whole life proving that he's stronger than all of us; the château is his revenge, his triumph! Damn it, if his father had seen this it would have driven him mad! It's incredible – Léon, the son of the poorest smallholder in the commune, Léon's going to buy the château!

'It's incredible,' he repeated in hushed tones.

'Does it surprise you so much?'

'All things considered, no. But still, it's a bloody great sum, three million!'

'Oh, that . . .' said Léon with a shrug.

'That's right,' admitted Pierre-Edouard, remembering that Yvette's father had died fifteen months earlier, leaving them a considerable fortune.

'You understand,' explained Léon, as if he needed to justify himself, 'if we buy it, it's only for the boy. You've seen what a good student he is; one day, maybe, he'll be a doctor or a solicitor, even a member of parliament. The château will be just the thing for him, more dignified than a plain house.'

'All the same, if someone had told me you'd be sleeping in the squire's bed one day . . . !'

'The wheel turns . . . Right, these fields on the plateau; I've calculated roughly, that makes them thirty thousand a hectare. Will you take them?'

'You're crazy!' protested Pierre-Edouard, 'at that price! And look here,' he added with a touch of bitterness, 'we took out our savings to extend the house, so . . .'

Léon shrugged.

'Is Mathilde around?'

'Yes, she's doing some mending in the bedroom.'

'Tell her to come. Where money's involved, I've more faith in her than you!'

Pierre-Edouard nodded his head and called his wife.

'If only we hadn't done all this work!' sighed Mathilde, as soon as she heard the news. 'If I'd known . . .' She observed to Pierre-Edouard with an unhappy look.

'What's done is done,' he said.

'Don't make me laugh,' Léon commented sarcastically. 'You won't get me to believe that you spent everything on the extension!'

'Of course not,' admitted Mathilde.

'That would have surprised me, because you've been getting me to buy napoléons for quite a time. You must have a bloody cauldron full by now!'

'No we haven't!' she protested, 'and well you know it! We do still have a few. But I don't want to touch them, that's our savings in case we fall ill.'

'Rubbish,' said Léon. 'Believe me, the best investment is land. Thirty thousand a hectare today, and maybe three hundred thousand in ten years' time! Yes, I tell you!' he repeated at his sister's sceptical look. 'Look, remember what I paid for land on the plateau in 1918.'

'Two thousand two hundred francs,' she admitted.

'And one year later, the lot we bought together was already three thousand five hundred,' recalled Pierre-Edouard.

'All the same,' she persisted, 'thirty thousand francs, it's impossible. With the overheads, ten hectares would cost us at least three hundred and twenty thousand francs, and that's too much . . .'

'Borrow,' suggested Léon. 'It's a good time for it.'

'We already have a loan for the house,' Pierre-Edouard reminded him.

'Sort something out,' urged Léon, 'you can't let a deal like this go. I asked for two weeks to consider it. At the moment we're the only ones in on this, but in two weeks the squire's daughter will put it on the open market . . .'

'If only we knew what Jacques wants to do,' said Pierre-Edouard. 'If we were certain he'd stay, we could buy half of it on his account; that would be a good start for him.'

'My God! Talk to him!' cried Léon. 'You're not going to tell me that you're frightened of him, that kid!'

'Well, no,' complained Pierre-Edouard, 'it's not that! But have you ever tried to talk about cattle-rearing with a mechanic! He doesn't care, it doesn't mean anything to him! It's like that with Jacques. He's not at home here, you see. Well, that's certainly what he feels, and I'm beginning to believe he may be right! Now, this land; we'll think about it.'

'Don't leave it too late,' advised Léon, as he headed for the door. 'And look, try and see what's up with Jacques. Really, he's beginning to get annoying, that boy!'

That evening, Pierre-Edouard waited until Nicolas had returned to his room, which was still fitted up in the stable, before rising from the table himself. He then went to turn down the radio and sat down on the settle.

Surprised at this manoeuvre, Jacques lifted his nose out of the newspaper and looked at his father. It had become almost a ritual: normally he remained seated at the table, reading and re-reading copies of *Chasseur Français* or *Rustica* while smoking a pipe or two, then went to bed.

'I must have a talk with you,' Pierre-Edouard said to him.

'Yes,' Mathilde backed him, as she plunged the plates into the washing-up bowl.

'That's convenient, because I need to talk to you, too.'

'Oh, good,' Pierre-Edouard said, somewhat astonished. 'Well, you begin.'

Jacques slowly folded the newspaper, lit a cigarette.

'I'm going to get married,' he announced.

'We knew that,' said Mathilde, smiling. 'Well, we thought so. It's little Michèle Mas from Perpezac, isn't it?' she continued, beginning to wipe a plate.

'That's right,' he agreed. He looked at his parents and his heart tightened to see them so happy, enlivened by this news. 'Yes,' he repeated, 'we're getting married next month.'

'What? Why so quickly?' demanded Pierre-Edouard,

suddenly worried.

'Because time is short,' admitted Jacques, and jumped as the plate his mother was wiping shattered on the tiles.

'*Nom de Dieu!*' shouted Pierre-Edouard angrily, 'so you couldn't be bothered to wait a bit!'

He was disappointed, hurt; furious too, for what his son had just announced was a betrayal. The Vialhes of Saint-Libéral had never needed to blush for their behaviour in that respect. Even when Louise had run away to marry Octave, she had been able to marry in white, proudly, without pretence. As for Berthe, her past conduct had not been within the framework of village life.

'Look, you little sod,' he went on, 'look what your mother thinks of a marriage where time is short!'

Mathilde was crying, silently, as always. But she seemed so devastated by the revelation that Jacques felt embarrassed.

'Listen,' he urged, 'it's not a tragedy, after all! Oh, I know, it used to be something to be ashamed of, but look, it's not like that now, it's 1946, not 1920! Try to understand!'

'Be quiet,' said his mother, wiping her eyes on her apron. 'We don't need any lessons from you in understanding! Because it's you who hasn't understood how things are now!'

'All right, okay, we were too quick. But look, we're not the only ones! And now, that's how it is and it can't be changed! Anyway, we're both adults, and we'll be getting married on the twenty-sixth of October; it's a Saturday.'

Pierre-Edouard sighed, knocked his unlit pipe against the hollow of the andiron.

'Fine,' he said, 'do as you like. You said you were adults! Right, so you'll go all alone to the Mas family to explain to them that you've made a mess of things, that's all in order, is it?'

'That's what I was meaning to do,' said Jacques drily. 'I'm not in the habit of running away.'

He had never considered sending his father as a mediator, for, as soon as Michèle had told him that she was pregnant by more than a month, he had allayed her fears by assuring her that he would take total responsibility and act

344

accordingly.

'We meant to get married on Midsummer's Day,' he'd said to her, 'but it'll be the christening then instead!'

But she had understood that he was showing off a bit, and that at heart he was contrite and upset.

'We've been stupid, haven't we?' she had continued.

'I'm the only one who's been stupid. You — you're just beautiful, that was all it took, it was bound to happen!'

'Our parents will take it badly . . .'

'Naturally, but that doesn't matter; it's our business, not theirs. And then, how do you expect them to understand!'

'Yes,' she had said, kissing him, 'I'm sure when they were young they didn't love each other as we do!'

'When is it to be, your . . . mistake?' asked Pierre-Edouard.

'End of May.'

'Right,' said Mathilde, beginning to pick up the pieces of plate, 'and apart from making babies and marrying, what else are you capable of doing? Any fool can do that, after all.'

Jacques was surprised at the coldness of her tone. He had certainly thought that she would take it badly, but that she would limit herself to simply rebuking him — it was not her way to nag.

'Yes, apart from making love, what were you thinking of doing?' Pierre-Edouard joined in bluntly. 'You're surprised to hear me talking like that? What do you think, little fool, that you were found in a cabbage patch? Good God, if your mother and I had followed our inclinations, you wouldn't have been born in 1920 but in June 1918, nine months after my leave! Only in our time, if we were thinking of the wrong side of the sheets, we considered the consequences! So, you dummy, what are you going to do, now you've made the wine before picking the grapes?'

Jacques was disconcerted. He would soon be twenty-seven and had never heard his father talk like that, nor his mother for that matter. He saw them as a couple united by great affection and long understanding, but he had always refused to imagine them as really in love, madly in love, like Michèle and himself for instance.

345

'Well,' he said at last, 'unless you don't want anything to do with us, we thought we could live on the farm, but . . .'

'Yes?' Pierre-Edouard pressed.

'That is . . . To prevent any difficulties, perhaps it would be better if we were independent.'

'That's exactly our feeling,' said Pierre-Edouard, and again his reply amazed his son. 'You want to take over the farm? All right, but I'm not old enough or rich enough to sit around doing nothing, so what do you suggest?'

Jacques had been turning over this problem in his mind. He had even considered going to work in the town. With his two baccalauréats, one year in veterinary college and five in captivity, he was confident of finding a job, as a civil servant for instance, in some administrative capacity.

But the idea of having to spend eight hours a day in an office, to carry out some boring task under the thumb of a departmental supervisor, had repelled him. He was not one to take orders, nor to fit in to fixed working hours, still less to wait placidly for his paid holidays and retirement.

Once he had wanted to be a veterinarian, because he liked the profession but also because he thought he could be his own master. Since this avenue was now irrevocably closed to him, it would be better to find one where he could at least keep his freedom, use his initiative, take responsibility and not be accountable to anyone but himself. The land gave him that, provided that his father understood his conditions.

'You let me work half the land as I think fit, we help each other with work, but each does as he wishes on his own ground, how's that?' he asked.

Pierre-Edouard deigned to smile.

'You're greedy, you devil! Half of it? If I'd said that to my father he'd have boxed my ears!'

'Tell him Léon's news,' interposed Mathilde.

Pierre-Edouard hesitated, wondering whether Jacques was motivated by love for the land or the need to find a job; he rejected the niggling doubts, and looked to the future.

'If you like, you could have ten hectares on the plateau, the château's fields; they're for sale. But if you want that land, you'll have to manage to buy half of it in your own name. Not got enough money? We had less than you when we got married; your mother made me take out a loan, and she was right. As for the rest of the land, we'll take care of it and make it over to you.'

'Really?' Jacques was ecstatic. 'You're not joking?'

'Really. We can't let you have the whole farm yet, because we've got to live, but you can definitely have those ten hectares belonging to the château.'

'Bloody hell, that's good news!'

'Yes,' said Mathilde, '*that* is . . .'

'Oh, and the rest too!' cried Jacques. 'You'll see, Michèle is perfect, you'll get on ever so well with her. And you can't be cross with us for ever about a little mistake like that!'

'I've already forgotten about your little mistake,' she said with a shrug, 'well, almost. And I'll forget how the people are going to laugh at us too – because, believe me, they'll enjoy that, for once the Vialhes have given them an excuse! Yes, I'll forget, but I'd be very surprised if you ever forget it! Well,' she murmured rather sadly, 'we each make our own beds to lie on, but it's no use being surprised or complaining if you feel the lumps later on.'

Léon burst into laughter when he was informed next day.

'I was afraid it would amuse you,' admitted Pierre-Edouard.

'Oh, the little beggar,' said Léon, 'who'd have thought it of him, eh? All the same, he's my nephew; I'll bawl him out a little, on principle, you know!'

'He doesn't care,' said Pierre-Edouard.

'But you and Mathilde do, I bet.'

'She's taken it badly – and then, it's so irresponsible. Dammit, everyone knows that Perpezac girls are as hot as bakers' ovens, but if you'd told me my son would go and burn himself before the loaves were ready!'

'Never mind burning himself,' joked Léon, 'he left a bun in there! I expect Mathilde's in a state!'

'Yes, and she's afraid that people will laugh at us.'

'If that's all you're worried about! You know, with the young people, things like that often happen, and just about everywhere. People soon get tired of laughing about it – and anyway, they don't dare, because they only need to have one

347

boy or one girl to think to themselves: it could happen to us as well!'

'Maybe,' admitted Pierre-Edouard. 'Anyway, it's irresponsible,' he reiterated. 'Right, about this land; we agree, we'll buy it. Jacques has decided to stay on the farm.'

'There, you see!' Léon was jubilant. 'Everything's falling into place, now your worries are over. And I'm truly happy for all of you! So you'll take the ten hectares on the plateau?'

'Yes, we'll get the money somehow. But you're going to buy the rest, are you? Oh, I'm only saying that because I know that Maurice, Edmond too and even Edouard, would have bought a bit of it, so if we do it behind their backs, without saying anything, they'll hold it against us and for some time to come!'

'I know,' said Léon, 'I've thought about that. But if they find out about it before the sale has gone through other people will find out too, and we'll all be in the soup! No, let me handle it, I've got an idea. The squire's daughter wants a big sum of money all at once; she'll get it. Perhaps not as much as she thinks, because I haven't started bargaining yet, and she'll have to come down a bit! But once I've bought it, don't worry, I won't keep it all. I'm interested in the château, the pine wood and the grazing; I'll hand over the rest to whoever wants it. I've already got a hundred and twenty acres of my own or rented dotted about the place, I don't need any more land that I can't use.'

'Are you sure?' insisted Pierre-Edouard.

'I give you my word,' said Léon. 'You know my word's my bond. Our friends'll do well out of the sale of the château. But just for now, let me handle it, and don't tell anyone. Once, about forty years ago, I talked too much in your father's hearing, about the meadow by the mill, and he stitched me up. That was a lesson well learned.'

Mathilde had suffered too much from sharing her living space to be one of those mothers-in-law who believe they should transform a couple into a trio. She had therefore no wish to interfere in the young couple's household affairs. She forced herself to welcome her daughter-in-law as best she could, but she had to work to suppress the bad impression the hastily arranged marriage had made on her.

Despite the quietness of the ceremony, the lack of ostentation and limited number of guests, Mathilde had barely been able to swallow her daughter-in-law's audacity – marrying in white, and in her own parish!

'We'd never have dared do that in our day!' she confided in Pierre-Edouard.

'That's right, and not so long ago they'd even have had to go to Rocamadour to marry, with just two witnesses. That's the way it goes, we have to accept it's all changed; well, we'll have to make the best of it and take life as it comes.'

All went well for the first few months, but probably only because the purchase of the château land and Jacques' restored energy masked the petty differences, the divergent views and idiosyncrasies of all parties.

Michèle was gentle, kind, polite to her parents-in-law, but she had a will of her own, knew what she wanted, and gradually got into the habit of running the house her own way. She kept a different timetable for her work from Mathilde, happily left the evening's dishes to be done the next day, postponing the time for tending the animals and thus the midday meal as well.

These were trifles, so Pierre-Edouard and Mathilde tried to adapt. Most of all they did not want to disturb the obvious happiness radiating from the young couple.

Stimulated by his wife, who, despite her pregnancy was still as affectionate as a lamb, Jacques was in seventh heaven. Now that he was master of his own land and free to work it according to his own theories, he was bursting with confidence and new projects.

However, despite the pride Pierre-Edouard and Mathilde felt in their son's capabilities, and their good intentions, they never felt on the same wave-length as the young people. And what had at first been insignificant details grew into a wall of misunderstandings.

Seldom did Mathilde and her daughter-in-law hold the same opinion on any subject. Concerning religion, for example, Michèle made a point of avoiding it for, she stated quite candidly, 'Only bigots bother with Father Delclos!' It was partly true; he was growing old, crotchety, embittered, and his sectarianism alienated all the young people. However, Mathilde, although she could hardly bear him, felt it her duty to attend the services. Then to hear her daughter-in-law talk about bigots!

The two women also crossed swords on the question of money, for, even though they did not operate a joint budget, Jacques and Michèle's happy-go-lucky attitude was worrying. Pierre-Edouard and Mathilde had never borrowed without first calculating the rates of interest and the consequences. Jacques relied completely on the support of the Crédit Agricole, and already planned to borrow to the limit to purchase equipment. In this matter he clashed with his mother, and also with his father, who recommended caution and reminded him that with land, sowing and working it are one thing, and harvesting quite another.

'All right,' Pierre-Edouard said to him one evening, when he had talked of buying a second-hand van, 'your wheat is magnificent. I'd heard talk that this Vilmorin was good, and you've proved it to me. But it isn't threshed yet, nor sold, so don't count your chickens before they're hatched. Especially to buy a car, which will be nothing but an expense!'

'With your system, nobody would ever get anywhere!'

'Maybe, but it's thanks to that system that five generations of Vialhes have got you where you are! Anyway, you do as you want, it's your problem.'

Then came the absolute parting of the ways that Mathilde had seen coming for months. She was so looking forward to welcoming her grandson or granddaughter into the world that she was terribly disappointed when Jacques announced that Michèle was going to give birth in Brive.

'But why?' asked Mathilde, 'why not here? I'll be there! I'll help her!'

'I prefer Brive, it's safer!'

'Bloody hell!' shouted Pierre-Edouard, who also felt thwarted. 'Safer than what? Your mother was alone at Coste-Roche when you came into the world; she didn't die of it and you didn't either!'

'Michèle would prefer to go to Brive, she doesn't like Doctor Delpy very much.'

'And why's that?' Mathilde wanted to know.

'He's too old,' said Michèle at this point.

'Now that, dammit,' cried Pierre-Edouard, 'is the stupidest thing I've heard for a long time! Too old? He's only sixty-nine!'

'And you think that's young, do you?' mocked Jacques.

'You little squirt!' His father was beside himself. 'At least it proves that he's got experience!'

'Granted.' Jacques avoided the issue. 'In any case, she's going to Brive, it's decided.'

'Right,' sighed Mathilde. 'Well, I shall have to apologise to Dr Delpy, I wouldn't like him to think that we'd fallen out with him.'

And that evening, despite the door which separated the old building from the new, Pierre-Edouard and Mathilde understood that there was one person too many in the Vialhe household.

Dominique Vialhe, Pierre-Edouard and Mathilde's first grandson, saw the light of day in Brive, and not in the village of Saint-Libéral like all his father's forebears.

A beautiful baby weighing almost six pounds, he came into the world without complications, and justified Mathilde's conviction that her daughter-in-law had made a lot of fuss about a completely natural occurrence.

In spite of everything, and because she was deliriously happy, she thought this baby would restore serenity to the house, and couldn't wait for her daughter-in-law and grandson to return. But it was fated that the two women should never understand one another, for Mathilde lost her temper when she saw that Michèle, despite her generously rounded breasts, was not feeding her son herself.

'Why aren't you giving him your milk, isn't it any good? '

'Yes, but the doctor said that it was better on the bottle,' explained the young woman.

'Your doctor is an imbecile, and you're a goose to have believed him! A baby should drink its mother's milk, and not any nasty old powder!'

Pierre-Edouard echoed her; Jacques joined in, and finished by saying coldly that he would not tolerate his parents' interference in things which were none of their business.

Pierre-Edouard gazed at him for some time, then looked over to his grandson and daughter-in-law.

'All right,' he sighed at last, 'we won't say any more. Come on,' he said to Mathilde.

'But where are you going?' she asked him, when she saw he was leading her out of the house.

'Come on,' he repeated, 'we need to take a walk and discuss this . . . That's it, we have to make another decision,' he said, when they had reached the track which climbed to the peaks.

She nodded her head, smiled a little sadly.

'Yes.'

'You've seen them; they're good children, they love each other, there shouldn't be quarrels because of us.'

'You're right.'

'Jacques is a fine, sensible chap, little Michèle is sweet, the baby is superb. They don't need us to be happy.'

He fell silent, broke off an elder twig and flicked it against his legs.

'And then?' pressed Mathilde.

'Well, you were right when you got me to repair Coste-Roche. When we did it, we thought it would be used by one of the children, but perhaps it's us who'll use it.'

'You want us to move up there?'

'Why not? I spent almost thirty years of my life fighting with my father, I don't want Jacques to be doing the same.'

'And wouldn't you mind leaving the house and village again?'

'Yes, I would,' he admitted, 'but if we stay together it won't work out. You know very well that you and young Michèle, I can feel it, you'll soon be fighting in earnest. So it's better to make peace before war is declared.'

'But what about the farm and the animals, all that? Coste-Roche is a long way!'

'We'll organise all that,' he assured her. 'You'll see, it'll be better for everyone.'

'All the same, the whole village will think we've fallen out.'

'People'll soon see we haven't. So we'll do it like that?'

'If you think it's for the best . . .'

'Then that's agreed. We'll tell them tonight after supper.'

'No!' said Jacques firmly, when his father had finished explaining his plan.

'Listen,' Mathilde said to him, 'it's for the best. We'll each be in our own home, we won't get on each other's nerves.'

'No,' now Michèle intervened, 'it's not you who should leave, it's us. And that's what we're going to do.'

'Exactly,' said Jacques. '*We*'ll move to Coste-Roche. It's what we should have done in any case when we got married, I should have listened to my godfather.'

Pierre-Edouard raised his eyebrows.

'What's the new squire of Saint-Libèral got to do with this business? That comes well from him, sticking his nose into other people's houses, now he's living in a château!'

Jacques smiled.

'He said to me: "In a herd, if you put the young animals with the very old, it works, they tolerate each other. But if you mix the first-time calvers with cows who are still strong, they fight. It's normal, they all want to graze the same patch of grass!"'

It was Pierre-Edouard's turn to smile.

'That's a stock-dealer talking . . .' Then he grew serious again. 'Are you sure, wouldn't it be better for us to leave?'

'No,' repeated Jacques, 'we'll move up there. There's not much needs doing to make that house comfortable; with a motor-pump we could even have running water.'

'You're forgetting that there's no electricity,' his mother reminded him. 'You know, that wouldn't worry your father and me, but you . . .'

'That's a mere detail,' interrupted Jacques, 'there'll be electricity by the time we move in. I'll put in the request tomorrow and my godfather will push it through. Yes,' he expanded, 'we'll go up there, but not straight away, because of the work to be done there and the baby too. We'll be able to spend the summer here, together and without fighting, won't we?'

'Of course,' said Mathilde, 'but if it comes to alterations, why not change things here? We'll build a kitchen on our side, lock the door and each have a home.'

'No,' decided Jacques, 'Michèle and you'll be meeting in the yard all the time . . .'

'He's right,' said Pierre-Edouard, 'when you're apart you always want to see each other, but seeing too much of each other makes you want to get away.'

Later on, when Pierre-Edouard was undressing to join Mathilde, who was already in bed, she raised the matter again.

'You knew, didn't you?' she asked.

'What?' he asked, feigning astonishment.

'That Jacques wouldn't let us go.'

'I was hoping,' he admitted.

'No,' she insisted, 'you were sure of it!'

'Do you blame me for playing a little game? Well, you played it with me, because you were hoping Jacques would react like that too!'

'Of course,' she agreed. 'Well, I'm very pleased that Michèle said what she did, even before Jacques; did you hear her?'

'Yes,' he said, getting into bed, 'she's a fine daughter-in-law.'

She moved over and snuggled up to him.

'It's still a pity that it had to come to this,' she sighed. 'And I am a bit cross with you, you know; for a moment I believed you were giving up, and wanted to go to Coste-Roche for good. Now I know you were only pretending, and I'm annoyed about that too.'

'You're wrong,' he said, passing an arm round her waist, 'I very nearly did give up, really. I wasn't pretending. Believe me, I didn't know what to do. Still, we had to find a solution that wouldn't hurt anyone – well, not too much. So if I'd said to Jacques: "Go and move to Coste-Roche!" he'd have thought we were kicking him out. I said to him: "We're going," and it's he who doesn't want to drive us out. It's good of him, and I'm sure he's feeling quite pleased with himself this evening! It's what I was hoping for, but you know, you can make wishes but they don't always come true!'

He leant on one elbow, looked down at her, smiled and slid his forefinger over the little brown mark decorating her

354

breast.

'It's still a teaser!' he joked, stroking her warm satin skin.

'Oh yes . . .'

'It's incredible, I've enjoyed it for almost thirty years and I'm not getting tired of it! And you, you're not bored, sleeping with a grandfather?'

'No, and I'll prove it,' she smiled, pulling him to her.

PART SEVEN
The New Wine

Chapter 24

JACQUES and Michèle's decision to go and live at Coste-Roche had the immediate effect of defusing all the sources of conflict between themselves and their parents. Since they had only three months to live under the same roof, mother- and daughter-in-law made an effort to avoid any grounds for dispute. As for Pierre-Edouard and Jacques, they worked together all summer, and even Nicolas became talkative again.

He had been present without speaking at all the family fracas, and was very happy to see them come to an end. He even initiated Jacques into the secrets of bee-keeping, and helped him to set up five hives on the border of the little oak wood which lay behind Coste-Roche.

When September came and the young Vialhe family moved, nobody in Saint-Libéral was shocked by the separation. Many even thought that Jacques was sensible to settle closer to his land. Anyway, in the village it was no time for gossip. Added to a very unhealthy general situation – strikes were starting up again, as before the war, and governments followed one another in quick succession; there was spiralling inflation and the latest stupidity of the politicians, who could think of no better way to revive private wealth than to cancel all 5,000 franc notes – the very life of the village was threatened.

In August 1947, the month of his seventieth birthday, Dr Delpy had announced his retirement. He felt tired, he admitted, and they believed him; for several months everyone had noticed his pallid complexion, bent back and lack of interest in conversation. Therefore, so as not to succumb to the temptation of continuing his work, which he was convinced would be the case if he stayed in Saint-Libéral, he chose to leave, and move into his wife's family home, not far from Saint-Yrieix.

The news of his departure, set for 15 October, saddened the whole community, for the doctor was loved by everyone. But beneath the sorrow lay a worry: from now on Saint-Libéral would have no doctor. Who would be crazy enough to come and set up in a village in decline, which the young left for lack of work, where the population dwindled year by year: 1,092 inhabitants in 1900, 979 in 1914, 701 in 1920, 594 in 1930 and now 452, many of them over fifty.

'At this rate,' said Léon from time to time, 'in twenty years there'll only be two hundred of us. I'm glad I won't be here to see it!'

Since nothing seemed to halt these death throes – already the markets were no more than a memory, Suzanne was talking of closing the inn, everyone knew that the ageing grocer would not be replaced – what did it matter that the Vialhe boy was migrating to Coste-Roche? At least he wasn't leaving the community, that was a bonus!

For the first time since their marriage, Pierre-Edouard and Mathilde found themselves alone. They were not accustomed to it, and had to make an effort to escape the incipient boredom. In unspoken agreement they threw themselves into their work and Mathilde, liberated from the burden of cooking and housework, returned to the fields full time.

She often needed to work herself to a standstill to deaden her anxiety for, whatever Paul might say in his letters, the news from Indo-China was not good. Nor was Mauricette's more encouraging. She was five months pregnant and had been forced to give up work, for she was supposed to stay lying down almost all the time. If no accident intervened she would give birth at Christmas, and Mathilde was gladly determined to be at her side.

Léon worried her a little, too. While helping to load a cow into a lorry, her brother had been kicked full in the chest; he had remained unconscious for almost ten minutes and, although there were no physical repercussions, his spirits were affected.

'If you can't bloody well get out of the way of a kick from an old bit of gristle, either you need to learn your job, or it's high time you got out of it!' he said bitterly.

To help him think more optimistically, Pierre-Edouard and Mathilde often visited the château. At the beginning they had felt almost intimidated as they entered the portals of the grand building and walked on the walnut parquet of the huge rooms. Léon too seemed a little lost in this environment, as if he were not quite at home. Then they gradually got used to the size of the reception rooms, the mirrored walls, the sparkling chandeliers on the main staircase.

Since the château was much too large for two people, Léon and Yvette only used four rooms, five when Louis was on holiday: the kitchen, where they took their meals, a bedroom, an office and the billiard-room, where Pierre-Edouard and Léon enjoyed meeting around the green baize. The other rooms, unoccupied, empty of furniture, with closed shutters, gathered dust.

'If I'd known it was so big . . .' murmured Léon occasionally. 'Well, the boy will enjoy it one day!' That was about the only satisfaction his purchase gave him.

However, he did use the salons of the château to organise, on 14 October, a convivial farewell party for Dr Delpy and his wife. There was a crowd of friends and all the town councillors.

But it was a sad occasion; nobody had the heart to tell jokes. With the doctor going, the last personality in the village was disappearing – apart from the priest, who was a pathetic sight, and, poor man, had little charisma. Now, however, he would be the only one fulfilling a public role and an office worthy of some respect.

Formerly the teacher had shared that privilege, but no longer. He was still morally a little superior to the villagers, but his situation had lost its aura of brilliance; many of the young people who had left the village were earning a better living than he, and knew as much, if not more.

Jacques and Michèle were happy at Coste-Roche from the start. There at least they could live and act as they pleased, without having to worry about possible criticism or comments from Pierre-Edouard and Mathilde.

With hindsight his parents' opinions now seemed quite unobjectionable, possibly because they were no longer affected by them, and Jacques was sometimes surprised that they had succeeded in poisoning the atmosphere. But he was not sorry to be out of the village. Down there, although his father had always left him completely free to manage his land as he thought fit, his position was awkward, for even without intending to, Pierre-Edouard dominated him with his strong character, professional ability and reputation. Jacques had once thought that his father had been overtaken by events, was out of touch with modern techniques and set in his ways, but honesty obliged him to admit that he had been wrong.

Far from being ossified, or behind the times, Pierre-Edouard was proving once more that his courage and enterprise were still sound. But his age, caution and experience had at first been mistaken by Jacques for opposition to change. He understood now that it was simply the reflection of good sense, steadiness and knowledge, the fruits of so many years spent watching over the land, listening to it, and shaping it too; not with the rough and ready energy of a beginner, but with the patient, attentive love of a man whom life had taught the language of the seasons and the value of time.

So, now that he had achieved his own independence, Jacques realised that he still had a great deal to learn. And it was no shame to admit this, for he had the feeling that he could also communicate to his father this new-found enthusiasm which was begging for an outlet. And because he felt a growing need for action on all fronts, he agreed to stand with Léon, his father and their friends in the municipal elections on 20 October 1947.

He was elected with a good majority, and unhesitatingly accepted the position of second deputy Léon offered him.

Pierre-Edouard laid down on the table the pages he had just been reading; it was a detailed plan of Jacques' proposed production.

'Well?' asked Jacques.

'Here,' said Pierre-Edouard, pushing them over to

Mathilde, 'you read it too, you know as much about it as I do. Yes, it looks sensible,' he admitted.

'You see,' persisted Jacques, 'here, mixed farming is finished – that is, the old sort. With my ten little hectares, if I go on like that, I'll soon have to shove the key under the door and walk away, and you know very well it's not for lack of effort!'

'I know.'

In the three years that Jacques and Michèle had been living at Coste-Roche, Pierre-Edouard had never found fault with his son. He had truly done all he could, thoroughly applied the techniques learned in his captivity, tried different sorts of crops and worn himself out at the job. Michèle too: the burden of heavy work had resulted in miscarriage in September 1949. But despite all their labours, their income constantly diminished. Jacques was right, now the problem had to be resolved.

'Yes,' said Pierre-Edouard, 'your ideas look fine, but you should beware of taking specialisation too far; it's sensible to have several irons in the fire. Having said that, I'm sure you're right not to want to grow wheat any more. I'm going to stop it too, it really doesn't pay, and whichever way we do it, our output is too small. You're wise to give up the spring vegetables as well, they take up too much time and manpower. That leaves tobacco, and there you're wrong to want to abandon it. Tobacco's good insurance against a rainy day.'

'Maybe, but I'd never be able to do all the work!'

'We'll help you,' promised Pierre-Edouard. 'Nicolas and I still have some strength left in us. Believe me, you should keep the tobacco.'

'And what about the other projects?'

'Well there, you'd better not make a mess of it . . .' said Pierre-Edouard, nodding his head. 'In his time your grandfather made a lot of money out of pigs, and he was thinking on a smaller scale than you! You're wanting to start off with at least forty sows – that's a lot you know, and they're greedy!'

'I know, but if I only plant crops for them I'll keep down the feed purchases.'

'On paper, yes . . . And then you'll have a big outlay on buildings!'

'I believe it could work,' said Mathilde, who had finished reading the plan, 'on condition that you keep the tobacco, of course, and that your second string is carefully organised.'

'You're thinking of the geese?' asked Michèle.

'Yes. You'll be looking after them, won't you? Well, you'll see, if you have the knack, they may bring in more than the piglets.'

'Good,' said Jacques, after lighting a cigarette. 'Now there's another problem, the biggest one, and it's not mentioned in my outline.'

'Oh,' Pierre-Edouard frowned, 'and what's that?'

'The time and the labour. Yes, I thought you'd overlook that. All the years you've worked, you've never counted your time or your trouble. The job was there and you did it, even if it meant a fifteen-hour day, including Sundays. We two have done exactly the same, up to now, but that's over; I don't want that kind of life any more, and neither does Michèle. It's nice to earn a bit of money, you need it to live – but that's just it, you need to live a little as well.'

'You'll have to explain more clearly,' said Pierre-Edouard.

'Our forty sows, our geese, various crops, our tobacco, since you insist on it – we couldn't manage all that except by working like beasts! And it's just not worth it.'

'And do you know any other way than by working?' asked Pierre-Edouard sarcastically.

'No, work is always work, but it depends what you mean by work, and above all, what you do it with! If we want to succeed, the way we mean it, we'll have to change, and for that I need your help. We need to buy a tractor and attachments.'

'Bloody hell!' exclaimed Pierre-Edouard, 'you think you're on a farm up in the north? A tractor? But that costs an arm and a leg, and it surely can't pay on our small acreage!'

'It'll pay its way,' Jacques argued, 'because it'll save us time, and you too. Yes, if you agree, you pay half of it; that way you could use it whenever you like. And instead of taking four or five days to plough one of your fields you'd finish it in less than a day, with much less effort.'

'I don't even know how to drive a car, let alone a tractor!'

'You'll soon learn, and you'll be so pleased with it, you won't be able to do without it. And your ploughing will improve as well!'

'How's that?'

'It'll be deeper.'

Pierre-Edouard smiled; he had given the same reason to his father when he bought his first pair of oxen.

'All the same,' he said, 'it's beyond our means.'

'Everything's expensive now, but money's not worth much!'

Pierre-Edouard meditated at length. His son's pronouncement was true, for even Mathilde, who always took care of the finances, and had known the inflation of the '20s and '30s, had difficulty in keeping pace with the astronomic scale of the figures. To the 1,100 francs Pierre-Edouard had paid Nicolas five years ago, he had been forced, as the years passed, to add more 1,000-franc notes: now, in April 1950, Nicolas was earning 10,000 francs! And a cow, previously a fair price at 3,000 francs, now cost twelve times as much! Léon had not been mistaken when he had urged them to buy land. As he had predicted, it didn't cost 30,000 francs a hectare any more, far from it! Their neighbour Maurice had just agreed on 120,000 francs for a patch of barely a hectare! Seen in that perspective, Jacques was right.

'Yes,' said Pierre-Edouard at last, 'I know money's lost its value, but I'm not like those good-for-nothings in the government, I haven't got a licence to print notes! And you know what your brother's going to cost us next year!'

If Guy passed his second baccalauréat, and all the signs were that he would not fail, he wanted to register at the School of Law in Paris in October. His parents had chosen Paris rather than Poitiers because Berthe had kindly offered to put up her nephew during his studies. With the price of a tiny room being what it was, that was an offer not to be refused: 'And I'll introduce him to people in Paris,' Berthe had said, 'that'll stand him in good stead.'

'Yes,' said Jacques rather bitterly, 'I hadn't forgotten that studying is expensive . . .'

'And this tractor, how much does it cost?' asked Pierre-Edouard.

'We need a twenty-five horsepower. With the equipment, it'll come to about nine hundred thousand francs, but I'll pay half!'

'And where do you think I'll raise the other four hundred and fifty thousand?'

'We'll find it,' said Mathilde quietly. 'Yes, think: if you buy a tractor, you won't need your oxen any more, so if you get them in good condition you might get a hundred and eighty thousand from the butcher. I'll find the other two hundred and seventy thousand . . .'

'If you go on dipping into your cauldron,' he commented sceptically, 'you'll end up scraping the bottom!'

'Yes, it won't be long . . .' she agreed. 'But just consider, in place of the oxen, you could feed four extra cows. Let's say it's only three, that still gives you three calves a year at forty thousand each; in a little over two years you'll have covered your investment.'

'Ever since I've known you, you've been counting your chickens before they're hatched!' he murmured.

'And with some success!'

'Yes, until the day you make a mistake . . . Now this tractor of yours,' he said to Jacques, 'I don't know much about it, but according to what I've read here and there, it eats too! And at almost fifty francs a litre for petrol!'

'Of course, but it's that or give up the struggle. Without this tractor I won't have the time to see to the sows and the geese, and Michèle won't be helping me. Yes, we wanted to wait a bit to tell you, but just so you understand: Michèle's expecting a baby at the beginning of November, and if we don't want the same to happen as last time . . .'

'That's lovely,' said Mathilde with a smile, 'really lovely; you were right to tell us, and we're very pleased. You'll be catching up with your sister – well, almost,' she joked. Mauricette already had two girls and was expecting a third child in July.

'Right,' said Pierre-Edouard, 'that alters the whole situation. You mustn't take any chances, and if you think this tractor will help you work better, with less trouble and higher returns, we'd better get it, even if it's expensive.'

'Yes, it'll make a world of difference to us,' said Jacques. He hesitated a moment, then smiled to soften his plain speaking: 'And it'll change everything for you as well, you . . . well, you're getting to the age when you shouldn't be crippling yourself with work, the way you've been doing.'

'Go on, say straight out I'm an old wreck!' protested Pierre-Edouard.

'No, no,' Mathilde calmed him with her quiet tone, 'but whether you like it or not, you're sixty-one and Nicolas is not far behind; it's beginning to get a lot for the two of you to manage! Jacques is right, this tractor will be useful.'

'Agreed,' he said. He sighed in amusement. 'After all, I moved on from the scythe to the reaper, from the sickle to the harvester, from the swing plough to the reversible brabant, from cows to oxen; I can change from oxen to a tractor. And I forget another thing: from paraffin to electricity! So it's just one more change in a long line!'

Jacques ordered a petrol-driven Massey-Harris, fitted with a small detachable plough fixed by ten screws, and a cutting bar, also detachable. But he had to control his impatience and wait for delivery until the beginning of September.

That year, the severe frosts which ravaged the surrounding area luckily spared Saint-Libéral, and Pierre-Edouard picked nine tons of plums which he succeeded in selling at twelve francs a kilo.

In July, Mauricette gave birth to a third girl, which inspired Pierre-Edouard to say, in his delight at being a grandfather again, that Mathilde's and Mauricette's features were like couch-grass, ineradicable — for the child, like her two elder sisters, was the image of her mother and grandmother. 'But,' he added, 'that's a weed I could wish on any man!'

Added to this good news came Paul's long-awaited leave; he had not returned since his posting to Indo-China. His arrival in Saint-Libéral did not pass unnoticed. Firstly because he turned up at the wheel of a splendid Ford Vedette, an indisputable sign of wealth; secondly because everybody very soon knew that he had just been promoted to captain.

Even Pierre-Edouard and Mathilde were impressed. Paul, matured and hardened by the preceding war, was now spare and chiselled, gaunt and nervous as a wild cat, always ready to spring, behind every glance the worrying little spark which shines in the eyes of those who have made war their first love. To him it was his *raison d'être*, his life and career, and his father – who himself had also fought ferociously – noticed with a certain alarm what differentiated men who were forced to defend themselves, not doing it of their own choice, from those, like his son, who married their warlike vocation body and soul.

Paul no longer strove to re-establish peace, but sought the thrill of battle. And Pierre-Edouard understood that he would search ever onwards for new conflicts: they were like a drug to him.

'But haven't you had enough of all this killing?' he asked one evening, when Paul had accompanied him to the Caput Peak to load a cart with heather for bedding down the animals.

'No,' said Paul, leaning on his fork. And because they were alone, man to man, he explained enthusiastically: 'This killing, as you call it, it's like love. There's all the build-up beforehand, that's very exciting in itself, and then the climax, when everything's let loose. With a woman you have the feeling you're dicing with a minor sort of death; in battle you're sure of it! Believe me, it's fantastic to know that you're flirting with death, and that she's always on the look-out for a moment's carelessness or a mistake which will win her the game! What I like about a battle is that you're not allowed the slightest weakness, you always have to do better than the time before, always prove that you're stronger! It's good, good like love!'

Pierre-Edouard shrugged.

'It's incredible, what rubbish you talk!' he said, 'and if it were only talk! Look, hearing you say you make love like you make war, I feel sorry for you, because love is more like peace. Yes, you'd have difficulty in extricating yourself from that hornet's nest, but then you don't want to, you like it. Basically it's what you were looking for fifteen years ago, when you wanted to leave for Paris: adventure, simply adventure.'

'Yes,' admitted Paul with a smile, 'it may be so, I've always had an insatiable curiosity.'

'I know, but what are you trying to prove?'

'Nothing. I live as I mean to live, that's all.'

'Oh, right, every man to his own taste. If that's how you see life, go on beating yourself unconscious, because one day you may wake up and realise that you've been fighting your own shadow, and you'll understand that no one has ever won that game!'

'Enough of this moralising,' said Paul with a laugh, 'you know I won't live long enough to wake up! So for the time being I enjoy my dreams – and believe me, they're superb, better than I'd ever hoped!'

Paul stayed three weeks in Saint-Libéral, helping his father in the fields and also with the large pig-unit which Jacques was constructing at Coste-Roche.

He even accompanied Léon to Brive market, for the pleasure of plunging into the atmosphere of his youth again, to hear the horse-dealers battling it out and to go and sit with them, towards ten o'clock in the morning, for a snack in one of those bistros on the Thiers Square which smelt deliciously of vermicelli soup, grilled meat, cheese and wine, and where the orders were given in dialect.

'I don't understand why you're going back there,' said Mathilde the day before he left. 'You've done your time, you could ask to stay in France!'

'In France? And do what? Work in an office? Teach kids how to dismantle a machine-gun and play at war with blanks and dummy grenades! No, thank you! You see, Maman, after the war, when I asked to be transferred to the Colonial Army, it wasn't so as to fall asleep in some town garrison.'

'But your confounded war in Indo-China will stop one day anyway!'

'Maybe, but the world is a huge place and the Colonial Army is all over it!'

And as she was about to continue, Pierre-Edouard placed a hand on her arm.

'Leave it,' he said, 'he needs his dreams.'

The arrival of the tractor at the Vialhes' attracted almost as many people as had gathered for the first demonstration of the mechanical reaper, bought by Jean-Edouard in May 1905.

Then a significant proportion of the elderly had at first regarded the machine with mocking scepticism, but nobody in September 1950 doubted for a moment that the tractor would prove extremely useful. Many even secretly envied the Vialhes, who had the courage and the means to acquire such a marvel.

It was magnificent, this Massey-Harris, with an impressive beauty and strength which made you want to touch the red bonnet, to stroke the swelling curves sculpted in the tyres, to climb on to the seat and gently handle the wheel.

As for its throbbing, both the soft, silky murmur of the pistons when disengaged, and the fierce growl of the cylinders exploding with energy, inspired respect, announced a power which had no equal amongst the best pairs of oxen in the community.

To test it, and also to prove that he was capable of steering and mastering it, Jacques decided to try opening a few furrows in the field called the Meeting. He had not driven a tractor since his captivity, and immediately appreciated the difference between the modern, manageable machine he had just acquired and old Karl's heavy, noisy Lanz.

Nevertheless, since he was being watched by all the neighbours, it was with some apprehension that he manoeuvred it to cut his first furrow.

'Will it work?' his father asked as he walked beside him.

'Yes, I think so. Well, we'd better see if the shares are properly adjusted.'

'Oh, don't ask me about that,' warned Pierre-Edouard, gazing at all the gadgets, 'I don't know a thing about it!'

Jacques lowered the right plough share, noted with a glance the proper opening angle, checked the distance between the coulter and the share and the correct slope of the mould-board.

'Fine,' he said, 'I'm starting.'

'That's right,' Pierre-Edouard encouraged him, 'let them see what you can do, and don't forget that some of them will have a good laugh if you bungle it!'

Jacques engaged first gear, pushed the accelerator and slowly let out the clutch. He noted the sound of the blades engaging, set his eye on a gate-post at the other end of the field which would give him the line, and powered the engine.

One glance over his shoulder was enough to tell him that the furrow was opening cleanly, the sods well turned, the depth even. Behind his back, hurrying their steps to keep up with him, all the neighbours were already crowding round with knowing and admiring looks. This ploughing elicited nothing but praise; it was a masterpiece of craft and speed that left them flabbergasted.

'Christ Almighty!' said Maurice. 'If he goes on like that all afternoon he'll have finished the field this evening! And he's a master at steering!'

'Yes,' said Pierre-Edouard with justifiable pride, 'he drives like a champion!'

Having reached the end of the field, Jacques lifted the plough, performed a fine loop on the headland, positioned the left front wheel of the tractor in the trench he had just made, lowered the plough and carved open his second furrow.

He experienced such satisfaction, such joy, that he cut four more before stopping. Then he jumped to the ground, admired his work and turned to his father.

'Come on,' he said, 'now show us what you can do.'

'You're crazy,' protested Pierre-Edouard, 'I've never driven in my life!'

'Of course not, but you're dying to!'

'Go on, Pierre-Edouard,' cried the neighbours, 'it's your turn! Climb up, and don't forget your goad, for when the tractor pulls to one side!'

'No, no,' he said quietly, torn between his desire to try out the machine and his fear of making a fool of himself.

'Yes, yes,' insisted Jacques, pushing him gently towards the tractor. 'Climb up; I'll stay beside you, on the mud-guard.'

'Don't upset your father, now!' interjected a rather worried Mathilde.

'Look, you see,' said Pierre-Edouard, delighted at the intervention, 'it'd frighten your mother. No, no, I'm not getting up on that!'

'Yes you are, they're all hoping you'll chicken out,' Jacques whispered to him, without believing a word of what he was saying.

'You think so?' asked Pierre-Edouard, happy to be able to use this completely imaginary excuse. 'Well, if that's the case, let's go!'

He climbed into the seat, pushed his beret onto the back of his head, and had it all explained to him. He very quickly understood the purpose of the two right-hand pedals, the brakes (which could be operated independently and each restrain one wheel at a time), and the left-hand pedal, the clutch. The gear-lever was soon mastered, and the throttle responded to his touch.

Then he started off and, happy as a child on Christmas morning, treated himself to a little test-drive around the field, to get used to the response of the steering-wheel and the play in the pedals. Then he turned slowly round and it was his turn to enter the trench.

'That's it,' said Jacques, who had just lowered the plough to make things easier for him.

'That's it? Are you sure? My God, it's fantastic,' he said, laughing with pleasure, 'fantastic!' He looked behind him. 'Bloody hell, what a piece of work! Have you see what I've been doing! Look at that: it's at least twenty centimetres deep! My word, if I met the fellow who invented this machine I'd give him a pat on the back!'

He reached the end of the furrow, turned, resumed ploughing, came back, set off again, with growing enthusiasm and confidence in himself. Only after the eighth row did he finally stop.

'It's incredible,' he said, climbing down.

He admired the shining brown surface that he and his son had just created, walked on to the soft earth, gathered a fistful and kneaded it in his hand.

'I've never seen ploughing like that,' he said, 'never! And if you'd told me you could do it as fine and regular as that, I wouldn't have believed it. I'm happy to admit it, we were stupid to wait so long before buying this machine! With this, things'll really take off now!'

Chapter 25

One more time, because the toddler had the knack of getting her to do what he wanted, Mathilde began to sing again, at the same time miming with her hands the words she was chanting, and once again the child burst into laughter when she got to: 'Your mill is turning too fast,' and speeded up her whirling arms. She smiled at Dominique, then rose from her cane chair.

'Right,' she excused herself, 'now I must see to your little sister.'

'She's always eating!' lisped the boy with a shrug.

'Well yes, that's because she's so little,' she explained, putting a pan of milk on the gas stove.

This was their latest purchase, and she was delighted with it. Thanks to this, it was no longer necessary to light the fire or the wood-stove every day, the sides of the pots were clean at last, and the cooking done more quickly.

In her moses basket, little Françoise reluctantly released the toes of her right foot, which she had been sucking voluptuously for several minutes, and began to protest unrestrainedly about the slow progress of the bottle her grandmother was preparing. She would soon be eight months old, and was as chubby and dimpled as a brioche and louder than half a dozen magpies chasing an owl. The whole Vialhe family was crazy about her, and Mathilde was delighted whenever she was entrusted with her while her daughter-in-law went into town to do the shopping.

It was a wonderful afternoon in June, just right for haymaking; not too hot, for the north wind lent it freshness. Once again Mathilde savoured the ability to stay at home without a guilty conscience, to look after her grandchildren. Thanks to the tractor and the hayrake, she no longer needed to gather up the cut grass with long exhausting sweeps of the wooden rake. Now two men accomplished the task: Pierre-

374

Edouard on the tractor, Nicolas on the tedder, and the work was done in a trice.

Then she thought of the coming holidays and felt happy, for Mauricette, Jean-Pierre and their three girls would be spending the summer in Saint-Libéral, in the enlarged house – it did serve a purpose, after all. Guy would also be returning from Paris, probably with Gérard and Berthe who, according to the latest news, had decided to spend at least two weeks in the village. In August Louise had promised to come too, with Pierre and maybe even Félix. And Mathilde was content, for she knew that Pierre-Edouard loved to see his family again.

She tested the temperature of the bottle by pouring a few drops of milk on to her forearm, bent over Françoise, who was now red with anger and running with perspiration, and took her in her arms. The child calmed down immediately with a great sigh of contentment.

'Crosspatch!' she called her, shaking the bottle to speed up the dissolving of the sugar, 'big bad-tempered Vialhe, I feel sorry for you, yes I do! Anyone would think you hadn't eaten for a week! Come on, my greedy love, feed yourself!' she said, stuffing the teat between the vainly sucking lips.

Holding the baby firmly in the crook of her left arm, she walked to the door to make sure that Dominique was being good and smiled to see him playing with the dog. The old mongrel displayed a touching patience with children. At the moment Dominique had passed a cord between his jaws, hung a rusty bucket round his neck and was sitting on his back. The dog cast Mathilde an imploring look, wagged his tail, then with a heavy sigh turned his head and licked the child's knee.

'Don't hurt him,' counselled Mathilde.

'We're having fun!' said Dominique. 'Look, there's Uncle Léon!' he called out suddenly, for he could see down the line of the main street from where he was.

'Léon?' she said as she emerged. 'What brings you at this hour of day?'

'Where's Pierre-Edouard?' asked her brother after kissing her.

'Making hay, on the plateau, why?'

'Ah!' he said in annoyance, 'I must warn him . . .'

'What about?'

'I'm just back from Corrèze market; it's full of foot-and-mouth disease up there, and it seems it's spreading all over the place!'

'My God,' she murmured, 'and you think we're in danger here?'

'Here like everywhere else! Which field is he in?'

'The lucerne.'

'I'll go up there.'

'Talk about a catastrophe if it spreads to this area!' commented Pierre-Edouard, as soon as Léon had relayed the news to him.

'You can say that again. Foot-and-mouth, that's fatal, you have to slaughter!'

'And what can we do?'

'I know what *I*'ll do,' said Léon with a meaningful look, 'but you – first you must sprinkle disinfectant in front of the cowshed, then you mustn't set foot near the markets. Believe me, that's where they catch it, that filth. And if your cows go to the bull, don't use Larenaudie, and I'll be saying that to everyone in the village.'

'But,' protested Pierre-Edouard, 'how shall I get my animals served?'

Since Léon had hastily disposed of his last bull two years earlier – the beast had almost disembowelled one of his workers – only Larenaudie, who lived in the locality of Fonts-Marcel, owned a breeding bull; an enormous Limousin with an evil eye and knotted shoulder-muscles, which, in return for the 350 francs pocketed by his owner, willingly and valiantly agreed to do the honours with all the cows in the area.

'You only have to apply to the artificial insemination service.'

'You think I should?' said Pierre-Edouard. 'That's what Jacques has been advising for a while now, but I don't like the idea. It seems a funny sort of thing to me, that insemination! And Larenaudie'll be cross if he loses all his customers!'

'I don't give a damn! I'm telling you what needs to be done

to limit the damage, but if you really want your animals to catch that plague . . .'

'No, no, I'll do as you say. But what are you going to do?'

'Oh, me,' said Léon warily, 'I'm going to stop, that's all.'

'You mean to say you're going to leave off the markets and all that?'

'Yes, I've had a basinful . . .' Léon sighed, spat through his teeth. 'A basinful, do you understand? I'll be sixty-five soon, and I've had enough of running round the markets. This business of foot-and-mouth disease, it's basically a good thing for me. That decided it for me in the end, you know.'

'Bloody hell,' said Pierre-Edouard, 'you're not going to give everything up, just like that?'

'Yes, I am. I'm tired, I'm telling you.'

'But you'll die of boredom!'

'Oh no. I'll potter about a bit on my own land to keep busy, but not the rest, I'm giving up the lease. As for shifting animals, that's finished. Look,' he said lifting his trouser cuff, 'I got another nasty kick the other day; in the last six months I've collected more than my share! I'm telling you, I'm too old to find it funny.'

Pierre-Edouard examined the purplish bruise mottling the white skin of his calf.

'No, that's not very pretty,' he agreed. 'But you've got workers; they can take charge of the animals, you don't need to bother with them!'

'I know, but I enjoy touching the animals, that's what I like, you see. But if I get a thwack every time I feel one over, no thank you. And then, I've got animals all over the place, what if they catch the infection? No, no, I'm going to sell the lot, and have done with it!'

'It's your business,' said Pierre-Edouard. 'If you think it's best . . .'

He was distressed to see his brother-in-law sinking into depression, sliding into old age. For a long time he had felt this change coming; certainly it was partly due to age and fatigue, but there was more to it. In fact, Léon was disappointed in his son. Louis had passed his baccalauréat creditably, but had no desire to pursue any of the avenues favoured by his father. He was not interested in continuing his studies so, instead of taking advantage of a deferment, he had left to do his military service.

On his return he intended to set up as an estate agent in Brive, Tulle or Limoges. It was a profession which Léon considered too close to his own. Buying, selling, making money on the transaction; he had done nothing but that since he was fourteen years old and, although he liked his job, he did not consider it particularly honourable. To see his son embark in business was no comfort to him.

As he had just admitted, the foot-and-mouth was just an excuse. He had more money than he could spend, no longer had to pay for his son's education – if he was a worthy progeny he'd soon be earning more than his father! So what was the point of labouring on, and above all, who was he doing it for?

Anxiety plagued the village throughout the summer of 1951, for all the farmers felt the threat of the disease hanging over their herds.

Fortunately they received Léon's advice positively; sprinkled their cowsheds and dung-heaps with lysol, refrained from touring the market-places, and stopped taking their animals to Larenaudie's bull.

As Pierre-Edouard had expected, the stud's owner was appalled at being put in quarantine and deprived of a substantial income. Furious, he declared categorically that Léon was talking rubbish and that anyway, the precautions were pointless, as almost all the animals drank from the same communal trough. It was the plain truth, except for the Vialhes, who were fortunate enough to have their own pond in the farmyard.

This harsh reality had the effect of making everyone wary and men who had got on perfectly well until then caught each other casting suspicious glances at their neighbour's stock. The few hustlers who continued to frequent the market-places on principle were severely judged. They were roundly informed that if by ill-luck the infection should reach the village, the culprits would be quickly found and suitably dealt with.

Finally, with the first October frosts, the danger diminished. But they had all been so frightened and so vigilant that it took several months for people to stop wondering whether their next-door neighbour, their friend, would be the one to bring in the contamination.

True to his decision not to interfere in his son's affairs, Pierre-Edouard hesitated a while before deciding to act. He was compelled to in January 1952 when Michèle admitted, after a concerned Mathilde had pressed her with questions, that their money worries were reaching critical point.

Despite the workload they accomplished, they were not succeeding in reaching a threshold which would allow them to survive and repay their loans – and also, more importantly, to save.

Due to lack of capital, Jacques had not been able to purchase a sufficient number of breeding sows. He should have had forty and he was rearing fifteen! As for the geese, they had not fulfilled their potential and their livers, sold at the Kings' Market at Brive, had not realised half the expected sum.

'They overstretched themselves and went too fast,' said Pierre-Edouard, when Mathilde had told him that her fears were confirmed.

'No,' she maintained, 'they don't have enough land, it doesn't produce enough.'

'Not enough! Ten hectares? My God, my father brought us three up on that area, myself and two sisters! With our grandparents, there were seven of us! Yes,' he accepted with a shrug, 'it's stupid, what am I saying, that was fifty years ago!'

'Exactly. At that time the money coming in wasn't paid out, or very little of it. Whereas now, there's more going out than coming in . . . And it's not their fault, you know that. We don't live like we did years ago, nobody does, and then all these loans!'

'You could see it coming, eh?'

'Of course,' she said, 'but after all, you can't reproach them for fixing up Coste-Roche, nor buying a van, a few bits of furniture, and a wireless, nor the tractor and implements!'

'No, no, I don't reproach anyone for anything, except

379

those puppets up there in Paris, who don't care if everything goes up, except the prices we get!'

'What can we do for them?' she asked.

'Hard to know! Give them some money? We don't have the funds any more, and anyway, that's not the solution.'

'Perhaps if . . .' she murmured. 'I thought . . . We'll always have enough to live on, because as soon as Guy has finished studying, we won't be spending . . .'

'Yes, I see what you mean. We'll do that, that's the best idea.'

And, like two conspirators who have no need of words to understand each other, they smiled.

Pierre-Edouard climbed up to Coste-Roche the following day, and was welcomed by his grandchildren with cries of joy. Since the cold was penetrating, he gladly accepted the cup of coffee his daughter-in-law offered him, and enjoyed it by the fireside.

'Would you like a drop of something in your coffee?' suggested Michèle, bringing out a bottle of plum brandy. He hesitated.

'No – or rather yes, but first call your husband; perhaps he'll take a drop with me, and it's him I've come to see.'

'He's busy with the sows, but Dominique will go and fetch him,' she said, knotting a thick woollen scarf round the child's neck. And as the boy ran to the piggery she slipped on her coat. 'I'll take over from Jacques,' she said, 'then you can talk things over quietly.'

'No, you stay, it concerns you too. Come on, take off your coat and sit down.'

'Bloody hell, it's cold enough to bring the wolves out,' said Jacques, coming in a moment later. He stamped his feet and shook himself, poured a big bowl of coffee and made himself comfortable on the settle, opposite his father. The fire flickered at their feet. 'What brings you here?' he asked.

'You two; no, you four,' said Pierre-Edouard, pointing to the children.

'Ah,' said Jacques rather bitterly, 'I bet Mother's managed to get Michèle to talk!'

'Don't blame your wife for a little thing like that. Mothers are born to listen.'

'Well then?'

Pierre-Edouard had not come earlier because he suspected his son would refuse financial support; his pride would forbid it. At the outset he had allowed his father to settle some of the instalments on the loans because he was still feeling his way into the management of his land, starting out in the profession, and had not found it humiliating to be helped to get off the ground. Now that time had passed, he made it a point of honour to feed his wife and children without having to ask for handouts from anyone.

Pierre-Edouard took out his pipe and filled it slowly and carefully, as he did whenever he had a difficult problem to resolve. He drew a brand from the edge of the fire, and lit it.

'Well, it's true; your wife has been talking to your mother, and she was right. This business, it can't go on. And don't tell me that you're going to take another loan!' he said, raising a hand. 'Quiet now, let me talk. Yes, yes, that's what you wanted to do, run to the Crédit Agricole and say to them: "Let me put off this year's repayment until next year, I'll pay you just the interest and that way I'll have a few months' breathing-space." That's a bloody stupid way of doing things!'

'Maybe,' said Jacques calmly, 'but this year I'll have eight more sows, and I reckon that . . .'

'Not a hope! All that to sell the offspring for barely four and a half thousand francs a time; you'll go a long way like that! Let's stop pretending, my boy. This is what we're going to do, your mother's agreed. From now on, you are going to take over the Vialhe land, what came to me from my father, the old farm, you know. I'll have to keep the Long Piece and the Big Field and also your mother's land and what we bought together, but that still leaves you fourteen hectares, and they're top class! We, that is your mother and I, will be happy with what's left, it'll give us nine hectares counting Louise's Combes-Nègres. For you it's not enough; for us, at our age, it's quite sufficient. You need to progress, whereas we can tread water now. I'll go to the solicitor in Ayen tomorrow to get it sorted out.'

'But that's impossible!' protested Jacques. 'I'll never be

able to make it up to the others! Where do you think I'm going to find the money?'

'Your brothers and sister will wait; besides, they're not short of a few pennies! And what I'm handing over is only part of it – there's the rest of the land, the house, the farm-buildings. Come on, don't worry about that, take what I'm offering and make it pay. You'll see, it's good land, the Vialhe land – you know that, anyway! Only, just for this year, you let me have half the value of the crops on it; I need that to pay for your brother's education.'

'Oh no!' said Jacques, 'not half, two thirds. What's left will be enough to make ends meet. And, well . . . All the same, I'm . . . I suppose I want to say thank you, that'll save us.'

'But won't it be hard for you to do?' asked Michèle.

'You mean to let go of my land? No, it's not going out of the family, and that's the main thing. Besides, I had such a dreadful time waiting for a settlement which my father had no intention of making! And your husband won't kick me out if I go on working the land with him, will he?'

'No,' Jacques reassured him, 'just the opposite.' He thought for a moment, and smiled: 'You'll see, we'll make it more beautiful than ever!'

'I'm counting on it. Oh, by the way, as to the stock; I'll keep six cows, the four calves which are ready for sale, and the ewes. The rest are yours now.'

'That's much too much,' said Michèle. 'We can't accept all that!'

'Yes you can,' joked Pierre-Edouard, 'better that than a kick in the teeth, eh? And now, you know, I haven't enough acreage to keep all my stock! Oh, one other thing,' he said, looking at Jacques, 'your mother and I thought that if you wanted to come back down, we could arrange things so that we're not in each others' hair . . .'

'No,' said Jacques and Michèle in chorus. 'You see,' explained Jacques, 'we're fine here, nice and quiet, so we'd rather stay put.'

'I understand,' murmured Pierre-Edouard, with a look of nostalgia in his eye, 'and if your mother were here, she'd understand too. It was here, at Coste-Roche, that we were happiest. So since there's no reason for leaving, stay and make the most of it.'

Without the revenue provided by his new lands and, most of all, by the ten cows which his father had given him, Jacques would not have been able to keep his head above water in 1952. It was a catastrophic year, for drought set in during April and continued all summer, not ending until mid-September. But by then it was too late, the damage had been done.

The hay-crop was thin, the maize wretched; the beets dried in the ground and even the tobacco wilted. As for the barley, it yielded less than twelve quintals a hectare, next to nothing. Only the plums helped the Vialhes to weather the blow, and saved Jacques in particular from sliding into complete bankruptcy.

For in July, at the height of the heatwave, a bout of pneumogastritis developed in the pig-unit and, despite the speed with which he treated it, carried off twenty-three piglets of 15 to 40 kilos each. Added to that (for troubles never come singly, as his father resignedly reminded him), three of his sows in the space of a month, perhaps upset by the insupportable heat — or out of pure evil — devoured their young at birth. The first gobbled up eleven, the second swallowed nine; as for the last one, as she lay down she crushed the only survivor from a litter of twelve.

'That's done me out of almost a quarter of a million francs!' said Jacques to his father. 'Good God, I can see the day coming when I'll get rid of all these filthy sows! It's true: they're noisy, they're greedy, they stink and they die!'

He was more angry than depressed, for the setback made him want to fight, to cheat fate.

'Remember what I told you,' his father reminded him. 'On the land, you can't make plans. The only money you can count on is what you've got in your pocket. The rest, what you're expecting or hoping for, can't be relied on, it's like a drop of water on oilcloth; sometimes you catch it, often it runs off! But don't give up the pigs because of a thing like that. Who knows, maybe it'll get better next year . . .'

'It was only talk. I'm not looking to give them up, nor the

rest of it!'

'The rest of it' was all the land which he was busy making productive by applying modern agricultural methods. Through the farming journals, he kept himself up to date with everything and already his voice had been heard at the meetings of the Departmental Union of Farmers' Co-operatives.

In the village itself, some were naturally jealous of him – he had the finest fields in the community, considerable livestock, a tractor, two beautiful children and a lovely wife – but others saw in him a worthy successor to his uncle and godfather, as leader in the mairie. For Léon, who now lived on his private income, made it plain that he would refuse the sash of office.

However, since he had stopped all his professional activities, he was bored. So to fill his time, he treated himself and his wife to trips to Paris, Nice and most often Mont-Dore, where Yvette took the waters. During his absences Jacques took care of matters at the mairie, for although his father was the first deputy mayor, he was quite happy to leave him to deal with ongoing business.

Jacques liked this work, did it conscientiously and with enjoyment, and he was preparing to take the mayor's seat when it fell vacant. If he succeeded in this, his dream was to revive the lost dynamism of the village. But he did not have too many illusions, and had already abandoned the idea of creating a study centre for farming methods in Saint-Libéral, through which he could have apprised all the members of the latest agricultural techniques.

But it was impossible, too revolutionary; that sort of thing upset too many traditions, infringing on each person's privacy and individual ideas. Few and far between were the young people still working family land. Apart from Jean, Maurice's son, Louis Delpy, Delpeyroux's son-in-law, and himself, the youngest farmer in the village was Roger Vergne, and he was forty-six. All the others were in their fifties or older.

It was not possible to get through to them. Not that they were opposed to all things modern, but they were held in the straitjacket of their own routines and opinions. They were glad to try something new, but you had to let them take their time about it; and when, after careful observation, they finally decided to do something it was always so late that the advantage was lost.

Only Pierre-Edouard, Léon and possibly Maurice were enlightened enough to be aware that Jacques was right and to encourage him. But they were no longer involved; they were over sixty and looking forward to retirement rather than new ventures.

Some time in March 1953 Father Delclos, now aged seventy-four, developed severe pulmonary congestion whilst digging the earth for his onion-bed.

In the evening the old lady who did his housekeeping found him all shivery with a temperature, crouched by the fireside. His skin was flushed with the fever, and his eyes were already glazed. As soon as he was told about it, the doctor from Perpezac-le-Blanc put him in his car and drove him to Brive, where he had him admitted to hospital.

Contrary to all the villagers' predictions, the priest did not die and recovered quite rapidly; but he remained weak, frail, depressed. As a precaution, the diocesan authorities sent him to a retirement home and informed the parishioners that Saint-Libéral would no longer have a pastor; only a peripatetic clergyman would conduct the services.

The announcement that the parish would no longer have an appointed priest shocked everyone. God knows, Father Delclos, with his changing convictions, his inappropriate attitudes and opinions, had succeeded in emptying his church; for several years the gathering of the faithful had constantly dwindled, and even the children in the catechism class managed to cut their lessons quite frequently.

Nevertheless, everyone was aware of the gap left by the departure of the priest, for, quite apart from the man himself, the office which he represented proved to all that they were not forsaken and that, in spite of the exodus, the ageing population and the paralysis which was gradually numbing the village, nothing was really lost as long as the structures and framework which had for centuries governed the community of Saint-Libéral remained.

Deprived of solicitor, doctor and priest, the village felt forgotten, rejected. Maybe they were subconsciously inspired by an almost suicidal instinct, an introspection and nostalgia for times past, but at the council elections in spring 1953, instead of voting in a mayor who could halt the death-throes, the electors turned to an older man. And because Pierre-Edouard had retired from the contest, between Jacques who represented the future and Maurice who embodied the past, they chose the greybeard. He was honest and certainly competent, and they felt that his sixty-four years were a measure of wisdom, good sense and experience.

Jacques felt hurt, and almost resigned from his seat as councillor, which the electors had awarded him in spite of everything. Convinced that nothing could now save Saint-Libéral, he withdrew to Coste-Roche and, to get over his disappointment, devoted himself more than ever to his work on the land.

That year – when the world was relieved to see peace return to Korea; when in France the feeble-minded politicians elevated incompetence to an established art-form and ministerial crisis to a method of government, whilst demanding peace in Indo-China, calm in Morocco, a stabilised franc, regulation of the vintners' problems and the organisation of a European Defence Community; when they required thirteen ballots to elect René Coty as President of the Republic – Saint-Libéral, silently and without protest, sank into a coma.

Within twelve months eight young people between sixteen and twenty left the area, tempted by the jobs and wages offered in the towns.

That year again, for the third time running, the number of deaths in the parish exceeded the births.

Guy Vialhe had deferred his conscription, but the young pupil barrister at the Paris Bar was called up in July 1954. He was not keen to leave work which he enjoyed and a way of life he appreciated in all its pleasures. Aunt Berthe, despite her age – she would be sixty-one in August – still managed the fortunes of her Paris couture house with a sure touch, now aided by Gérard. Thanks to her, Guy had discovered all the charms of Parisian life.

To him, Saint-Libéral and the Vialhe house were now no more than distant, tender memories and his parents charming, emotive representatives of the past. As for his brother Jacques, he remained an enigma. He never understood how someone of his intellectual weight could prefer the land, with its responsibilities and even trials, to any job in town.

However, Guy did like to visit his village, his parents. He felt a deep and sincere gratitude towards them, which amply repaid all their sacrifices. But his need to return to his roots did not stretch further than two weeks a year. After that he · was overcome with boredom, and with it the desire to resume his work and a more exciting, eventful life, filled with friends and relationships.

He joined his garrison in Stuttgart two weeks before Paul, on sick leave — he was riddled with amoebic dysentery and recovering from two successsive attacks of jaundice — finally quit Indo-China, which, since 20 July and the Geneva Conference, was no longer French.

Exhausted, looking older and a little bitter too, but still full of spirit, Paul arrived in Saint-Libéral at the end of August. He really rested up for two weeks, savouring with delight all the attention his mother lavished on him, the succulent little dishes she cooked with loving care, the infusions of herbs sweetened with honey.

Then one morning, because he was a man of the Vialhe stamp and idleness hung heavy, he followed his father and Nicolas and went to spread muck with them on the field called Léon's Letters. And in the evening, after having drunk the lime tea his mother handed to him, he went to his mess-chest in search of a bottle of cognac, poured some for his father, tipped a generous measure into his still-warm bowl, and talked.

He had not yet mentioned his long spell in Indo-China since his return. He evoked it now with an affectionate nostalgia which amazed his father, and opened his eyes to an unknown world, unimagined landscapes and incomparable smells. And Pierre-Edouard, who retained horrifying visions of butchery from the war of 1914, noticed with astonish-

387

ment that his son preserved fond, almost loving memories. And this despite the ambushes, the slaughter, swamps, mosquitoes, leeches, the climate and all the lost comrades. To listen to Paul, however horrible it might have been, this war featured as one of the most gripping periods of his life, the richest and most exhilarating.

Thus words which up till then had been if not foreign, at least meaningless to Pierre-Edouard, Mathilde and Nicolas, were brought to life by Paul. With him they discovered the grinning coolies, the compliant women, smelt the fragrance of Chinese cooking, heard the bustle of Catinat Street in Saigon, stepped into the bars of Cholon and Hanoi, experienced the death-throes of Lang Son and all the battles.

Above all, they understood what Paul had left there: a part of himself, for ever. Whatever he did, for him Indo-China would now be a sort of paradise lost, and also probably an ever-open wound.

Chapter 26

As soon as her grandson Pierre left for boarding-school, in October 1954, Louise felt overwhelmed by loneliness, idleness, and her age too.

Until then she had filled her time by trying to replace in some way the mother whom her grandson had never known. With Pierre gone she knew that Félix did not need her there; that she was possibly even in his way and preventing him from enjoying to the full that solitude he so loved, which he craved and lived for.

Through the years spent in the deepest forests, thickets and plantations, Félix had acquired complete peace of mind; this allowed him to live alone and not seek for company except amongst the oaks, beeches or hornbeams. To have as his only companions all the birds he so loved, which he observed and protected, and all those animals, both high and low, which filled the forest. He set off in the early hours and quite often did not return until evening, preferring to eat a snack at midday seated at the foot of a tree or the edge of a pool.

At first Louise was worried to see him withdraw from the world in this way, and had tried to jog him out of what she took for a state of depression. Then she had understood that, far from sinking into morbid melancholy, Félix sought and discovered in solitude the strength to live and be happy, showing his son the face of a man at peace with himself.

'Well now,' she said one evening in October, when the forest all around echoed with bending boughs as the east wind made it sing like an organ, 'now the boy has gone, I feel there's nothing left for me to do here.'

He pushed away the notebook in which he had been entering the results of his daily observations, looked at her and smiled.

'That's not a very kind thing to say. What about me then?'

'Oh! You! You haven't needed me for the last twenty-five

years or more!'

'You want to go back to Saint-Libéral, don't you?'

She agreed with a smile, and he noticed that the mere mention of her birthplace rejuvenated her.

'You've always pined for your home,' he continued, 'although you've been living here for more than forty years, you should have got used to it by now!'

'It's true, but this is not my land,' she said. 'Here it's too flat, you can't see far enough.'

'I know,' he joked. 'You Vialhes, I finally understood you while talking to my godfather down there, at your place, on the White Peak. You're not happy unless your eyes are level with the sky! You know, they say that in the past some knights had the right to enter churches without dismounting from their horses; you Vialhes don't like to have to raise your eyes to talk to God. I'm convinced you discuss things with him by getting up to his level!'

'Maybe,' she admitted, 'but that's not all I miss.'

'Your brother?'

'Him and the others. Everyone in the village. And the smells of home too; heather and bracken, the chestnut trees in flower and the black mushrooms you find beneath the oak trees. And the sun, the air, the wind – from the Auvergne with its taste of mountains, from the south with the feeling of heat, from the west with its odour of water and from the north bringing us the scent of fine weather. Here your wind smells of nothing, except mud!'

'To me it smells good, it tells me just as much as yours down there tells you. To understand it, you need to love it, but you never wanted to love it.'

'That's possible. I was just passing through here by accident.'

'Passing through for forty years, that's a long time!'

'Oh, yes! But now I want to return home; I'm old, tired. If I stay here, in this country full of forest and water, I'll soon lose the will to live. But down there, on our land, you'll see how we grow old gracefully! I'm going to write to Pierre-Edouard; I know he's expecting me and I think he may even say that I've left it too long.'

'Of course,' said Félix. 'But aren't you worried you may

put them in an awkward position?'

'No,' she reassured him with a smile, 'I know there'll always be room for me in the Vialhe house as long as Pierre-Edouard is there, and even afterwards.' She nodded, and continued quietly: 'At the Vialhes' we only kick out the young ones, and only for a while. But the old ones always have the right to a home; none of us die except under our own roof.'

Despite the disappointment he had felt when the electors rejected him as mayor, Jacques did not feel himself beaten for ever. If for a while he devoted himself solely to his farm, the urge to operate on a wider scale, beyond the borders of his fields, did not desert him.

Intellectually, he had the need to grapple with other problems than those of his land and animals. So he attended the co-operative meetings more frequently than before, became known and respected within the Chamber of Agriculture, the Crédit Agricole and the Insurance Association.

But he was conscious that his age – he was only thirty-four – was a handicap to effective action at the heart of this rustic world, now controlled by a majority of men over fifty, who had no desire to relinquish to him positions or responsibilities which they wished to hold for themselves.

His first reaction was outrage at a state of affairs which ran directly counter to the revolution convulsing the countryside. Everything was on the verge of collapse. Already, here and there, mechanisation was arriving in force on the farms, speeding up methods of working in the first instance and even giving the illusion of prosperity. Then in the second phase it often accelerated the downfall of those who thought it was enough to acquire a tractor in order to increase their yields, and who realised, too late, that the expenses incurred would never be covered by the modest profits from their tiny farms.

When he understood that it would take him years before his point of view prevailed, Jacques changed his tactics and decided to go at it in a roundabout way, aiming for a role which would eventually allow him to expound his opinions.

They were clear, and based on an analysis of the current situation.

He predicted, for everything pointed to it, that a certain way of farming had finally been superseded, and it was therefore necessary to work towards the development of a competitive, modern agricultural system, regrouping with fewer men, and still producing more. But he wanted, at the same time, to control the cruel pace of the rural exodus. Without that, he felt, given the example of Saint-Libéral, entire regions would fall into decline, for lack of people.

It was to try to promote his theories in a practical way that he took the decision, at the beginning of October, to stand in the regional elections on 17 and 24 April 1955.

'You'll be beaten hollow,' forecast Pierre-Edouard as soon as Jacques informed him of his plans, 'and what an idea, to want to get mixed up with all those scoundrels!'

The older he grew, the less time Pierre-Edouard had for those who went in for politics. And he did not hesitate to say that every other one of them should be hanged, to make the rest put their hearts and souls into their work!

'Let your son alone, he's right!' said Léon, who had come to spend that evening at the Vialhes'.

'And after all,' added Jacques, 'the regional council, it's not real politics!'

'Much you know!' scoffed Pierre-Edouard. 'There are just as many toads in there as anywhere else! Well, if it amuses you!'

'Don't listen to your father, he's an anarchist!' said Léon.

Pierre-Edouard shrugged, and turned towards Mathilde to seek her support. But she was chatting with Yvette and Michèle by the fireside, and had not even heard the beginning of the conversation.

'Fine,' said Pierre-Edouard, suddenly serious. 'After all, why not, you're a cut above plenty of others I could name! But it's a far cry from that to getting elected!'

'I'm going to help him,' decided Léon, delighted at the thought of all the days he could fill supporting his godson. 'Yes,' he said, 'if you want to have a chance of succeeding, you'll have to get yourself known, everywhere. I know everyone, I'll introduce you. We'll go round all the farms, the markets too, and you mustn't be afraid to drink a glass or two, to talk and shake hands.'

'That's right,' mocked Pierre-Edouard, 'dance around, like that bear a gypsy promenaded through the village before the war – the 1914 war, I mean!'

'Don't listen to your father,' continued Léon. 'You'll see, as soon as you're elected, he'll be the first to say it was thanks to him!'

'Possibly,' admitted Pierre-Edouard, 'but in the meantime, who's going to look after the animals while he's running round the countryside?'

'Yourself and Nicolas of course,' decided Léon. 'You can do that, can't you?'

'Oh, I get it,' Pierre-Edouard smiled, 'while you two are stirring up a lot of hot air, Nicolas and I will be stirring manure and buckets of pig-swill! Well, I prefer my place to yours! At least my work serves some purpose!'

'What are you talking about?' asked Mathilde, who had only just started listening to them.

'Your son wants to stand as a regional councillor, and thinks he's already there.'

'He's right,' she said, 'and he should be elected, that would teach the people in the village who didn't want him as mayor! Yes, that would teach them!'

'Now look at that!' cried Pierre-Edouard. 'First Léon, now your mother! Well, my boy, I'll end up believing you could be elected, because with two Dupeuchs to support you, you'll see, everyone will vote for you, just to get rid of your uncle and your mother!'

'Don't pay any attention to your father,' said Mathilde, 'he doesn't believe a word he's saying! Right,' she pressed on in a serious tone, looking at her brother, 'you know the mayors of all the towns involved?'

'The mayors and everyone else.'

'Good. So before announcing Jacques as a candidate, you'd better find out the way they're thinking; what they want, what they're expecting, all that sort of thing!'

'*Miladiou!*' said Léon with a smile to Pierre-Edouard, 'there's my sister trying to teach me my job! What are you thinking of,' he said to Mathilde, 'getting your son elected, it's like selling a cow! You show all his good points and none of his faults! With him, I'm in luck; I don't even need to tell any lies – well, not too many, just a few for the fun of it, eh!'

Louise came back to Saint-Libéral for good on 29 October. She was greeted by magnificent weather which warmed her heart and threw her, overflowing with emotion, into her brother's embrace.

As she had said to her son, Pierre-Edouard and Mathilde had not hesitated for a minute to reply that she would be welcome; that her bedroom stood ready, and they would both be delighted to see her return at last.

That same evening, because she wanted everything to be above board, she suggested to her brother that she give him part of her pension to pay for her food. He rejected it outright.

'Keep your cash, you won't see the day when I allow my sisters to pay me for a room in the house where they were born!'

'Yes, yes,' she insisted, 'because if you won't take anything, I'll soon be embarrassed to be eating your soup!'

'Rubbish,' he interrupted, 'save your money. You'll need it if you're going to get that house built on Combes-Nègres one day.'

'Yes, but meanwhile I don't want my being here to cost you anything. And if you won't accept any money, I'd rather go and move into Suzanne's!'

'You'd have a job,' he said laughing, 'she hasn't kept any rooms for three years! Now she only runs the bistro.'

'Well,' decided Louise, 'I'll work with Mathilde on the farm, in the cowsheds, the garden, all over!'

'That I agree to; I can't argue with that.'

'And I'll go and mind the cows on Combes-Nègres, as I did in the past,' she added with a touch of nostalgia.

'You can mind them if you like,' he said, 'but it won't do much good; we closed off all our meadows a long time ago with barbed wire or Jacques' electric fence.'

'That's a pity,' she murmured in disappointment.

'Maybe, but it's more practical. Besides, who minds cows

these days? You know, my dear, cowherds don't exist any more.'

Three days later, on 1 November, the news on the radio told of the tragic events which had plunged Algeria into mourning on All Saints Day. But in Saint-Libéral, as elsewhere, nobody paid much attention to these massacres. Algeria was far away, like Morocco or Tunisia, and there was always trouble with the Arabs, conflicts without apparent reasons.

And because the political situation was no worse than usual since Paul had been posted to Djibouti, and Guy was still in Germany, neither Pierre-Edouard nor Mathilde thought for a minute that a fresh war had just broken out.

Rejuvenated by the goal which he had set himself, of getting his godson elected, Léon spent part of the winter running round the hamlets and villages. After considering the problem he had calculated, in agreement with Jacques, that it was unwise for a candidate to reveal his intentions and plans too soon, and thereby to present his competitors with the time and the wherewithal to attack him.

His judgement was correct, and he was jubilant when he realised that the majority of electors, as a result of seeing him beating about the countryside, firmly believed that he was preparing for his own candidature. Secretly delighted, he let them talk, amused to see his godson's future adversaries exhaust themselves by directing their blows at himself.

Then, when he had studied and researched the canton and learned everyone's needs – this village had no running water, that isolated farm was waiting for an electricity supply, others demanded surfaced roads – he faded into the background and pushed Jacques into the ring.

Even the people of Saint-Libéral were surprised at this dramatic turn of events. As for the other candidates, they were forced to change their target hastily, and look for arguments designed to denigrate young Vialhe. But just as it was easy to invent a hundred accusations against Léon – his former profession and his inordinate riches were a gift to his detractors – it was extremely difficult to attack Jacques. On his side he had the honesty and good reputation of the

Vialhes; he was a serious professional, a pillar of one section of the farming world and of the young people in the Young Christian Farmers.

With all these advantages came an ease of expression and best of all, thanks to the information supplied by Léon, an excellent knowledge of particular situations.

Despite that, when all seemed set for him to gain a commanding lead at the end of the first ballot, he only came second, far behind an old war-horse who, as Pierre-Edouard said, had been lining his own nest for more than thirty years.

Sad and embittered, Jacques was within a fraction of abandoning the struggle.

'Out of the question!' said Pierre-Edouard, irritated by his son's partial failure, 'you have a week to climb back up the slope!'

'A slope of almost three hundred votes!' sighed Jacques, 'and I haven't even any money to pay for posters and leaflets!'

'Don't worry about money, that's my business,' cut in Léon. 'Starting tomorrow we'll go round all the farms again, and at the double! You'll see, the other old Arab is so sure of winning now that he'll sit back. We're going to get moving, and too bad if you're drunk every evening from buying rounds for everyone, I'll bring you home!'

'That's right,' Pierre-Edouard encouraged him. 'Look, we'll study the results, village by village; we'll have to give the ones who voted the wrong way a good working-over.'

'And then you must make a fuss of the women,' Mathilde reminded him. 'Well, what I mean is,' she said, smiling at her daughter-in-law, 'get them to vote, you know! They've had the right for ten years; tell them that now's the moment to exercise it!'

Jacques started his electoral campaign again on the Monday morning. He conducted it briskly, undertaking visits to the most remote farms and hamlets, never hesitating to walk into the fields to have a discussion with some elector busy sowing his beets or planting his potatoes.

On Wednesday, the day of Ayen market, he spent the morning in the market-place; strolled among the calves, gave his opinion on the heifers on sale and his views on the latest tractor models, agreed with everyone in deploring the lack of control over prices and the spiralling rise in the cost of commodities.

But to be forced to try to outbid his rival in this way depressed his spirits, and strengthened his impression that the battle was lost before it had begun.

'That's all very fine, but I really feel I'm prostituting my soul, and I don't like it one little bit,' he confided to Léon, when they went to recharge their strength, towards ten o'clock, by taking a bowl of soup with a little something in it at the nearest bistro.

Léon shrugged.

'Yes,' he admitted as he poured a generous measure of wine into the bottom of his soup-bowl, 'but your rival's doing the same, and not as well as you! So you may be in with a chance; when it's between two whores, it's seldom the poxy one that's chosen! Now, back to work. And don't be scared of making them promises!'

'Even if I were elected, I could never keep half the ones I've already made!' protested Jacques.

'Never mind,' Léon assured him, 'they know that perfectly well, but it's part of the game! Come on, my boy, let's go and get you the missing votes.'

It was on their way back to Saint-Libéral on Thursday evening that Léon was taken ill; a mixture of weakness numbing his left arm and a heavy-headed fuzziness in the back of his skull. Luckily he felt himself losing consciousness, and had time to stop the car before collapsing over the steering-wheel.

'My God! What's the matter?' cried a worried Jacques as he supported him.

'Tired,' whispered Léon, 'take me home, quickly . . .'

'It'd be better to go to Ayen and see the doctor!'

'Home,' repeated Léon, 'you can call him from there. Drive on, my boy,' he muttered, sliding into Jacques' seat, 'drive on, it's getting better already.'

'But the interior light revealed a pallor and an expression which contradicted his words.

'Go home,' he insisted.

'All right,' said Jacques, feeling more anxious than ever, 'but at the next village I'm going to call the doc.' And the Citroën roared off towards Saint-Libéral.

'A classic start to a stroke,' diagnosed the doctor, 'it doesn't surprise me, with that sort of blood-pressure! How old is he?'

'Sixty-eight,' groaned Léon.

He opened one eye, and looked at Yvette, Jacques, Pierre-Edouard and Mathilde who stood at his bedside. Then he noticed the young doctor.

'Who's this then?' he asked in a weak voice.

'The locum from Perpezac, the other one's on holiday,' explained Yvette.

'Right,' said the doctor, closing his bag, 'I've done what's needed for the moment, but he must be admitted as soon as possible. Do you have a telephone?'

'I'm staying here!' said Leon, trying to sit up. He realised that his left arm felt like cottonwool, and raised himself on his right elbow.

'Out of the question!' cut in the doctor.

Léon closed his eyes; he seemed to be gathering the remnants of his strength.

'I'm staying here!' he insisted.

'Come, come, don't be so childish. No arguing! We'll take you down to Brive, you'll be very comfortable there. They'll nurse you and get you back on your feet in no time,' declared the doctor in the jocular, slightly patronising tone he reserved for his patients.

'Pierre-Edouard,' called Léon without opening his eyes, 'chuck him out, the young fool! Out!' he repeated in a remarkably firm voice, 'in memory of Drs Fraysse and Delpy . . .'

'Forgive him,' stammered Yvette.

'It doesn't matter,' the doctor assured her, although he was turning red, 'I'm used to sick people's peculiarities. Get your husband's things ready while I telephone.'

Pierre-Edouard looked at Léon, then at Yvette, and finally at the doctor. Suddenly he understood the strength and reputation of the old country doctors. They strove to treat the sick without removing them from their familiar surroundings, their homes and families, except in cases requiring surgical operations. Without depriving them of that reassuring, soothing environment, punctuated by the noises and incidents which chronicle the life of a farm or village; the whistle of the wind in the slates and the branches of the lime tree, the lowing of the animals in the barn, the children's shouts at playtime, the neighbours chatting beneath the window. And at night, punctuated by the solemn chime of the church clock, the dogs barking to each other, the plaintive whoop of the tawny owl, the screech of the little owl, and in the loft, the quick patter of mice suddenly halted by the cat springing from its ambush behind the grain sacks.

This was the life to which the sick clung, and even if the treatment given by the doctor was sometimes lacking, at least it was accepted with complete confidence and total faith in the man who hurried to their aid at any hour of the day or night. His presence alone was a relief, an immense comfort.

But all that was gone for ever. Saint-Libéral had no doctor now, and the stranger – possibly capable, possibly incompetent – who stood at Léon's bedside was dealing with a routine matter. To simplify things, and to off-load the responsibility, he preferred to send this unknown patient to some equally anonymous treatment centre. Léon's wishes cut little ice with him; he was only one case among many, an old man whose name and appearance he would soon forget.

'Pierre-Edouard,' began Léon weakly, 'remember Dr Fraysse and Dr Delpy, they would have left me here; don't let them take me away . . . They'll kill me over there.'

He tried to sit up once again.

'I'm going to give him a light sedative,' said the doctor, opening his case, 'it'll calm him for the journey to Brive.'

'Leave him,' said Pierre-Edouard suddenly, 'and go. I've seen enough of you, too!'

'But . . .' protested Yvette.

'He's right, let him say it!' whispered Léon.

'Are you related?' asked the doctor coldly, delicately severing the neck of an ampoule.

'Yes,' said Pierre-Edouard.

He was conscious of the enormous resonsibility he was taking. If Léon stayed in Saint-Libéral and died in the night, everyone would say it was for lack of positive treatment which, according to the doctor, he could only receive in hospital. But if he died over there, Pierre-Edouard would never forgive himself for having let him die alone and far from home.

Léon wished to stay under his own roof; he had a right to do so, his last right maybe. They should not betray him by disregarding it; it was unthinkable.

'Yes,' repeated Pierre-Edouard, 'since my brother-in-law doesn't want to go to hospital, no one can force him. He'll stay here.'

'I've never heard of such a thing!' protested the doctor. He observed Léon and pulled a long face. 'This man needs hospital treatment; he's already partially paralysed, any professional practitioner would tell you the same thing!'

'We don't give a damn about professional practitioners, we're not asking them!' said Pierre-Edouard. 'All we want is an ordinary doctor, a real one, who knows how to look after people without sending them off the devil knows where!'

'And what is Madame's opinion?' queried the doctor, turning to Yvette.

She looked at Léon, saw his imploring eyes and forced herself to give him a faint but reassuring smile.

'He'll be staying, I'll take the responsibility. I'll find a colleague of yours who'll agree to treat him here, and if need be, I'll get a home nurse in.'

'If you enjoy complicating things and taking risks!' said the doctor, throwing his syringe into his case and closing it briskly. 'I've done what I had to do; now, don't come complaining if the paralysis spreads to the whole left arm.'

'Bah!' spat Léon, placing his right hand on his stump, 'it's been half cocked-up for the last forty years, so . . .'

Watched over in turn by Yvette, Mathilde and Pierre-Edouard – Jacques had returned to Coste-Roche lest Michèle became anxious at his prolonged absence – Léon passed a peaceful night. He woke in the early hours, when the truck from the milk co-operative passed through Saint-Libéral with its churns clanging, saw Pierre-Edouard seated at his bedside and smiled.

'I was far gone, wasn't I?' he asked him.

'Maybe . . . How are you now?'

'Okay, but I think that little squirt was right, my arm feels like lead!'

'It'll get better, but who's going to treat you now?'

'The doctor who looked after my father-in-law. He didn't stop the poor old fellow from popping off, but at least he died at home, in peace! Look, I'm hungry . . .'

'You're hungry?' exclaimed Pierre-Edouard, delighted at this indisputable sign of recovery.

'Dammit, with this going on, I didn't eat a thing last night! Go down to the kitchen and fetch me a hunk of bread and a big bulb of garlic, I hear that's good for high blood pressure. I'd ask you to give the crust a good coating of lard and bring me a half bottle of white wine, but I don't think you'd do that!'

'No, I would not!'

'Well, go and get the slice of bread and garlic, we've got a battle to fight!'

'Yes,' Pierre-Edouard smiled, 'and we'll have the best of it, like in 1914!'

'Well?' demanded Léon anxiously, when Mathilde came to inform him of the election results.

'It's still neck and neck . . .' she said, holding out a sheet on which Pierre-Edouard, standing guard by the telephone at the mairie, had written the figures for the last known count.

Léon scanned the page, made a face and put down the paper on the bedside table, amongst the medicine bottles. He had accepted without protest the draconian course of treatment prescribed by the family doctor. He knew that he was ill and must take things carefully. That was logical. So, on condition that he was left in peace at home, he was quite disposed to follow the doctor's orders, which included, among other things, staying in bed.

God knows how much he had wanted to get up to go and

vote, but Yvette was firmly opposed to it and even Pierre-Edouard had sharply reminded him of the threat hanging over him: at the next sign of trouble, it was into hospital with him!

'I'd rather die!' Léon had grumbled.

'You're not that bad yet,' Pierre-Edouard had reassured him. 'As for the election, one vote won't decide it.'

'Good God, no! But what if everyone did the same as me?'

'Stay in bed and be patient. Would you like something to read? I've got some magazines at home.'

'Go to the devil, you and your reading! You'd do better to go and watch the polling-station!'

'It's not open yet!'

Léon had been a bag of nerves all day, and now the results were arriving his fears were not abating. He picked up the figures again and studied them.

'Those bastards,' he said, 'they prefer a city type to a local lad!'

'That's to be expected,' said Mathilde resignedly. 'The countryside is growing emptier, people are forgetting about us. Right, I'm going back down to the mairie, maybe there's something new.'

'Wait, call Jacques on the telephone; maybe he knows more about it in Tulle.'

'No,' she said, smiling sadly. 'Leave him be, he wanted to be over there, at the préfecture, because he'd be calmer than here; we're not going to disturb him. And then, you know, if it's to tell him that even in this village he didn't do all he should have done . . .'

'You're right,' he agreed, 'go to the mairie, but come back as soon as you have any news!'

When she arrived in the council chamber, Mathilde felt that something had changed. There was not the same hubbub, and the looks she was getting were different. She saw that some were triumphant, others disappointed, and understood that one of the candidates was beginning to forge ahead.

'He's gaining!' Pierre-Edouard called as soon as he saw her.

Then she sighed with relief, rushed towards him and

examined the figures.

'He's a hundred and twenty-eight votes ahead,' Maurice explained to her, 'it's fantastic! The other one can't make that up now; there are only two villages left and they're right behind Jacques!'

She looked at him and could not resist the impulse to tease their old friend, the good man whom the people of Saint-Libéral had chosen as mayor rather than her son.

'Well, well,' she said to him, 'I think, Mayor, you'll be seeing a regional councillor on your town council . . .'

'Yes,' he said, placing a hand on Pierre-Edouard's shoulder, 'and I'm proud of it. Not as much as you two, but almost. And Léon'll be proud too, and so will the whole town. You'll see; everyone'll be there to set up a maypole in front of the Vialhe house!'

'I'd better go and tell Léon,' she said.

But she stopped because the telephone was ringing. Pierre-Edouard lifted it, nodded his head.

'You can go now,' he said, putting it down again, 'that was the préfecture. Your son is elected with a majority of a hundred and eighty-seven votes!'

'Jacques has been elected!' shouted Maurice, and everyone there cheered with delight.

But Mathilde, beside herself with pride and happiness, was already scurrying through the darkness towards the château.

'He's won! He's won!' she called as she stepped into the hall.

She reached her brother's bedroom and stopped in amazement. Seated in his bed, well propped up against a pile of pillows, a beaming Léon was drinking a glass of champagne.

'What about your diet?' she stammered.

'Jacques telephoned us,' Yvette explained to her, 'so Léon absolutely insisted on toasting the good news, and since he was threatening to get up if I didn't bring the champagne . . . I thought it would be better if I served it up . . .'

'Come and drink to him!' he said, 'and give me a kiss, we can be proud, we have the right. Half an hour ago, the grandson of Jean-Edouard Vialhe and Emile Dupeuch became a regional councillor for the Corrèze!'

'Wait,' said Mathilde. 'I'll drink to it when Pierre's here, because without him there wouldn't have *been* a Vialhe-Dupeuch grandson.'

Chapter 27

JACQUES and Germaine Sourzac, teachers in the village since 1932, finally left Saint-Libéral in July 1955. Since they had never mixed very much in the life of the village, except during election times, and had no close, long-standing friendships, the villagers saw them depart without any great regret. All the more so because it had been known for two months who their replacements were to be, and everybody was delighted to see them arrive.

When it was announced that Jean-Pierre Fleyssac, Pierre-Edouard's son-in-law, was to be the next schoolmaster, many people thought that Jacques had cleverly used his mandate as regional councillor to promote members of his family. He was at pains to deny it and confirm that his brother-in-law had applied for the post two years earlier, but the majority remained convinced that it was thanks to his intervention that Mauricette, her husband and three girls were able to move into the school in Saint-Libéral. In the end Jacques let them talk, for he quickly realized that, far from reproaching him, they saw it as a sign of his power and effectiveness, and his electors respected him all the more. They could not, of course, know that Jean-Pierre had only been appointed to what was to be a single teacher school from now on – there were only twenty-one pupils – because Mauricette had given up teaching.

If the departure of the Sourzacs raised little interest, the same could not be said of the butcher; everyone understood that his dwindling clientele did not provide him with a livelihood, but people still lamented his disappearance. It was worrying, for if a man like him was forced to go and earn his living elsewhere – he was taken on as an employee by a meat-curer in Allassac – it stood to reason that the other shop-keepers would shortly be following his example. What was to become of Saint-Libéral then?

Already robbed of their priest, doctor and solicitor, more and more isolated, forgotten, the villagers foresaw the time when they would have to trek all the way to Perpezac, or still further, to buy the merest loaf of bread, litre of oil or three pounds of stewing-beef.

That summer of 1955 two other farmers in the commune acquired a tractor each; the era of working with cows or oxen was past. But during the same season five young people who had been helping on their fathers' farms left the village. Two set off for Paris, pleased to have been taken on as unskilled operatives by Renault; one enlisted in the army, and the last two went to work at the hinge-maker's in La Rivière-de-Mansac: they, at least, returned each evening to Saint-Libéral to sleep.

For Pierre-Edouard and Mathilde, Mauricette's return was a real joy. This happiness somewhat relieved their worries over Paul, who had been in Algeria since August, and over Jacques – despite all his effort and labour, the revenue from his land was not increasing as he had hoped.

The price of pigs was subject to incomprehensible and violent fluctuations; calves were hard to sell; cereals, given their yield, were no longer viable. As for fruit and vegetables, they did not stand up to competition from the citrus fruits and early produce from North Africa and the Midi.

Jacques still gathered in enough to support his family, but the accounts kept by Michèle were there to prove they were simply marking time; it was impossible to expand without taking out further loans.

'It's up there it's happening, in Paris,' said Jacques from time to time, 'they don't want to know about us, we're too small. I think they're hoping we'll disappear; some people don't balk at saying as much, too . . .'

And even Pierre-Edouard, who had long believed that the Vialhe land formed a great and untouchable holding, ended up assessing just how small, modest and vulnerable it was. Occasionally he was haunted by the idea that the time would come when maybe, despite the presence of his son to care for it, this property, fruit of the labour of five generations, would founder – just as in the past all those little smallholdings had gone under, the ones which his fathers and grandfathers, confident in their ten hectares, had considered wretched and without a future.

'It's not possible,' he told himself, 'for if we were to disappear, we who have the finest lands in the commune, who could then survive?'

Mauricette's return was therefore a great joy to him. It cheered him up, made him laugh at his granddaughters' pranks; he bounced them on his knees and in the evening wove baskets of willow or chestnut for them. Trifles for which they thanked him with cries of pleasure and kisses warm and wet as ash leaves after a June shower.

The winter of 1955–6 was treacherous and cruel, like an asp which pretends to sleep beneath the heather and coils with a hiss at the approach of a silhouette; you think it torpid and replete, but it reveals itself keen and ready to attack.

Thus January 1956 was mild, rainy, occasionally almost warm, even with the scent of spring some afternoons which deceived everyone. Even the bees were fooled when, on the 20th, a pale but pleasantly warm sun encouraged a few workers to leave the shelter of the hives and buzz about the shelf at the entrance.

'I don't like this weather,' said Pierre-Edouard to Nicolas one day as they were making up bundles of firewood. 'Look at that,' he said, pointing to the swollen buds of the sloe bushes, 'they're ready to burst, the fools; I don't mind if *they* get frosted, but I bet you the plum trees are doing the same . . . I'm telling you, the weather's going mad!'

'It's the atom bomb that's upsetting it!' joked Nicolas.

'It may be that,' said Pierre-Edouard, smiling. 'The trouble is, I remember winters just as crazy before the bomb! At that time, before 1914, people blamed in on the aeroplanes!'

The end of the month was wet and mild. On the evening of 31 January everyone fell asleep to the patter of rain-drops falling on the flagstones, but on the morning of 1 February the silence was astounding. A frozen, glacial silence. In the night, without warning, winter had fallen like an axe; the thermometer registered minus 12° at eight in the morning, and minus 14° by eleven o'clock.

Paralysed by the cold and amazed at the suddenness of the attack, the people of Saint-Libéral closed their shutters, stopped up the doors to cellars and cowsheds with great heaps of straw bales, and huddled in their chimney-corners around blazing fires.

The cold set in and, encouraged by a wind that cut like glass, tightened its grip. Even the snow, which fell in abundance from 10 February onwards, did not succeed in raising the temperature, which remained stationary at about minus 15°. On the 11th, the River Vezère froze over. But they had to wait until the 18th, Ash Wednesday, to experience a cold snap such as very few in the village had ever known. Even Pierre-Edouard admitted that the winters of 1899, 1917 and 1939 had not recorded such temperatures. Only a few former prisoners, like Jacques, and also Nicolas, maintained that they had seen worse; on the thermometer at the mairie the mercury fell to minus 24°. And the wind went on blowing.

It was because of this that Nicolas decided to go out in the middle of the afternoon. He was worried about his bees, for he feared that the wind surging from the east would tear off the thick wrapping of rye straw and jute sacks which protected the hives.

'Are you going out?' Pierre-Edouard was astonished to see him pulling on his fur-lined jacket. 'It's not time to see to the cows yet!'

'I know, but I'll be back soon,' Nicolas assured him, as he slipped on the thick woollen mittens which Mathilde had knitted for him the winter before. 'I'm going to the hives,' he explained. 'I'm afraid this infernal wind will rip away the straw.'

'Wrap up well,' advised Mathilde, 'it seems to me it's even worse now than this morning!'

He went out; the door was only open an instant, yet an icy blast swept through the room. Pierre-Edouard shivered and stoked the fire.

'By God,' he murmured, 'he's brave going over there in this weather!' Then he returned to reading his newspaper.

Nicolas was soon reassured. Even before reaching the apiary he noted from a distance that the straw was holding well; it was covered with frozen snow and was not moving under the buffeting wind. Nevertheless he climbed up to them, for the pleasure of contemplating the fine line of hives.

He was bending towards the first one when an agonising stab seared through his chest. Lashed by the pain he straightened up sharply, wavered for an instant, and collapsed like a tall poplar felled by the wind. And his hair, although so white, made a little patch of grey on the snow.

When Pierre-Edouard found him half an hour later, he could not even fold the arms across the body – they were already stiffened by the frost.

In the village they very quickly learned that death had struck at the Vialhes. And because everyone knew that Nicolas was almost part of the family, many came towards evening, despite the intense cold, to pay a last visit to the strange man who had landed up in Saint-Libéral a quarter of a century earlier and had made it his home, and the Vialhes his only family.

Even Jacques, informed by a boy, walked down from Coste-Roche, for the frozen snow rendered the track impassable by car. He came and was not surprised, any more than the neighbours were, to find his father dejected and his mother in tears. Their sorrow was heartfelt – and so was their gesture. For Nicolas, who in his lifetime had never wanted to leave his cubby-hole in the cowshed, now lay in one of the bedrooms of the Vialhe house.

For the two nights preceding the burial Jacques, Pierre-Edouard, Mathilde and Louise, but also neighbours and friends, took it in turns to watch over the mortal remains. Only Léon could not come; for him too the cold might prove fatal.

The weather broke on the day of the funeral and heavy rain accompanied the cortège, making the snow slippery and dirty and the red soil in the graveyard as sticky as grease. Despite that, the neighbours came in great numbers for, having been twenty-five years in the parish, Nicolas had eventually made them forget that he was a foreigner. Many were quite astonished to discover his name on the plaque which Pierre-Edouard had ordered to be engraved:

Nicolas Krajhalovic
30 juin 1893. 17 février 1956

For them all, he was simply Nicolas at the Vialhes'.

Nobody needed to wait for the complete thaw to discover the extent of the catastrophe. Besides a number of water-ducts burst by the frost – pipes can after all be replaced or repaired – not a single cereal field in the commune escaped destruction. But this loss, however burdensome, was not as devastating or far-reaching as what had happened to the walnut trees.

On every side were split trunks, gaping scars, through which their life would flow away as soon as the sap began to rise. And the damaged trees which might perhaps have survived would have their wounds open to every parasite, infection and fungus; attacks which would undermine the trees until they withered away in years to come.

With a heavy heart, when he foresaw the extent of the damage, Pierre-Edouard counted the victims. The frost of 1939 had cost him four trees; that of 1956 carried off another thirteen. Of the thirty-one walnut trees which he had planted long ago with his father, there remained only eleven. Eleven magnificent trees, in their prime, their beauty and value accentuated by the loss caused by the frost. Besides the harvest of nuts which the victims would have provided, their wood itself was spoiled. That wonderful wood for carving which, to the owner of a walnut planta-tion, is like a living investment, to be drawn on in dire need.

'How many?' asked Mathilde, when he came back down from the plateau. She had no doubt that the losses would be significant, but she wanted to know the extent.

'Thirteen,' he sighed.

She saw him unhappy, distressed by this fresh blow; Nicolas's death had affected him deeply, and the lost trees increased his sorrow.

'We'll have to replant,' she decided, 'this year. Promise me you'll plant some more!'

'Of course,' he said. 'What did you think, that I'm too old now to fight on?'

She smiled, held out her hand to him, and her small, delicate fingers were lost in his hard, calloused fist.

'No,' she reproached him, 'I didn't say that, but . . . in the long run, aren't you tired of always having to start again?'

'Yes, a bit,' he admitted, 'it's natural, I'm not twenty any more. But that won't stop me replanting our walnuts!' He turned to Louise, who was knitting by the fireside: 'Do you remember when we planted them, thirty-one of them, up there?'

'Of course! It was on St Catherine's Day, in 1901!'

'How old was Grandfather?'

'Oh, he was ancient, and his rheumatism was giving him a terrible time!'

'Yes,' she said, looking at Mathilde, 'he was seventy-one then. He still wanted to come up to the plateau on the last day of the planting. Well, I'm sixty-seven next month, so you mustn't think I'm going to sit about doing nothing! And I haven't got rheumatism – well, not much . . .'

The call-up for the class of 1952 in May '56, and the departure for Algeria of Guy, now a sub-lieutenant in the reserves, surprised and shook the Vialhes like a thunderbolt from the blue.

They suddenly understood, as did all the parents in the village with sons of an age for military service, that the so-called peace-keeping operations – as the politicians hypocritically named them –were a war; a new sort maybe, but a real war.

Until now, the people of Saint-Libéral had not taken much interest in the events in Algeria. They found them disturbing because they complicated and aggravated the political situation and the general malaise, and they could do without that, but they did not feel directly affected. Until spring 1956 it had never occurred to Pierre-Edouard, although he knew what was going on from Paul's letters, that his youngest son would one day have to face war.

Admittedly Paul wrote rarely, and his information was vague; but he had never given them to believe that it would ever be necessary to call up conscripts to subdue a rebellion amongst a few goatherds!

So the shock was severe for Pierre-Edouard, and above all for Mathilde; cruel and lonely because, beyond the first moment of amazement, those villagers who were not directly concerned – and they were the majority – continued their lives as if nothing had happened. But for the Vialhes and several others, the wait for letters began; the worry after reading a newspaper article reporting actions; the careful listening to the bulletins and, between the mothers, the exchange of news.

Mathilde, who had finally got used to the life chosen by Paul – he was a professional soldier, therefore, she thought, more capable of defending himself – suddenly felt very worried about Guy. He himself, stationed in Biskra, might sometimes forget to strike off the days which separated him from his discharge, but his mother certainly kept count of them. She calculated that her son had spent almost two years in Germany; the length of service was thirty months, and he would therefore be home to celebrate Christmas with them.

In September, Paul spent the last week of his leave in Saint-Libéral. Although Mathilde was secretly hurt when she learned that he had already taken three weeks' holiday in Paris without even telling them, she did not reproach him with it.

'You must understand that we don't mean much to him now,' Pierre-Edouard explained to console her. 'Here there's nothing to distract him; no friends, no cinemas, no bistros, no women,' he murmured almost to himself, 'and we're old . . .'

'There's still his brother!'

'Jacques? Yes, but you know they've nothing in common, you must realise that! Look how Paul lives, and what he earns! Poor old Jacques, in comparison . . . And then to Paul, Jacques' whole life is routine, peace and quiet, the family – everything he was trying to escape!'

For the first few days Paul talked very little about his life in Algeria. He made an effort to reassure his parents as to the risks Guy might run, but Pierre-Edouard was convinced that he was not saying what he was really thinking; that he was ill at ease when anyone urged him to talk about the war. So one evening, when Mathilde and Louise had gone to bed, he tried to find out.

'Now that the women can't hear us, tell me what's really happening over there?' he asked, as he watched his son pour himself another measure of plum brandy.

Paul inhaled the bouquet, swallowed a mouthful.

'Over there?' he said with a bitter grimace. 'It's foul, completely rotten. We comb through the Jebel Mountains, we trudge about, we lock people up. All that to pick up a few lousy vermin, and we don't know whether they're partisans by choice or force! But we put a bullet in anyway, to clean up the countryside . . .'

He emptied his glass in one draft and refilled it.

'You're drinking too much,' commented Pierre-Edouard.

'Yes, I know; over there, we drink too much, what else do you want us to do? It's such a bloody mess, and we're doing such disgusting work! It's not a straightforward war, you see,' he continued fiercely. 'How can I explain it to you! The Viets were vicious, deceitful, but at least they were soldiers and in the field; when you could pin them down, there were real battles! Besides, over there, I knew who I was fighting against; against the Marxists, that was plain. But with the fellaheen, it's a complete shambles. You don't know who they are nor where they are, everywhere or nowhere, like shadows, you know! Bloody ghosts ambushing us and then disappearing. Or they're chucking bombs or grenades into the bistros and cinemas, poxy things, I'm telling you! Then we have to search through the hamlets, check the papers, drag about everywhere, interrogating, questioning. It's a copper's job, that, and I'm no copper, but I'm doing their work!'

'You chose it,' his father reminded him.

'Yes, to make war, not be a policeman! And to add to it, now they've stuck these boys in amongst us, kids like Guy! It's not their job either to track down wogs! Those kids, all they want is their demob. You can't blame them; they don't give a damn about Algeria! That's natural, in France you don't care either, I soon saw that in Paris during my leave!'

'I care about it!'

'Of course, you've got two sons over there! But suppose

neither Guy nor I were there. Come on, be honest, you'd do the same as everyone else, you'd wait for it to blow over!'

'Maybe,' admitted Pierre-Edouard. He relit his dead pipe, and sighed: 'And do you think it'll last much longer, this war?'

'How should I know . . . If they fought like the Viets, we'd soon have them on their knees! But the way they do things, it's not so simple.' Paul thought for a moment; contemplated his empty glass. 'Anyway,' he continued, 'we'll fight to the finish on the ground; over there we won't get screwed up in another battle like Diên Biên Phu, and they haven't got a leader like Giap either! Yes, we'll wring their necks, but I'm not sure there's any point in it!' He smiled rather sadly, and added: 'You see, I'm in a position to know that you can never hold on to those who really want to leave. You left the house a long time ago, and Aunt Louise and Aunt Berthe and I went away as well! And no person or reason could stop us. The Arabs will do the same – in fifteen or twenty years may be, but they'll be off. That's to say they'll kick us out, it amounts to the same thing! So we're already in a bloody mess, and the longer we wait the sillier we look!'

'So you think it would be better if we saved ourselves the trouble and stopped straight away?' asked Pierre-Edouard, surprised by his pessimism.

'Oh no!' said Paul pouring himself another half glass of alcohol, 'we've got this far, we might as well try to salvage something out of it; anyway that's what they're paying me for!'

'I thought you didn't want to do a . . . a policeman's job!'

'I know, but after the two bouts of jaundice in Indo-China and the amoebic dysentery, I shouldn't drink alcohol either, and still . . .'

Following Nicolas' death, Jacques lost several hours each day coming down to the village to help his parents look after the cows.

So in the spring, he reckoned that the most sensible and cost-effective course would be to take his own animals to Coste-Roche. And he would doubtless have moved them up there without more ado if the little byre attached to the house could have accommodated his fifteen Limousin cows,

414

but it was only intended for three. He was therefore forced to consider the construction of a cowshed.

He talked to his father about it, and was surprised at his reaction. Without trying to dissuade him outright, Pierre-Edouard presented all the arguments which tended to demonstrate that this solution was neither the simplest nor the best. He spoke of the expenses of the building; assured him that Louise, Mathilde and he were still quite capable of seeing to the cows, and that he did not need to come twice a day if it took up too much of his time.

'And anyway,' he said, 'you're driving the children down to school and picking them up in the evening!'

'Of course, but as soon as they're big enough, they'll walk or bike it. No, really, it wastes so much of my time. And it's not practical, nor good for the animals. Our land is up there, the cows tire themselves out climbing up to graze and again coming back down here; it's not viable. Besides, soon it'll be too small here; I've got to get to the stage where I keep more than twenty cows, and I'll get there.'

'If you move your cows to Coste-Roche, that means you'll never come back here,' said Pierre-Edouard finally.

And Jacques understood that this was the real reason for his reservations.

'Here or there, it's still a home!'

'Yes, but this is the real Vialhe house. Coste-Roche is different, and it's too small anyway!'

'That's no problem; as soon as I can convert the loft, I'll make three bedrooms there.'

'And who'll look after your mother when I'm gone?'

'You've got Mauricette, and after all, good God, we've still got time to think about that!'

'You never know . . . Well, if you prefer to stay up there for good, you'd better do it,' conceded Pierre-Edouard. He sucked his pipe, which had gone out, then smiled mischievously: 'Oh yes,' he said, 'I know what you like up there; that's where you were conceived and born. At heart you feel it's the new Vialhe home, for the young people. Here, with your mother, aunt and me, it's almost like an old people's home, just like the rest of the village!'

*

415

Pierre-Edouard let his son draw up the plans for his future cowshed, calculate the cost of the project and discuss it with the Crédit Agricole. But he would not compromise when, at the beginning of November, the moment came to plant the walnut trees, and Jacques proposed the establishment of a modern orchard, for quick returns and ease of working, planted with half-standard, fast-growing trees.

'No, no,' insisted Pierre-Edouard, 'I saw you coming, I know what you want me to do, I've read about it somewhere, but I won't have it here! Do that on your land, if you like, I'm sure you're right, but leave me the satisfaction of planting real trees, the sort that take fifty years to reach their prime; at least they'll remind my grandchildren that I planted them for them! Your half-standards, with trunks like cabbage stalks – I don't want any of them, don't think I'm going to put them on my land!'

'But they're the most cost-effective,' attempted Jacques. 'You'll have nuts in less than ten years, whereas with the others you'll need to wait twenty-five! If they haven't been destroyed by the frost before then . . .'

'I know. If I were your age, I'd probably think the same way as you. You young people, you must work for yourselves, grow whatever gives quick returns and lots of it. And your sons'll have to follow the same system because you won't be leaving them much that's lasting; no big beautiful trees, no fine stone and slate buildings, nothing solid, you know, like so much wind . . . Whereas I'd like to leave behind some real nut trees, just for the sake of it. I'll never pick their walnuts but I don't care, because when I go, the trees you're going to help me plant will still be young. And if all goes well, in eighty years' time they'll be a memorial for me, and for you too.'

Since he was much younger than his brother, and in no way prepared for the hate, racism and violence, Guy was profoundly affected by the months he spent in Algeria. And he, whose vocation and profession was to defend the guilty – or the presumed so – discovered with horror the law of retaliation, an eye for an eye, applied indiscriminately and immoderately. A corrupt law which escalated, quickly attaining a bloody and irreversible momentum of its own.

He saw its ravages in bodies torn by a grenade thrown at aperitif time between the legs of the drinkers peacefully sipping anisette. He measured its vileness as he watched the ragged fellaheen – maybe innocent, maybe real cut-throats – disappearing towards a mountain pass with doomed expressions and dragging step: they set off, well guarded by several squaddies in a deceptively peaceful way, on a supposed wood-gathering party, which would be suddenly interrupted by the long furious volleys of submachine-guns.

Immediately disheartened, he attempted at first to understand, to analyse, to plead for both sides equally, without differentiating between clans and races. He refused to choose between the young shepherd boy who, from sheer panic, fled at the sight of troops rather than coming towards them and was cut in two by a burst of machine-gunfire, and Private First Class Durand from La Ferte-Saint-Aubin or Calais, riddled with bullets twenty days before the discharge which he had looked forward to for twenty-nine months.

However, he very quickly understood that it was impossible to sustain the position of passive witness. It could only be maintained by those who were not at the heart of the tragedy, who did not experience it every day; those who far away, in France for example, had the opportunity to fulminate and argue – but at peace, without risk and among friends – and even to pronounce definitively on the facts of a situation of which they only saw one side, one tiny part.

Guy's arguments and ideas of one day were destroyed by the events of the next, for the clandestine execution of a suspect followed the mutilation or massacre of a comrade surprised in an ambush. Because he was an unwilling participant in this terrible guerilla war, but did not want to succumb in his turn to the blind hatred, not to say sadism, of the torturers on both sides, he developed a melancholy cynicism. He compelled himself not to feel anything and, like many of his companions, tried to view the events and the corpses with the indifference of men who know that they are merely counters in a game which they have neither willed nor chosen; who submit to its demands and even inconsistencies, required only to obey, to act, and to remain silent.

Nevertheless, despite his wish to be only an unthinking tool – a position which prevented him from seeing war with the eyes of a real fighter, that's to say, to love it and live by it – he was aware of the conflicts within himself which he was forced to endure from the moment he noticed that, as a civilian disguised as a soldier, he was thinking and reacting like the lawyer he was to become, whilst behaving as the sub-lieutenant he now was.

Constant struggle between the man who rebels against a senseless war, and the Jebel scout who feels the heady exhilaration of the hunter, the instinct to fight. He was never one of those who rejoiced at the sight of enemies finally stretched out on stony ground – from that moment the game became a nightmare – but he did have to admit that he experienced a sort of barbaric satisfaction, participating in this horrifying game of hide-and-seek, where everyone knew the rules, and the stakes.

It made it impossible for him to speak of the war on his return to Saint-Libéral at Christmas, as his mother had expected. From now on it was a secret, an episode of his life, a memory to be shared only with those who, like him, had discovered all its facets, its occasional delights, frequent horrors, constant paradoxes. Civilians could understand nothing of all that, for on this matter they saw things with different eyes from those who returned from Algeria; they did not speak the same language.

Between them lay the chasm which isolates actors from audience; an unbridgeable orchestra-pit, crowded, for Guy and many others, with colonists who were not all exploitative, Arabs who were not all killers, beautiful *Pied-noir* women, tantalising but forbidden, the smiles and the glib chatter of the little shoe-shine boys, the smell of anisette, mint tea, burning spices, roast sheep and couscous. And behind it, on the stage – rendered all the more poignant by the incomparable brilliance of the sun – tragedy, in all its violence, horror and complexity.

The people of Saint-Libéral could not perceive any of that. They wanted everything to be black or white, good or bad; that someone should analyse logically for them a situation born of confusion and incomprehension and poisoned by a thousand nuances.

So they would have grasped nothing if Guy had told them that, despite the revulsion he still suffered at the memory of certain days, already a sort of nostalgia hovered within him, for a land which he had detested for its murderous fury, and loved so much for its gentleness, beauty and charm.

He only stayed a week in Saint-Libéral; was taciturn with his parents and grumpy with the neighbours, who all wanted to understand the inexplicable. They took him for a veteran, proud of his deeds and actions and happy to talk of them; he was no more than a man lost amongst them, almost a stranger.

Pierre-Edouard was worried about him, but remained silent. In former times he too, during a war, had measured the breadth of the wall which forever divides those who watch and comment from those who act and say nothing.

'But what's he been doing over there to have got like that?' Mathilde asked him, saddened to see Guy so distant and cold.

'Nothing,' said Pierre Edouard; 'well, yes, he's aged, and that's a lot.'

PART EIGHT

The Gold Ring

PART EIGHT

THE GOD GAME

Chapter 28

JACQUES installed his animals in the new stable at Coste-Roche in August 1957. All of a sudden the old Vialhe farm seemed really empty, almost dead. It was with nostalgic disappointment that Pierre-Edouard now tended the three cows which Mathilde and he had kept. Thanks to them, to the two sows, ten ewes, the hives and farmyard fowl, some fruit and vegetables, and also Pierre-Edouard's modest pension, they could survive without calling on either Jacques or Louise. Because they did not spend more than the absolute minimum, were almost completely self-sufficient and had finally paid off all their debts, they even managed to put by some savings. The work provided by the animals, the cultivation of the last few hectares they had kept for themselves, and the help they gave Jacques, prevented the boredom which lies in wait for the idle.

Besides, Pierre-Edouard did not feel old, and although he no longer had the strength and dynamism of former times, at least he retained a clear, open mind, with a remarkable ability to adapt. So he understood and even approved, after a pause to consider and observe, the sometimes perplexing way in which Jacques managed his farm.

He therefore quickly realised that moving the animals to Coste-Roche was the best possible solution, and he appreciated all the benefits of it. With its short, easily cleaned stalls, metal tether-rails, feeding passage, automatic drinking troughs, gulley for dung and urine, and accessible feed-store close by, the cowshed was beautiful, and the line of eighteen animals impressive.

During the two years that Jacques had concentrated on breeding, Pierre-Edouard had found the time to assimilate and appreciate the techniques which he cleverly applied. Even the tonnage of fertiliser which he spread each year no longer surprised him, and he ended up recognising that the results were spectacular.

Jacques now grew grass with the same care that his ancestors had formerly taken over wheat. Pierre-Edouard had been rather downcast to see his cornfields transformed into artificial prairie, but had quickly admitted, faced with the stretches of rye grass, cocksfoot and lucerne, that his son was heading in the right direction.

Only one shadow disturbed his complete peace of mind; he knew the total of his son's debts and was appalled by it, for he was also aware that his annual revenue was not increasing. The demonstrations, sometimes violent, which were currently shaking the countryside did nothing to reassure him.

They proved to him that Jacques, like hundreds of thousands of other farmers, was reduced to fighting a sort of rearguard action, an almost hopeless struggle.

Since he was bored, no longer had a taste for travel – on the rare occasions when he set out with Yvette, it was now she who drove – and was reluctant to hunt alone, Léon bought himself a television set in September 1957. It was the first receiver in the village.

For Léon and his wife, but also for Pierre-Edouard, Mathilde and Louise, who did not need to be asked to go and spend several evenings a week in the château, this acquisition was truly revolutionary.

Accustomed until then to learning the news only by reading the paper and listening to the radio; to considering the cinema, theatre and circus as luxuries reserved for townsfolk, they leapt straight into the world opened up by the screen, and were fascinated.

They, who had all known the era of the paraffin lamp – not to mention the cruse of oil with a wick poking out of it, for Léon and Mathilde – had experienced the arrival of the first cars and the clumsy flight of aeroplanes built of wood and canvas, marvelled at this prodigious wonder which allowed them, by simply pressing a button, to witness the life of the universe.

The television changed their entire existence. It offered them amusement every evening and, especially for Pierre-

Edouard, Mathilde and Louise, who had never gone out as such, the unexpected chance to visit the cinema, theatre, circus, even the parliamentary chamber, without so much as leaving Saint-Libéral.

For several months they were regular, model viewers, to such an extent that the women hardly dared knit during the transmissions. Then, gradually, their interest in the pictures waned; Pierre-Edouard and Léon began to comment loudly on the news, to choose between programmes and even to criticise them.

Then, one evening, as *La Piste aux Etoiles* was beginning and the delighted women were comfortably settled in their armchairs, Léon tapped his brother-in-law's shoulder, tilted his chin towards the set and winked.

'What a drag, this carry-on! It's always the same!' he said peremptorily.

'Ssh!' replied Yvette, Mathilde and Louise.

'Léon's right,' said Pierre-Edouard, getting up, 'it's fine for children, but we've got better things to do!'

And they went off to the billiard room where they had not set foot for six months.

'Television, it's like women,' declared Léon, 'shouldn't overdo it, it'll end up driving you off your rocker! Which reminds me, what would you say to a drop of plum brandy?'

'Well, since you're not allowed it, I think . . .' said Pierre-Edouard, taking out his pipe.

'True: failing a cure, the quacks forbid things, that's all those charlatans can think of doing,' said Léon, grasping a bottle and two glasses, 'but a little brandy once in a while . . . It's like tobacco, eh? Come on, roll me a cigarette, Yvette's hidden my Gauloises again.'

'I'll get told off by your wife, and by Mathilde too!' said Pierre-Edouard, taking out his packet of Old Job cigarette papers.

'The women? You must be joking! They're much too busy watching that carry-on, reckon they won't be moving!' He inhaled the bouquet of the brandy and smiled: 'Say what you like, basically television's a bloody fine invention!'

Since he disliked both pandemonium and politicians, and

was incensed by the government crises and incompetence of the fly-by-night personalities who succeeded each other in the political arena, Pierre-Edouard was amongst those who rejoiced at the return of General de Gaulle, following the events of May 1958. But his happiness was somewhat disturbed by the reserve with which his son greeted the arrival of the general.

Wisely, Jacques mistrusted the military; from 1939 he retained a much too sinister memory of them. In addition, he had not lived through the period of the resistance, was close to thinking that the general had the makings and ambition of a dictator, and had not hesitated, with the support of his wretched United People's party, to make a virtual alliance with the Communists. Consequently, unlike his father, Léon and so many others, he was not charmed or reassured by de Gaulle's character.

'But who put those ideas into your head?' grumbled Pierre-Edouard, when Jacques had communicated his scepticism with regard to the new President of the Council of Ministers.

'I don't need anyone to give me ideas! Your general, I don't trust him, that's all!'

'But, good God, you couldn't want it to go on like it was! You said yourself something had to give! Haven't you had enough of all those halfwits who've been ruining us since the end of the war?'

'Maybe there was a way of saving the situation without taking over by force!'

'What takeover? For goodness' sake, Coty sent for him, yes or no? And all those stuffed-shirt deputies agreed, yes or no?'

'Not all, not all. Well, time will tell, we'll talk about him some other day, your de Gaulle!'

'But dammit! Who the devil are you going to put in his place, eh? Can't you see we're in the soup? And with this war in Algeria to add to it! Here, you go and ask your Aunt Louise what she thinks of it! You'll see what she's expecting; that de Gaulle will stop this business, and Pierre and all the boys of his age will come home at last!'

'I know, but I'm not sure that he'll sort it all out the way you're hoping. Your de Gaulle's not God, you know!'

'That's for sure,' said Pierre-Edouard, 'but joking apart, who d'you want to put in his place? Find me just one decent person among all the dregs we've seen marching by for the last twelve years. Come on, I'm listening!'

Jacques shrugged his shoulders.

'They're not all dregs. It seems to me that someone like Mendès France, for example, or Gaillard or even Bidault . . .'

'Look, they've tried, haven't they? What have they achieved? Nothing, except regulating private distilleries and distributing milk in schools! And not forgetting the kicks up the backside we collected in Suez and Indo-China! Come now, trust me; with de Gaulle it'll change, and high time!'

But Jacques was not convinced, and for several months his father and he avoided talking politics.

Guy's marriage hurt Pierre-Edouard and Mathilde deeply, for although they accepted that their son had every right and was of an age to marry without their consent or presence, they viewed his attitude as a denial and rejection of his own origins.

'He's ashamed of us,' said Mathilde sadly when Jacques, in great embarrassment, told them that he had just seen the request for registration of the banns at the mairie.

'Bah,' scoffed Pierre-Edouard, to mask his disappointment, 'we wouldn't have been there anyway. But damnation, the little devil could have told us some other way!'

'Yes,' repeated Mathilde, 'he's ashamed of us, that's what it is.'

'I'd like to know what's going through his head! It may well be that he hasn't even told Berthe – although she wouldn't put him to shame, she knows how people live up there! And anyway, who's this girl? This Colette, where's she from?'

They had to wait three weeks for the arrival of Berthe to spend a few days' holiday in Saint-Libéral before hearing the details of the story.

'Well, I told him to write to you,' said Berthe with a shrug.

'Oh, we understood!' cried Pierre-Edouard, 'he was ashamed of us, that's all! He'd better not forget where he's from and who paid for his education!'

'That's not how it was at all!' she protested. 'Do you think I would have let him do it if that were the case? It's much simpler than that! Colette's parents didn't want anything to do with this wedding, so Guy and she married with two witnesses, that's all; I couldn't even attend, I was in Rome.'

'By God! You could have told us!' Pierre-Edouard was cross. 'We would have gone up ourselves for the ceremony! And why were her parents against it? Because Guy wasn't good enough for them? Because he's the son of peasants? Is that it?'

'Yes,' admitted Berthe with a smile, 'but it's not worth getting annoyed about it, those fools don't warrant it!'

'It doesn't matter,' said Mathilde sadly, 'he was ashamed of us too; the proof is, he didn't invite us.'

'But that's not how it is,' continued Berthe, laughing. 'Oh, you know, you two are amazing! Right, listen, let's be frank. We're in August 1958, not 1920; Guy and Colette have been living together for more than a year, that's all. So, as the girl's parents were opposed to it, they didn't consider it necessary to bother with a ceremony. You're not going to make a fuss about it, are you? It happens every day, marriages like that!'

'Ah!' gasped Mathilde, biting her lips. 'So she's expecting a baby, is that right?'

'Absolutely not! What are you thinking of! They wanted to regularise their situation, you're not going to complain about that!'

'No,' sighed Pierre-Edouard, placing his hand over Mathilde's, 'when you come down to it, he was right not to tell us, he knows us well; he must have thought we wouldn't put ourselves out. A wedding, that's a celebration; well, for us, it should be a great celebration. Regularising a situation, as you put it, is just a formality; they don't need us for that.'

'Now calm down and be happy,' said Berthe, to try to lessen their disappointment. 'You'll see, Colette's a fine girl, really nice, healthy and everything, and very pretty, too. You're bound to like her. And now she's a Vialhe, she's one of the family.'

'Of course,' Mathilde smiled sadly, 'she's one of the family, especially if hers has rejected her. But apart from Guy, will she want anything to do with the Vialhe family? At the moment, seeing the way she's come into it, you'd think she was trying to avoid it.'

Champing at the bit in an out-of-the-way post more than a hundred kilometres east of Beni-Ounif, Paul sought every chance to escape from the B2 Namous camp. One of those isolated stations, forgotten in the middle of the stony desert, established at the far edge of the *mesa* of El Medjbed, on the rutted track which led towards Benoud, Al Abiod and Brezina.

Pounded by the sun, which at the end of August maintained a temperature of 45° in the shade even at five o'clock in the afternoon, it was often scoured by fearsome, burning sandstorms, which blasted from the south with extraordinary strength and violence.

Paul was bored, and almost longed for his previous posting. In Kabylia, where he had spent more than a year, at least there was something happening; there was unrest, shooting, and the campaigns, even if they were dangerous and testing, made things lively and broke the monotony of the days. But here, nothing. Emptiness, absolute silence. Desert as far as the eye could see.

A natural hell into which even the fellaheen were not crazy enough to stray, especially in mid-summer. Despite that, it was still necessary to guard the sector; on principle, as a discipline, and in case, which was unlikely, the rebels from the mountains of Grouz and Antar, having broken through the frontier towards Ben Zireg – instead of crossing towards Figuig – tried to reach the mountains of Bou Amoud, Bou Lerhfad and the peaks of Ksour by the eastern route.

So, because it was in their orders, but mostly to keep the men busy, for they were ravaged by the heat and undermined by idleness, Paul organised raids; theoretically to detect possible rebels who might venture into this forbidden zone, but in fact to hunt gazelle, whose succulent flesh wonderfully improved their dreadful everyday diet. Besides these sorties he had to send three trucks, including a tanker, to Beni Ounif every ten to twelve days; they returned in the evening laden with stores, cases of beer and water.

On Monday 25 August, to amuse himself, escape the humdrum daily round and give the impression of doing something rather more useful than playing poker or dice, Paul decided to accompany the convoy.

He entrusted responsibility for the camp to Lieutenant Verriet, promised to bring back a good supply of cognac, anisette and cigars, and climbed into the cabin of the leading truck.

'Come on, roll it,' he said to the driver, 'let the lads behind us taste a bit of dust! And if you want me to buy you a beer when we get there, try not to shake up my guts too much.'

Pierre-Edouard put down the sledgehammer, stepped back to admire his work, and smiled at Mathilde and Louise.

'Not bad,' he said, 'not very big, but not bad, and with a fine view!'

To please his sister, who three months ago had made up her mind to have the house of her dreams built in the pasture of Combes-Nègres, and since the plans had arrived that morning, he had just marked out with four poles and a ball of string the ground where the building would stand.

'Yes,' said Mathilde, 'it'll be very good, due east.'

'It seems rather small,' noted Louise, as she stepped over the string into what was to be the kitchen.

'Don't go by that,' said Pierre-Edouard, 'like this it looks small, but wait until the walls go up and you'll see!'

'Anyway, just for me . . .' she murmured.

Pierre-Edouard shrugged, sighed, but kept his counsel. When his sister had talked to him of her project, he had tried to show her that it was quite unnecessary; from the moment Jacques had decided to move to Coste-Roche, Louise could stay in the old Vialhe house for the rest of her life. She was certainly not in anyone's way, but was good company. Besides, building a house, even if you owned the plot, was expensive, very expensive.

It was a waste of time; Louise had not wavered. She herself had contacted a small building contractor in Perpezac and taken all the necessary steps. She wanted her house, she could now afford to get it built, and nobody was going to rob her of the satisfaction. Faced with this stubbornness and determination, Pierre-Edouard had eventually understood, and done nothing further to dissuade her.

It was not for herself that Louise desired this house; maybe she would never even inhabit it, preferring to continue to live under the roof where she was born rather than alone here, almost a kilometre from the village. But this house, she wanted it for Félix and Pierre, to leave them one day tangible, solid and lasting proof of all the affection she felt for them.

She had already devoted the greater part of her life to them, and wished now to present them with something which, after she was gone, would perpetuate her memory and her love. And to that Pierre-Edouard had no reply; had he himself not planted walnut trees for his great-grandchildren?

After two hours on the potholed track, which was choked with sand but passable, the little convoy of three vehicles reached the pass of Tamednaïa. Here the stony desert, stretching flat as a table as far as the encampment and even beyond, was broken by a huge, deep fault which overhung the valley where the dry Zousfana wadi sprawled like a fat grey snake.

The track tumbled down towards it in a multitude of breathtaking bends, of lethal sheer drops. It crept through the black scree, clung, twisted, coiled against the rock face, to emerge eventually thirteen kilometres lower down on the pebble plain which bordered the wadi.

Paul jumped to the ground. He had not needed to tell the driver to stop; Private Lavaud knew the road well. Here there was a compulsory halt. First to have a breather and a drink, but above all to work out the descent carefully.

It was crazy, so terrifying that even in the evening, on their return, after a climb of thirteen kilometres the convoy would stop at the same place and the men walk to the precipice to observe with relief what they had just survived.

Not only was the defile as dangerous as a mountain path; it was also well suited to all sort of ambushes, traps. There, fifty rebels could conceal themselves in a thousand different places and fire on the lorries as at a target. There one single fellah, just for the pleasure of christening his brand new weapon – made in Czechoslovakia – could dispatch the three trucks into the ravine; three drivers, three cartridges and goodbye, or rather *msa el khir*!

Since it was impossible to clear this pass as it deserved – that's to say with four platoons of well-trained men who would have taken hours to search through the smallest crannies – the convoy leaders threw themselves into it, foot on the gas, hoping, if it came to the worst, that the vehicles, launched like rockets, might perhaps have a chance of escaping; unless the driver miscalculated a bend.

'It really is a bloody filthy hole,' said Paul, lighting a cigarette.

'Would you like a drink, captain?' suggested the driver, offering a cool damp *guerba*.

'What a joke!' said Paul, grasping the goatskin. He drank deeply, then observed the trail. 'You see,' he said pointing to a bend, 'if I were the Viets – or rather, the fellaheen – that's where I'd hide, but they won't be there, too stupid! Ready, my boy? Right, off we go, and don't chuck us over the side!'

The three trucks rattled off and charged towards the incline.

The unexploded 105 shell, recovered four kilometres from the Duveyrier encampment, primed and buried in one of the turns of the track, detonated under the right wheel and pulverised the entire cabin of the heavy duty transporter.

It was only by the three stripes still clinging to the bloody, lacerated fatigues, that the horrified men in the following trucks could identify the body of Captain Paul Vialhe. He was thirty-six.

As soon as he saw them, all awkward and self-conscious, climbing slowly, as if reluctant, from their blue car, Pierre-Edouard understood. Before they had even spoken, he knew. And when the military police sergeant and his colleague, a corporal, still without having spoken a word, clumsily took off their kepis, he almost told them not to say anything.

He guessed what they were going to announce for,

although he denied it time and time again, did everything possible to banish the insidious premonition which lurked within him, he had been expecting their visit for years. He dreaded it, but foresaw that it was inevitable.

His instinct had not deceived him: the two gendarmes who twisted their kepis between their fingers, looking at him with sad, guilty eyes, proved that the hour had come to hear the terrible news. He was so resigned, so shattered, that the policemen, although still silent and trying vainly to show their compassion, understood that they were the incarnation of death, and that this old man knew it.

'Good day, Monsieur Vialhe,' began the sergeant humbly, 'we are here to . . .'

'I know,' said Pierre-Edouard, 'but speak more quietly; Mathilde might hear us, and it's not for you to tell her about it.'

'Of course,' murmured the sergeant, shuffling from one foot to the other. 'I . . . Well, you may have some idea, possibly . . .'

'No, I know. When? How?'

'Yesterday morning,' stammered the gendarme. 'A mine, he didn't suffer at all, that was it.' He sighed. 'It'll take a week to bring back the body . . .'

'Yes,' whispered Pierre-Edouard, 'go away now, I've things to do. I must tell Mathilde, my dearest Mathilde, you understand?'

He turned on his heel and walked slowly towards the house. When he pushed open the door a flood of sun and light filled the room, but he knew that he was entering into darkness.

Chapter 29

ONE supporting the other, responding to every sigh, look or burst of sorrow, with a determination full of consideration and a wealth of affection, Pierre-Edouard and Mathilde helped each other to emerge from the abyss. And since he believed himself stronger and better equipped to react than Mathilde, who thought herself the more robust, each persisted in wanting to carry the burden alone.

Pierre-Edouard compelled himself to suppress self-pity, to silence the mournful anger which thundered against this intolerable injustice: that he, an old man whose life was already so full and future so restricted, should survive his son. It was illogical, against nature, repellent. But he said nothing, for the sake of Mathilde.

And she, whose loins and flesh still held the memory of this son, she whose memory rang daily with his baby cries and childish laughter, she who had been so concerned yet so proud to see him become a man – she also remained silent, stifled her moans and hid her tears, for the sake of Pierre-Edouard.

So, in order not to increase their shared agony, each conquered their distress, attempted to stifle it, with the sole aim of shouldering their partner's pain.

Then gradually, because they had constrained themselves to conquer their sadness, they emerged together from the tunnel and the darkness lifted for them.

During this long period punctuated with pitfalls, setbacks, words and sighs which needed to be silenced – with worry too, at the thought of seeing the other stumble or fall – they were supported, watched over, surrounded. Besides the help of Jacques, Mauricette and Louise, and even Léon, who himself was a sorry sight, they received comfort from Berthe.

She arrived in Saint-Libéral the day after the gendarmes' visit and with her, embarrassed at introducing themselves

434

under such circumstances, but conscious of being in the right place, came Guy and his young wife Colette, to whom Mathilde opened her arms, quite naturally and without restraint.

Félix also appeared two days later and, as the women were comforting Mathilde, and Jacques and Guy did not know what to do for their father, he dogged his footsteps, hardly left him. He listened to the old man when he needed to talk, and knew to keep quiet when he sought silence.

Neither he, nor Guy and Colette, could stay long after Paul's interment. In contrast, Berthe, already semi-retired, moved permanently to Saint-Libéral. It was she who made sure that the Vialhe house was now always enlivened by the presence of Pierre-Edouard and Mathilde's grandchildren; she who encouraged her brother not to neglect his jobs, his hives, his garden, his vines. It was she, again, who placed a fat ball of wool and knitting needles in Mathilde's hands to begin the layette which Colette, one month pregnant, would need for her baby. Berthe again who, for Christmas, arranged for a television to be installed in the Vialhe house, since Pierre-Edouard and Mathilde, on account of being in mourning, did not wish to go and spend the evenings at Léon's — the neighbours would not have understood such behaviour.

She, finally, who, after Colette's confinement, succeeded in persuading her brother and sister-in-law to accompany her to Paris — where she had retained her apartment — to meet their grandson Jean and thereby prove to Guy and his wife that their offhand behaviour the previous year was forgiven. Pierre-Edouard and Mathilde had to be begged; they put forward the argument of their work, the care of the animals and the hives, and ended up accepting.

So it was that in May 1959 Pierre-Edouard, who had not set foot in Paris since 1918, helped Mathilde discover the capital which she had never seen. Mathilde, at fifty-nine, had never yet left the Limousin.

Elected mayor of Saint-Libéral in the polls of March 1959, Jacques had donned the sash of office with pride and satisfaction, but with no illusions as to his chances of reviving the community.

Everything indicated that it was without a future, without inner resources, in its death throes; deadened by its ageing population, deprived of strength by the haemorrhage of young people who, after their school certificate, fled to the towns to learn a trade, and it was never farming.

Saint-Libéral vegetated like very old chestnut trees which still grow a little greenery each spring, but the number of dead branches increases from year to year and the arteries of the whole framework harden. In Saint-Libéral now, the total number of full-time farmers did not exceed fifteen. As for the other local people, half-workers, half-peasants, they cultivated their plots on Saturdays and Sundays, or in the evening, on returning from the work in town which was their only means of survival.

However, in the '60s Jacques regained hope, for, one after another as if Louise had taught them how, several houses were constructed on the edges of Saint-Libéral, on land sold by Louis, Léon's son, estate agent in Brive.

For a while Jacques believed in the resurrection – or rebirth – of the village, but he was quickly disillusioned. The new inhabitants, retired people on small pensions, or commuters, did not live within the community of Saint-Libéral, nor join in the life of the village. The former were there to sink into peaceful retirement, the latter came to sleep, or perhaps at the weekends to tend their gardens jealously. Some of them proved to be pleasant neighbours, but their mode of existence, their rhythm of life, created between themselves and the natives of the village a wall of incomprehension which was difficult to surmount.

As the years passed, Saint-Libéral changed in appearance and in character. Whereas not long ago everyone knew everyone else and greeted them daily (apart from quarrelling neighbours), now many villagers got to the stage of no longer bidding good day to individuals who, out of diffidence or pride, did not even respond to their greeting.

At the same time the spirit of mutual co-operation disappeared, which had been the strength and foundation of the whole community. Busy with their dual activities, the worker-farmers had neither the time nor the energy to help out their neighbours. As for the last farmers, they were forced to compensate for the vanished farm-labourers with the maximum number of implements, placing themselves further in debt without increasing their turnover to an equal extent.

Re-elected as a regional councillor in 1961, but disappointed to be unable to pull the village out of its slump, and worried also over the future of his farm, it was with a sceptical eye that Jacques watched the birth of the agricultural directives of 1960 and 1962. Certain aspects of these laws reconciled him somewhat to the existing government, but others reinforced his certainty that he was one of the rearguard of a fast-disappearing agricultural system, condemned because it was not sufficiently productive.

Nobody was interested in it any more, for it was practised by simple farmers who, whatever was talked of or decided, were incapable of transforming themselves into those business managers who, it was claimed, represented the future on the land. Even Jacques, despite his abilities, knew that his modest enterprise, lost among a collection of tiny farms, many of them already in their death throes, was also on the slippery slope to economic stagnation, and therefore extinction.

Since he had a wife and two children to feed, was of the type which deplores passivity and surrender, and held fast to the idea that maybe the one who lasted out the longest would be the winner, he clung on to his land, cared for it, devoted all his energy to it. Thanks to his work, in the face of all logic, the Vialhe farm remained the finest in the commune.

He neither wished nor was able to retrench, he felt forced to rush forward, and therefore never hesitated when, in April 1964, the axle and gearbox of his first tractor gave up the ghost: he acquired a new machine, this time a 35CV. He paid 25,000 new francs for it and, for good measure, since he was going to get into debt, he also bought a bailing machine for 9,500 francs. It had become as indispensable as the tractor and its accessories, for he and Michèle were now bringing in the hay alone. His father might well be strong still, but he was seventy-five; his help was not sufficient.

It was Léon who got wind of the business. He hardly went out these days – dabbled a bit in his garden, but mostly watched out impatiently for Pierre-Edouard, who walked up to the château every afternoon just after siesta time.

It had become a ritual. In former times they would probably have gone to the inn to talk, but it had been closed for four years, and the bistro previously run by Noémie Lamothe – the only one in the village, now, managed by her daughter Nicole – still had as bad a reputation as at the beginning of the century, at the time of Ma Eugène.

Pierre-Edouard therefore climbed up to the château, kissed his sister-in-law, then joined Léon in the billiard room. The two men still played the occasional game, but more often they preferred to settle into the huge armchairs. There, with a conspiratorial air, although they had known for a long time that Yvette was not fooled, Pierre-Edouard rolled a cigarette for his brother-in-law – only one, but as thick as a finger! – whilst Léon poured a thimbleful of plum brandy into glasses. They then resumed their conversation of the previous day; commented on the local and world news, dissected the newspaper, discussed politics, evoked their memories and vanished comrades. They were well informed and interested in everything.

On that day, 17 October 1965, despite his haste to tell Pierre-Edouard what he had just learned, Léon bowed to their customary ritual; only after he had lit his cigarette and placed the little glass of brandy in front of his brother-in-law did he announce:

'Louis came by this morning . . .'

'I know, he dropped in on us.'

'That's good,' commented Léon, happy to discover that his son was not neglecting his aunts and uncles. 'And he didn't say anything to you?'

'No.'

'That's good,' repeated Léon. 'I understand why he's successful in business, the devil: he knows how to keep quiet . . . And you know why he came?'

'Oh, that, yes! To check on the staking out of the three

438

plots he's sold on the edge of the track up to the plateau!' grumbled Pierre-Edouard.

He did not like all these settlements of houses in the middle of the country. Up until the last few years, the plateau and the peaks had remained as he had known them in his childhood: wild, isolated, quiet, reserved for crops, herds, chestnut trees, collecting butterhead and chanterelle mushrooms, for hunting.

Then the road leading up there had been surfaced – likewise the one climbing up to Coste-Roche. And then the houses had appeared, incongruous eyesores ruining the countryside with the prominence of their tiled roofs and white roughcast walls; they frightened off the game, disturbed the silence, and gave the villagers the feeling of no longer being quite at home when they went out into their fields.

'I know,' said Léon, 'you don't like those shacks, nor do I, but you have only your son to blame; he's the mayor!'

'He believes it'll revive the village; well, he used to believe . . .'

'Never mind, I've something else to tell you,' interrupted Léon, anxious not to continue on this subject, for he viewed with a fairly jaundiced eye the way his own son was using the good ground which he had handed down to him.

'And what's that? Your son's going to do the same as Jacques and not vote for de Gaulle? I know that, he told me so this morning, the idiot!' said Pierre-Edouard sarcastically. His mood had clouded over at the thought of the new houses which would spoil his view.

'It's nothing like that! Let the young people vote as their fancy takes them, that won't stop the Big Fellow from giving the other rogues a good hiding! No, what he told me is much more serious: the Bouyssoux boy's selling his farm.'

'André Bouyssoux? From the Heath?'

'Yes, Léonard's son, that fool your father wanted as a husband for Louise!'

'Oh, bloody hell! And why's he selling?'

'What else can he do? While Léonard was there, it worked; with him dead it's a right mess of a farm.'

'And his mother?'

'She's in hospital — and for a fair old time, if she ever gets out at all. Put yourself in André's place, all alone over there! Anyway, he's incompetent and bone idle, so the land . . .'

'That's a damn fine farm, at least fifteen hectares and almost all lying together!'

'Fourteen hectares, fifty-five acres,' said Léon. 'He wants nine hundred . . . no eighty, well, nine million in old francs! Now it's up to you.'

'You're crazy.'

'I wanted to tell Jacques.'

'I see,' murmured Pierre-Edouard thoughtfully. 'Heath Farm, yes; that would suit him down to the ground. But it's a lot of money, and a long way off!'

'Three kilometres from here, four from Coste-Roche. Going over the plateau with a tractor and these good surfaced roads, that's nothing!'

'It was Louis who tipped you off?'

'Yes, André went to see him at his office in Brive. So Louis thought that might interest Jacques. He hasn't said anything to anyone else yet.'

'We'd better tell Jacques, straight away,' decided Pierre-Edouard getting up.

'Yes,' smiled Léon, 'we'll go there; Yvette'll drive us. But first, let me finish my cigarette.'

'And where am I supposed to find nine million — ten even, with the fees! If I told you what I'm already repaying on loans each year, at your age, it could kill you!' commented Jacques ironically.

He felt bitter, for as soon as he heard, he realised that these fifteen hectares could save him, that they represented the chance, perhaps his only one, which he must seize no matter what it cost. But his enthusiasm quickly waned at the thought of the sum required to purchase it.

'You'll have to sort something out,' said Léon. 'First you can bargain on the price; in my opinion he needs to come down to seven million. That would be about half a million a hectare, which is fair. If you like I'll go and bargain with him myself, and I'll eat my hat if . . .'

'Dammit! Sort something out! You must be joking! I've no

ready money!' cried Jacques, tapping his thumbnail against his teeth. 'And I'm fed up with always grubbing around for cash! The devil take your Heath Farm!'

'Calm down,' said Pierre-Edouard. 'This land, you absolutely must have it. First for you and later for Dominique, if he wants to come back one day.'

'Huh, he'd better not! Why do you think we've paid for all his education, and he's still costing us an arm and a leg? For him to come back and do what I do, work himself to death for damn all? Oh, no!'

'Be quiet,' said Pierre-Edouard brusquely. 'You don't know yet what he'll decide to do.'

This was a contentious subject between himself and his son, which they usually avoided mentioning. Dominique had followed in his father's footsteps, had passed two baccalauréats and was at present pursuing his studies at the college in Grignon, hoping to become an agricultural engineer.

Originally Pierre-Edouard had been very proud of his grandson, and had presented to him, on the day of his first bac, that twenty-franc napoléon which his own grandfather had given him for his school certificate on 11 July 1902.

Subsequently, Jacques' remarks and his grandson's choice of career had slowly undermined his contentment. He had realised that an agricultural engineer is not likely to return to clean out the pigsty, look after the cows, cart the dung. Although he was very happy about Dominique's achievements, the thought that one day there might be no one to succeed to the Vialhe land filled him with sadness. To overcome this he clung to the idea that, against all logic, despite his diplomas, his lily-white hands and head full of books, his grandson would – in his own time, but one day – return to the land.

'That's it exactly,' he repeated. 'You don't know what he'll decide to do later.'

Jacques shrugged. 'It'll never be to come and bury himself here! Not unless he goes mad first!' he grumbled.

'This business is getting boring,' cut in Léon. 'That's not the problem; it's this land at Heath Farm which we mustn't miss out on!'

'That's true,' said Pierre-Edouard. 'I hope time will take care of the rest. For the moment, you've absolutely got to buy,' he insisted in milder tone.

'I'd like nothing better, but I've no money, so don't let's talk about it any more!'

'We'll try to help you,' pleaded Pierre-Edouard, 'we could lend you some, er, not much, but a million perhaps . . . I'll need to speak to your mother, you know me and money . . . You must have this land. You've always said that you needed at least forty hectares; with Heath Farm you'd have them. Go for it, my boy, go for it! You should never let land go, never!'

'But you must understand that I don't want to spend my life paying for it! It's no way to live, in the end! All that to live poor and die rich!'

'Don't talk stupid,' Léon interrupted him. 'Your father's right: land, that's the only thing you can rely on. So, your problem, we're going to solve it. I say the older ones who can should help the young ones; that's about the only useful thing old beasts put out to grass like your father and me are fit for! So look: your parents can lend you a million, I'll add five to that myself. You give it back when you can, to me or to Louis, later, right . . . We'll put it on paper, that there's no hurry; because money, at my age . . . And believe me, if I could have, I'd have done more, but Louis has cost me a pretty penny with this new agency he's just set up in Limoges! So, five million, will that do?'

'You'd do that? Really?' asked Jacques.

'I give you my word; right away, if you like!'

'Oh well, that changes things,' said Jacques. 'There's less than half left for me to find!'

'Yes, but where?' speculated Pierre-Edouard. 'From the Crédit Agricole?'

'Oh yes. It should work. Next year I'll have finished paying off my first loan, for the château land, so I'll reschedule it for the Heath. You see how it is,' he joked, 'when I said I'd spend all my life paying for my land! But that's less of a worry; four million's not a fortune!'

'Maybe,' said Pierre-Edouard, 'but if I were you, before going to see those gentlemen at the Crédit, I'd talk to Berthe;

she gives sound advice, and maybe she'll lend you a few sous too.'

Once informed, Berthe never hesitated for a second, but took out her cheque book and smiled at her nephew.

'At least you make less of a fuss than your parents,' she said. 'Since I came back to live here, they haven't taken a sou from me. I even have to fight to go and do the shopping. Ah, that Vialhe pride! How much do you need?'

'Do you mean . . .?' stammered Jacques in surprise.

'Here,' she said, and held out a cheque to him. 'You just told me that you were four million short; there it is, and don't mention it again.'

'The thing is, if . . .' he said, 'for the repayment, if you could wait a bit . . .'

'Yes of course,' she laughed, 'I'm seventy-two; if you can give it back in about thirty years, I think that will suit me fine!'

'But I'm not joking!' protested Jacques. 'Either I pay you back, or you keep your money!'

'Don't be silly, dear boy, you remind me of your grandfather Vialhe! Oh, I can see you've still got a lot to learn, and I hope you live long enough to understand that the value of money is only what it's worth to you. For me, it's a pleasure to write you this cheque, it's a little treat to myself, and it's not excessive, whatever you may think! For you, it sorts things out, so don't bore me with the rest. In my life I've earned lots of money, but I've never liked talking about finance. So don't make a fuss. Take this, but if it really bothers you, I'll tell you that when Guy and Colette got married, I helped them too. And then as now, it was a pleasure to be able to!'

Jacques became the owner of Heath Farm a month later. Since he was the only local buyer SAFER, the land development agency, did not intervene. It was therefore Léon who, by choice, bargained over it with the seller.

After a month of holding out valiantly, the vanquished André Bouyssoux laid down his arms, losing two and a half million old francs in the battle, but still certain that he had been the craftier; Léon had convinced him that the next presidential elections would bring a Marxist to power and that all fallow land – which his was – would be nationalised!

Thus, in return for six and a half million old francs, the Heath farmland, on which Jean-Edouard Vialhe had wished to establish his daughter about the year 1910, came into the Vialhe family in November 1965.

Chapter 30

PIERRE-EDOUARD and Mathilde judged the events of May 1968 harshly, despite the explanations and justifications offered by Mauricette and Jean-Pierre, and Jacques' arguments — for without approving the form adopted by the movement he was with them at heart.

They disliked waste, civil disorder and strikes, and did not understand how people who enjoyed a comfortable existence, in comparison to what they had lived through, could have the impertinence to complain. They, who had spent their whole lives working, who in nearly fifty years of marriage had only ever taken ten days' holiday, listened in amazement to the demands streaming out from all sides.

It was not the demonstrations by the working classes which shocked Pierre-Edouard the most. Since 1936 he had rather mistrusted them, knew they were quick to flare up and rarely satisfied, and, as he expected no good of the unions, he was not surprised to see them take industrial action. In contrast he was scandalised to his soul by the attitude of the teachers who sided with the protesting students.

He, who all his life had respected those who possessed knowledge, who had done so much and worked so hard to give his own children the opportunity to pursue their studies as far as possible, was outraged to learn that affluent and privileged children — they were students, after all! — not only had the audacity to spit in the soup, but also to create havoc in the streets, and that with the blessing of their professors.

'And is that what you find so good?' he challenged his daughter one evening, after watching the demonstrations shown on television.

Mauricette and Jean-Pierre had come to dine with their parents, as they did once a week, but, knowing their father's point of view on the current events, they carefully avoided broaching this controversial subject.

'You have to understand them,' attempted Mauricette, 'if you think their life's easy —!'

'Christ Almighty! You dare say that to me! Life has never been as easy as it is now! When I was the same age as those young good-for-nothings, I was working twelve hours a day, summer and winter, and my father didn't even pay me! Why are you laughing, eh? What's so funny about that?' he asked Berthe.

'Nothing,' she said, slipping a Gauloise into her cigarette-holder. 'But it's all very well you saying that: when you were their age, you wanted to break the system too! And that's what you did by leaving here, and me too, and Louise the same! When you think about it, we Vialhes were great anti-establishment types; that's what's making me laugh.'

'That has nothing to do with it!' he protested. 'Besides, we never preached revolution!'

'That's true, but we made it happen, in our own way.'

'That was quite different,' he insisted. 'In the first place we worked; they do damn all and demand the earth. Good God, what they deserve is a kick up the backside! And when I think that the teachers have sided with the little whingers!'

'It's not always easy to be a teacher!' pleaded Jean-Pierre.

'What's that? You're complaining too, are you?' mocked Pierre-Edouard. 'With your four months' holiday, your salary, your housing, your guaranteed pension, and all for looking after fifteen kids! You've got a nerve, my fine fellow!'

'I'm not speaking for myself — although I'm entitled to complain, having only fifteen kids to teach, in a village that's being left to die, abandoned by the state! Leaving that aside, I assure you that a number of my colleagues have good reason to demand changes!'

'Not at all!' contradicted Pierre-Edouard. 'A student who refuses to work is a scrounger, and a teacher who goes on strike is a jackass! You won't change my opinion about that!'

'Now, now,' Mathilde quietly intervened, 'we're not in the Latin Quarter now, or at the Sorbonne! I find it quite upsetting enough to see all those people fighting over silly things; so don't you do the same!'

'You're right,' said Pierre-Edouard.

But since he felt himself boiling with anger, and the May evening was still light and clear, he rose and marched to the door.

'I'm going to see my bees,' he called as he went out; 'at least they don't bloody strike, and they don't muck anyone around!'

Although from then on he avoided talking about the demonstrations when Jacques, Mauricette or her husband were present, Pierre-Edouard made up for it each afternoon with Léon. Together they followed the unfolding situation, and were appalled at the way it escalated as the days passed.

Léon remained enraged – even going so far as to advocate a good clean-up with heavy machine-guns and flame-throwers to get all the protesters off the streets – but Pierre-Edouard began to see things differently. After his first fury came mixed feelings, of sorrow, doubt and an inability to comprehend what motives inspired the young people, of an age to be his grandchildren, to act as they were doing.

'I don't understand any more,' he said one day to Léon. 'Either I've really turned into an old fool, or these youths are crazy. Did you see the TV last night?'

'Yes, they should all be shot!'

'But why did they do that? Why?'

'To make barricades, of course!'

'Maybe,' murmured Pierre-Edouard thoughtfully, 'but maybe to destroy everything that existed before them, too . . .'

Until that day, however scandalous he had considered the thoughtless vandalism which set fire to cars, broke windows and ripped up cobble-stones, however grotesque he had found the posturing of the politicians, at least he had seen nothing sacrilegious in all the madness.

He had even felt a tremor of fear when a few hotheads – there were some in the village – had declared that the real proletarian revolution and the time for settling accounts was fast approaching, but the attitude of those who hankered after purges had not surprised him. He knew these old enemies well. They were the sort who had failed to seize power in 1944 and aimed to make up for lost time in 1968. Although their threats called for a few elementary precautions – for a week he slept with his hunting rifle within arm's reach – at least they were logical, understandable, not to say obvious.

But since yesterday, what was to him an irreparable act had been committed; even Jacques, who was in the house, had muttered angrily when, on the television screen, they saw and heard the plane trees topple in the Boulevard Saint-Germain, briskly felled by the demonstrators.

That was the straw that broke the camel's back, the point of no return, the unpardonable crime; and for Pierre-Edouard, who had spent his life planting trees for the sake of his grandchildren, it was the parting of the ways with a generation crazy enough to destroy trees in their prime for pleasure and no other reason.

So, despite the relief he experienced when the crisis was resolved, after the elections on 30 May and in June, he remained hurt by this episode. It had compelled him to take real heed of a fact he had known for years without wanting to consider it particularly significant; that he was a man of the nineteenth century, and a chasm separated him from these youths who were preparing to confront the twenty-first.

It was not years which lay between them, but the sad image of the plane trees needlessly sacrificed on the Boulevard Saint-Germain.

In order not to wake Mathilde, Pierre-Edouard rose as quietly as possible, opened the big wardrobe by lifting the door slightly so that the hinges did not squeak, took his Sunday suit, a white shirt and a black tie, and shut himself in the bathroom.

There, having shaved and washed, he dressed with care, combed his white hair, moistened his temples with a few drops of lavender water, then crossed the bedroom, the living room, and finally emerged into the yard.

The night was just fading in the east and despite the time of year it was mild, with no wind. He examined the sky, and was happy to see stars, without the shadow of a cloud; the day would be fine.

Today, this Saturday, 21 December 1968, Mathilde and Pierre-Edouard were celebrating their golden wedding, and he was as excited as a young bridegroom.

Despite his shoes, which pinched a little, and to pass the time while waiting for Mathilde to wake – she would sleep another hour – he walked along the road, then turned off up the track which climbed to the plateau; the grit in the tar crunched under his leather soles. He strode along for five minutes, then stopped and turned round.

At his feet Saint-Libéral was barely awake, only the houses of those who were about to leave for work in Objat, Ayen, Terrasson, La Rivière-de-Mansac or Brive lighting up one by one. He noticed also that lights were on in the cowsheds of Maurice, Delpeyroux and Duverger; reckoned that it would not be long before Brousse's shone out too, and sighed to think that no other would ever light up again. In the village there were now only four herds, and in the whole parish just eleven farms still active.

'This area is like me,' he thought, 'it's old, worn out, tired, it's standing upright out of habit . . .'

He tried to banish these bitter thoughts, but did not succeed. The previous day Jacques had confided in him that he would only be registering three births in the year 1968, a miserable number. As for deaths, the least said the better; they were too numerous and too frequent.

So today Saint-Libéral, which seventy years earlier had contained almost 1,100 inhabitants, held no more than 322. Already, in spite of the protests and the intervention of Jacques – still a regional councillor – the administration had warned that the post office would be closed down from January 1969.

The rumour was also running round that the school would be closed, too, if the number of pupils remained so low. At the beginning of the school year in October Jean-Pierre had only welcomed eleven kids; if he nevertheless retained hopes of keeping his job, it was only thanks to the arrival of four Portuguese families – they had a swarm of young children whom Jean-Pierre counted on enrolling when they reached school age. And maybe, with a bit of luck, other strangers would move into the village.

There was no lack of empty houses, nor gardens in need of clearing.

Mathilde awoke as he entered the bedroom, frowned at first to see him so smartly dressed, then remembered and smiled at him.

'Happy anniversary, dear wife,' he said, bending over her.

'Happy anniversary,' she mumbled, offering a cheek still warm from the heat of the pillow.

He kissed her on the edge of her mouth and sat down beside her. And with his large hand, all calloused and knobbly, he gently stroked her face.

'Let me see your hand,' he said, 'the left one.'

She held it out, and he was moved to see the little wedding band of nickel silver which he had slipped on to her third finger fifty years before. The ring was quite worn away, as fine as wire.

Then, almost as awkwardly as fifty years earlier, he pulled a box from his pocket, opened it, took out a gold ring – a solid, broad, heavy one – and placed it on his wife's finger.

'I've been wanting to give you a gold ring for fifty years,' he explained; 'there it is, it was now or never.'

'You're crazy,' she murmured in delight, looking at the wide band with the little nickel silver ring almost invisible beside it.

'Yes, maybe,' he said, pulling her against him and stroking her hair, 'but it's lasted fifty years and I've got used to it now, and I like it very much.'

Her cheeks all pink from the champagne and her eyes sparkling with happiness, Mathilde leaned toward Pierre-Edouard.

'I'd really like us to go for a walk, in a few minutes, when the meal's finished,' she whispered in his ear.

'Like lovers, eh?'

'Of course, just us two.'

He smiled at her. 'Are you happy?'

'Oh, yes!'

'Well, so am I.'

Everything had been wonderfully organised by Jacques. Thanks to him, Pierre-Edouard and Mathilde had experienced one surprise after another, joy after joy.

First of all, as ten o'clock struck, Pierre-Edouard and Mathilde – who, for the first time in ten years, laid aside her mourning and wore a gorgeous cream ensemble presented by Berthe – had been summoned outside by a chorus of hooting. Then, because it was very fine, they had moved out into the sun on the steps and had seen at one glance that all the children were there, laden with flowers and presents.

Behind them stood Louise, Félix, as well as Pierre, his wife and their baby, and Gérard, too, with Berthe on his arm; finally, at the back of the group, Léon, Yvette and Louis. And one by one, in order of age, the families had approached the old couple, who awaited them arm in arm at the top of the three steps, their smiles trembling with emotion.

Firstly Jacques and Michèle, with Dominique and Françoise between them – real Vialhes; then Mauricette and Jean-Pierre and their three girls, Marie, Chantal, Josyane; and finally Guy and Colette and their four children, Jean, Marc, Evelyne and little Renaud, barely a year old; they were Vialhes, too.

And it was a noisy, happy procession which set off together for the church, where the vicar of Ayen, who generally only came to celebrate Mass every fortnight, had gladly agreed to officiate in honour of this venerable couple who, fifty years earlier in this same church on a cold snowy day, had sworn each other love, fidelity and support.

After the Mass, whilst the bells pealed out, Pierre-Edouard and Mathilde, like newly-weds, had shaken the hands of old friends and neighbours, and even posed for the two reporters whom Jacques had advised of the occasion.

Subsequently the whole family had assembled in silent meditation around the war memorial where, amidst so many other names, was engraved that of Paul Vialhe. Forcing a smile, for the day was not made for tears, Mathilde had placed a huge bouquet of roses at the foot of the stone cockerel which was crushing a pointed helmet, both flecked with lichen over the years.

Then they had all regrouped in the cemetery, where again

Mathilde laid flowers on the Vialhe tombs, that whole line of Edouards who had forged the family. Finally, before leaving, she had not forgotten to go and put a few white carnations on Nicolas' grave.

Under cover of the noise which reverberated around the village hall where the long table had been set up, Pierre-Edouard and Mathilde stepped discreetly towards the exit.

'Going to pick wild strawberries? At your age? Aren't you ashamed of yourselves?' Léon whispered to them with a wink.

'Jealous!' replied Pierre-Edouard passing his arm around Mathilde's waist. 'If you hadn't picked so many in your youth, you could still be gathering them!'

'Boasting again!'

'What are you saying?' asked Mathilde.

'Oh nothing,' Pierre-Edouard assured her, 'it's only that old man, your brother, complaining about his age again!'

Outside peace and quiet welcomed them; even the church square was deserted, and they met only a dog as they walked up the main street. Shut up in their homes, the inhabitants of Saint-Libéral were watching television.

Still with their arms around each other they passed in front of the old Vialhe house, then quite naturally turned along the track which rose towards the peaks. They had no need to talk to know where their steps would take them.

Pierre-Edouard turned his head away as they passed the new houses which stood beside the track. There were now six of them; they ate into the edge of the plateau, and their positioning hinted that other buildings would shortly encroach upon the countryside.

They emerged eventually on the plateau. It was still magnificent, for the Vialhe land was spread out there, luxuriant, rich, full of life. All the more beautiful now that it was gradually being encircled by fallow land, heath and even brushwood, which, since men had fled the land in disgust, was establishing itself firmly, and yet waging a losing battle against the inexorable march of the houses; much of this ground belonged to Louis, who some day or other would divide it up into plots.

'Come,' said Pierre-Edouard, pulling Mathilde along.

They walked on to their land, crossed the Long Field with its walnut trees, the very old and the very young, all beautiful, then the Malides – fine, fertile lucerne – Léon's Letters and At Mathilde's – thickly planted with rye grass, sheep's fescue and cocksfoot – and finally the Meeting Field, covered in a rye and vetch mixture, which petered out at the foot of the White Peak.

This had not changed, and the junipers, box, gorse and rush-leaved broom still covered its flanks, as on that day in September 1917 when Pierre-Edouard, on leave from the army, had met little Mathilde, all beautiful, impulsive and pure in her seventeenth year.

'Shall we climb up?' he suggested.

'Of course.'

Slowly, because his legs were no longer those of a young man, they scaled the peak.

'Look,' he said, stopping on mid-slope to catch his breath, 'it was just here that I came with your brother and Louise to empty the thrush snares. It was so cold! It was the twenty-fourth of December 1899, you weren't even born!'

'I know,' she smiled, 'you've told me a thousand times! And it was as you set off again that you heard the wolves and threw away your thrushes!'

'You're right, I'm rambling,' he said, sitting on a large flat stone.

'Don't catch cold on me now!' she worried, leaning towards him to tighten the knot of his scarf.

'No, no, it's fine. Sit down, there.'

She settled down beside him and they nestled against each other.

'Do you remember?' she asked indicating a clump of broom with her chin. 'That's where you stopped my cows. It's a long time ago, all that . . .'

'Oh yes,' he sighed, 'a very long time. And yet it's as if it were yesterday.'

'Don't be sad,' she said, for she knew how to interpret his every look and tone of voice.

'I'm not sad.'

She saw that he was gazing at the Vialhe lands; knew what

453

he was thinking.

'Don't worry,' she insisted. 'Now, thanks to Heath Farm, Jacques is saved. They'll remain the Vialhe fields.'

He gently shrugged his shoulders.

'Yes they will!' she continued. 'Jacques is still young, he can hold them for twenty-five years.'

'And after that?'

'Dominique will be forty-six,' she calculated, 'maybe he'll be glad to have them.'

'Maybe . . . But you know, an agronomist, they don't like bending down.'

'*He* does!' she decided. 'And if not him, there are other young Vialhes – Guy's children, Jean, Marc, Renaud, or perhaps even a son of Dominique's!'

'Perhaps,' he repeated. But he sighed once more: 'There'll be no more fields in ten years,' he murmured. 'They'll all be gobbled up by the houses!'

'Not ours, Jacques will keep them!'

'That may no longer be possible. He may well stop working for almost nothing on ground which is worth a fortune as building plots. Look,' he said, pointing his hand, 'from here you can already see the roofs sticking up. The wood pigeons never make a mistake; since the houses have come closer, the doves have moved further away, it's a sign. One day they won't fly over any more; then it'll all be finished, I mean the Vialhe land. Luckily I won't be here any more to see that . . .'

'Don't say that!' she protested, putting her arms around his neck. 'Don't say that! You must trust all our children; they'll guard it, just as we did. They've already taken over!'

He looked at her and was cross with himself on account of the tears which he glimpsed brimming in her eyes; it was he who had provoked them with a few bitter words.

'I'm nothing but an old ass,' he said. 'It's you who's right, as always. The children are there, they'll watch out, and others'll come along – I'm hoping to see you a great-grandmother. Forgive me for being so stupid on such a beautiful day. I have no right to complain. It's true, life is wonderful and basically we've had lots of luck, we two, and lots of love. Sorrow and hardship too, but who hasn't? Now smile for me. That's it,' he encouraged her, 'like that, yes. You're very beautiful.'

'No, old and covered in wrinkles.'

'Young to me, and beautiful,' he insisted, placing his large hands around her face.

He gazed at her, then, with his forefinger, traced the network of lines.

'You are beautiful, I love your wrinkles and I know them all, they're your very own medals. This one,' he said stroking a little furrow at the corner of her mouth, 'that's the first, it dates from 1917, when I returned to the front line, and my wound in 1918 etched it in. Those ones, those are from the children, their births and the worry they caused you. There,' he murmured, putting his finger in the middle of her forehead, 'that's Paul's, our dear Paul, the deepest one . . . And all the others – that's life; me, us.'

'Exactly what I was saying: it makes a lot of lines altogether!'

'What does it matter! Saint-Germain apples are covered in wrinkles too, when they've lain on the straw all winter. And you know very well that they're the best, the most wholesome and tasty, the ones I prefer above all.'

'You're saying that to please me. Anyone would think you wanted to seduce me, or eat me up!'

'Of course I'd like to! And that's nothing new, you know very well!'

She leaned towards him and kissed him.

'We're a bit ridiculous, aren't we?' she said. 'What if people saw us!'

'They'd say we loved each other, and at our age it's a good sign.'

'Come on,' she said, getting up, 'you'll end up catching cold. And down there, the children are going to worry if they can't find us. They don't even know where we are, perhaps they're looking for us already . . .'

'You said they'd taken over. Well, if they're worried, it's their turn now. I think we've done all we had to do, and we didn't do it too badly. So we've every right to rest a while or go for a stroll. Come on, let's climb to the top of the peak; from up there you see better, and further.'

Hand in hand, like two lovers who have an eternity before them and are careless of time, years or the weather, they ascended the heights of the White Peak.

Marcillac, avril 1979
— mars 1980